EDW

Edward the Sevent

A NOVEL

Tyler Whittle

W H

HEINEMANN : LONDON

William Heinemann Ltd
15 Queen Street, Mayfair, London W1X 8BE
LONDON MELBOURNE TORONTO
JOHANNESBURG AUCKLAND

First published 1975

SBN 434 86490 0

Printed in Great Britain by
Cox & Wyman Ltd
London, Fakenham and Reading

To my godson

Richard Bowyer

great-grandson of one of
King Edward's steadier friends

PART ONE

1

Battleships, cruisers and destroyers of the Royal Navy were moored in two lines all the way from the Isle of Wight to Portsmouth. Through this great fleet steamed a file of four royal yachts. Aboard the little *Alberta* which led the way was the coffin of Queen Victoria. The time was a little after three on a sharp February afternoon in 1901. Already the sun was setting in a coral-coloured sky.

England's longest reigning sovereign had been tended by her own. Her dressers wept over her as they did their work. Her Bedchamber and Linen Room Women had clothed her tiny body. Her Physician, and her grandson the German Emperor, had measured her for her coffin. When the inner casing arrived the Emperor and her son, the Duke of Connaught, laid her carefully inside it. Both were struck by her pathetic lightness. Over her face they placed the bridal veil she had worn sixty years before and they laid her wedding dress beside her. They gave her a Cross to hold, lined the coffin with fresh flowers, and sealed the three lids themselves. A chapelle ardente was made in the Osborne dining-room, and there, surrounded by her family who received the Sacrament for the last time in her presence, her old friend and counsellor Bishop Randall Davidson celebrated the Holy Communion.

But it was so long since the death of a reigning sovereign that, inevitably, there had been muddles. At first the 60th Rifles stood guard over her until it was discovered this was the particular privilege of the Queen's Company, Grenadier Guards. The Queen's Household and the new King's intermingled and did not appear to know where their duties began and ended.

Exact in all things, Victoria had left a carefully drawn-up Will naming her Privy Purse, her youngest daughter, Princess Beatrice, and her youngest son, the Duke of Connaught, as her executors, giving specific details as to how her funeral was to be managed.

Yet, as is usual with such laid-down instructions, they could not be carried out to the letter. The Queen had ordered no mourning black because she was rejoining her beloved husband, but her son scotched that at a stroke. She had been a great Queen Empress. Mourning could not possibly be put aside.

She had also wished that her son should reign as Albert or Albert Edward, yet at his Accession Council, in a short and impromptu yet excellent speech, he said that for England there could be only one Albert, his father, Albert the Good, and that he intended to reign as Edward the Seventh. By this title he was proclaimed by the heralds. His sisters Lenchen, Louise and Beatrice, watching over their mother's remains at Osborne were not in the least surprised but they were saddened. The Scotch did not like it either. To them he was Edward the Second.

The Queen had directed that the ceremony should be simple. This, too, was an impossibility.

Sensibly deciding that her Household knew more about such things than his own, the King put her Equerries and Secretaries in charge, but they were at a loss for precedents. There was no one at Court, and no one in the Earl Marshal's office who could recall the full and correct procedure. Most of the arrangements were made by the Queen's Secretaries and had to be guessed at and improvised. . . .

No one watching the small royal yacht *Alberta* steaming through the avenue of warships could fail to be moved. Only a few were aware of the difficulties that might still lie ahead.

Over everyone hung a cloud of apprehension. The Queen as a person was being mourned by very, very few. Her oldest and closest friend Jane, Lady Churchill, had died three weeks before. Her Ladies grieved. So, in degree, did her children, especially her youngest, Beatrice, who had lived with her, and her eldest, Vicky, who, though distant in Prussia, had kept in touch with her for many years through long and intimate letters. Her son and heir, King Edward, had grown to be proud of her and without her he felt lost, in some sense unmanned. But the majority of her family and friends and courtiers and subjects suffered from an overwhelming sense of incredulity and foreboding. The great majority of her people were young. Indeed about forty-three per cent of the whole population had not yet reached the age of twenty. And yet all shared a feeling of uneasiness. Four days after her death the *Illustrated London News* expressed the general shock.

> *Think what it means that we can never again sing the National Anthem in its present wording!*

The Queen had lived very much in retirement, but she had always been there. Without her everyone felt rudderless.

As a genuine expression of her own feelings the King's consort Alexandra announced she would not allow anyone to address her as Queen or kiss her hand until after the funeral. Cynics observed she need not trouble herself to make such a gesture. Victoria had been doyenne of reigning sovereigns for decades. She had had thirty-nine grandchildren and it was an interesting speculation that had each of these lived and produced the same number there would have been over six thousand blood relations by the fourth generation. Many of her grandchildren bore the name of Victoria. Many were queens. But for a long, long time the title Queen could apply to only one person.

That person lay within the third of three coffins aboard the *Alberta*, made fast to a jetty at Portsmouth while the other royal yachts and warships rode at anchor in the Solent.

On the following morning the funeral train took her body, the chief mourners and their Households, to London. Getting everyone ashore in steam pinnaces had taken more time than the equerries had calculated. The train left Portsmouth nine minutes late and the driver, urged on by courtiers who knew the new monarch's hatred of unpunctuality, did his best to make up the time. As a result the train roared with indecorous speed through the countryside where people stood hatless in the fields, not a few crying, all bowing and curtsying. Ninety miles an hour was reached and on one or two reverse curves there was a serious danger of derailment, but the driver managed to reach Victoria Station with two minutes in hand – there to receive the congratulations of the German Emperor through an equerry.

The Sovereign's body was carried on a gun carriage through the streets of London from Victoria to Paddington. Huge silent crowds lined the route. And there, with perfect co-ordination, men of the Coldstream carried the coffin into a second train.

At Windsor another disaster threatened. When King Edward and visiting sovereigns had taken their place behind the gun carriage, the drums began to roll the *Dead March*, and the gunner lieutenant in charge failed to give the command 'Walk march'. Sensing the order, the two wheeler horses started off before the leaders. Finding the load heavy, they began to plunge and rear, and away went the traces. The procession was halted. With a thunderous expression on his face the King gave his consent to an improvised scheme of sailors dragging the gun carriage up to the castle. The gunners felt equally thunderous. A third disaster threatened when the cortège arrived at St George's Chapel because the Earl Marshal's department had failed to allocate seats in the choir, but this was quickly rectified, and the first part of the funeral service took place.

A Sunday intervened in the obsequies.

The King was determined that nothing should go wrong with the second part of the funeral at the Frogmore Mausoleum on the Monday. Reluctantly he consented to the suggestion that the Artillery be allowed to redeem their mistake at Windsor Station by pulling the gun carriage – but he warned Captain Ponsonby, his mother's Assistant Secretary and one of her equerries whom he intended to take into his own Household, that if anything went wrong he would never be forgiven.

Ponsonby went for advice to Lord Esher, an intimate friend of the late Queen and of her son Edward. Esher was an astute man. He considered, threw out a suggestion or two, and eventually, between them, they decided on a plan. A rehearsal was arranged for eleven o'clock that Sunday night. Two bearer parties, one from the Life Guards, the other from the Foot Guards, met at the Frogmore Mausoleum. A coffin of the same weight had been quickly knocked up by the Office of Works, and this was shunted in and out of the Mausoleum doors until every possible problem had been ironed out. It involved intricate manoeuvring by the light of flash-lamps and flickering torches, but certainly saved the final service from being a ridiculous farce.

The King was suitably grateful, though he wondered why there was an English officer in khaki in the German suite and why Ponsonby led him out of the Mausoleum. Ponsonby was, in fact, giving the officer a lecture for intruding on a family service and asking his name and regiment. But afterwards the officer popped up again; this time right in the middle of the royal family on their return to the Castle. He chatted amiably with King Carlos of Portugal until Captain Ponsonby spotted him and once more ejected him. It turned out he had been invalided home from the Boer War with sunstroke – and had dearly wished to be at the funeral of his Queen.

And so Victoria of England at last reached the place she had longed to be for forty years of widowhood, beside her beloved Albert in the Mausoleum she had built for them.

Queen Victoria was at rest.

But her country was not. For the fortnight between her death and elaborate burial at Windsor and Frogmore the public houses had sold more beer than usual, but had been unnaturally quiet.

Nor was her Empire at rest. The Great White Mother to so many of her subjects all over the world had gone and they were lavish in their expressions of grief.

Nor was her Court at rest. Some of her servants had to go. It was inevitable, though a few would be kept on by her son.

Nor by any means was her heir at rest. Temporarily quartered in Edward III's tower, Edward VII viewed the present and his future with the deepest gloom.

He was vexed with his guests. His close relative the King of the Belgians had scandalized everyone. A monarch of sixty-five should not have behaved like a randy tup when over for a funeral. Edward decided he would not have him in England again. Nor, though he was pleased with the way Willy had behaved at the time of Mama's death, did he want to see the German Emperor for a long time. To show his gratitude he had made Willy a Field Marshal and given his son the Crown Prince the Garter. But Willy was a second Jeremiah. Already he had complained about some of the funeral arrangements, and had made a terrible fuss because his rooms at Windsor were next to George's, and George had German measles. Moreover both he and the Crown Prince strutted like gamecocks and this was unbearable. So was their love of tittle-tattle. How Willy's eyes had sparkled when he passed on the information that the detestable Ferdinand of Bulgaria had celebrated with a gala luncheon on the previous Saturday, the first day of Mama's funeral.

Death frightened Edward. Mama had died peacefully enough, but his brother Alfred had died of cancer the year before in the greatest pain. His sister Vicky was dying of the same disease also in the greatest pain at that very moment in Germany. He himself was fifty-nine, felt ten years older, and, owing to constant over-smoking and colossal overeating, he was in poor condition.

The King was inclined to feel low about everything – and especially about his own immediate family. He and his surviving brother, Arthur of Connaught, had been at odds for years. His sisters were scarcely any better. Lenchen was a bore, keen on good works and needlework, and married to a bore only really interested in eating, smoking shag, and shooting – in that order. Louise was a flighty intellectual who refused to live with her husband, and Beatrice, the youngest, was going to cause the very devil when he told her he planned to give up Osborne. He would be able to manage better if Alix supported him but she seemed to enjoy claiming, with justice, that she was a wronged woman, was not in the least inclined to put herself out, and absolutely maddened him with her infantile attitude to important matters, her unpunctuality, her moments of waspishness and her stubborn refusal to part with their unmarried daughter Victoria. The rest of his children were simply dull: Louise married off to the elderly Duke of Fife, Maud who had married into her mother's Danish family, and young George – now his heir because poor Eddy was dead – George was merely a serious-minded Naval officer who had married May of Teck and already given him four fine grandchildren.

Momentarily the King's gloom receded as he thought of his adored grandchildren, David, Bertie, Mary and Harry. But the depression returned. There he was, Edward VII in Edward III's tower, far, far too old and ill to be of much use as a king.

The Times had preached a sermon at him on the first day of his reign, reminding everyone that as Prince of Wales he had been 'importuned by temptation in its most seductive forms' and that he must often have prayed 'lead us not into temptation . . . with a feeling akin to hopelessness'. It was damned impertinence, of course. His mother had had a particular antipathy to newspapers which he fully shared, and he could never understand why the radicals and socialists and riff-raff democrats didn't see the press for what it really was – a self-elected power without responsibility to anyone save a few rich proprietors. *The Times*, as usual, had been ruder than the rest, but none had actually welcomed him to the throne. He felt aggrieved, misjudged, unwanted.

But then his pout turned to a tired smile. Frankly he had enjoyed many of the compensations of being kept from affairs of state by Mama. It had allowed him to lead a Prince Hal sort of life and, while no one in their senses would expect him to blossom into an elderly Henry V, he planned to leave some sort of mark behind him.

He threw his finished cigar into the fire, lighted an Egyptian Dambergi cigarette, and tickled the scruff of his terrier Caesar who lay by his chair.

Ill and old or not, and despite the Irish sneer that he'd never be the king his mother was, he was determined to show Society he still had a shot or two in his locker.

Already he had let it be known that the Duke of Westminster's projected marriage with Shelagh Cornwallis-West must, in view of the Queen's death, be quiet almost to the point of silence – and that despite the fact Shelagh's mother had once been his mistress and they were still on the very best of terms.

He would also show the statesmen that he valued his prerogatives and did not intend to be squashed or ignored. Only that morning he had ordered his name to be placed at the head of the Navy List, something Mama had never done; and he had dismayed the Prime Minister, Lord Salisbury, by calmly announcing before Mama's funeral that George and Mary's projected tour to Australia must be cancelled and George sent as Viceroy to Ireland instead. Salisbury was a Cecil and so would get his own way in the end, but a little firmness at the beginning of his reign, however short it might be, could do no harm. Without reference to anyone he had decided what to call himself as King and had added to the royal title 'and of the British Dominions Overseas'.

Then of course, though one had off days, and this was certainly one – February in Windsor being impossibly draughty and uncomfortable to a man of fifty-nine – he felt there might be consolations as well as work ahead. Alice Keppel had a most comfortable drawing-room in Portman Square. Agnes Keyser mothered him in the apartment above her hospital in Grosvenor Crescent. Jeanne de Sagan's hospitality at Cannes, Deauville, or at her great Paris house in the rue St Dominique, was invariably silky. There were other delights as well. He pulled a bell cord and his second valet Hawkins came into the room. Dinner had been substantial, but the new King's appetite was large. 'Have we, Hawkins,' he asked, 'anything by way of a titbit in this draughty tower?'

'A dish of *cailles cecilia*, your Majesty? A *pâte de poulet*? Or should I send down to the kitchen?'

The King considered. 'The quails,' he decided. 'Thank you.'

Hawkins had a journal in his hand. 'It is Saturday's *Queen*, your Majesty, and contains an article which might be of interest.'

Edward let go of Caesar's scruff and took the offered journal. 'Thank you, Hawkins.'

The valet retired to get the dish of quails while his master read a flattering description of himself. Part amused him.

> *A well-known physiognomist has formulated the axiom that full, blue eyes are generally associated with a cheerful and happy disposition; that they evidence a candid and generous nature and belong to those who make the best of unpleasant circumstances. . . .*

He rose to his feet and looked at his reflection in a wall glass. The candlelight was soft. No electricity at Windsor yet. That would have to be altered. But there was no denying the blueness of his eyes.

'Hawkins,' he said when the valet re-entered with a tray, 'are my eyes definitely blue?'

'Most definitely, your Majesty.'

In his London house the American Henry James was dipping a steel nib into an inkwell. The son of a noted theologian and himself the famed author of such books as *Portrait of a Lady*, *The Bostonians*, and *The Awkward Age*, James was not at that moment adding to his list of works, but scribbling an idle, acid comment about the ruler of the country of his adoption.

> *Now we have lost mysterious little Victoria,* [he wrote] *and are to have fat, vulgar, horrid Edward.*

2

To the north of Berlin, with a seaboard on the Baltic but hedged about by Prussia, lay the nominally autonomous Grand Duchy of Mecklenburg-Strelitz. From the Schloss at Neu Strelitz reigned the old and blind Grand Duke Frederick, whose principal pleasure was music and re-hunting in daydreams grand runs of the past with his famous pack of boarhounds and the equally famous Grand Ducal beagles.

His Grand Duchess, Augusta, was a Princess of Great Britain and Ireland, and she shared his liking for music – preferring Donizetti and the music of her youth though she also managed to appreciate newer composers like Puccini and Leoncavallo. But, above all, she loved England and politics.

Since the age of eight the Princess had been an ardent reader of newspapers. Her English newspapers and letters came to Neu Strelitz a little stale, but each year railways and steamships brought them more speedily. She devoured them, just as her very fat younger sister the late Duchess of Teck had devoured food: keeping in touch with beloved England, reading the newspapers herself through a powerful lorgnette, for she was in too much of a hurry to absorb information to permit her lady-in-waiting to read aloud. The coming of the telegraph had been a boon. She was an ardent telegrapher. But she could not bring herself to use a telephone. Each year she slipped off to England to live in a small house in Buckingham Gate which she re-named Mecklenburg House and which she filled to overflowing with family souvenirs.

In January 1901 she was much grieved to hear of her cousin Victoria's death. They had not always got on. As an attractive princess at the young Victoria's Court she had atttracted many personable men – which had not always been to the Queen's liking. On one famous occasion Prince Albert's brother Ernest was physically prevented from dancing with her at a Court Ball. But her marriage and virtual exile to distant Strelitz and the passage of time had softened their differences. Augusta never forgot her English background. In Strelitz she kept Primrose Day after Disraeli's death, an action which Victoria had thought touching. And since that awful day when the Grand Duchess discovered her grand-daughter Marie was carrying an illegitimate child by a footman, and Victoria had shown more sympathy and practical common sense than anyone in the family, they had been fast friends. Therefore Augusta of Strelitz genuinely mourned her cousin.

She was not, however, very pleased when one of her own courtiers attempted to comfort her with the tactless remark that Victoria had been in her dotage. Dotage! She, the Grand Duchess, was a mere three years younger. And now, assuredly, they would be needing her in England. Only she and her brother George remained of all the progeny of George III who could recall an English Court ruled by a king and his consort.

Her lady-in-waiting, Frau von Heyden, known to all as 'Oh! Matilda!' on account of some joke in the distant past, insisted that they could not comfortably reach England in time for the funeral. But the little Grand Duchess did not distress herself. She knew that she would be sent for sooner or later, and her eyes sparkled in delightful anticipation. Her brother George would not have the least recollection of past coronations. She could count on that. Only she knew the ins and outs, and plenty else besides, of the coronation of a British sovereign.

The Season at Strelitz always began with a carnival in January and ended in March. On account of the Queen of England's death it had been drastically curtailed this year. Fretting with impatience, the Grand Duchess waited.

She was sister to the old Duke of Cambridge, cousin-german once removed to the new Queen, and aunt to Princess May who had married Prince George, the Duke of York, and all felt themselves more closely bound than by mere blood relationship. They were heirs of a Landgrave of Hesse who had married a daughter of George II of England, a nobleman with so strong a sense of family that he had bequeathed his magnificent Schloss at Rumpenheim on the bank of the river Main to be used for regular reunions. By law it belonged equally to his children and their successors, a widening yet select and intimate group known in European royal circles as Rumpenheimers. Vexingly to the Grand

Duchess, however, Alix chose to write chiefly to her family in Denmark, and George, while a dutiful and painstaking correspondent, never quite gave his sister the sort of information she wished for. Therefore it was a great relief that Princess May liked to write long, factual and careful letters which absorbed her aunt. From May she heard of the moving funeral services. From May she received some pressed flowers which had been taken from Queen Victoria's bedroom at Osborne. From May she heard that while George automatically became Duke of Cornwall in addition to York as Heir Apparent to the throne, his father had not yet made him Prince of Wales, nor had he any intention of doing so yet awhile. A serious-minded girl, not given to concerning herself about rank, even May thought this was wrong. As for Aunt Augusta, she was almost beside herself. It was disgraceful.

> *. . . when my tears were dried my* ire *was up & hot that the legitimate historical Title is not to be continued by you & George! Oh! what a terrible mistake so to upset old traditions. . . .*

After that Aunt Augusta heard that George's German measles had cleared up, but he had suffered a relapse and could not be at the State Opening of Parliament which May herself attended and described as '*very fine & one felt very* emotionée'.

May then disclosed that her father-in-law had been persuaded to let them go to Australia as arranged. Lord Salisbury had been most insistent, and they were to leave in March.

> *How plucky you are, dear Love,* [replied her aunt] *I admire you . . . but oh!* the voyage! *the distance, the leaving the darling Chicks behind!*

The practical Duchess of Cornwall and York was more concerned with the abrupt changes which were taking place in England.

The King had not thrown over his old friends, Prince Hal fashion, in fact he had thrown over no one. Amongst his intimates there were the Devonshires and Carrington, and Redesdale to steady him, the Rothschilds, Sassoons and Sir Ernest Cassel to advise him on finance and entertain him with all the extravagance such a celebrated voluptuary required. There were also other intimates, his Private Secretary, Sir Francis Knollys, his acknowledged mistress, Mrs George Keppel, his enigmatic friend, Sister Agnes Keyser of the hospital in Grosvenor Crescent, the boisterous Admiral Sir John Fisher, Sir Charles Hardinge from the Foreign Office, the Portuguese Luis de Soveral, and that *éminence grise* in British affairs, Lord Esher.

Members of the old English aristocracy were, of course, unexceptionable, but Princess May was not inclined to care for the obtruding of newcomers and especially European financiers to the heart of England's Royal Court. She wondered if it was a wholesome innovation.

Her Aunt Augusta joined her in regretting certain alterations in protocol, though with a sprightliness which made her niece seem staid, she said they were now in the twentieth century and changes *will* happen! In her heart she could understand the substitution of evening Courts for afternoon Drawing-rooms, yet she thrilled with horror to hear from May that some Court functionaries appeared to be so blind to certain aspects of ceremonial importance that unseemly music was often played at Courts, Levées and Investitures. No girl could wish to be presented while the band played *'His nose was redder than it was!'*

Aunt Augusta was also shocked to hear of radical alterations at Windsor and Buckingham Palace. With a team of advisers the King had gone from room to room exclaiming with a guttural roll of his *r*'s that he might not know much about a*rrrr*t but he liked to think he knew something of a*rrrr*angement. And, with an undignified vindictiveness, he had personally destroyed dozens of trophies of Mama's Highland servant, John Brown. Photographs, casts, carvings, portraits, large statues, and chinawork collected from all the royal palaces, houses and gardens, had been smashed by the royal hands. He left not a trace of the servant who had caused him such personal annoyance....

As the news came in daily from England, the Grand Duchess decided she positively must go there at once. She could wait no longer. She ordered her luggage to be packed, everything in jet black, with a becoming grey dress or two in case it happened to be anyone's birthday, and she fully intended to set out unannounced for London to satisfy her curiosity when the long-expected letter arrived. It was from May.

I send you one little line to tell you from At. Alix that she has been told that on the demise of a reigning sovereign Queen the Mistress of the Robes exists no more – Now At. Alix can hardly believe that this is so, so she begs you will let me know what happened when William IV came to the throne & who Queen Adelaide had . . .

It was an irresistible invitation.

On the day following, the Grand Duchess bade her blind husband farewell and swept through a throng of bowing and curtsying courtiers in the grand *Saal* to the Grand Ducal carriage waiting in the *Platz*. She was accompanied by her disgraced granddaughter Marie, now the Comtesse Jametel, so that she might be reinstated in the eyes of Europe at the English Court, and, of course, by 'Oh ! Matilda !' Heyden.

The Grand Duchess' brother, the Duke of Cambridge, greeted her at Mecklenburg House.

How rosy he looked, she thought, though sadly he had never overcome the shock of being dismissed from his post as Commander-in-Chief, and it had amounted to that because, despite pleas from the Queen and her family, he had refused to resign and make way for someone younger and less conservative. He had spoken of Staff officers as 'nasty *fellahs* who don't wash' and had had to go.

With him were two of his sons, that is, his bastards, for he had married an actress and the wedding was illegal by the laws of England. But the Grand Duchess Augusta held this was nonsense. Fitzgeorges or not, she gave them her hand to kiss. One of them glanced appreciatively at the famous Cambridge sapphires which she always made a point of wearing in England. He supposed they would pass to her son. It was regrettable.

After dinner everyone excused themselves and left the elderly brother and sister to talk in private. There was much to say. The Duke was eager to tell her about some sort of machine which caught noise waves in the air; a wireless it was called, and just invented. He was also interested in a dust-collector called a vacuum cleaner which was going to revolutionize domestic economy. But his sister, though for a moment she indulged his liking for gadgets, declared she had not travelled so far to hear about radios and vacuum cleaners. She tapped his wrist with her fan and asked about Bertie and Alix. How were they managing as King and Queen? . . .

The Duke's close resemblance to their pop-eyed father grew stronger than ever. 'Eh?' he said.

She repeated her question, to which he replied. 'Oh, well enough I gather. Well enough, Augusta.'

'May writes that Alix is not anxious to move from Marlborough House.'

'Eh?'

'Are you getting deaf, George?' The idea worried the Grand Duchess. Their own father had been deaf for years. In royal circles it was an especial disadvantage.

'Deaf? Certainly not. You ask the oddest questions.'

Deafness however reminded the Duke of something he had heard in his club. As the new King and his deaf Queen had been touring Windsor Castle with a view to seeing what needed to be done, Edward had drawn his wife's attention to a sculpted figure of a young child in the repose of death, in fact, the daughter of William IV and his Queen Adelaide. Generally, because of the depth and tone of his voice, the King could make his wife hear easily, but too many cigars that day and the dust they had kicked up had obliged him to roar at her. 'If it hadn't been for that,' he bawled, pointing with his cane at the sculpture. 'You and I wouldn't be here.'

George chuckled over the story. His sister thought it a little undignified. But she did not say so. She had no chance. Straight away he was telling her once more about the new invention for cleaning carpets, curtains and so forth; an extraordinary sucking device which cleaned houses through an eight-hundred-foot tube and made such a racket that cab horses were bolting. . . .

Two days after her arrival the King himself called at Mecklenburg House.

To say the least, the Grand Duchess was surprised. The sovereign had not moved about like an ordinary person in Great Britain for sixty-four years. She appreciated the courtesy.

She curtsyed but he quickly seized her wrinkled hands and raised her again.

'My dear Cousin,' he murmured, kissing her on both cheeks.

'I intended to drive to Court as soon as possible, Sir. You do me great honour.'

'No honour, Ma'am. Cousin to my Mama and to my wife. Aunt to my son's wife. The consort of a reigning prince. I welcome you, Ma'am, on what is truly a sad occasion.'

For a time they spoke of Queen Victoria, both drawing on their best reminiscences of that remarkable and indomitable figure. Then he described her last hours.

Augusta of Strelitz had heard it all before from a variety of sources, and at great length, but it was the right thing to do. Deathbed scenes were a central topic in any family. In a royal one they were particularly important.

Offered refreshment the King declined.

'How, Sir, may I serve you?' asked the old lady.

'In many ways, Ma'am; first, by keeping my people informed as to the correct protocol – for Uncle George hasn't the least idea and no one else appears to know. Muddles have resulted.'

She smoothed the silk at her lap. 'I think perhaps my memory will be of use, Sir.'

'And there are two other things, Ma'am.' Edward longed to smoke, but knew that it was out of the question in this faded drawing-room. 'If you could soothe a family sore, I'd be obliged.'

He explained. A week after the Queen's funeral he had made Alix a Lady of the Garter, a unique distinction as she was the first non-sovereign lady to be given the Garter since 1488.

The Grand Duchess inclined her head and smiled her approval. It was a generous, happy sign of his affection for his wife.

'But the devil, Ma'am, if you'll pardon the expression, is that the ladies in the Royal School of Needlework went prudish and instead of embroidering the naked female figure on the Irish harp in Alix's banner, they substituted a plain stringed instrument. There's been trouble ever since. Trouble from the heralds about altering the Royal Standard. Trouble from the Irish who say they've been slighted. Trouble from Alix and trouble, as you might guess, from my sister Lenchen. . . .' He paused.

'Ah yes,' breathed the Grand Duchess. She did not need to be told more. Princess Helena, or Lenchen as she was called in the family, had founded the School of Embroidery in a small house in Sloane Street almost thirty years before and, though it had earned the patronage of Victoria and the prefix 'Royal' and moved to a larger establishment, it was still very much her own special interest. She and Alix had never got on well. This Irish harp affair must have ruffled their feathers badly. And apparently, from what the King was now saying, something worse had come between them. Without reference to anyone, Alix had announced that she wished to see the formation of a really efficient Army Nursing Service which she would personally lead. This cut right across the small Service which already existed and which was headed by Lenchen. A miracle of a compromise had been arranged. Alix was to be head of a new Army Nursing Service, Lenchen was to supervise a new Army Nursing Reserve. 'But,' the King spread his hands expressively, 'there is small love between them.'

'I shall do what I can,' promised the Grand Duchess.

'With your authority, Ma'am,' said the King. 'You might reconcile them.' He hesitated. 'There's yet another matter. . . .'

She waited patiently. Suddenly he burst out with it all, and evidently it sadly bothered him for he slipped unconsciously into the old relationship, addressing her as 'Aunt Augusta', and letting his tongue run away with him as was his habit when very excited. It appeared that Alix was being more stubborn than usual. She did not wish to move from Marlborough House where she had lived for so long and she would take no interest in the renovations at Windsor or at Buckingham Palace or in the economies which were being introduced by Lord Esher.

'Economies, Sir?' He might 'Aunt Augusta' her, but she was too much of a Princess of Great Britain and Ireland to call her sovereign 'Bertie'. Nevertheless, she permitted a note of warning to enter her tone. 'I recall your Papa making adjustments to the Royal Household many years ago. They did not go down well with everyone.'

'Esher, I assure you, Aunt Augusta, knows what he is doing. There's been a great deal of slackness in these latter years. Mama was not always well served. Esher's discovered that at least fifty of the three hundred and fifty indoor servants at the Palace are totally unnecessary. But Alix won't interest herself in the least.'

'Again Sir, I shall do what I can.'

Much relieved the King got to his feet. 'It occurred to me you might be willing to help. There are not many to whom I can confide the stubbornness of England's new Queen.'

'I am both willing and happy to serve you,' sad the old lady.

Aunt Augusta was as good as her word. She called on the Queen at Marlborough House and was received with floods of tears.

'Come, come,' she said to the still beautiful woman whom she had wheeled years before in a pram up and down the swept paths at Rumpenheim. 'Come, come, my love.'

With great felicity she made Alix understand how much she sympathized. She could *feel* for her so – to lose her home and move into strange, huge palaces; to lose sight of her beloved George and May who were soon to leave for their tour of New Zealand and Australia. It was indeed hard. But there were compensations. George's children would be with her for eight months, and there was always familiar Sandringham to fall back on should the Palace or Windsor or the other royal establishments prove uncongenial. *Not*, cried Aunt Augusta loudly so that Alix thoroughly understood, *not* that they could possibly be uncongenial with their wonderful treasures and collections and historical associations. . . .

She was checked by a further flood of tears. From the subsequent wailing which went on, the Grand Duchess discovered that Osborne was to be offered to George, and, if he didn't wish for it, it was to be got rid of; that Balmoral was fusty and marmalade-coloured and had little to commend itself. As to Windsor and the Palace: all Alix's interest in the former was to have one small room in which she would hang her own water-colours; and in the latter was how her beloved Woman-of-the-Bedchamber, Miss Charlotte Knollys, could most comfortably be lodged.

Aunt Augusta gave up at this. She postponed mentioning that unpleasantness with Lenchen. Nor did she offer any hints on what was expected from a Queen consort taking Queen Adelaide as a precedent. These could wait until Alix was more tractable. Meanwhile, yes, she would be glad if her carriage could be called.

Once inside the landau with her large coat of arms painted on the little doors, the Dowager Duchess reflected that Bertie might have given Alix much cause for complaint in the past, but that in no way justified her present hysteria. She inhaled from her lace handkerchief scented with English violets. The afternoon had been a waste of time; what Alix's down-to-earth mother-in-law would have reprobated as a most unroyal boo-hoo.

Generally the Grand Duchess enjoyed her visits to England. For a variety of reasons it was difficult on this occasion.

There was a sudden and quite inexplicable recurrence of the Malta Scandal which declared that Prince George, while serving with the Mediterranean Fleet, had morganatically married an admiral's daughter and, therefore, could not be legally married to Princess May. Actually it was more of an upsurge than a recurrence because, despite many attempts to expose it as a lie, it had remained totally unsquashable – and was to remain so until Prince George took the matter to law many years later. The Grand Duchess' instinctive reaction was to be seen in public as often as possible to show that at least the little Court of Mecklenburg-Strelitz regarded the story as a libel. Many other influential people followed her example. Busy as she was preparing for her voyage to New Zealand and Australia, May saw the necessity for making a show and was suitably appreciative of her family's and her friend's efforts to help. George was less so. He grumbled, saying it was all a lot of women's nonsense. But at his mother's urgent request, and May's, and positively pushed into it by Aunt Augusta, he did what was expected of him. Temporarily, at any rate, the whispers died away.

While this gesture of solidarity was being organized in London, King Edward quietly slipped away to see his dying sister.

The Grand Duchess hardly approved of his taking a suite of only two: his physician, Sir Francis Laking, and his new Assistant Private Secretary, Captain Ponsonby, and she was appalled to hear that at Flushing he had been greeted by a huge crowd singing the Boer National Anthem. How misunderstanding people were, but, then, there were traitors in Britain who were strongly pro-Boer – even a radical Member of Parliament, a wretched solicitor from Wales named George, who had had to be rebuked for lack of patriotism by his own party leader.

Nor did the Grand Duchess like hearing that a loyal headmistress had brought all her girls to sing 'God Save the King' on Edward's arrival at Düsseldorf and no one had thanked them. It was beside the fact that the headmistress happened to have a shrill and penetrating voice and that her carolling was at two in the morning. The King ought to have dressed and appeared in person to thank her.

She told him so when he returned, politely of course, but with the firm authority of an older and wiser person. But she did not pursue the matter. The poor man was evidently very distressed about his sister. Tearfully he told her that it had been out of the question for Laking to challenge Prussian medical practice. He had been permitted to examine the Dowager Empress, but not allowed to give her the morphia he had taken specially with him and which would have eased her terrible pain. The whole of her house had been overhung with a feeling of menace and he had not been at all surprised when Ponsonby told him the Empress had begged him to smuggle her correspondence out of the country when they left. Nor was the Grand Duchess surprised. Her own little country being so enclosed by Prussia she knew Prussian methods. The Empress had never been popular, and the liberal views which she had shared with her short-lived husband were anathema to her son and his militant régime. Almost certainly she would be traduced after her death, especially if the Emperor could lay his hands on her private papers.

'Captain Ponsonby succeeded?' she asked quietly.

For the first time a smile crossed King Edward's face. He told her Ponsonby had expected a package or two which he could slip inside his own valise. Instead, melodramatically at the stroke of one in the morning, four men had staggered into his bedroom under the weight of two large studded boxes. Labelling one *CHINA* and the other *BOOKS*, he had risked smuggling them out from under the Emperor's nose.

The Grand Duchess also smiled. 'Willy will *not* care for that!' she declared 'At any rate, thank God they are safe.'

Both nodded. Then the King said: 'While we are mentioning letters, I need your advice.'

To the old lady's astonishment he confided that Lord Rothschild had just given him a packet of letters from Queen Victoria to her dear Lord Beaconsfield. As the latter's executor, Rothschild had held on to the letters, and had now handed the packet over.

'What am I to do with them?'

Without any hesitation at all, she replied: 'Burn them.'

She was certain there had never been anything in the least scandalous about Victoria's hothouse relationship with her First Minister, and, as an ardent admirer of Disraeli herself, the Grand Duchess would dearly have liked to read the letters, but she knew the royal value of discretion.

The King accepted her advice and burnt the letters.

Not everyone, however, was willing to listen to Aunt Augusta. Alix remained obdurate about moving from Marlborough House. Even May refused to consider dropping Mrs Derek Keppel from her list of Ladies for the tour. It was unfortunate that the King was clearly determined to continue his liaison with Derek Keppel's sister-in-law, but she had no intention of allowing this to interfere with her plans. Derek had been George's faithful equerry for many years, and Mrs Derek was her own excellent friend. If she had a fault it was a tendency to vanity and at present she was complaining at the difficulty of finding any sort of variety in the black toques they would all have to wear. Otherwise no one could be a better companion for so trying a trip.

Aunt Augusta gave way on this, but she went down to Portsmouth herself to see the *Ophir*, an Orient liner which had been converted for the round-the-world voyage. She approved May's choice of pale blue brocade furnishings with deep pile carpets, though later she confided to her brother George that what they call 'every comfort' was not in the least comfortable and hardly sufficiently commodious for anyone who suffered from sea-sickness. Like some gloomy sibyl she conjectured that for a good part of the eight-month journey her niece was going to be prostrated with that miserable malady.

Through May Aunt Augusta also tried her best to impress Alix with the necessity of being punctual, which was a virtual impossibility, and to follow protocol more strictly. Remembering what Queen Adelaide had done at Drawing-rooms she was concerned to discover that Alix stood silent and appeared to take no part in the Presentations. This was not only wrong, it was un-royal. It was Alix's *duty* to greet all duchesses, marchionesses and countesses with a kiss on each cheek, then with one kiss down to earls' daughters in the scale of precedence, after which she simply offered her own hand to be kissed. Aunt Augusta remembered it well.

She could recall washing Queen Adelaide's hands after a quantity of kissing more than seventy years before.

There was the most appallingly un-royal boo-hoo when May and George actually left. The King gave a farewell banquet at Marlborough House the evening before and, to Aunt Augusta's astonishment, he broke down and a tear or two rolled down his cheeks. A small rigid stick of self-control, she contented herself with saying goodbye to the party at Waterloo. The others were already boo-hooing, and many miles of railroad and a farewell luncheon aboard the *Ophir* before she sailed still lay before them.

Two days later the Grand Duchess went to Marlborough House to console Alix.

The weeping and wailing was quite awful. It could hardly have been worse had the *Ophir* sunk with all hands. She cried over the heads of May and George's children as though they were orphans and on the parish too. Briskly Aunt Augusta said she quite understood and she would return the next day to accompany Alix to the Palace.

'Oh, no!' cried the Queen. 'Oh, no!'

Aunt Augusta was firm. Prostrate with grief or not, Alix really must rouse herself to take an interest in her future home. Was the King himself to make all the necessary arrangements? Was it to be left to Lord Farquhar, the Master of the Household, or to Mrs Johnson, the Palace Housekeeper?

Alix did react to this challenge. Yes, she said, she would be ready to go with dear Aunt Augusta to the Palace.

It was not, however, an agreeable afternoon. Though the Grand Duchess tried to encourage her, saying how well this would look and that with a little alteration, and how pretty many of the rooms were, Alix was still only interested in finding suitable apartments for Charlotte Knollys and making sure, too, that in one of his strange moods of iconoclasm, Edward did not dismantle Mama's room and do away with all her precious souvenirs.

The Grand Duchess reported to the King that she had not been able to carry out all he asked, but at least the Helena–Alix sore was healing, and Alix seemed reconciled to moving to the Palace 'though with no more liking than Marie Antoinette had for the scaffold'. Did he, in fact, intend to dismantle his Mama's apartments? Yes, replied the King. It really was necessary. The keepsakes of years no longer had any meaning and the clutter was abominable, but he would make sure that nothing of interest or artistic value was lost and that the clearing should be done while Alix was in Denmark holidaying with her parents.

'Very wise, Sir,' the old lady approved. Then, because her visit was drawing to a close she thanked Edward for his kindness to her poor grand-daughter Marie. 'She has been misfortunate,' she said frankly, 'and is disposed to a natural melancholy. Being given the entrée to your Court has given her an éclat which will be of great benefit at home.'

The King admired the old lady for standing by her grand-daughter.

'For you, Aunt Augusta,' he murmured, kissing her cheek, 'anything is possible.'

Her wrinkled face broke into a shy smile. She curtsyed.

Edward bowed and took his leave.

From her drawing-room window the Grand Duchess saw the horses start up.

Again she curtsyed.

Then she turned to summon her grand-daughter Marie and 'Oh! Matilda!' Heyden. It was time they left Mecklenburg House and went home.

3

Three of the King's sisters awaited him in the Durbar Room at Osborne House. Lenchen, Princess Christian, had come down the day before from Cumberland Lodge in Windsor Great Park and stayed with her sister Beatrice, Princess Henry of Battenberg, at Osborne Cottage. The tall, stately Louise, Duchess of Argyll, had walked up the hill to Osborne from her own property, Kent House.

The Durbar Room was the latest addition to the royal apartments; a handsome room of fine plaster filigree work designed by Rudyard Kipling's father but alien really to the rest of the house. Queen Victoria had used it solely for ceremonial occasions and to her daughters it was far less redolent of the atmosphere which had always surrounded Mama. This was almost certainly why the King had chosen it as a rendezvous. To have met in the private apartments, the drawing-room or the Queen's own sitting-room, would have put them at once under her dominating influence. Apart from Princess Beatrice, and the housekeeper and cleaning servants, no one had regularly been into the private apartments since the general upheaval of the Queen's death and the subsequent pensioning off of her Indian attendants.

It was a hot August day. Lenchen and Beatrice, both stout and encased more than dressed in voluminous petticoats under their black dresses, suffered from the heat. Princess Louise, always the odd one out, stood by the window cool and poised, draped in soft hangings of thin lilac-coloured silk.

Their brother had telegraphed to say he would arrive at three at the Durbar Room. Ever punctual, he would be there on time. It still lacked four minutes to the hour. The sisters had already exchanged all the words they wished. Now they were waiting in silence; Louise looking forward to the meeting and the discomfiting of Beatrice; Lenchen a little distrait and sorry for Beatrice; Beatrice herself, determined not to show her feelings if she possibly could.

Hints of all kinds had been communicated to her: through various members of the family; through lawyers because, with Arthur and Mama's Privy Purse, she was executrix of the Queen's Will; and even one through official channels because she still held the office Mama had given her as Governor of the Isle of Wight. It was as plain as it was painful that Bertie was not going to keep on Osborne. The estate had been willed to him as had Balmoral, but he had Sandringham and Abergeldie as well as the Palace and Windsor. Balmoral he would keep. He liked the stalking and shooting. Abergeldie could go to George. So could Osborne if George wished, but Beatrice happened to know that, though May shared her feelings of reverence for Osborne House, just because it had been Mama's and was a shrine to her memory, George shared his father's passion for shooting at Sandringham.

The clock from the campanile struck the hour. Simultaneously there was the sound of horses at the outside entrance to the Durbar Room; the crunch of hooves and wheels on gravel. Edward was not even using the correct entrance to the house, thought Beatrice in dismay. He came in through the Durbar entrance hall and vestibule carrying his hat and cane. He kissed his sisters one by one, then gave a hasty glance round the room. He had been there on several state occasions, but he had not lived in the house as she had, always at Mama's beck and call for years. It was an unwanted legacy to him. To Beatrice, although she and her sons lived a little down the Cowes Road at Osborne Cottage, the place was home.

'It is hot,' he said. 'Shall we take a little air? My carriage is outside. We could drive to the Swiss Cottage.' He offered Lenchen his arm. As they walked out to the crimson royal carriage he patted the gun captured at the battle of Tel-el-Kebir in 1882. Beatrice panting behind Louise, saw his careless gesture. He was not even bothering to stay in the house. He wanted to get them away, right away.

She was quite right. The carriage took them round the Durbar Wing and the Royal Pavilion to the Italian garden. There Edward called for a halt. Too impatient even to reach the Swiss Cottage given to the royal children by their parents he walked his sisters round the Italian garden speaking deliberately in German so that the coachman and footmen could not understand.

He explained the situation and with a delicacy which did him honour.

Through the advice of his Jewish financier friends and the care of his Privy Purse, Sir Dighton Probyn – and frankly, because he had come by a great deal of money through his stables – he had ascended the throne without any debts, but he must be prudent and look to the future. The bulk of Mama's private fortune she had rightly willed to her younger children which left him, as King, in receipt of an adequate Civil List voted by Parliament, but not a great deal else. It was, of course, no secret that Alix was quite outstandingly extravagant, which meant that he had to look after her debts and, as May had not brought George any sort of *dot* worth speaking of, he had to look after them too. It followed that he must practise certain economies. Lord Esher had already put a number in hand, and things looked well, but he felt unable, quite unable – and here he avoided Beatrice's pug-dog eyes and looked directly at the pool with the fountain at its centre – quite unable to accept Mama's gracious bequest of Osborne House with its contents and the estate.

'It might be,' he added hurriedly, 'that George will decide to take it on and maintain it as Mama wished, but again I have to remind you that he took May without a fortune and his own income is limited.'

Beatrice's eyes had already filled with tears. So had Lenchen's, she was so sorry for her sister.

The King trailed a hand in the lily pond. 'Vicky is too ill to be concerned. She in any case, is well provided for. All of you, too, have your portions – which are adequate. But this house . . .' He waved a wet hand towards the Royal Pavilion; 'this house is too large for any of you and I cannot use it.'

Beatrice was many years younger than he and held him in respect which he hardly deserved. 'Too large,' she burst out. 'But made by Papa. It was his creation, and Mama loved it with all her heart.'

'It is not to my taste,' drawled Louise. She was considered the authority on art and literature in the family, but whether she meant what she said there was no means of telling. Only one thing was certain. She and Beatrice disliked each other intensely. Barren and not quite like other women, Louise had left her husband, but this had not prevented her setting her cap at other men – one of them Beatrice's adored husband, Prince Henry of Battenberg. To prevent her daughters scratching and clawing at each other the Queen had got Prince Henry out of the way by allowing him to go on the Ashanti campaign, and there and then he had died. A sore place had been further exacerbated.

Lenchen, happily married to a bald, easy-going German prince who loved roses and gardening and pipe-smoking and shooting, and who only had one eye (the other had been shot out by his brother-in-law, the Duke of Connaught), generally followed her husband's practice of counting to thirty whenever faced with a problem; but Louise's taunt had made Beatrice bristle like an angry hen.

'Your taste,' said Lenchen firmly, 'is beside the point. When you are not gallivanting you have Kent House.'

'Beatrice has Osborne Cottage,' snapped Princess Louise. 'And I will not be accused of gallivanting.'

'Ladies,' urged the King. 'Dear sisters.' He glanced towards the waiting coach. 'Shall we walk towards the sea?'

'I see no point,' said Beatrice angrily. 'The matter is decided and done with.' Her tears ran freely. 'Already Mama's precious keepsakes have been turned out of Windsor and Balmoral and the Palace. Only here are they left as she wished.' She sobbed. 'Since the day he died Mama has left Papa's rooms as they were. Nothing has been changed. Now you wish to alter everything.'

'Beatrice, Beatrice.' Edward tried to calm her. 'Hear me out.' He soothed her. 'I shall give the estate as it is to the nation, but with certain provisos. Nothing shall be altered in the State apartments. Nor in Mama's private suite. Servants will be kept on to clean and maintain them as they are; but Osborne, I fear, cannot any longer be regarded as the Sovereign's Marine Residence . . .'

'It is a great white elephant,' cut in Louise maliciously.

'That will do,' said the King sharply. He put his arm about Beatrice and deliberately led her away from her sisters. 'If you can, take no notice of Louise's unkindness. She has never been the happy one in our family. And believe me, this has to be. You will be at hand to visit whenever you wish and see that dear Mama's things are kept as they should be. I promise that neither her suite nor the State apartments will be altered. As to the Household wing – that is less treasured because Mama barely ever entered it, and I am considering putting it to two uses. One part can be a convalescent home for our poor officers who are invalided home from the front. The other I intend to use as a shore training establishment for naval cadets.' Shrewd, he had chosen well. Beatrice would interest herself in looking after convalescents, and she knew that his own grandsons David and Bertie were destined to be naval cadets. She would be able to mother them while they were at Osborne.

'Dear Bertie,' she said; and, then, quickly, 'I beg your pardon, Sir, but for the moment . . .'

He squeezed her arm. 'We are brother and sister,' he said encouragingly, 'and I am more sorry than I can say that we cannot keep on Mama's house here; particularly sorry,' he added, 'because I know how much it means to you.' He handed her his pocket handkerchief. 'That scrap of cambric is no use. Now wipe your eyes and blow your nose and we'll return to show Louise that her spite cannot hurt you.'

4

On the day following the meeting of the three sisters at Osborne House, their eldest sister, the Empress Frederick of Germany and Princess Royal of Great Britain and Ireland, died at her home in Kronberg. It was a release from a long and patiently borne agony.

Beatrice, who had visited her only three weeks before, was gratified to hear that at her passing a butterfly flew out from her bedroom and whirled away towards the forest. She took consolation in this sort of sentimental manifestation. It did not always go down well with her family. Not long after Mama's funeral she had been at Windsor with Alix looking for a suitable room to display the new Queen's water-colours, and a robin had come in the open window, circled round the room they were inspecting, and flown out again. Beatrice had clasped her hands and exclaimed that the robin must have been the spirit of Mama. Alix, not usually so practical, had put her down. 'I do not think, Beatrice,' she had said in her still guttural English, 'that that could have been Mama, because Mama would not have made a mess on my hat.'

Nevertheless when she left for Germany with the King Alix gratified Beatrice by showing great sensibility. She took with her a small wreath of wild flowers gathered at Windsor, the English home Vicky had so much loved.

Edward was at his lowest. Next to Alice he had loved and admired his sister Vicky more than all the others. The German practice of allowing her to die in such pain he castigated as downright cruelty, and he said as much to the German Emperor, who met him at Frankfurt to travel with the English party north to Homburg.

His nephew did not care at all for this lightly veiled criticism. Outright he said that just as Aunt Alix had shed Denmark when she married the Prince of Wales, so his mother had shed England on the day she married the Crown Prince of Prussia. And with England she had shed English medical practices which German physicians believed were of small practical value and sapping to the morale, in other words, soft.

King Edward's blue eyes blazed for a second. He recognized, he said stiffly, that this was no occasion for quarrelling but his nephew ought to realize that far from shedding Denmark on her marriage Aunt Alix had gone regularly there each year for several weeks, a liberty not allowed to the Empress Frederick who, although married to a German, had remained the Princess Royal of Great Britain and Ireland.

After this frank exchange the journey was not comfortable for anyone.

On arriving at Homburg where the first part of the funeral was to take place the King was astonished and very angry to hear that his sister's house had been surrounded by soldiers. He knew they were not there to honour her or guard her mortal remains, but to prevent anything from being removed. They were simply policemen. He felt ashamed to be wearing the uniform of his Prussian regiment which politeness obliged him to wear on meeting the German Emperor, and he was so upset that he made the first serious mistake of his reign.

Lord Lansdowne, the Foreign Minister, having great confidence in the King's diplomatic powers, had decided the occasion would be useful to sound out the genuineness or otherwise of the rapport which was said to be growing between Germany and England. With this in mind he had given the King a sheaf of confidential notes, outlining the position as he saw it. Generally much more astute than his traducers would allow, on this occasion the King allowed his feelings to get the better of him. In his sincere grief at the death of his sister, and his anger with his nephew – whom he was to meet officially for confidential exchanges of opinion after the funeral – he simply handed over Lansdowne's notes. In fact it did no harm save that it made the King and his Foreign Minister look foolish, but Lansdowne was understandably annoyed and he let the King know. It was an added chafe to an already difficult position.

The two parts of the Empress Frederick's funeral went well enough, but Edward regarded his nephew's cold attitude as heartless.

Alix was so outraged that when the time came for her to leave she could scarcely bring herself to say goodbye to Willy. As a Dane she hated Prussians, as a woman she heartily disliked the German Emperor, as a relation by marriage she was ashamed of him. But she did her duty, as Queens must, and went icily on her way to her stay at her father's palace in Copenhagen.

Edward returned to Homburg, a watering-place he had always found relaxing and enjoyable, but this was the first time that he had been there as King. His photograph was in every shop and he found himself being mobbed. He disliked it exceedingly.

A few old friends helped to keep curious trippers at bay, but he continued to be irritated. Only one consolation offered itself. Aunt Augusta's brother, the Duke of Cambridge, was taking the cure at Homburg accompanied by one of his old flames, the rich Mrs Vyner, and by his eldest son Colonel FitzGeorge. The King was relieved to have their company because 'Uncle George', as the King had always known him, was evidently in the highest spirits. They took tea together and, as those on a cure will, and especially those who are fond of food as these two were, the old Duke and the King talked almost exclusively of delicious dishes. After they had dined too well that evening they decided, for the sake of their diet, that it was wiser not to meet again.

King Edward went to see his sister's home once more before it was altered out of all recognition. He and Captain Ponsonby, who was acting as Private Secretary in his suite, went informally to Kronberg. The house had already been ransacked. The King and his Secretary exchanged glances. The Dowager Empress had known what she was about when she smuggled her papers from Germany. The King asked quietly if Ponsonby had them safely. Ponsonby had.

After stumping through the quiet house the King resolved never to return there again. He was sickened that a sovereign could be so devoid of good taste and a son so devoid of ordinary human feeling as to have had his mother's private apartments searched by a lot of common soldiers.

Nevertheless, for public and family peace, the King was prepared to stifle his feelings of repugnance when he made an unavoidable private visit to his nephew the Emperor at Wilhelmshoehe. Dressed once more in his detested Prussian uniform which, because of its tight fit and short tunic and his own barrel shape, was scarcely becoming, he travelled a four-hour train journey simply to have luncheon with the Emperor. Any hope that Willy might show some faint trace of being abashed was quickly lost. To the contrary, he was pert and smiling and apparently full of irrepressible energy. Naturally he had flown in the face of good taste and massed fifteen thousand soldiers to greet the King although the visit was a private one. And he put his uncle in a sulk by making facetious remarks about what he called 'the Lansdowne despatches'. Edward himself, and his ambassador, made it plain the memoranda had been simply memoranda, but the Emperor continued to tease. Then he produced a present for his uncle to mark the occasion: a gold cup for flowers with gold railings round it to support drooping blooms – a special invention of his own. Not expecting anything at all, this being a private visit, Edward had not brought a present himself. He was distinctly put out.

That afternoon he made the long, four-hour train journey back to Homburg and thence, as soon as he could, to England. He had done with Homburg and done with Willy for the time being, and he was not disappointed when Lord Lansdowne announced that the state of public opinion in Great Britain and Germany precluded the possibility of an Anglo-German alliance.

5

It was good to be home again yet he was upset to find his Private Secretary, Francis Knollys, in a sullen mood simply because Fritz Ponsonby had acted as Secretary on two visits to Germany. Knollys had resented Ponsonby's appointment in the first place, declaring obstinately that an Assistant Private Secretary was quite unnecessary – and especially one from Queen Victoria's Household. Now that the King was working independently through Ponsonby on foreign tours he was deeply offended. Up to then all information had passed through his hands. He had been the pivot. For a week or two after their return from Germany Knollys showed his resentment by denying Ponsonby information and not giving him enough to do.

The King considered. The truth was that he owed Knollys a great deal and Ponsonby, in comparison, very little. Yet he already knew the latter's worth and he was determined to be master in his own house. Given plenty of time, he was fairly certain that Knollys would get over his objection.

Frankly he explained the matter to his Assistant Private Secretary and, tactfully, Captain Ponsonby reported to his regiment and went to the front in South Africa.

Much more of a difficulty in the Royal Family was the Queen's continued objection to going to the Palace. She was determined to stay at Marlborough House until the last possible moment.

At luncheon soon after Edward's return he urged her to realize that they must move, and soon.

Young Prince David was at the table and tried to enter the conversation by saying: 'Grandpapa!'

The King frowned at him. He and his sister and brothers had been somewhat spoilt during their parents' absence in New Zealand and Australia.

'Mind your manners, David,' he rumbled – and continued listing the advantages of moving into more spacious apartments at the Palace and at Windsor. He made little impression on Alexandra. She seemed more taken up with the children. Really it was very aggravating.

He turned back to his grandson. 'Well, David,' he asked. 'And what was it you wished to say?'

'That there was a tiny slug on your lettuce, Grandpapa,' piped the little boy. 'But it doesn't matter now. You've eaten it.'

The King pushed his plate away.

On 1 November when George and May returned from a triumphant tour there were as many tears of happiness as there had been tears of misery at their departure. Through streets lined by cheering crowds the King and Queen drove the Duke and Duchess of Cornwall and York to Marlborough House.

A week later the King created his son Prince of Wales. It partially placated May, who had been piqued to discover that her parents-in-law still had not moved and how much her children had been indulged – taken from their lessons and their routine altered at the whim of their grandmother who used them as playthings.

The King groaned in spirit at the grievances which were in the air: felt but never expressed.

Alix was aggrieved because she knew that one day or other she would have to move to the Palace. She was aggrieved, too, by her daughter-in-law's unspoken condemnation of the way she had spoilt the children. To the King's dismay she spitefully remarked on May's inability to see things 'through royal eyes'. Far less sensible than Queen Victoria, she saw May's morganatic blood as some sort of stain, and had no idea that once Queen Victoria had said exactly the same of her because she came from a very minor royal family. 'Not a *real* princess,' her mother-in-law had remarked. Now she was saying the same of May.

May did not retaliate. She was more sure of herself now than she had been as Princess May of Teck. She owed respect and love to her mother-in-law, and sincerely pitied her deafness which made her so withdrawn and apparently indifferent to the feelings of others, but her judgement of Alexandra was not lacking in shrewdness. Complaining loudly that she was left out of things and that apparently a Queen Consort had no laid-down duties was really an excellent excuse for retiring to dear, dear Sandringham with dear, dear Charlotte. Nevertheless May amazed her father-in-law by announcing what alterations she proposed to make when she took over Marlborough House. No one wanted to leave it more than King Edward but he was pained by her wish for changes. What had been good enough for him ought to be good enough for his son. But May was resolved on this. She wrote a stern little note to her husband about it:

> *'Surely he must know we really cannot go into a filthy dirty house* – not *even to please him.'*

George rather agreed with his father, but said nothing. Still, he was aggrieved by his mother's unfair attitude to May. He was a simple sailor, no linguist like his father and preferred stamp-collecting and shooting to the pleasures of the King's fast set. Moreover he had married for reasons of state not love, engaging himself in duty bound to his dead brother's fiancée. Nevertheless in the eight years of their marriage he and May had become deeply attached to one another, and while he loved his mother with a deep and abiding passion, he considered she was being unfair. He was also aggrieved by the pressure put on him to take on Osborne House, which his father formally offered him as a country home.

The King was quite insistent.

Even more so was Aunt Beatrice who pleaded with him to respect the old Queen's wishes. George had dearly loved his grandmother and found himself in an uncomfortable position but, trained as a sailor and with May there to bolster his resolve, he squarely faced the facts. They had York Cottage at Sandringham, and Frogmore House was promised to them as well as Abergeldie. He could not afford Osborne. Besides, there was nothing to shoot at Osborne.

Princess Beatrice, her last faint hope gone, retired sadly to Osborne Cottage. She let her brother know that she would always do her duty as a royal princess and attend Courts and the Opening of Parliament at his bidding, but otherwise she wished to live quietly and privately in her widowhood.

His sister's decision and her attitude hurt and aggrieved the King. He considered he could not have managed the matter of the Royal Marine Residence with more courtesy and sensibility, and yet Beatrice had cut herself off from the mainstream of the family.

He was a worried man; worried about the Boer War, a remote leech which was sucking the country's blood; worried about his family; worried about himself. He showed symptoms of overstrain, drinking more than was his habit as a stimulant and eating even more. He fell asleep suddenly at odd times for no reason. Once he even nodded off in the middle of a meal.

He had such feelings of inadequacy that he confided to friends like Carrington and Redesdale and Devonshire he had a mind to abdicate. All three sympathized, but none thought it a good idea.

Carrington with the privilege allowed a boyhood friend reminded him of his mercurial temperament; however deep a low he was in at present he would be up and out of it soon enough.

Redesdale helped him to see things in a more realistic light by remarking dryly that threatening to abdicate was a particular malady of the Hanoverians. George IV had gone in for it a good deal. Even William IV, who so much enjoyed being King – had done it once or twice. As for Queen Victoria, there had been occasions when the smallest frustration had made her a prey to this melancholy speculation. Was it any wonder, he asked, that King Edward should catch the same disease?

But it was Devonshire, in his gruff, dreamy way who really made Edward see sense by pointing out that the Prince of Wales, ably helped as he was by his wife, still had a lot to learn. When he knew as much about statecraft as he did about philately that was the time to hand him the throne. Until then Edward, King and Emperor, had better stay where he was.

6

1901 slid into 1902 – and in a Boer War uproar.

The Colonial Secretary, Joe Chamberlain – with all the bellicosity of a former radical-pacifist turned imperialist-jingoist – defended his policies with all his might. Chief of England's critics were the Germans. Chamberlain retorted that the behaviour of British troops in South Africa very favourably compared with German atrocities committed in the Franco-Prussian War of thirty years before. It caused a sullen roar of anger through the German Empire. Bülow the Chancellor seized on the occasion to make himself popular with the masses by announcing in the Reichstag that anyone who cast aspirations on the glorious German army would find 'he was biting on granite'.

The statement won him momentary credit amongst his countrymen, but only contempt from those he had hoped to intimidate. Unfortunately, perhaps unwittingly, he had borrowed the phrase from Frederick the Great, undoubtedly a great soldier but, as the British were quick to remember, one who 'knew love only in the arms of his drummer boys', and just at that particular time there was evidence that many high-ranking Germans were also falling victim to the charms of handsome young men. Friedrich Krupp, Member of the Chamber of Lords and of the Council of State of Prussia, and the world's largest armaments manufacturer, had at last been found out. He did what was expected and shot himself in Essen, though it was given out that he had died of apoplexy.

Again to the surprise of Europe, the German Emperor personally attended the funeral and sent a wreath inscribed *'To my best friend'*. This was solely because no one with anything to hide had dared to sue the radical newspapers which printed the accusations, and the facts were easily kept from the Emperor because he only read one newspaper, his own, a personal imperial daily, printed in gold, of 'welcome' excerpts chosen from other papers.

Joe Chamberlain gleefully rubbed his hands together while all the Fatherland – except the Emperor William – writhed in temporary mortification. The mischief Bülow had tried to create had been entirely undone by his own stupidity.

But not only the Germans sympathized with the Boers.

The radical Welsh lawyer David Lloyd George was publicly waging a pro-Boer campaign – though largely, King Edward understood, because of a personal vendetta against Mr Chamberlain.

Though a turncoat and a parvenu and a Unitarian from Birmingham, Chamberlain was genially accepted by a society which would never be elastic enough to receive the lapsed Baptist farmer's son from Wales. Not that Lloyd George cared a scrap. He had attacked the establishment from the days he attended a village school; as local reporter, dissenting agitator, hard-working student, and small-town solicitor; and he had the courage – or the effrontery, it depended on how one looked at it – to carry his war on Joe right into the heart of Joe's own country, to the Town Hall in Birmingham. At least he tried to, arriving disguised in a worker's cap and heavy overcoat. But speech-making was absolutely out of the question and he had to give his written oration to the press before escaping from the Town Hall, this time disguised as a policeman, marching in a rank of others with bull's-eyes and truncheons for all the world like the chorus in the *Pirates of Penzance*. Denied Lloyd George's head, the mob turned the Town Hall into a Roman circus. Two men were killed, dozens were seriously injured. One thousand, one hundred and ninety-eight windows were broken. Everything smashable was smashed.

This sort of public exhibition by a Member of the Commons irritated the King intensely. Lloyd George's pro-Boer views positively enraged him – which possibly was good for him at this juncture. Reflecting on these 'stabs in the back to our men at the front' might send up his blood pressure, but they also took him out of himself. He was also enraged by the Irish nationalist Members of Parliament who treacherously cheered news of Boer victories in the House. Indignation gave him a fresh decisiveness. He was thoroughly woken up. Abruptly he cancelled a projected tour of Ireland. His mother had honoured the Irish troops for the part they had played in the war, but he was determined not to hold any traffic with these seditious Celts. They were as bad as the pestiferous Lloyd George – another Celt.

That one of his former mistresses, Lady Warwick, should also have pro-Boer tendencies did not surprise Edward in the least. His Darling Daisy, as he called her, had always had more heart than head, and the immensity of her riches almost exactly matched her compassion for the weak and the poor. Darling Utopian Daisy. As a socialist, pro-Boer Countess, she was a bore, but only in that, and just at this very time Edward knew she was suffering hell from a disastrous love affair. Their own affair was dead, though it was happily recalled by each of them, and so were all Daisy's other adventures of the heart, but now, poor woman, at an age close on forty, she had fallen head over heels in love with one of the most irresistible men of his generation, the dashing Major Laycock who placed a secret wedding ring on her finger (though she was, of course, married at the time) and had returned her devotion in bits and pieces. There was no other way of putting it, wailed Daisy. The other bits and pieces he had been regularly bestowing on Lady Downshire and had allowed himself to be caught out by her husband's private detectives. Promptly, because custom and prudence demanded it, detectives were set on to Lord Downshire in the hope of discovering anything discreditable which might be used as a lever to prevent him divorcing his lovely marchioness. But Downshire led a blameless life morally, despite his oddity of dressing each morning in a butcher's apron and driving a cart round his Irish estate selling chunks of meat to his tenants. The case was heard that spring and Kitty Downshire found herself divorced. Joe Laycock would have to do the right thing and marry her when the decree absolute came through. Meanwhile poor, pro-Boer Daisy was desperate, playing any card she could, bombarding him with passionate letters, aware that she was about to lose the love of her life.

Her friends were concerned to see her frenzied attempts to hold on to Joe, none more than the King. He overlooked what he considered her eccentricities and assured her of his constant devotion.

Queen Alexandra, usually self-immured at Sandringham and refusing to take an interest in anything very much at all, suddenly arrived in London. She had heard of Daisy's trouble and contrived to knock the last nail into the coffin of her relationship with Edward. In England he had his Agnes Keyser and Mrs George Keppel, both of whom she liked and trusted, but she suspected that Daisy Warwick, in the agony of losing Joe to Kitty Downshire, would try anything to get him back, and even involve the King. She wrote a kind but firm little note to Daisy, then asked the *éminence grise* of Windsor, the obliging Lord Esher, to call on her and explain that she must never entertain Pompadour ideas of being a power behind the throne.

Daisy accepted the inevitable. She had to this time. But she adored Joe so much that she was unscrupulous to the last. When he did marry Kitty Downshire and they went off to Paris for their honeymoon, he was recalled by a telegram to say Daisy Warwick had taken poison and he was to come at once. Obediently he did, to be met by a radiant Daisy who fell into his arms and had her share of the honeymoon before he felt compelled to return to his bride in Paris.

In the months before his Coronation the King's close friends realized quite well how difficult he found it to relax. They took great pains to keep up his spirits and provide the novelties his restless nature craved for.

Lord Carrington attempted, without a great deal of success, to persuade him that politics was an exciting business. Of no real party, the King just did not believe him. Nor did Lord Redesdale do much more than calm him with his reasoned arguments, his views on diplomacy, and his enthusiasm for plant-life. The Rothschilds did their very large best. Lord Natty discussed, had made up, and tasted with the King exquisite dishes. He also begged the King to go down to Tring where his son had assembled thousands of stuffed birds and the largest collection of fleas in the world. Natty's brother, Leopold, talked racing with the King by the hour and confirmed that once, seeing a poor little chap at a Rothschild garden party, and thinking he must be in some sort of need, he had only just been prevented from tipping the Prince of Wales half a crown – a tale which the King just accepted without a frown because it was in danger of lessening the dignity of the throne. Natty's youngest brother, the bachelor Alfred, kept his sovereign endlessly amused with the eccentricities of his sybaritic life: conducting his own private symphony orchestra with a flawless ivory bâton encircled with diamonds; driving a four in hand of zebras; and serving pheasants out of season at grand banquets, by eating them young and calling them *Poussins Haltonais* after his country seat at Halton. The Sassoons added a less opulent yet no less genuine concern for King Edward's relaxation, as did those of the former Marlborough House Set who entertained him in the country.

The King's ladies also did their duty by him.

Agnes Keyser did her best to calm him. She refused to allow him to mention any excitable subject in her presence, and obediently he submitted. He also permitted her to feed him with nursery food which, she said, was the only way to fortify his nerves, cheer him up and cut down his weight.

Mrs George Keppel was equally assiduous in trying to get the King to look after himself. Fractious because his tailor was for ever adjusting or replacing suits which had become too tight, the King agreed that as soon as he could he would take a cure – but not, he exclaimed, holding up podgy hands in protest, *not* at Homburg. He had done with being stared at and mobbed. Mrs Keppel soothed him. There was no need to return to Homburg. There were plenty of other spas....

Most successful of all was Lord Esher who cleverly persuaded the King to stage-manage his own Coronation. He had always been an expert on ceremonial and together they looked out precedents. The King's great-uncle George IV had been crowned at great cost amidst mediaeval splendour and an extraordinary number of calamities had occurred. His other great-uncle, William IV, had practised the strictest economy, but again there had been some strange mistakes. His Mama's coronation was best remembered for the quality and quantity of food and drink provided by the Dean and Chapter of Westminster in a refreshment alcove constructed behind the High Altar, and the fact that the newly crowned Queen had gone straight home to give her dog a bath.

Edward's enthusiasm waxed fast. He wished, he said, for magnificence and correct procedure. Esher, who alone could prevent him from plunging into ostentation, undertook to supply both. Wisely he advised against giving the motor car industry a fillip by arriving at the Abbey in a gilded Panhard.

The Grand Duchess of Mecklenburg-Strelitz was again consulted. She had attended William IV's Coronation and Queen Victoria's, yet her advice was not always accepted. To her dismay she heard that the traditional colour of Princesses' trains had been changed; that the Queen Consort had decided to choose her own robes.

'Can *it be*?' She wrote from Strelitz.

Indeed it was. Not even Lord Esher could move Queen Alexandra when she was determined on something. She made this perfectly clear:

> '*I know better than all the milliners and antiquaries, I shall wear exactly what I like and so will all my ladies* – Basta!'

The Grand Duchess concluded that Alix was simply being awkward. She most certainly could be, as her closest relatives and friends well knew. Sometimes the popular picture of a gracious and lovely and deeply wronged woman collapsed. Alix's amiability was limited and not constant. For example, though generally she was kindness itself to her Maids of Honour, vanity made her choose the tallest to attend her on the most sparkling Court occasions while the little ones had to be content with drearier duties; and her Ladies-in-Waiting dreaded her flashes of anger – which is not surprising considering that once she thrashed one with a long, steel umbrella. Fellow Rumpenheimer or no, Aunt Augusta decided it was not prudent to persist. The King and Lord Esher had already come to the same conclusion and left the Queen's robes entirely to the Queen.

At last everything was in the Esher notebooks. The King was more content than he had been for a long time. Only two problems weighed on his mind. Would the ancient Archbishop of Canterbury survive the long ceremony? and how could Willy be prevented from making a nuisance of himself?

The former had to be left to providence; apparently the latter was an impossibility.

Crowned heads did not attend a coronation but sent their heirs. However, the German Emperor would not allow the Crown Prince to be there because, on a previous occasion, he had mixed with the fastest of people, and bounded from bed to bed with a most unprincely abandon. Prince Henry of Prussia, Willy's brother, would be sent instead.

So be it, said the King grimly, putting Prince Henry after all the heirs to thrones in precedence.

The Emperor was not pleased.

Possibly the greatest of the King's solaces in the months which led up to the Coronation was the establishment of the Cavendish, a very, very private hotel recently bought by Mrs Excelsior Lewis.

For years the King had liked Rosa Lewis' cooking and on special occasions at his friends' houses Rosa was generally hired to make the complicated but not over-rich dishes of which he was especially fond, and now that her husband Excelsior had fallen prey to the butler's temptation and become an alcoholic, she had obtained a quick separation and sunk all her savings into the Cavendish. The King quickly took a set of apartments and was intrigued by the decorations and the convenient arrangements made for slipping in and out at will. Rosa's Cavendish was perfectly safe – even for the King of England, and there she provided the aristocracy with two highly valued assets: delicious food and wine and absolute discretion. Her motto, she told the King, was 'No letters, no lawyers, and kiss my baby's bottom'.

7

Just in time for the Coronation the Boer War ground to a halt, with small advantage to the victor. And when Captain Fritz Ponsonby returned from South Africa to take up his duties at Court again, he found Sir Francis Knollys was to be given a peerage in the Coronation Honours list, and his own job had been cut in two. If Assistant Private Secretaries *were* necessary said solemn

Knollys, let there be two to take turn and turn about. The implication was obvious; only working for six months in the year neither of the Assistant Secretaries could obtain any real influence over the King, not influence, that is, as Knollys understood it.

Ponsonby complained ruefully to his co-Assistant Secretary – not because he had to share the work with him for they happened to be old friends, but because, after seven years in the royal service, he had suddenly lost £200 a year and been given only half a job. Then, more forcefully, he complained to Knollys. The latter received his protest in chilly silence. It had been decided, he declared, the decision had been made. He spoke as if the declaration had the authority of Holy Writ.

But though he regretted his loss of income, Ponsonby found himself more and more in the confidence of his master. King Edward had not forgotten all Ponsonby's father had done for Queen Victoria over a period of many years, nor that it was Fritz Ponsonby himself who had risked her grave displeasure by pointing out the obvious failings of her loathed Indian servant, the Munshi. Moreover Edward liked his company. Advising him to be tolerant and keep out of Knollys' way until the Private Secretary was more used to the idea of having official Assistants, the King gave Ponsonby many responsible tasks which required tact and discretion. Soon he was as close to him as to any of the members of his Household, and he used Ponsonby as a liaison officer between six of the seven highly placed counsellors Mrs Asquith had denigrated as 'the Court Pests'. The seventh, Knollys, still maintained a deep mistrust of anyone who had worked in the old-fashioned household of Queen Victoria.

Ponsonby also maintained close private contact with the King's Ministers; soothing the latter when they were angered by Edward's straightforward – and, therefore, unstatesmanlike – way of going about things, and soothing the King when he believed his royal prerogatives were being nibbled away by 'those damned rats in the Cabinet'.

He was not always successful and very seldom with the Marquess of Salisbury.

The Prime Minister was a tall and heavy man, deeply religious and markedly eccentric. He wore, for example, the shabbiest clothes and pretended to be a philistine, but this was simply to tease, because his wardrobe was rich and vast and he habitually read Goethe or Sophocles to cleanse himself – as he put it – from politics. And though in many ways he was ultra-modern, interesting himself in electric light, the telephone, tricycling, steam cars, and in chemistry, he was more of an eighteenth-century statesman in mood, in points of view, and in action. Having been three times Prime Minister and never fond of Queen Victoria, he hardly took her son seriously at all, and remained unimpressed by his sovereign's attempt to regain certain powers already lost. With olympian calm, he declared that the King's claim to see Cabinet Papers while matters were under consideration was totally obsolete.

King Edward was exceedingly put out, especially as the pronouncement came from a man generally regarded as far past his peak of usefulness to the country. 'Why he can't even recognize his own family!' declared the King angrily – which was perfectly true. Salisbury considered such things as of small importance, and had once asked at Court for the name of the young man who was beaming at him so amiably across the room, only to be told that it was his eldest son.

Ponsonby had to call in the aid of Mrs George Keppel, Lord Esher and even Sir Ernest Cassel, to quieten the King's indignation with his Prime Minister.

He was hardly more successful in reconciling his master with the Foreign Secretary, Lord Lansdowne, and found himself being used as a punchball between sovereign and minister over the matter of whether or not the Shah of Persia should be given the Order of the Garter. The Shah was due to make a State Visit soon after the Coronation and let it be known he expected the Garter. This had been promised by Lansdowne, who considered it politically expedient. Not on any account, roared the King; though his mother the Queen had been cruelly pressed to bestow the Garter on a brace of infidel monarchs, he had no intention of doing so.

Happily for Ponsonby the affair of the Shah's Garter was temporarily eclipsed by the Coronation which loomed before everyone. . . .

Lord Esher had everything at his fingertips. The fourteen-mile procession route wore an unusual look because of the tiers of stands, barricades, flag poles and Venetian masts. The military had drilled themselves into perfection. The Navy, given no less an important part to play, rehearsed for weeks. So did the many bands. The clergy and peerage practised their parts; that is, all save the ancient Archbishop who was living largely on port and meat jellies and whose strength had to be preserved. The Grand Duchess of Mecklenburg-Strelitz bombarded London with letters, giving and demanding information. As 26 June approached deputations from the Empire and Dominions and Colonies with representatives from the Courts of Europe, began to arrive in a bedecked London. A small sensation occurred amongst those who were hostile to masonic orders when the special United States representative arrived with a portrait of George Washington got up in Masonic regalia as America's coronation gift. Another sensation took place when an oriental mission arrived and commenced to turn their hotel suite into the replica of a caravansary.

Twelve days beforehand the King went to review his troops at Aldershot. With him travelled the Queen, George and May, and other members of the family.

Accustomed to his tempestuous bursts of rage, they were, nevertheless, alarmed by the King's passion when he discovered the Royal Pavilion was damp and distinctly uncomfortable. He already had an attack of lumbago for which he required warmth and rest. How the devil, he bellowed, could he get either in such a place? His own servants plus a score of soldier servants scurried to light fires and make the Pavilion more habitable. They knew someone would have to pay for this.

At twenty minutes past midnight the Pavilion rang with cries of pain. Everyone was woken. Two doctors arrived. They conferred with the Queen and the Prince of Wales. The King's illness was certainly not lumbago. His face mottled with a mixture of pain and anger the King declared it *was* lumbago. That, at any rate, was what he insisted the doctors should say. 'Otherwise all the arrangements will go to the devil.'

The Queen conferred with her family. They agreed to humour the King for fear of exciting his condition. But he was persuaded to forgo attending the Garrison Church the next morning, and in the afternoon the Queen had to go alone to visit three hospitals and a library.

When circumstances forced her to be less introspective, Alix could summon up reserves of courage and face almost any situation. The royal physicians insisted that the King could not possibly attend the ceremonial review. Therefore she took his place, driving on to the parade ground in an open landau despite a thin trickle of rain which, in the march-past of two and a half hours, soaked her through. Afterwards, she changed and consulted with her son and the physicians as to how best they could get the King from Aldershot to Windsor. Clearly he could not endure the jolting of a motor car. He positively refused to travel by special train which would give rise to public alarm. As a compromise he agreed to travel the twenty miles in a carriage. Pallid and occasionally groaning, he clutched his wife's hand as the carriage rolled to Windsor. At a discreet distance followed a second carriage crammed with physicians.

'I must get to Ascot,' he kept repeating. 'I must get to Ascot.'

There was no question now but that he was seriously ill. Despite all forecaution the news leaked out. He was quite unable to drive down to Ascot. Again Alix bravely took his place, and was greeted by a vast crowd in absolute silence. There was simply the rattle of wheels and carriage springs and harness, the whinnying of horses; nothing else. The race-goers could not have given a more moving demonstration of their sympathy, nor of their own sense of anxiety.

On the following Sunday the Prince of Wales sent for Captain Ponsonby. As he had such influence over the King could he please try to persuade him not to get up and tire himself; and if he insisted, would Captain Ponsonby stay close by to attend him in any way that might be needed? King Edward was very ill and yet persisted in entertaining friends to luncheon – they included Mrs Keppel – and afterwards despite the most outspoken warnings of his Assistant Secretary, he walked them round the Castle, moving faster and faster, hurting himself more and more as a child will jig endlessly at an aching tooth. Ponsonby, Mrs Keppel, eventually all his guests begged him to stop and rest, but he went on and on – so rapidly that they themselves were tired out. After the party's departure, he sat on a marble seat and Ponsonby just caught him as he fell forward in a dead faint.

The Prince and Princess of Wales went quietly to their apartments. He was deeply alarmed, more moved that she had ever seen him. He paced their sitting-room. 'Poor Papa!' he exclaimed. 'Poor, poor Papa!' Unlike most Hanoverians with their heirs, he and his father were excellent friends and devoted to one another. George was appalled by this sudden calamity. Then something else occurred to him. 'I am not ready,' he cried, bursting into tears. 'I am not ready. He must not die.'

The Princess put her arms round him and he sobbed against her shoulder. She was carrying her fifth child, and not feeling in the best of spirits, but she tried her best to cheer her husband. Her own private feelings were that someone in authority should tell the King, and as forcefully as possible, that it was his chief duty to get well and not concern himself wholly with the impossibility of trying to deceive the people. But there was no one with sufficient authority. Much of the Queen's influence as a wife had been lessened by his relationships – the Princess would not call them affairs – with Mrs Keppel and Sister Keyser. She herself had little or no influence. Otherwise – she pursed her lips as she soothed her sobbing husband – otherwise she would most certainly have used it.

On the next morning the King and Queen were due to arrive at Paddington and drive in semi-state with a Captain's escort of the Household Cavalry to the Palace. The physicians forebade it. Flushed with a high fever and in great pain the King told them to go to the devil. He refused to abandon the drive. The Queen resigned herself to a nightmare journey. Having heard he was gravely ill, the crowds were amazed and brightened to see the King driving through the streets. He was red-faced and swayed and sometimes he winced when the carriage passed over an uneven patch, but Queen Alexandra beside him waved and bowed and smiled to them all. They responded with cries of joy, fluttered their handkerchiefs, threw their hats in the air. The King was all right after all.

At the Palace he collapsed. The Queen sent out an order. Two hundred guests would attend a state banquet there that evening but the King himself would not appear. She would preside herself attended by her son and her daughter-in-law.

At 4.30 the King woke from a deep sleep induced by a draught of sedatives. His Physician to the Household, Sir Thomas Barlow, and his Surgeon-Apothecary, Sir Francis Laking, were standing beside his bed.

'Laking,' he exclaimed. 'Barlow, I feel a good deal better.'

'You are not better, Sir,' said Sir Francis gravely. 'You have a seriously inflamed appendix, and if it is not operated on peritonitis will assuredly follow, and you will die.' He looked at the Household Physician who took the hint.

'You will die, Sir,' he echoed.

'Nonsense,' rumbled the King and tried to sit up. 'Help me, damn you both.' And as neither moved he called for Chandler, the Superintendent of his Wardrobe, who genially acted as his whipping-boy whenever he was angry. Summoning Chandler was tantamount to announcing the King was about to lose his temper very seriously. 'Chandler,' he roared – and then crumpled in the bed with pain.

'Lie still, Sir,' ordered Laking. It truly was an order.

The King regarded him balefully while Barlow took his pulse.

'You have a high fever, Sir,' observed Laking. 'It is more prudent to lie still and not fret yourself, otherwise the pain will get very much worse.'

The threat was effective, or appeared to be. The King lay there gasping while Barlow told him a special room had been made into an operating theatre. His Honorary Sergeant Surgeon, Sir Frederick Treves, who was unequalled in appendectomy, had made all the preparations, and, after a night of rest, he was prepared to operate.

'The Coronation, I fear, Sir, will have to be postponed,' said Laking firmly. 'But as your life is at stake . . .'

'Laking,' shouted the King furiously. 'I will stand no more of this. I am suffering the most awful mental agony any man can endure. Leave the room at once.'

A pre-arranged signal took place between the two physicians. Instead of Laking leaving the room, Sir Thomas Barlow did.

'Laking!' exclaimed his master. 'I have given you an order.'

'Obedience, Sir, in this case is impossible. My duty to you is a physician's to his patient. In this case my Hippocratic oath comes before my oath of allegiance.'

There was a soft pleading in his tone which brought a slow alteration in the King's stubbornness. They were old associates. Laking had been in his Household when he was Prince of Wales. Laking had gone with him to Germany to try and help his sister Vicky in her last agonies.

'I am devoted to you, Sir; and I have been long in your service. I cannot, cannot let you die without making some attempt to prevent it.'

The King eyed him warily. 'You are sure of it?'

'Absolutely. If you wish I will give you the exact medical particulars, though they do not make pleasant hearing, and I will tell you what sort of death it is you face.'

The King held up his hand. Anger and pain had wearied him. 'I trust you, Francis,' he said suddenly. 'Do as you wish.'

Laking caught his breath in relief. 'Thank you, Sir. Now the first thing is to make you comfortable and give you a further sedative so that you can enjoy a long and strengthening sleep.'

Charles, Earl Carrington, the Duke of Devonshire and Lord Redesdale stood in the doorway of the Upper Chamber that afternoon when Lord Spencer rose to ask the Prime Minister a question. Redesdale was courtly and old-fashioned and generally accounted a good influence on the King. Both the others at some time had competed with Edward for the favour of certain ladies. Carrington had known him since childhood. Devonshire, as Lord Hartington, had gone racing with him and given him the splendid hospitality of his country seats. All three were devoted to him.

The House was full when Lord Spencer put his question. Could the most noble Marquis inform their lordships as to the state of the King's health?

At this point every peer in the House removed his hat, except for the Queen's Lord Chamberlain, poor Lord Colville who was eighty-four and who was sitting on the sacks looking at the ground and weeping.

Lord Salisbury who was unwell himself stood up, unfurled his great height and massive form like a waking seal. He was impressed by his colleagues' mark of esteem for a King he himself thought little of. Perhaps he had been mistaken. The possibility made him more expansive than he would ordinarily have been. He informed the House of the critical nature of the sovereign's health, of the hope that an operation for the removal of the appendix might be successful but the King was very ill indeed, that the Coronation would have to be indefinitely postponed. . . .

Carrington, Redesdale and Devonshire and a few other of

Edward's intimates in the House who had heard this Job-like utterance were hardly reassured. A deep gloom descended on them. Old Lord Colville continued to cry salt tears on to the sacks.

Queen Alexandra presided at a muted State Banquet. The menu was worthy of a happier occasion. How, she thought moodily, Bertie would have loved it: trout, quails, poussins, Basque ham, ortolans, asparagus, anchovy canapées....

She had not been told what the Medical Household was planning for the next morning. They had thought it kinder not to worry her. As it was she was striving to fight down a panic of apprehension simply because she did not know.

Her son was fighting panic of a different kind. The physicians had thought it proper to inform him, and he foresaw the worst.

Despite a widely circulated rumour to the contrary, which persisted for decades, and which probably originated from his loud voice and laughter, allied to the flushed and mottled complexion he had had ever since an attack of typhoid ten years before, the Prince was normally an abstemious man. Nevertheless at that particular banquet, his appetite altogether cut by the physician's warning, he permitted himself to be helped liberally to the sherry laid down in 1837, the year of Grandmama's Coronation, an 1853 Madeira, a sparkling Rudesheim only eight years old and at its perfection. The champagnes he missed, preferring a claret, Château Langoa of 1874, to help down the ortolans and salad, and then he took a royal Tawny Port of 1863. His head buzzed as it had not since he paid off his last command. He caught his wife's eye. She nodded to give him courage from a distance. He needed it. He simply was not ready. Not ready at all.

When the banquet was done, and they were free to go, the Waleses went to the apartments which had been set aside for them. The Prince at once went to smoke nervously in the sitting-room. Without being summoned the Princess' old governess and friend, Mlle Hélène Bricker, had arrived to do all she could at this awful moment. Princess May threw herself into Mam'selle's arms. Only with her could she comfortably be her real self: 'Oh, do pray that he may get well,' she sobbed. 'George says he isn't ready yet to reign.'

. . . .

Sir Frederick Treves cast a last searching look round the room which had been prepared as an operating theatre. All was exactly as it should be. Three of the Royal Medical Household were with him. A fourth, Sir Francis Laking, ushered the royal patient into the room.

The King had insisted on walking there himself. Queen Alexandra, with commendable courage, had insisted on being with him.

To Treves' concern she remained whilst the anaesthetic was administered. Inevitably this was almost as difficult a proceeding as the operation because the King was an addicted smoker and his waist measurement of 48 inches actually equalled that of his chest. Growing black in the face the King thrashed and flailed about.

The Queen struggled with the others to hold him down. 'Oh, why don't you begin?' she cried.

It dawned upon the surgeon that she believed it was her duty to be present at the actual operation. He looked appealingly at Laking who took the Queen's arm and led her gently from the room to where her daughter Victoria and George and May were waiting with clasped hands. Treves gave a sigh of relief. His royal patient's heavings ceased. He took off his frock-coat, put on an apron, tucked up his sleeves and began. It was 12.25 p.m.

Forty minutes afterwards Treves resumed his frock-coat and went to tell the Queen and her family that the operation had been a complete success. The King had just woken from the anaesthetic and asked for his son. 'Where's George?' Such are the commonplace utterances of men who return from the threshold of death. On recovering from typhoid many years before his first words had been to ask for a bottle of Bass' beer. But the Press gingered up both utterances. In this case 'Where's George?' was changed to the more moving phrase: 'Will my people ever forgive me?'

That afternoon an unpostponable rehearsal for the Coronation took place in Westminster Abbey. A good many had absented themselves, but those most closely concerned with the ceremony were there. Hearing the good news the Bishop of London showed great presence of mind and turned the rehearsal into an impromptu Service of Thanksgiving for the recovery of the King.

On the day he should have been crowned the King gave an order that all the perishable items prepared for the Coronation Banquet should be given away. The caviar could be pressed on ice, so could the two thousand, five hundred quails; but there were huge excess quantities of chicken, ptarmigan, partridge, royal sturgeon, and cutlets, not to mention dozens of side dishes. These were distributed to the indigent of Whitechapel by the Sisters of the Poor. Frankly they would have preferred a dish of winkles or jellied eels or a cut at a leg of mutton to the *Côtelettes de bécassines à la Souvaroff* and *Consommé de faisan aux quenelles* and so forth which had been prepared for princes and diplomats. Still, it made a change. . . .

8

Despite his vast chest and stomach measurements and his prowess as a trencherman and smoker, the King's wound quickly healed and his physicians said that it ought to be possible to hold the Coronation within a matter of weeks if he took proper care of himself. A convalescent cruise was decided on as the best way to keep him from doing too much. The Queen seriously considered the idea of inviting Sister Keyser to take charge of him. No one was better at keeping the King from going on the rampage, but, under the circumstances, she thought it might not be circumspect. She asked George and May for their opinion. George thought it would not matter. May most certainly thought it would. Sister Keyser was not invited, but she supervised from a distance, writing out diet sheets and daily timetables which the Queen found very useful. It was planned that the convalescent cruise should begin on St Swithin's day, 15 July.

Three days before the King showed he was very much on the mend by quarrelling with his Prime Minister. Lord Salisbury, after making suitable congratulations on his sovereign's marvellously rapid recovery, begged him to discuss afresh before his departure the question of Coronation Honours.

On his own initiative the King had recently founded an Order of Merit, for which he personally proposed to nominate members, and he reserved the right to confer the Royal Victorian Order at his own discretion. All other honours lay in the hands of the Prime Minister, and Salisbury was not eager to give them too freely. He was in accord that Treves and Laking should be rewarded with baronetcies, but he was opposed to a considerable enlargement of the Upper Chamber and on this occasion to the inclusion of a certain nominee of the Duke of Devonshire, who had recommended a Liberal–Unionist M.P. The Duke's nominee would have to wait until the next Birthday Honours.

The King had a natural regal manner exactly like his mother. *Son métier est Roi* was said of him everywhere in Europe. But any hint that his prerogatives were being lessened induced in him a callow and offensive hauteur. He was rude to his Prime Minister, quite insistent, and when Lord Salisbury said in his tired old voice: 'That, Sir, is impossible!' he drew himself up and replied: '*I* wish him to be given a peerage, and he must have it.'

Ordinarily perhaps Lord Salisbury might have given way, but his dearly loved wife had died two years before and ever since he had looked and felt old and bent and ill. Personally devoted to the old-fashioned conservatism which had been aristocratic, paternal and landed – in fact, really Whiggish – he privately deprecated the new and alien Conservatism which was middle-class, managerial and industrial. Yet he had struggled through the end of the Boer War and had intended to resign after the Coronation; but now, in a flash, he saw an opportunity of retiring to recoup his strength at his French home on the Riviera and stimulate his flagging intellectual zest with chemical experiments in his laboratory at Hatfield. . . .

To Edward's astonishment his solemn, ponderous Prime Minister was bowing and saying that as his advice was unacceptable he had no other course but to resign. And resign he did, refusing inflexibly to change his mind. He would hand in his seals of office at once and recommend the King send for his nephew, Arthur Balfour, First Lord of the Treasury to form a new ministry.

King Edward found his tongue, graciously thanked Salisbury for his long years of public service, and undertook to send for Balfour. But when the old man had bowed himself out, the King nervously tapped the arms of his chair.

What had he done?

He had not cared for Salisbury. The old Marquess' talents and piety and his Cecil detachment had made him a dependable Minister of the Crown, but they had also given Edward a profound sense of inferiority. And yet Salisbury was nowhere near as aloof or intellectual as his nephew Arthur Balfour. He had often met Balfour at country houses for Saturdays to Mondays, and, naturally, as a statesman in the ministerial scheme of things. Therefore in theory they were well acquainted. In fact they were not. While Edward had been on the rantan with La Goulu and Liane de Pougy in Paris, Balfour had been publishing a *Defence of Philosophic Doubt*; and while Edward led the fast Marlborough Set Balfour had led the equally smart set called 'the Souls', a pair which ran parallel but seldom intermingled with each other. Then, of course, while Edward had worked his way through a long list of mistresses and demi-mondaines Balfour had been having affairs of the heart – so it was said – with only two, Lady Elcho and Lady Desborough, which the King guessed were principally platonic. Balfour had a sexless insipidity about him which a full-blooded man could easily detect.

The King suddenly roared for Chandler, who came running from the Wardrobe. Ordered to find a certain reference book, he quickly returned with it and, because his master was in too impulsive a haste to find the reference, he found *Balfour, Arthur James* for him. The King seized the book and read the entry with increasing panic. It was worse than he had expected. His about-to-be Prime Minister had quite recently published *The Foundations of Belief, being Notes introducing the Study of Theology*, was a Fellow of the Royal Society, and had honorary doctorates from the universities of Edinburgh, St Andrew's, Cambridge, Dublin, Glasgow and Oxford....

From Uncle Salisbury to Nephew Balfour was very much a frying pan and fire affair. Poor Chandler had a bad hour or two.

The next day Lord Kitchener arrived from South Africa and went to the Palace to congratulate the King on his recovery and receive the King's congratulations on his successful campaign against the Boers.

At the King's request he knelt beside his bed and was invested with the Order of Merit – a procedure which overwhelmed the emotional Queen, who burst into floods of tears and had to rush from the room. Edward was not sorry that she had gone. Because he admired the Field Marshal and thought him a steady rocklike figure, Edward told him the surprising news that Salisbury was out and Balfour in. Would it, he wondered with an air of innocence, be good for the country? Kitchener was a man of few words. He considered for a moment. Then he said 'Yes, Sir, it will.'

So control of the Kingdom and the Empire was handed to a handsome bachelor philosopher and the King went off for his convalescent cruise.

Daily the King's strength built up. His temper, at first uncertain, also improved. At Divine Service on the first Sunday of the short cruise the Commodore of the Royal Yacht Squadron officiated but, being unable to intone the versicles, he snapped them out like military commands.

The responses were tremendous. The whole ship's company, plus the Royal Family and Household, accompanied by a full Marine Band sang at the top of their voices: especially after the petition *'O Lord, save the King'*.

The object of their prayer had had his bed wheeled to the window of his deck cabin where he lay fondling Caesar and secretly smoking a long cigar. He beamed benevolently at his subjects as they sang *fortissimo*:

'And mercifully hear us when we call upon thee.'

9

The King's recovery was so speedy and complete that his physicians consented to an abbreviated ceremony of the Coronation to take place on 9 August. By that date, of course, all the official foreign representatives had gone home, excepting the Abyssinian Mission who had not dared return to Africa in case they lost their heads. It was therefore principally a domestic event, which to the King and his family made it that much more pleasant.

The King dressed for his crowning and sent for his grandchildren and a few of their friends to come and see him. They gaped at the transformation. None of them could speak. He found it necessary to reassure them. 'Come, come children,' he said – and uncharacteristically, for he was never one to make light of the majesty of his office – 'Am I not a funny looking old man?' They giggled shyly and were led away.

Aunt Augusta of Mecklenburg-Strelitz was appalled by the Queen's unorthodox appearance. She had chosen to wear an embroidered dress of golden Indian gauze and the Dagmar Cross as a compliment to Denmark. 'Denmark!' exploded the irrepressible old lady when she heard of this. 'Denmark! When she is Queen Consort of Great Britain and now a Lady of the Garter in her own right! Ugh! Ugh!' It was surprising, she added, that Alix had bothered to wear the traditional train of violet velvet.

Whatever her dress, inevitably Alix failed to get into it in time. She was as late as usual, and her exasperated husband, fully robed and with the Cap of Maintenance on his head, rushed into the room, half tripped over one of her many dogs, drew out his pocket watch, held it before her and said: 'My dear Alix, if you don't come immediately, you won't get crowned.'

Alix did, then, move very quickly indeed. To her the Coronation had a special religious significance which she reverenced. Always a staunch High Churchwoman, she insisted that at her anointing the oil should touch her head and not simply the bank of artificial hair which she wore across her forehead. As a result, the Archbishop of York overdid it, a little trickled down her nose to drop on the golden Indian gauze.

She should, of course, have been crowned by the Archbishop of Canterbury, but this was felt to be quite beyond that tottery old man's capacity, and so York crowned and anointed the Queen while Canterbury did his best for the King. The King was in a continual state of anxiety about the Primate. Already he had suggested through the Royal Family's favourite bishop, Randall Davidson of Winchester, that the Archbishop be given a strengthening meat lozenge. But the old man was obstinate. 'What's the good of it, Davidson? What's the use? My trouble's in my legs, man, my legs; not my stomach.'

He managed to do all that was required – just. But not without help from the King who acted as his leaning-post for a large part of the service, had to catch and support him when he approached carrying the crown up the steps of the dais – or both prelate and crown would have fallen; and was actually obliged to raise him to his feet after he had knelt to pay due allegiance to his sovereign on behalf of the Church. George as Prince of Wales was the first to do homage to his father. Their beards met. Both were moist with tears.

There had been little rehearsal for so important an event, and a number of unforeseen calamities occurred. But no one seemed to mind. One which amused everyone was that either by accident or design Mrs George Keppel sat in a box with a number of ladies all of whom had enjoyed Edward's favours in the past. Instantly it was dubbed 'the King's Loose Box'. Another calamity – at least to her – was caused by Princess Beatrice who, admiring the embroidered copy of the Service which had been presented to her, turning it this way and that, eventually dropped it with a clatter into a display of Abbey Plate arranged below the Princesses' stand. Then the eccentric Duchess of Devonshire, called the 'Double Duchess' because she had been Duchess of Manchester in her time, decided that the arranged conveniences were inconvenient, and set off by herself to find one just as the royal procession formed to leave the Abbey. Stopped by a line of Grenadier Guards she poked them in the back, upbraided their officer and, in trying to slip past, she somehow slipped, shot between two guardsmen right down a flight of steps, lost her coronet, and fell prostrate at the feet of the Chancellor of the Exchequer. One of the King's seven Olympian influences, the Marquis de Soveral, instantly took charge, lifting the heaving Double Duchess to her feet, taking her coronet from the hands of Mrs Asquith who had caught it bouncing along the stalls, placing it on her head, and leading that angry and exceedingly uncomfortable lady away on his arm.

Afterwards the King declared he felt a little lazy but not in the least tired and did justice to a huge banquet.

It was fine weather and everyone was in the holiday spirit. Rosa Lewis had cooked no less than twenty-one Coronation Dinners in that week. The indigent of Whitechapel, secretly grateful there was to be no further palace largesse, chewed cheerfully on whelks and winkles. They had cheered themselves hoarse as the carriages went to and fro between the Palace and the grand houses and the Abbey. Now they settled down to an evening's drinking and sentimental songs. From all the pubs came beery renderings of 'Dolly Gray' and 'The Honeysuckle and the Bee'.

10

There had to be a Coronation Naval Review and receptions for the defeated Boer Generals and the Shah of Persia – before the King could escape for a further strengthening cruise.

The Review was a splendid occasion. It rained, but nothing could douse the King's high spirits as he sat on the bridge of the *Victoria and Albert* taking the salute of each of his warships in turn. They were anchored in long lines, the royal yacht going up and down between each line, and they seemed endless. Now Crowned and Anointed King and master of this great fleet, Edward allowed his emotions to get the better of him and tears trickled down his cheeks. Eventually the *Victoria and Albert* returned to the centre of the fleet, the King pressed a button, and all the ships about him were suddenly illuminated. After a sumptuous dinner with his admirals, the King pressed the button a second time, and all the lights were doused.

Edward had his emotions in strict control when the Boer Generals trooped up the side of the royal yacht and gravely took off their hats. They were in civilian dress and looked like a group of undertakers in their black frock-coats and trousers, black gloves and tall black hats. Kitchener and Roberts were with them. Civilities were exchanged. No more. The King had strong feelings about rebels and *lèse-majesté*.

He held an equally strong view about Lansdowne's promise to give the Garter to the Shah of Persia, and waited in glowing impatience for the Foreign Minister to untangle the imbroglio before the Shah arrived at Portsmouth.

Lansdowne's solution was not a happy one. As the King's objection was to an infidel being given a specifically Christian Order, he ordered a special Garter Star to be made with a Muslim Crescent instead of the Cross of St George.

A design of his new invention arrived on the King's desk in a Foreign Office box which the King opened in his cabin. He stared at it. Incredulously he read Lansdowne's explanation that this might be an ingenious way out of their mutual problem.

Ponsonby who was in the small suite acting as Private Secretary, and who was standing by the desk noticed that the veins at his master's temples began to throb. His face took on a dangerous plum colour. When he found his voice it was to rumble, then roar, then bellow with rage at his Foreign Minister's preposterous suggestion.

Suddenly he grabbed the prototype design. Instinctively Ponsonby ducked. The design shot over his head, across the cabin and out of an open porthole.

The King's bellow could be heard from stem to stern.

The Queen, who enjoyed smoking with Miss Knollys, hurriedly and nervously put out her cigarette, and in case the King should come in they fanned the smoke out of the portholes with cushions and shawls. Sir Seymour Fortesque, Equerry-in-Waiting, who was drinking a glass of gin, paled with fright. Only the Bishop of Winchester, on board for a brief visit, permitted himself to smile. Dr Davidson had seen similar outbursts at Osborne and heard of many others. On one occasion Queen Victoria had swept everything from her writing-tables. On another she had destroyed a number of plaster casts. King Edward was certainly the son of his mother. The Bishop rather expected to hear crashes and a little smashing from the royal cabin. But there was no more noise.

Jettisoning the odious prototype seemed to have relieved the King's feelings. He began to dictate a reply to his Foreign Secretary which might have proceeded from the pen of Ivan the Terrible or perhaps Napoleon, but which could not possibly emanate from a constitutional monarch to his Secretary of State for Foreign Affairs. Ponsonby nevertheless wrote down each withering, blistering expression. Afterwards he bravely suggested that, in such an important matter, perhaps Lord Knollys ought to convey the message, but he was cut short by the King who acidly reminded him that Knollys had already gone ahead to Balmoral where they were to meet him in a month's time. Ponsonby bowed and asked if there was anything further for the present. Puffed after his roaring the King said no. Business for the moment would have to wait. Let Ponsonby write out a fair copy of that letter and have it sent to London by special messenger right away.

The Secretary bowed himself to the door, and had just reached it when there was a knock. The King growled something and in came his Equerry, Seymour Fortesque, with something on a salver.

'A stoker, Sir,' he explained, 'has just found this in the steam pinnace which lies alongside. . . .' He faltered because his master's eyes were beginning to bulge. 'Believing it might be of some value,' he rushed on. 'He brought it to me. . . .'

Edward held up his hand. Believing, as Ponsonby had, that Lansdowne's odious infidel Garter design was at the bottom of the Solent, it shocked them both to see it on the salver. It must, thought Ponsonby, have shocked the stoker too.

Not another word was said. Ponsonby and Fortesque rapidly bowed themselves out and closed the door. Not until they were well out of hearing did Ponsonby try to explain. Then he went to tackle the immensely difficult job of watering down the King's salty letter to Lord Lansdowne so that the King would not discover the adulteration, and Lansdowne not be too offended.

How successful he was could be judged by the appearance on the day following of the Prime Minister himself. Urbane, handsome, with that slightly weary, vexed look of a busy minister who has better things to do than wait on constitutional monarchs, Arthur Balfour came aboard and asked to see the King. He was at once given an audience, though the King, almost in self-protection, insisted on Ponsonby remaining in the state-room. With an enviable clarity of expression, and in a regretful tone which immediately neutered any suggestion of impertinence or hostility, the Prime Minister explained that owing to Lord Lansdowne's impulsiveness he had entangled himself and England's word in a wretched muddle. Therefore the Foreign Minister was prepared to resign and place his office in the Prime Minister's hands. But the Prime Minister himself believed this ought not to be necessary. . . .

'Balfour,' interrupted the King. 'I'll not give the Shah a bastardized sort of Garter. His father had the real thing from my mother, and so did two Sultans of Turkey. But at least no one suggested eliminating St George's Cross.'

That, the Prime Minister said, had been a first-class blunder. But England's word was at stake....

'Balfour,' interrupted the King again. 'If any infidel ought to have the Garter it should be the Emperor of Japan. We have a treaty with him, whereas the Shah is simply the Shah.'

'I quite agree, Sir; though events in the Near East suggest that the friendship of Persia might one day be of importance.'

Quite quickly the King calmed down. It was agreed between them that Lansdowne should be left where he was.

'After all,' conceded the King – using clichés and mixing his metaphors in the fashion he had deliberately practised since his boyhood in order to torment a hated tutor, and which pained Arthur Balfour greatly – 'After all, he does know the ropes and has a trick or two up his sleeve even if he does take a toss at times.'

It was also agreed that whatever the Shah expected when he made his visit to the *Victoria and Albert* on the following day, he should not then be given the Garter. Later, the matter could be re-opened and discussed. For the present the Shah would have to do without.

And really, said the Prime Minister, it would do him no harm. He was something of an autocrat. A day or two before he had been visiting a prison and had shown interest in the gallows, asking to see it in use. The governor explained that just at that moment there was no one to be hanged, but the Shah cut him short. 'Then take one of my suite,' he had said, and had been hurt when his offer was courteously refused.

The King laughed. 'I remember his father telling me on one visit years ago that Sutherland was far too rich and powerful and I'd have to have his head off when I came to the throne. Then, on another visit, he wanted to buy Theresa Londonderry. I tried to explain she wasn't for sale, but it simply put him in a sulk.'

On this note the King's quarrel with Lansdowne began to diminish. The Shah when he did arrive was disagreeable and sulked, so did many of his suite. But Edward held out. Then, much later in the year, he conceded and the Shah got his Garter after all – though with the Cross of St George, not the Crescent of Islam.

His royal duties done the King set off on a cruise up to Scotland. Everyone looked forward to a leisurely, luxurious voyage, but the King's sudden decision to drop anchor and visit the Isle of Man caused an unexpected furore.

It appeared Edward was the first British Sovereign to land there since King Canute, and as soon as the word got about, thousands of people took the boat over from England and the island's six policemen gave up all attempts to control them.

It also appeared that although there were distinguished Manxmen in the House of Keys and a President of that House, the man who considered himself the most important islander was the journalist Hall Caine who had turned out any number of preposterous melodramas. To the King's astonishment Hall Caine took over the royal party. He pushed everyone into the background including the President of the House of Keys. After luncheon a commemorative photograph was taken and there right in the middle was not the President nor any other distinguished Manxman, nor even the King and Queen, but the beaming and irrepressible Hall Caine.

The rest of the voyage round to Dunrobin, the Duke of Sutherland's place, was, as had been intended, both a rest and a cure for the King. By then thoroughly fit again, and thinner than for years, he stumped ashore and took a train south to Balmoral where Knollys, at his command, had already instituted some changes.

Fritz Ponsonby, who had served the Queen for six years, and for part of that time at Balmoral, was slightly shocked to find the tartan drawing-room had been made to look like an hotel room.

The King himself instituted more changes. He believed his mother had been put upon by her faithful Highlanders. Certainly they had consumed huge quantities of whisky at the royal expense and this he stopped immediately. It had not been uncommon for a vast majority of the outdoor servants and estate workers to be three parts under by teatime. Supplies were withdrawn. A fresh bottle of whisky was no longer put into the royal carriage each day 'in case of accident'. Nor were as many bottles as there were stalkers taken out into the heather. Coachmen and gillies, deprived of the perquisites, were inclined to be sullen. It made not the slightest difference to the King, and he startled everyone by his determination. On a rainy, misty morning a projected deer drive was cancelled and the men sent to their cottages. When, unexpectedly, the sun came out and the King changed his mind about the drive, one stalker showed he had already been at the bottle. He was at the garrulous stage and insisted on going up to the King and talking in the middle of the shooting luncheon. He had been thirty years in the royal service, but the King had him dismissed on the spot. He could not be persuaded to change his mind although there were serious grumbles on Deeside, but characteristically, as soon as the fuss had died down, he arranged secretly with Ponsonby that the man should be given a permanent pension provided that he never returned to Balmoral. At length it was thoroughly understood by the faithful Highlanders that shooting and stalking, gillies' balls and commemorations of the Prince Consort's and the Queen's birthdays were no longer to be an excuse for substantial bouts of drinking.

Edward by now was at the top of his form. He was almost as buoyant as Teddy Roosevelt, once cowboy and big-game hunter, Colonel of his own 'Rough Riders', and now, because a tuft-hunter had assassinated the elected President McKinley, a shrill-voiced, bouncy Head of State himself.

On his return to England the King felt quite up to facing his formidable Prime Minister, even, so to speak, on his own ground – the appointment of a new Regius Professor of Modern History at Cambridge. Balfour thought that the American Admiral Mahan would suit the chair well. The King was moved to expostulate. An American for a royal chair at Cambridge! He would prefer John Morley, to whom he had given an O.M. and for whom he had the highest regard. Balfour was not having this. Morley, known to his friends as 'Priscilla', was a Gladstonian Liberal and, though an eminent biographer, he was agnostic enough to spell God with a small 'g' in his writings and could not be counted a serious historian.

As was the case with the Shah's Garter, a compromise was reached. Neither the American nor 'Priscilla' Morley was appointed. The appointed man really pleased neither the Monarch nor his First Minister because he insisted on treating history as a science.

11

Toned up by long cruises, carefully studied dieting, settling the hash of Mama's gillies, and enjoyable brushes with his philosopher Prime Minister, King Edward faced a visit to Sandringham by the German Emperor with unusual calm. Under normal circumstances he would have dreaded it, knowing that his nephew would be patronizing, over-talkative, and quite unappreciative of anything done to please him. But on this occasion Edward refused to upset himself which – human nature being what it is – very probably increased the Emperor William's insufferability.

The King had hoped he would not bring too large a suite. It was a forlorn hope. Sandringham was packed. The British and German Ambassadors were also there, and the Prime Minister with Lord Lansdowne. The King had hoped that Balfour would dazzle his overbearing nephew with his brilliance, but this was a forlorn one, too. Balfour, possibly wisely, kept very quiet. Finally, the King hoped to teach Willy bridge – a game of which he was particularly fond, but this was the most forlorn hope of all. Willy turned down the suggestion at once, largely, guessed Queen Alexandra, because he knew that to do so would irritate his uncle. And, if anyone was going to do any teaching, it was he. He gave a long lecture to the Household on fuels for the combustion engine, with bottles of this and that and some other apparatus to prove that potato spirit was the best. The English, of course, used petrol. Every effort was made to please him. The guns went out each day and the shooting was excellent. The food was exquisite. No one over-taxed him with affairs of state. Special entertainments were arranged. Jan Kubelik, the violinist, came down to play for him. Albert Chevalier came down to sing 'My Old Dutch'. An illusionist was imported. Finally, at great expense, Sir Henry Irving and all his company were hastily summoned from Belfast, to give a single performance of Conan Doyle's *A Story of Waterloo*. But nothing, absolutely nothing, pleased His Imperial Majesty. He never seemed to be satisfied. He politely said thank you, but his tone was restrained. If he wished to anger his uncle he certainly succeeded, yet King Edward controlled his hurt feelings for the sake of Anglo-German relations. Nothing, however, could prevent him from exclaiming in the hearing of his Household on the departure of the Emperor: 'Thank God he's gone!'

Afterwards he went to Windsor to welcome easier and far more appreciative guests: the King and Queen of Portugal.

King Carlos, a short, round man with bandit moustachios, was a merry monarch. Given all the out-of-doors sport he wished and shown the great treasure of the Castle by his attentive host, he was asked at the end of his stay what had impressed him the most. Without hesitating he replied: 'English roast beef.'

King Edward was delighted. 'And from *everything* else, what next?' he asked.

His guest did pause at this question. Evidently it was a difficult choice to make. Eventually he replied: 'English roast pork!'

Science was opening out in 1903. Gillette had invented a safety blade. Beards and whiskers would soon give way under the attack. Just after King Carlos and his Queen had returned to Portugal, King Edward heard that Wilbur and Orville Wright had constructed a flying machine, set off in it and landed safely. True, the flight only lasted twelve seconds, but it was an extraordinary advance. On New Year's Day the King and President Teddy Roosevelt exchanged greetings across the Atlantic. It was not easy to be exuberant in Morse Code, but both managed it.

Edward was in excellent form at the Chatsworth house party early in the new year. He felt it was exhilarating to be at the head of the largest Empire in the world and on the edge of an age of discovery. He was devoted to his old friend Devonshire who had almost married a whore and had been saved by Louisa Manchester just in time. For years, until the Duke of Manchester died, Devonshire had been consistently loyal to his Louisa, and then taken her to the altar and made her the Double Duchess. Though a shrewd and honest statesman – too honest to last – and, with 'Priscilla' Morley, the King's great friends in the Liberal Opposition, Devonshire had developed eccentric little ways. He wandered about Chatsworth as though he was a guest, failed to arrange the shooting properly, and often forgot that Albert Edward was no longer

Prince of Wales but his Sovereign Lord. However, the King did not mind in the least. With a Cavendish one did not stand on one's dignity. Nor did Devonshire stand on his. He did not in the least mind being laughed at. 'D'you know, Sir,' he said confidentially to the King, taking his arm soon after his arrival, 'the oddest thing happened to me not long ago.' Edward was not surprised to hear it. Odd things frequently happened to his friend. 'Well?' he said encouragingly. 'The oddest thing,' repeated the Duke. 'When my man drew the curtain and I woke up I could see a dense fog outside. So sensibly, as I thought, I went to sleep again. And I slept all morning. Wouldn't you have done, Sir?' Before the King could reply he went on. 'Well, at about time for luncheon in comes my man and prods and shakes me and says don't I want to get up? No, I tell him, not in such a filthy fog. I'd have my luncheon on a tray. But d'you know, Sir, it wasn't a fog at all. It seems Louisa had arranged some sort of garden party and they'd put the marquee outside my bedroom window.' He squeezed the King's arm. Both laughed a great deal.

The King was also devoted to the Duchess, his hostess, who kept her husband in strict order, and thoroughly enjoyed entertaining guests. Though over seventy she wore clothes more suited to a young matron and greeted her King and Queen ablaze with rubies and wearing a wreath of bay in her red wig. There were to be amateur theatricals, she announced, because that she knew would please the Queen. There would be bridge for the King. Indeed her own passion for bridge and raddled appearance had earned her the nickname of 'Ponte Vecchio', though by some long-standing intimates she was still called 'Grand Slam'. She was almost as passionate about race-going. She would sit there thinking hard about form and then come to a conclusion which she announced like a sibylline utterance. Coming to life she would take a purse from her many petticoats, snap it open and call up a relation standing close by. The year before at one race meeting, with wig askew, she had commanded: 'Put two pounds on *Cream Tart*.' It had earned her yet another nickname.

Louisa Devonshire went to immense trouble to please her royal guests. Soveral was there to amuse the Queen. Mrs Keppel was there to amuse the King. Their apartments could not have been more comfortable.

At Chatsworth Edward found it easy to relax. He liked to

see Paxton's waterworks in full play, or wander with the Duke through the innumerable conservatories, invariably followed by a gardener's boy in case His Grace should forget the way or even where he was. Or he would sit at a single bridge-table set in a great saloon with his hostess and another pair. Or he would sit alone in the library, or work with his secretary in his private sitting-room.

At this particular party there was little in the despatch boxes to command his interest, except for reports on the Duke of Connaught's journey to India as his representative at a Coronation Durbar. Privately he was not sorry that Arthur was out of the country. They had never got on well. In moments of great candour the King would admit to himself, though to no one else, that jealousy had something to do with it. All his life he had wanted to be a soldier but, as Heir Apparent, it had been denied him, whereas Arthur was a professional, had commanded the Guards Brigade at the Battle of Tel-el-Kebir, and, on his return from India, he was to be Inspector General. It appeared from the reports that he was keeping great state on his journey out. From perusing a list of the suites he saw that the Connaughts had taken the Leslies with them. Odd that, considering how correct Arthur liked to think himself. Everyone, including John Leslie, knew that the Duke had lost his heart to Mrs Leslie. Edward had frequently wondered if there was any real passion in the affair and had decided probably not. But one never knew with tall, spare military men.

He pushed back the despatch box and chuckled to himself. At least Arthur's affair kept things in the family because Leonie Leslie's sister, Lady Randolph Churchill, had at one time been in his own string of ladies, and he had actually stolen Alice Keppel from John Leslie.

How curious it was, he thought, still to have passionate affairs and, at the same time, discover that one's mistresses' children had become an anxiety. There were Alice's daughters for instance. The little one, Sonia, he rather liked but she had a habit of racing bits of buttered toast up and down his trouser legs which made him feel foolish and sticky and which absolutely maddened Hawkins. Her elder sister, Violet, was more of a problem as she showed no sort of fancy for anything male. And there was Lady Randolph's son Winston, mercurial in politics and for ever causing trouble, at present sulking in Egypt because he had been crossed in love. Then there were Patsy Cornwallis-West's children. She'd done well for her girls: Daisy was Princess of Pless, though not liking it much, and finding her husband a bore; and Sheelagh was Duchess of Westminster. But her son George had actually handed in his papers and married Lady Randolph who was literally old enough to be his mother – he was about the same age as Winston – and had superintended a tramcar company in Stoke-on-Trent. It was something of a come-down. Patsy must be feeling it. Daisy Warwick, poor darling Daisy, had hardly done any better. Her son was far too precocious. And as for Jeanne de Sagan's children. . . . He managed to laugh now at the memory of Jeanne's elder boy dumping his clothes in the Mello fountain, whence they were poled out, covered in weed and goldfish, by terrified servants, but at the time it had been mortifying.

Dear Jeanne. Madame la Princesse de Sagan, Duchesse de Talleyrand-Périgord, and proud to be his acknowledged *Maîtresse en titre* in the Republic of France. When, he wondered, would he see her again? The gossips who spent their waking hours counting on their fingers up to nine declared her second, blue-eyed boy was his and not her odious, faithless husband's. He would like to see the boy as well. But the Boer War had kept him from his beloved France for over two years. The people were so anti-English that he had been consistently advised to stay away.

Yet in France there was Jeanne. Jeanne at Mello. No, Mello had passed to another member of the family, but she still had her château on the Riviera and her mansion in the Rue St-Dominique. And in France there were many, many other attractions. . . .

On an impulse he scribbled a note, summoned his sergeant footman, and asked him to deliver it to the Prime Minister, who was a fellow guest at Chatsworth. In less than a quarter of an hour Mr Balfour was knocking at the door.

'Ah, Prime Minister,' said Edward genially. 'Do come in. I am sorry to disturb you with work. But I have a thought.'

Balfour bowed.

'It seems to me,' went on the King, pulling a diary towards him, 'that I might reasonably extend my visit to Lisbon, Gibraltar and Malta.'

'You are also expected in Italy, Sir.'

'Yes, yes. But after Rome, why do I not return by Paris?' He snapped the diary to and regarded his Prime Minister through half-closed eyes.

'The French press has been particularly hostile,' Balfour reminded him.

The King did not need reminding. French caricaturists had treated his accession with undeserved bitterness. They had been worse than the Germans. One, in *L'Assiette au Beurre,* had shown a woman lifting her skirts to reveal a naked and hirsute fundament which closely resembled the features of His Britannic Majesty, Edward the Seventh.

'It has, of course, been discussed before,' continued Balfour. 'But I should like to raise the issue again. We are in accord that relations between the two countries should, must, be improved and, if I may be permitted to say so,' and here he smiled his sad smile, 'I believe no one could initiate a better feeling of understanding than you, Sir.'

Edward found himself going pink, he so throughly appreciated the compliment. He knew it was sincere.

That evening over a superb dinner of royal natives, sole, Alpine morels, chicken breasts in a champagne sauce, lamb cutlets, artichoke hearts with truffles, and the inevitable quails, the King confided in his hostess that he hoped soon to breach the wall of hostility France had raised about herself. She warmly approved. She had never permitted the wall to affect her personally and had continued going to the Cannes casino each spring – arriving in a curiously bent posture because she scorned sleeping berths and sat bolt upright all through the night as the train took her south. Once there she was the object of some anxiety to the local police because, since she was immensely rich and grand, money meant nothing to her and so if she saw a pile of it lying about in the casino and she wished to bet, she would simply help herself. To Edward's surprise and delight she echoed what Balfour had said, though expressing it rather differently. 'Only you, Sir, can check the cheek of those Frogs.'

12

The King saw off his Queen, who was going to her old home in Copenhagen, and then set off himself for Portugal.

The royal suite was comparatively small. It included Ponsonby as Secretary, Laking as Physician, Fortesque as Equerry, and, for the official visit to Lisbon, Soveral the Portuguese Ambassador to London. This was the King's first state visit abroad as a monarch, and he broke with tradition by not taking a Minister in Attendance, but Charles Hardinge, an Under-Secretary of State from the Foreign Office, instead. Hardly commensurate with the smallness of his suite were the seventy pieces of personal luggage hauled aboard the royal yacht, thirty personal attendants, and three dogs.

On the evening of 30 March the royal yacht left Portsmouth escorted by two cruisers and was off Lisbon by 2 April.

Jolly Don Carlos, with his son and heir, came himself to greet the King in a green and gold barge rowed by eighty men in red. It was an impressive sight. Less impressive was the King of England who, to honour his host, wore the uniform of the Portuguese cavalry regiment of which he was the Colonel, and the tunic of this was even shorter and more tight-fitting than his Prussian uniform. As a result he showed an immense expanse of breeches. The Portuguese, accustomed to rotundity in their own Monarch, were obviously impressed by the size of his royal visitor. The Kings and their suites were rowed ashore and driven up to the Palace in gilded Cinderella-type coaches. Though they looked beautiful they were, in fact very old and worn. Ponsonby admitted afterwards that the floorboards of the one he rode in were so rotten that he feared the passengers would fall through and have to run inside the wreck. Nevertheless the entertainment was truly royal.

Alexandra being in Copenhagen, Queen Amélie of Portugal had gone away so that it could be a meeting between Kings alone. King Carlos' mother briefly received the visitors. After that everything was in his hands.

Remembering the roast beef and pork of England, he had personally supervised the menus. At the suggestion of Soveral his English guests had whisky and soda placed in their rooms at night-time together with small delicacies in case they should wake up and feel hungry, and tea with thin bread and butter in bed every morning. There was a bullfight which offended no one because, as in Southern France, the bulls were not killed, nor even the horses in danger of being hurt. There was a visit to a museum, a pigeon shoot, gala performances at the opera, receptions and a good deal of motoring. The last was unnerving to those who had the misfortune to drive with Don Carlos' brother, the Duke of Oporto. Driving intoxicated him. He liked nothing better than to accelerate, reach a rumbling fifty miles an hour, then brake abruptly so that all the cars behind were obliged to ditch themselves. Or he would drive madly at crowds of his brother's subjects, stopping dead when they scattered, never touching or hurting anyone. And his method of returning to the Castle was sheer lunacy – careering over a narrow drawbridge, through an archway barely two feet wider than his motor car, and shooting into a large courtyard where he circled tootling on his horn and whirring the press klaxon for all he was worth.

When the two amiable sovereigns said goodbye to one another it was with real regret. Further visits were promised.

The King's programme slowly unfolded, drawing him closer to the place he really wanted to be.

He stayed at Gibraltar, where an anarchist, armed with pistol and dagger, had to be locked up on a trumped-up charge; then at Malta, where the Governor was mortified to discover that the French chef, especially imported to please the King, turned out to be a complete fraud. After that he moved to Italy, passing Sicily where his darling Daisy Warwick was hiding her misery from the world because she knew that Kitty Laycock, as she had now become, was carrying Joe's child.

Theoretically he travelled *incognito,* though as the royal yacht was escorted by eight battleships, four cruisers, four destroyers, and a dispatch vessel it was within anyone's capacity to guess who was at the heart of this British fleet.

Stromboli obliged by erupting beautifully as they steamed past –

'Italy salutes your Majesty!' cried a member of his suite euphorically; and off Capri they dropped anchor while the British Ambassador to Rome and the British Consul at Naples came aboard. Edward, remembering all the recent stories of Capri and her inhabitants was momentarily tempted to go ashore but it would have interrupted his itinerary and that was out of the question.

At Naples he received courtesy calls from the Crown Prince of Germany and his brother Eitel Frederick who were returning from Cairo, from the Queen of Portugal who was delighted to hear Edward had enjoyed his visit to Lisbon, and from Mrs Vanderbilt who had long striven to bring the aloof Mrs Astor to her knees, and who – so it was said – was enjoying a romp with Willy's brother, Prince Henry of Prussia. What, wondered Edward, did Mrs Vanderbilt want? It appeared she wished to show him the artistic treasures of Naples. Politely he refused. He did accept one invitation, to dine with Lord Rosebery at Posillipo. Lord Rosebery he admired, and had it not been for Alix's positive refusal to part with her last unmarried daughter, that cultivated, sporting, immensely rich and sensitive earl might have become his son-in-law. As it was he was happy to be entertained at one of the most beautiful villas on the Bay of Naples. Unfortunately Rosebery suffered the same calamity as the new Governor of Malta. He had put a twenty-course luncheon in the hands of Neapolitan caterers who turned out to be incompetent. It was a fearful meal.

At Naples Edward left the royal yacht and, with his suite, travelled in a special train to Rome. He had three solidly built but quite unostentatious private coaches for travelling on the continent. One was furnished like a club-room which he used as a work-room and to which he invited friends and members of his Household for a talk and a drink. A second contained his considerable wardrobe, bathrooms and bedrooms. The third was a dining saloon complete with dining-room, stores and kitchen with gas cooking equipment and three refrigerators. It hardly matched the Emperor William's brand new train of twelve gold and blue coaches; nor the Russian Imperial train, a string of royal blue saloon cars containing studies, sitting-rooms, bedroom suites, and even an anteroom for the serving of *zakouski* before each meal. But the King was fond of his train and would not dream of having it altered. It suited him. For a good part of each year it was his snailshell.

In Rome he was greeted by the King of Italy and taken in state to the Quirinal. The weather was hot and oppressive. Caesar stretched himself out on the marbled floors and went to sleep. His master, in a very peppery mood, considered the floods of telegrams which had come in from Low Church and dissenting bodies protesting against his projected visit to the Pope. The King would permit no Roman Catholic pretensions in England, but bigoted Black Protestantism did not appeal to him either, and he reserved the right to be courteous and see his fellow sovereign the Pope just as he had done on his first visit to Rome as Prince of Wales. The visit was made and appreciated.

Then, his heart beating a little faster – either with pleasure or with apprehension – the King left the hospitality of Italy and the Vatican and set out for France.

The French crowds were restive as they waited for the King of England to arrive at Bois de Boulogne station in Paris. They had liked him as a Prince of Wales full of wit and gallantry, but now he represented *perfide Albion,* which they had been taught to despise by politicians and journalists.

As restive were the great hostesses in the Faubourg Saint-Germain and Faubourg Saint-Honoré, the legitimate patricians and parvenu imperial aristocracy who were chiefly friendly on two accounts: their dislike of the republic and their deep attachment to King Edward. The Princesse de Sagan had arrived at her house in the Rue St-Dominique from Cannes. The mansion was astir, preparing to honour its most illustrious guest. Her husband, a dandy and philanderer, known in society as *Fleur des Pois,* was preoccupied in his own establishment elsewhere. The once exquisite Anna, Duchesse de Mouchy, was equally busy preparing for her old friend Edward. Her model husband sent for cart-loads of violets from the markets. They were to be placed everywhere. Mouchy's cousin, Frank Standish, and his wife Hélène, who liked to think King Edward would use their houses as his own as he had in the old days, were more restrained in the preparations. The royal suite was turned out, upholsterers, gilders, carpet layers and plumbers set to work, and Madame Standish had her celebrated rope of pearls cleaned by an expert.

The *demi-monde* also stirred expectantly and hopefully. Courtesans worked hard for a short time. Some of le Prince's *cocottes* were still kicking their pretty heels in the air, but a younger generation set its heart on winning the royal favour which in France was a guarantee of permanent fame and fortune, far better than a diploma on the wall, and the equal, it was estimated, of winning a racing sweepstake.

Most anxious of all was President Loubet and his ministers who waited on red carpeting for the arrival of the royal train. It was 1 May and a brilliant day. In their frock-coats the dignitaries became more and more uncomfortable.

At last, and exactly on time, the train drew in to the station. The King, wearing the scarlet of an English field marshal, stepped down from his carriage. State trumpeters blew a fanfare. A band played the two national anthems. The two Heads of State embraced.

How he looks and smells like a dentist, thought the King.

How truly royal, thought Loubet, who, like most republican leaders, could not help envying those who are born to rule.

The King and President and their suites were arranged in six carriages each drawn by four horses with postilions. There was also, the King noted grimly, a vast escort of cavalry as though the President was playing for safety.

The carriages set off. There were thick crowds on either side of the Champs-Elysées, and to begin with they politely cheered the President while shouting little or nothing at the King of England. What they did shout made their feelings plain: 'Vivent les Boers!' 'Vivent les Boers!' A curious historical hark back was the cry 'Vive Jeanne d'Arc'.

The King smiled graciously. Beside the dentist-like Loubet he looked magnificent, the brilliancy of his uniform throwing his grey beard into relief. He was just the sort of spectacle the Parisians loved, but they did not cheer him.

At the British Embassy in rooms hurriedly but splendidly furnished for the King, Captain Ponsonby expressed the opinion that the French reception had been very cool. 'They don't seem to like us much, Sir,' he said indignantly. To his surprise, the King calmly replied: 'Why should they?'

But the King was less composed when presented with a printed list, issued by the Chef du Protocole, of what he was to do and to wear throughout the visit. With a blue pencil he crossed out everything concerning himself, made a few suggestions in the margin and sent it back where it had come from. There was consternation in the department but they bowed to the royal will.

Having paid a formal visit to the President and Madame Loubet, the King spoke to the British Chamber of Commerce and, that evening, he went to the Théâtre Français to see *L'Autre Danger*. The Loubets were also there, but the general atmosphere was chilly. Edward was determined not to mind, or, rather, not to show it. To the consternation of the police who were there to protect him from anarchists, he insisted on walking about during the entr'acte and meeting by chance a great French actress whom he had seen perform in London, he at once held out his hand and greeted her. 'I recall, Mademoiselle, how I applauded you in London for there you personified all the grace and the spirit of France.' She was enchanted. So were many others who overheard the King's gracious remark. Thereafter the audience was slightly less hostile, but only slightly.

Edward worked hard. By now it was clear to him that on this, his longed-for visit, he would have to sacrifice private pleasure to public duty. As never before he was in Paris as a diplomatist for his kingdom. He sent affectionate messages to all his old friends to say that, though desolated, he could not pay formal or even informal visits on this occasion. He sent letters and flowers and made telephone calls, especially to his beloved Jeanne Sagan. But nothing more. His friends were disappointed but they quite understood.

Nevertheless the *demi-mondaines*, when they realized le Roi Edouard was there on business only, were distinctly put out. One who had invested a great deal of her savings in clothes, scent, redecorating her rooms, and paving the way to an introduction, went to the length of saying it was a disgrace and she ought to be reimbursed by the British Ambassador.

In this case unaware of what he was missing, Edward reviewed troops, scrupulously saluted every flag he saw, and said at the Hôtel de Ville: 'I can assure you all it is with the greatest pleasure that I return each time to Paris, where I feel exactly as if I were at home.'

It was this which finally broke the ice. Delighted Parisians passed the phrase from one to the other: 'où je me trouve toujours comme si j'étais chez moi'. As he sat down there was a sudden burst of cheering. It grew louder and louder.

That afternoon the King attended a race-meeting at Longchamps arranged especially in his honour. He attended a state banquet at the Elysée, a gala performance at the opera, a luncheon given by the French Foreign Minister, and a dinner at the British Embassy for the President. At each he spoke in fluent distinct French and at each he won more hearts than before.

There was only one discordant note – caused not by the French but, as usual, by the King's nephew, the German Emperor. It had been suggested that Edward might go on to pay a State Visit to Berlin, but Willy had said no, he was not feeling up to it. And now the King heard from his ambassador in Rome that, immediately after his own departure from the Quirinal, the Emperor had turned up there. It was so deceitful, and maddening the way Willy followed in his footsteps.

As the royal train pulled out of the Gare des Invalides, leaving Monsieur Loubet looking more like a dentist than ever, Edward had fulfilled and far surpassed the hopes of his ministers at home of bringing the two countries to a closer rapprochement. In four days of hard diplomacy and tact he had altered the French crowds jeers of 'Vivent les Boers' to 'Vive notre Roi Edouard', 'Vive le Roi'. He could justly claim the credit for initiating the Entente Cordiale which followed.

13

The King returned with romantic notions of tilting a lance for his only unmarried daughter, the Princess Victoria. Poor Toria, as she was called, or Beck-and-Call, being exactly that to her Mama, was perceptibly wasting and pining. Remembering Rosebery's handsome, melancholy face while presiding over that dreadful luncheon in Naples, and fresh from the city of intrigue and love, Edward determined to tackle his Queen.

First he sought the advice of his son and daughter-in-law. May sensibly remained silent. Inheriting the excellent taste of her father, and the capabilities of her mother, beloved Fat Mary of Cambridge, she had been well schooled by her governess, and had her own considerable accomplishments. To no one, save perhaps to Aunt Augusta of Strelitz, would she have admitted what a bore she found her husband's family; their vacuous lives devoted to little but superficialities; and that she had to bite her lower lip when her mother-in-law played her sickly part as poor, defenceless Motherdear. She knew that she could do no good, even by giving sensible advice. She simply supported George's view that Motherdear would never let Toria go, and wished the King well in his attempt to do something for his daughter.

Then Edward sought the advice of his *éminence grise*, Lord Esher. Theirs was an especially close relationship. Esher had an immense number of important contacts and, being Lieutenant and Deputy Constable of Windsor Castle, he had direct access to his sovereign, which gave him great power behind the scenes. Being a devious man he enjoyed this far more than the open political power he could have had at any time he wished. To this liking for power he brought a shrewdness of judgement and knowledge of affairs and people which made him invaluable to the King. Indeed, of the seven intimates who most influenced Edward during his reign, it is likely that Esher was the wisest. Certainly he would do anything for him, from directing a circumspect enquiry into the mishandling of the Boer War to seeing that private apartments were always kept available on an island platform at Swindon station for discreet dalliance after the King's arrival in the royal train from a strenuous day's racing at Newbury. But Esher confessed himself at a loss when the King asked his advice on how to prise Princess Victoria from her mother.

'You have someone in mind, Sir?' he asked.

'Good gracious me, no, not yet,' replied the King, though he still thought a marriage with Rosebery would be good for each of them. 'I should expect your help with that in due time of course.'

Esher bowed.

'But first we have to persuade the Queen,' went on the King. He pondered 'Could it be done through Miss Knollys?'

Esher thought not, but he said he would try. Meanwhile

Edward was to be outspoken with the Queen during their stay at Dalkeith Palace.

This had been planned for the 11–14 May – and included a large number of engagements in Glasgow and the Scotch capital. Edward considered it ought to be done in style. His mother had possessed a remarkable interior pomp, as it were, which he shared in some degree, but he understood better than she had ever done the importance of outward pomp, that it was in itself an *instrumentum regni,* and he and Alix took such outsize suites to Scotland that the Duke and Duchess of Buccleuch had to move out of the Palace into the factor's house. They did it without the least complaint. They, too, realized that the pomp and circumstance which surrounded the King and Queen would bring excitement and a dash of colour and enormous satisfaction to the thousands of poverty-stricken who lived in the squalor of Glasgow slums and in the alleys and courts of Edinburgh.

Having been so recently in a Paris springtime it was something of a mortification for Edward to ride through the thin May rain in an open carriage smiling and waving to his northern subjects. However, he played his part well, as, when driven to it, his mother had always done. He opened things and laid foundation stones and made a great number of speeches, stopped to talk to the ordinary people, and put himself out to please. He even confounded a section of disapproving Scotsmen – who, oddly, insisted on calling themselves by the old English word Scots, and refused to receive him as Edward the Seventh – by saying, very well, he was perfectly ready to be simply King Edward in the northern Kingdom. On the last day of what was evidently a triumphant visit, in which the Queen had played her own difficult and exhausting part to perfection, the King sought her out in the Duchess of Buccleuch's private sitting-room. It was filled with dogs and caged birds. At a glance from the King both Princess Victoria and Charlotte Knollys curtsyed and asked permission to retire.

Putting his hands to the logs blazing in the fireplace Edward congratulated Alix on her endurance during the visit, and said how much he appreciated what she had done. It was never easy for her, being so deaf, though she was adroit at lip-reading or guessing by intuition what was going on. Because of the deepness of his voice or because she was so accustomed to its tone, she could hear her husband better than most people, and she coloured at his compliment.

'We each have our duties, Bertie.'

He leapt at the opportunity, taking her hand, and saying: 'Indeed we have, my dear. Duties of all kinds, though sometimes they are unpleasant.'

It was so long since he had involuntarily taken her hand that she was immediately on the defensive. She pretended not to have caught what he said. He repeated it, adding: 'There are, for example, our duties as parents.'

'Now George and May have been complaining to you,' said Alix, pouting. 'They think I spoil their children. Well, so I do. And what of it?' she added defiantly.

Edward shook his head. Neither had complained, he told her, though he was surprised to hear she had been spoiling the children. It would not be good for them....

'They are my grandchildren,' broke in Alix. She spoke petulantly, like a child herself.

'And mine, my dear,' he reminded her, forcing a laugh. 'We share George's children, and Louise's, and soon we shall share in Maud's baby.'

Alix called to a dog who jumped into her lap, and she talked of Maud's coming child. It gave Edward another excellent opening.

'We must hope that Victoria, too, will be blessed one day in the same way, and present us with other grandchildren.'

He said it carefully and she heard every word. He could tell that by her face. But she continued to pat her lap-dog and talk of Maud's approaching confinement. Then quite definitely she changed the subject and spoke of George and May's recent move into Marlborough House and their trip to see Hampton Court. So determined was she not to mention Victoria that she even moved further by saying how frightening it must have been for poor Stanley Smith the aviator who had recently flown an airship from the Crystal Palace over St Paul's and had been unable to return to his starting point....

Not long after the King left the room.

Lord Esher reported that he had met with no success. Miss Knollys had positively snubbed him.

The King put an arm round his neck. 'We'll not accept defeat yet, Reggie. It wouldn't be fair to my poor daughter.'

The King's poor daughter did indeed look a wan and unhappy woman at the State Ball given at Windsor in Ascot Week. It was the first of its kind to be given in the Waterloo Chamber for half a century, and was magnificent.

There were nine hundred guests and yet plenty of room. There was an innovation in the Supper Room generally kept exclusively for royalty. It now also included a table for Ambassadors and other special guests. The *Queen* in the week following published a detailed list of the most magnificent gowns: that the Countess of Wicklow had long sprays of pink roses on her gown of tulle and was covered with rose petals; that the Marchioness of Lansdowne was in cream satin, trimmed with chiffon and old lace, with very wonderful diamonds; that the Countess of Cromartie's grey iridescent and mother-of-pearl embroidery mingled with white tulle, grey pearls, and grey and white hyacinths; that Lady Ermyntrude Mallet's superb gown was of tulle and mousseline de soie, embroidered with crystals, topazes and chains of precious stones....

Poor, wan Princess Victoria; so sharp and black and sour beside the Queen's radiant beauty. She was asked to dance, or rather, required to. It was her duty. And of course it would fall to her lot to be partnered with fat Prince Dolly Teck, May's brother, who bounced her round the ballroom until his spurs fouled Mrs Keppel's chiffon train and he and Victoria fell flat on their backs before all the company. It was too, too humiliating to trip over Papa's mistress. An account of the event naturally reached the Court of Mecklenburg-Strelitz. The Grand Duchess Augusta wrote:

> *'Oh! poor Dolly's and Victoria's fall, truly grievous, she who is already so delicate!'*

Edward would have felt his daughter's humiliation far more, and probably would have dressed down Prince Dolly for putting her at such a risk, had he not received grave news from Belgrade. There a military junta had entered the royal palace at night-time and murdered King Alexander, his Queen and the Prime Minister.

They had not been liked and a more popular King named Peter was elected to replace the assassinated monarch, but King Edward refused to recognize King Peter. He sent for Lansdowne and said that diplomatic relations must be withdrawn until all the assassins had been dealt with. As he put it expressively to envoys who waited on him later and tried to make him change his mind, 'I cannot be indifferent to the assassination of a member of my profession, or, if you like, a member of my guild. We should be obliged to shut up our businesses if we, the kings, were to consider the assassination of kings as of no consequence at all.' He always loathed any threat to the monarchic principle, and not for three years would he consent to a resumption of diplomatic relations.

On 4 July he perforce had to think of his daughter's unhappy situation once again. He went down to the Isle of Wight, was received by his red-eyed sister, Princess Beatrice, in her capacity as Governor of the Island, and formally opened the shore establishment which replaced the training ship *Britannia* in part of Osborne House.

'Come, Beatrice,' he said gruffly when it was over. 'I want to see your new garden.'

As a consideration for her consent to his plan for Osborne House, he had ordered that the grounds of Osborne Cottage should be enlarged.

'You may if you wish,' said Beatrice, weeping once more. 'But I personally never go into the new part. I do not care for change.'

'Yes, yes, dear, I know,' exclaimed the King pettishly. He was irritated by her stubbornness but more by her lack of gratitude.

'You do not know, Sir,' said Princess Beatrice with sudden spirit. 'There are those about you, I dare say, who tell you what you wish to know; but you are spared the sort of difficulties the rest of us have to face.'

Her brother reddened. He laid his hand on the latch of the garden gate. Quickly he looked to see no one could overhear. 'Now that, Beatrice, is as large a piece of nonsense as I've heard for years. Nonsense, I said, and I mean it.' His sister began to take in a breath to speak, but he cut her short. 'For example, tell me, and in the quickest, simplest way, how I am to get my daughter Toria married when her mother is so against it? I am *not* spared difficulties as you suggest. On the contrary I have dozens. Marrying off Toria happens to be at the forefront of my mind because

I think it important and I can see no solution to getting her away from her mother.' He opened the gate, and the Princess preceded him through it. 'Now can *you* make a constructive suggestion?'

Beatrice wiped her eyes and apologized for letting her feelings smother her. It had not been an easy day but she regretted now having spoken so plainly. As for poor Toria, no she had nothing to suggest. 'Mama hated it when I married, as you recall,' she said and Edward nodded. 'But then she was extremely fortunate in her son-in-law. And long ago Mama herself spoke several times of the necessity of marrying Toria. She even spoke to Alix. Of that I am certain.'

'Yes,' said the King, miserably, 'I remember.' He poked at the ground with his stick. 'But I am resolved to go on trying, if I can, to prise them apart. Alix remains astoundingly young and healthy, while Toria daily ages and sickens.'

His sister took his arm. 'If you can spare ten minutes, Sir, we will go into the house and I shall ask for tea to be sent in.'

The King was no closer to a solution when President and Madame Loubet paid a return State Visit to London. This passed off well, though the President could not be given the Garter because, like the Americans, he was unable to appear at Court in stockings and breeches and for no one in the world would Edward the Seventh fasten the Garter over the trousers of an elected president who resembled a dentist. The thought was as bad – no, worse – than Lord Roberts' suggestion that, for reasons of economy, all sheepskins, horse-cloths, shells, browbands, rosettes, plumes and bit-ropes should be abolished from the saddlery of officers excepting those belonging to the Household Regiments; an outrageous submission which made the King speechless. These things *did* matter, he told Lansdowne, who was busy setting up the machinery for an Entente Cordiale on a negotiated basis; and M. Loubet had to be content with jewelled boxes and a portrait of his host.

Nor was Edward any further forward when he and Alix made a State Visit to Ireland at the end of July, though he hoped their proximity might give him a suitable opportunity to reopen the matter. Fate seemed to help him. The Corporation of Dublin refused by three votes to offer him an Address of Welcome, which at once made the Queen protectively sympathetic towards him.

Then, soon after their arrival, one of his favourite dogs, an Irish terrier named Jack, died without warning. Alix went to comfort him. He was genuinely moved, but she swiftly began to doubt his sincerity when he used the chance to put in a word about letting Toria fly from the nest and have her own establishment. She coldly remarked that he seemed less concerned about the death of the ever-faithful Jack, than he was about the Supreme Pontiff Leo XIII whom he had met once in his life and who had also died that day.

'Alix,' he said reproachfully, 'Ireland is a Catholic country and it was politic to send my commiserations to the College of Cardinals. It was also polite. The Pope is a fellow sovereign. But that is beside the point. I am anxious about poor Toria. . . .'

'Toria,' snapped his Queen, 'has her usual headache and a cold in the nose. And if you keep me waiting I shall be late for the ceremonies which have been arranged.' This sort of threat made him pant with apprehension. Glumly he watched her curtsy and sweep from the room.

It was no use, he decided. Toria's uncaging would have to wait. Meanwhile he concentrated on his work as sovereign of Ireland, never itself an easy task. He recalled that during one of the many troubles a leading but puzzled statesman had asked what the Irish really wanted from the English to which he received the enigmatic but characteristic reply that whatever England had in mind to offer, the Irish wouldn't be wanting it.

The Viceroy who welcomed the King was, rather embarrassingly, Lord Dudley, the son of one of Edward's most engaging mistresses in the 'nineties, but he was kindness itself. So was the Chief Secretary, George Wyndham, who acted as his Minister in Attendance and who could not do too much for him. The King himself did his best. He reviewed troops and not without danger because the enthusiasm of the mob thoroughly frightened his carriage horses. The review was in Phoenix Park. He would have liked to get down to the Curragh in Co. Kildare – for it was there when he had been soldiering as a boy of eighteen, that a girl had been smuggled into his quarters and opened up a world he had now been enjoying for forty-three years. What had been her name? After all this time it had slipped his memory. He recalled sharing her with Charlie Carrington at Cambridge until his father had found out about it. Then he remembered. Nellie was her name.

Nellie Clifden. It would have been good to get down to the Curragh to shake up a few memories. But his brother Arthur, who was Commander-in-Chief in Ireland, had not put it on the list of events – which was typical of Arthur. Speaking to officers at Vice-Regal Lodge the King asked after the Curragh and if it was much changed. No one, of course, could say. Could any officer describe changes at Aldershot, which was the English equivalent? But Edward was delighted by the story of the exceedingly portly wife of a high-ranking officer who, entitled to official quarters, had lately gone to inspect the place, ending up in the basement kitchen. There she found a corporal of engineers cementing in a new grate which, she declared forcefully, was not to her liking. The corporal looked over his shoulder at the massive lady of the house, and made a marvellous mistake. 'Don't you worry about that, Cookie, my dear,' he reassured her. 'It'll soon sweat the belly off you.' The King stuck to his programme and daily grew more popular. Evidently the Corporation did not wholly represent the people of Ireland. Eighty-two deputations presented addresses of welcome, and the King was charming with them all, especially those from the remoter parts of Ireland who were somewhat confused to be in the royal presence and forgot all they had been told by the ushers outside. One mayor managed to miss the King and shoot his address straight into the wastepaper basket. 'Just pick it out again,' whispered his sovereign in the friendliest fashion, 'and hand it to me.' They all adored him. Two carmen, who brought an address signed by 1,200 jarveys, went back to their mates with the comment 'his Honour's a true Honour!' Trinity College, Dublin had ever been loyal to the Crown and so Edward went there. Then, knowing that the Roman Catholic Church was a real force in the land, he chanced protests from Black Protestants – which he ultimately received – and visited the seminary at Maynooth where young Irishmen were trained to be priests. There he was delighted to discover that they possessed a huge picture of his Derby winning horse 'Persimmon' and, in his honour, had decked it with ribbons of his racing colours.

Finally he held a Court at Dublin Castle and received a crowd of pretty young girls. He regretted it was no longer the custom to kiss the girls as they were presented. The Viceroy, Lord Dudley, told him of a predecessor who had also enjoyed this part of Court ceremonial, and, having a long red beard, he had retired after each batch of fifty girls, to have it brushed, powdered and scented; then back he came to represent his monarch and enjoy a further batch of fifty.

After this the King and Queen and Toria went north to stay at beautiful Mount Stewart with the King's old friend the Marchioness of Londonderry and her silent husband, the bad-tempered, bandy-legged Minister of Education.

Theirs was a sad history. Married when Londonderry was twenty-three and his bride nineteen, they had bred heirs before she fell in love with one of the greatest gallants of all time, Harry Cust, a man of charm and taste and intelligence who read Virgil on the way to a meet, but whose infinite promise never came to very much. And, though a famous lover, Cust was not discreet and handed out too many latch-keys to his apartment. One of Queen Alexandra's closest friends, Lady de Grey, became jealous of the attentions he was giving to Lady Londonderry and, after finding a tied-up wad of letters in Cust's house, had the incredible effrontery to steal them and then, with cold deliberation and unbelievable spite had sent them under plain cover to Lord Londonderry. When he opened the packet and read the letters, many of which were most abusive about himself, the Marquis was thirty-two and his wife twenty-nine. He re-wrapped the letters, added a curt note: 'Henceforth we do not speak', and sent them to his wife by a footman. Thereafter he devoted himself to politics and never addressed his wife with a single word except necessary announcements in public. They arrived at Court and at balls or the opera in separate carriages, and, when receiving guests at Londonderry House or Wynyard or at Mount Stewart, they invariably stood a little apart.

The King considered Londonderry an odd stick to keep it up for nineteen years and was as delightful as he could be to his witty and charming hostess. He had had trouble about writing letters himself, not once but several times. His mother had warned him against it and Mama had been right. But Alix, who naturally took Gladys de Grey's side – apparently overlooking her infamous behaviour – considered Lord Londonderry a deeply-wronged man, and set out to be charming to him. In such a spirit of division, there was no chance of the problem of Toria being solved. In a photograph of the House Party at Mount Stewart Princess Victoria herself stood well to the left looking piqued. The silent Marquis, bandier-legged than usual in a tight-fitting uniform, was separated from his Marchioness by the Viceroy, Queen Alexandra, King Edward and the ubiquitous Charlotte Knollys. It was a dull picture, no doubt of a dull party.

Devoted as he was to Lady Londonderry, and beautiful as the gardens of Mount Stewart were during the two hours out of every twenty-four when it was not raining, the King was not sorry to get away on the *Victoria and Albert* and go ashore at various places on their way south to Cork. But he had his father's social conscience and was disturbed to see so many poverty-stricken turf-roofed cabins, and find evidence of such appalling ignorance. Dumbly they gazed at the royal party. The few who at last guessed who the strangers were, remained absurdly muddled as to their actual identity. Edward found himself being addressed as Henry the Seventh.

On returning to England the Royal Family went almost at once to Cowes, staying partly ashore and partly aboard the royal yacht. Patsy Cornwallis-West was there with her daughter and son-in-law, the Prince and Princess of Pless. Edward chose to regard it as an excellent opportunity to seek the advice of his dear Patsy. But Patsy was either feeling flighty or she did not grasp what he was saying, for she called him an old worrier and refused to take anything seriously. Edward scowled and growled. He dined Patsy, and Daisy and Hans of Pless twice, and he put up with Daisy's singing – on which she rather fancied herself. Alix turned the pages of the music. May embroidered. Patsy chattered. Hans gaped. George evidently was thinking about stamps. The Equerries politely stood in attentive attitudes. Toria merely held a lace handkerchief to her nose – she had yet another cold – or, sometimes, a phial of salts to refresh her in the stuffy August weather. The King desperately tried not to go to sleep, and came to with a guilty start when Daisy's last shrilling note had died and she came directly over to him. 'Sir,' she said, 'I declare you were asleep.'

'Not in the least,' he replied sharply. He was not especially fond of Daisy. She was too German in England and too English in Germany, which could never work. And she trilled rather than talked. Moreover she hadn't the modesty he expected in a young lady, and took liberties just because she was Patsy's daughter.

Before dinner she had begged him to do something about cleaning up the Solent. She like an early swim, she said, and the water was deliciously cool, but there were salad leaves and bits of paper in the water which she found quite horrid! What was he going to do about it. The King had turned quite red. What a subject for discussion with a young lady! And did she regard him as overseer of the waters of the Solent? He had as good as turned his back on her. Now she showed a spirited revenge. 'Of course you were asleep, Sir; and so I shall sing another little song, if the Queen would be so kind as to turn the pages.'

Alix declared herself willing. The King groaned in spirit and glowered at the piano. Daisy of Pless inhaled deeply, and then she was off. . . .

Agnes Keyser took the commonsense line. She gave the same sort of advice as Beatrice had. If Queen Victoria had been quite unable to prise Princess Victoria from her mother, it was exceedingly unlikely that he would be able to do so. 'Your mother, Sir, had a certain power over the present Queen which you have forfeited.'

'Then my poor daughter is to be condemned to a solitary life, always at her mother's beck and call?'

Sister Keyser nodded. 'A solitary life is not always unacceptable,' she reminded him. After all she was unmarried herself. And he was not to fret his nerves by attempting the impossible. 'Come, Sir, sit in your usual chair and I will ring for something to soothe your stomach.'

Mrs George Keppel, voluptuous Alice, said much the same, though in a different manner, on the night before King Edward left for a cure. It was his custom to dine with her on leaving and returning to England; the next day he was due to leave for Marienbad, not noisy Homburg where he had been mobbed, but little Marienbad which had the triple advantage of being small, in beautiful countryside, and in Austria not Germany.

Over the exquisite little dinner she had had prepared for him he explained quite candidly his total lack of success in liberating his daughter.

Alice did not contradict him, not even when he said bitterly that he had bred a daughter who had been turned into a lap-dog. She soothed him with her sympathy, her food and wine, her considered opinion that no blame could properly be attached to him, and she soothed him with her love.

The King's campaign was over. Far from tilting a lance for his only unmarried daughter, he had not even been able to draw it. Alix had seen to that.

14

On the following morning when Fehr, his Swiss courier, reported that everything and everyone was ready for departure, the King walked to the Queen's apartments to say goodbye. She was still in bed, wrapped in swathes of lavender-coloured lace.

'I hope you enjoy your cure, my dear.'

'Thank you. And I wish you *bon voyage* to Denmark.'

'Thank you. We shall, I expect, enjoy ourselves as usual.'

'Charlotte is to accompany you, naturally?'

'Yes. And Toria, of course.'

'Ah, yes, Toria. I ought to say goodbye to her.'

'Really, dear, you need not trouble yourself. Toria is in bed.'

'At this time of the morning. . . ! There is no reflection on you, Alix, but Toria is a young woman. She ought to have been up hours ago.'

'Toria is not feeling quite herself. She has another cold.'

'Yet another?'

'Another. And I understand from her maid that she is feeling low, somewhat depressed.'

'But no doubt she will be cheered by the invigorating atmosphere of your father's Court.'

'Now, Bertie, please don't be tiresome. You've made it plain a score of times that Denmark does not suit you – or your way of life. Marienbad will be so much better.'

'Then goodbye, my dear. A kiss to poor Toria from me.'

'Yes, thank you, a kiss for poor Toria. Goodbye.'

. . . . .

Marienbad: so small and intimate and friendly; with shooting or golf, walks and gardens, those astringent waters, and infinite resources for what the old Marlborough House Set had termed 'roguey-poguery'.

All this, at least, is what Marienbad promised. Edward had stayed there before and loved it, and again he was at the Hotel Weimar with his own comfortable suite in which each year, the bedroom, dining-room and sitting-room were freshly furnished. On the train out the King looked forward to a restful cure and to losing a little weight. He was travelling incognito as the Duke of Lancaster, but the German Emperor managed to smash that by meeting his uncle at Frankfurt with a large Guard of Honour, and the Burgomaster of Marienbad did not help by putting up notices round the spa begging people to respect the King's incognito. In any case his choice of title was unfortunate. Someone in England had the effrontery to say that it was not his to use, and Fehr, the courier, angered the King by labelling the luggage LORD LANCASTER. 'Do you,' snapped the King, 'want everyone to think I am an ennobled gunmaker?'

Edward swiftly discovered that being at Marienbad as Prince of Wales was very different from being there as a reigning sovereign. Whenever he walked with friends or members of his small suite he was followed by a dense crowd and this enraged him. If he sat down on a park bench and glared they formed a circle and photographed him. It was not as bad as it had been in horrible Homburg, but sufficiently bad for him to protest personally to the Austrian Emperor, and Franz Joseph solved the problem by sending a force of plain-clothes policemen from Vienna. In one way or another they cajoled people to leave the Duke of Lancaster alone, and, dieting apart, at last he was able to enjoy himself.

Most of the visitors were exceedingly fat and therefore the company on the whole was jolly. The majority were Austrian, though there were a few bearded and ringleted Polish Jews who wore long overcoats, tall top hats and high boots. There was also a sprinkling from international society. Alix's brother, the King of Greece, arrived – also under a transparently obvious incognito. The two kings and their suites were entertained by a charming Frenchwoman, Madame de Ganay; and the Princess Murat and Madame de Chévigné were bidden as well. Despite the diet champagne flowed. The English suite looked to their master for a lead. He was resisting temptation, but displeased that it had been placed in his way. On the other hand, the King of Greece and his suite went at the champagne as hard as they could.

Odd people, knowing that King Edward was at Marienbad, would arrive there in the hope of meeting him. He was good-natured about it, taking up with a middle-aged Paris beauty married to a man half her age who had assumed a title, as one could in France. At least he had been modest enough to choose a barony for he could have made himself a duke. Then there was a lady, described by Captain Ponsonby who was in the suite, as 'with an eye-glass, short skirts, and a murky past'. She was invited to luncheon. A less questionable luncheon guest was Madame Waddington, the widow of a French Ambassador in London and herself an American who spoke in torrents of French, English and American. Then there was a very old friend of the King's. Harry Chaplin had first met him at Oxford and the rich young rip who hunted like a demon with the South Oxfordshire and was strong meat even for the Bullingdon, had taken to the shy young Prince of Wales. Known as 'Magnifico' because of his fortune, he did everything on a grand scale, driving his own coach and four and keeping two packs of hounds so that his friends could hunt six days a week. Eventually he had run through most of his money, married the Duke of Sutherland's daughter, settled to a respectable career as politician, and had served in Lord Salisbury's third administration. Now he was Viscount Chaplin, a connoisseur of food and wine, and under a grey exterior as ebullient as ever. Edward was delighted to see him. They had never lost touch, played 'baccy' together, gone racing together, and been fellow guests at dozens of Saturdays to Mondays.

Captain Ponsonby, who never failed to be freshly surprised by discovering new depths of character in his master, noted how he received his diverse guests; his generous affability to the faded beauty and her young 'Baron', his keen interest in the lady with the murky past; his surprising patience with the gushing Madame Waddington, his joyousness and sparkle when he was with Lord Chaplin. He also gave luncheon to the Abbot of Tepl, a monastery of the Premonstrant Order which was very rich and virtually owned Marienbad. With the Abbot the King was suitably respectful. Finding it so difficult to keep to the rules of the cure, he admired men who had self-discipline, though this particular order had the advantage of spending two years in seclusion and two years out in the world, a feature which was characterized by their unusual uniform, a monk's white habit and a black top hat.

As a diversion, Captain Ponsonby suggested they drive one day to Carlsbad, famous for more than its plums. Aware that the King liked nothing better than to be unrecognized in a crowd, he told Fehr to order a car from Vienna and book an outside table at a restaurant in Carlsbad in his own name.

King Edward thought it an excellent idea.

He thoroughly enjoyed the drive, urging the driver to put his foot down with deep cries of 'Schnell! Schnell! Schnell!' And, when they left the steaming, dusty motor car, and walked along the pavements looking into shop windows, he was in the highest of spirits.

Ponsonby noted with dismay that some of the shop windows contained postcard photographic portraits of the King, but he hoped that they would have luck and not be recognized. He was being over-sanguine. Whatever Edward might call himself he was still a king, and however much he pretended to be like other people, he was not. Accustomed to being instantly obeyed he found the waiters' slowness and their insistence on treating clients in order intensely irritating.

His fat fingers began to drum on the table, always an ominous sign. Ponsonby risked muttering a warning. 'As the party is Fehr's, Sir, we cannot expect any sort of preferential treatment.' Having been born to it, the King did expect it. He really could not help it. It was part of his nature.

His exasperation soon made itself felt by the waiters. They and others in the restaurant were not long in coming to the conclusion that the fat, grey-bearded man in Herr Fehr's party who looked so very like the King of England was, in fact, the King of England.

The outside table where Fehr's party sat was ringed in by a garden fence. This was soon packed with people gazing in. The restaurant itself began to fill. No one dared approach the King's table. One party sitting at the next table actually left, backing away with mumbled apologies. Waiters scurried like rabbits. Food was on the table in a minute.

By this time Fehr's appetite had gone. He guessed that he and Captain Ponsonby were in for an uncomfortable afternoon. Ponsonby's appetite had also gone, for the same reason. But the King, having absolved himself from the strict Marienbad diet because they were in Carlsbad, had ordered a substantial meal of favourite dishes. Growing pinker every minute he champed on his fish and meat. Nevertheless when a hastily gathered band, their uniform half buttoned and their hats askew, began to blast out 'God Save the King', he put down his knife and fork, pushed away the plate, and asked Fehr if he would be good enough to settle the bill.

All plans for wandering through the streets and parks of Carlsbad and enjoying the afternoon there had to be abandoned. With difficulty Ponsonby squeezed through crowds, found the hired motor car, dragged the protesting driver from a near-by inn, and went back to the restaurant. There he found the King wearing his hat, and giving a fixed smile to the citizens who peered at him and pointed at him through the garden railings, and clutching his gold-knobbed cane so hard that his knuckles were white.

Way was made for him through the crowd. To Edward's intense disgust people touched him for luck and babbled obsequious compliments. At last they were able to move. Carlsbad policemen led the motor car to the edge of the city. The same band, by this time buttoned up and efficient, played 'God Save the King' for at least the eighteenth time.

The King gritted his teeth, politely raised his hat to the crowd and bowed. In a few minutes they were out in the country again.

This time it was Captain Ponsonby who begged the driver to hurry: 'Schnell! Schnell! Schnell! Schnell!'

At the end of August the King's skeleton suite was enlarged and he paid a State Visit to Austria.

The Emperor sent his own train to Marienbad so the journey was exceedingly comfortable, and at Vienna he was there to greet his fellow sovereign. They embraced, and Edward who was a very sentimental man, felt his heart go out to poor old Franz Josef. For years and years his Empress had lived apart from him, and had come to a nasty end as the victim of an assassin's bullet. His brother Maximilian, the Emperor of Mexico, had been literally chopped to pieces by rebellious subjects and the pieces auctioned off as souvenirs – which, hardly surprisingly, sent his widow off her head. His only son and heir, the Crown Prince Rudolph, had shot his mistress and then himself in a royal hunting lodge. The Emperor called himself a *Pechvogel,* a bird of misfortune, and now had only two pleasures left to him, shooting in the company of a solitary gamekeeper at Bad Ischl, and sipping coffee with a handsome retired actress named Schratt. Otherwise he worked all day at a standing desk, scratching away like a lawyer's clerk, and, when bedtime came, he lay in a soldier's iron cot. Edward determined that, if he could, he would try to cheer up this aged *Pechvogel* who was his host.

As it turned out this was not very easy. Given every comfort at the Hofburg, Edward was taken on the usual visits to the Viennese opera, the royal tombs, and to other formal functions. At a gala dinner he made an impressive impromptu speech and ended by announcing that he wished to create the Emperor a British Field Marshal. There followed an uproar; everyone shouting 'Hoch, hoch!'; and the *Pechvogel* seemed very pleased. He promptly announced that he was making King Edward a Field Marshal of the Austro-Hungarian Army. More thunderous cries of '*Hoch, Hoch!*'

But the fact of the matter was that their hours were so very different, host and guest saw little of each other.

Edward had to keep to his host's meal times: luncheon at twelve and dinner in full uniform at five o'clock, but, whereas the Emperor went to his iron cot at 7.30 and got up at four the following morning, his guest liked to see Viennese night life until at least one or two and had only just gone to bed when the Emperor was scratching at his desk again.

On the rare occasions when they actually met and had the chance of a private word, Edward was at pains to show particular respect for the doyen of European sovereigns and was as friendly as the *Pechvogel* would permit. But by now the Emperor had really shut himself off from the world and, though he thought Edward of England a reasonable fellow sovereign, certainly better than many he was obliged to meet, he was not expansive. Edward was disappointed, but felt he could say and do no more without being obtrusive.

At the end of the visit the imperial train took them swiftly to the frontier where they transferred to the King's own royal carriages. It was only then that he learnt his objectionable nephew Willy was carrying out his usual practice of following him everywhere. He was due to pay a State Visit to Vienna in exactly a week's time.

A shade slimmer, rested, and certainly feeling fitter for his cure and a little 'roguey-poguery' in Marienbad and Vienna, Edward returned to find himself the target of much hostile comment from that powerful organ the *Tailor and Cutter*. Being a leader and arbiter of fashion, he was known throughout Europe for his absorbing interest in clothes. The seal of his approval was generally sufficient for everyone to follow his lead, and already he had introduced the dinner jacket for very informal evening wear, the Norfolk jacket, the Homburg, and grey felt hats, and had mercilessly squashed the upsurge of a craze for wearing Panamas. He was a stickler for correct dress on every occasion, and not even Lord Roseberry, who had a very special position as an ex Prime Minister, twice winner of the Derby, and a great friend, could get away with appearing at Court in trousers rather than the regulation knee-breeches and stockings. The King had eyed him coldly and said he presumed for the evening Rosebery had attached himself to the suite of the American Ambassador. The *Tailor and Cutter* was generally whole-heartedly on his side, though the editor had correctly foretold failure when, on a whim, Edward had tried to popularize the idea of putting trouser creases on the sides rather than the front. Now, in their issue of 17 September, 1903, the editor spoke scathingly of a report that Marienbad the sovereign had gone down to meet a friend at the station in 'what approached fancy dress: a green cap, pink tie, white gloves, knee-breeches, grey slippers, and a brown overcoat with loud checks'. His Majesty might be on holiday, but the *Tailor and Cutter* considered he was not at liberty to dress up so eccentrically.

> *Loyal subjects* [wrote the editor] *must sincerely hope that His Majesty has not brought this outfit home.*

His Majesty was nettled that someone had given him away, but he was chastened nevertheless.

15

King Edward was extremely careful about his wardrobe when he went north to stay with his old friends Lord and Lady Savile at Rufford Abbey for the Doncaster Races. He took vast quantities of luggage and a brusher as well as Hawkins, to make sure that he was sartorially perfect all the time. But at Rufford he found irritations worse than the *Tailor and Cutter.*

He had stayed with the Saviles for the Doncaster Races since that unfortunate Tranby Croft scandal when he had been unwise enough to stay with the shipowner, Arthur Wilson. And he considered the Saviles his good friends. But Lady Savile tearfully confessed that her nerves had been shredded by the malice of those who wanted to offer the King their hospitality but who knew that it would not be acceptable. By now he was of an age to have fixed his close friends and he stayed with them almost by routine. It had not occurred to him that other members of Society would so bitterly resent their exclusion. 'I can't be everywhere,' he told Lady Savile. 'They must realize the impossibility of it.'

'But the jealousy, Sir!' she cried tearfully. 'The way they hate us!'

'Hate you?' he said astonished.

She nodded. 'All of us. The Sassoons and Ernest Cassel – perhaps because they are Jews. But the others who love to have you as their guest as well: the Vincents and Lawsons and Wests, the Devonshires, and Derbys, and Lord Iveagh, the Willy Jameses and the Grevilles....'

'Come, my dear,' he said kindly to his hostess. 'You are feeling the strain of the races. Perhaps I have overburdened you with too large a suite.' Certainly he had not stinted himself on this visit. His two Equerries with their valets, plus Hawkins and the brusher, two telephonists, a pair of chauffeurs and an Arab boy to make his coffee, had saddled the Saviles with eleven to provide for in addition to himself.

'No, no, Sir,' she declared. 'But the jealousy is so wearing.' She dabbed at her eyes. 'Forgive me for breaking down, but they believe we owe your favours to obsequiousness, and that is horrid. In some quarters they refer to the Saviles and the Grevilles as the Civils and the Grovels. . . .' Once more she broke down.

The King was much put out, but decided there was absolutely nothing he could do. He was too old now to change his routine. Still, because of Lady Savile's wounded feelings, he enjoyed his stay less than usual and when the Doncaster races were over, he went north to Balmoral.

Ordinarily not overfond of business, he found it something of a relief to turn to political issues. Balfour travelled up to Balmoral to talk over a reconstruction of his Cabinet. He had the personal belief that occasional reconstructions were good for administration, the party, and the country, but this one had been forced on him by the findings of Esher's Royal Commission of enquiry into the mishandling of the Boer War. Evidently there was great need for Army reform, and naturally St John Brodrick, who had been Secretary for War since November 1900, resented the Commission's interference and hated its findings. Advised to resign in August 1903, he was still holding on to office in the third week of September.

The Prime Minister knew this was not going to be a peaceful arrangement because that galvanic admiral, Sir John Fisher, and the ubiquitous Lord Esher were also guests at Balmoral, and the King immediately made it clear that he had some very definite views which he intended to air extensively and loudly.

One was approving of Fisher's scheme that the Austro-Hungarian idea of uniting War Office and Admiralty under one Minister of State ought to be adopted. It took all Balfour's powers to persuade him that one day it might be worth considering, but, for the present, he was sure that neither the generals nor the admirals would stand it.

'At any rate,' said the King, coming to his second definite view: 'Brodrick must go.'

This was mutually agreed, though Balfour did not wish to dismiss a useful colleague. He could be transferred to the India Office.

'And,' said the King, arriving swiftly at his third point, 'Esher, here shall be War Secretary.'

Again there was almost mutual agreement. Balfour thought it poetic justice to put the Army's chief critic in a position to reform it. Fisher, who got on splendidly with Esher, considered it an excellent idea. Edward as good as commanded it. Esher himself refused.

'Reggie,' exclaimed the King in horror. 'You cannot mean it.'

'Sir, I do. I should positively hate to be War Secretary.' He explained that he was engaged in a lucrative arrangement with Ernest Cassel which he would have to abandon if he became a Cabinet Minister. The truth was, of course, that he preferred to continue as the *éminence grise* of Windsor. He far preferred the power of palace intrigue to that of a Secretary of State.

Edward was put out. 'Then I propose, as you have been the means of moving Brodrick, Reggie, that at least you propose what reforms should be made. Is a three-man commission possible, Prime Minister? Reggie could chairman it, and Jacky Fisher could be a second.'

Balfour weighed the matter carefully. At length he agreed.

Then there came the incendiary question as to who should be Secretary for War. Balfour had only one candidate in mind, H. O. Arnold-Foster, a versatile man of high intelligence who was nephew to the poet Matthew Arnold....

'No, no, no,' said the King sharply. He held his hands over his ears as if to shut out the offensive recommendation. 'I can't help it, Balfour, I can't help it, but I *detest* that man. There's no reason for it – except that he's common, and I don't trust these jumped-up people. I heard he absorbed all his intelligence, as you term it, by knocking up a series of textbooks for an educational publisher. Now who wants a publisher's hack looking after the Army?'

Wisely the Prime Minister left the question unanswered.

'He's uncouth,' snapped the King. 'Absolutely uncouth.' He warmed to his theme. 'My senior officers could neither respect nor accept the authority of such a man. It really wouldn't do at all.'

At dinner the King continued protesting, though both Fisher and Esher had told him Arnold-Foster might do – at a pinch, and Balfour found the meal, generally so jolly at Balmoral now that King Edward had taken over, an oppressive one. He respectfully declined to admit any of the King's charges against his nominee.

In the end Matthew Arnold's unpolished nephew became Secretary for War. Edward had been well brought up by his father and mother, and he knew exactly how he stood as a constitutional monarch. Balfour's advice had to prevail. But giving way did not make him like Balfour any more.

The King growled and he snapped and nothing pleased him for weeks – not even the saucy news that Daisy of Pless, in doing a turn at Alloa House, had lost her drawers before the audience.

'That girls of yours,' he said bad-temperedly to Patsy Cornwallis-West when next he saw her, 'that girl of yours is over here far too much. She ought to be with Hans in Germany. And why is she forever singing and dancing and going in for amateur theatricals? It is disgraceful.'

Patsy warmly defended her daughter. 'Journalists never leave her alone. Never. And the things they say! An American paper says she dyes her hair a copper-colour, and is languishing for love of the Prince of Wales.'

The King started. 'Eh?'

'And the same paper says poor Princess May has sleepless nights because of her husband's devotion to Daisy!' Mrs Cornwallis-West twice said 'tch! tch!' and went on: 'Why, losing her drawers at Alloa House is absolutely nothing, Sir.'

He scowled at being put down. 'No doubt you and your daughter will soon be leading members of the Women's Union?' he sneered. Like his mother the King loathed the possibly reasonable, but, to him, totally unfeminine claim for women to have equal rights. A Manchester Registrar of Births and Deaths, called Mrs Pankhurst, had recently formed the Women's Social and Political Union, which was determined to press its views forcibly.

'Very probably,' said his former mistress, quite unmoved, 'we will.'

The King had to endure several further minor annoyances that autumn.

He went to stay with the Londonderrys at Wynyard, and in no time at all he felt thwarted.

To begin with he had hoped to effect some sort of reconciliation between his host and hostess. Theresa Londonderry was his confidante and adviser in many matters and, although she affected not to mind being put into Coventry by her wronged husband for nineteen years, and had conducted a series of affairs throughout that period, she really felt it deeply. Edward, in the spirit, as he hoped, of a friend and guest, rather than as sovereign to his Minister of Education or King to Marquis, strove to soften Londonderry. But his host stiffened even at the hinting stage, before the actual words were said, and the King wisely forebore. If Londonderry was that implacable the situation was hopeless – and exceedingly thwarting.

Then his old friend Devonshire who was a fellow guest made him impatient by suddenly deciding to resign from the Cabinet. He had already held up Balfour's final reconstruction by dithering for over a month. The King was sharp with him about being so dilatory. As Balfour chose Londonderry to take Devonshires's place as Lord President of the Council and there were sufficient Privy Councillors in the house, the King decided to hold a Council then and there. Almeric Fitzroy, Clerk of the Privy Council, was summoned by telephone and arrived with the necessary documents, seals and so forth; though as no Council had been held outside a Royal Palace since the reign of Charles II, he hoped, he said, that it was in order.

The King looked at him coldly. 'Fitzroy, the Court is where the King is,' he declared, and further ordered that the transactions of the Council be headed 'At our Court at Wynyard'.

Lady Londonderry was delighted at obtaining such a cachet. Her quiet strange husband seemed entirely unmoved – though he was not unmoved on the next day when, at one of his famous rabbit shoots, the Duke of Devonshire plainly showed he was bored by lighting a cigarette. The new Lord President of the Council was exceedingly curt to his predecessor in office, and not a great deal mollified by the fact that the sport was so good that over three thousand rabbits were shot on that single day. Most of the men had headaches in the evening and there was still a whiff of cartridges about Wynyard when the company settled down to poker – except for the King and Captain Ponsonby, who played bridge at a special table with Mrs George Keppel and Louisa Devonshire. The last had her wig askew and was so rouged she resembled a port-drenched don, but she played expertly and the

King and Mrs George lost and lost, to Edward's increasing vexation.

In October King Edward went to open the new Gaiety. To make the occasion entirely respectable he took with him his Queen. She was intrigued to see Gaiety Girls in the flesh. They had character and a reputation as well as beauty – unlike the girls at the Empire Music Hall – and they were fast becoming an institution in the new century. One or two had already been married into the ranks of the small gentry. It was believed, and correctly, that some would soon rival the American millionairesses and be absorbed into the highest ranks of Society. Queen Alexandra reflected. A little American, May Goelet, had just netted the Duke of Roxburghe. Perhaps one of the vivacious soubrettes she was watching that night might aim as high....

The King of Italy, little Victor Emmanuel, when he was at Windsor on a State Visit soon afterwards, said he had heard of the Gaiety Girls and would very much like to see them; but neither his host nor his ambassador thought this would be very politic. And Queen Elena very firmly said no.

King Leopold II of Belgium would also have liked to feel welcome in England so that he could drop in at the stage door of the Gaiety – just as, once, he had crossed the Channel to call on Lillie Langtry at the strange hour of nine in the morning. But Edward was not having that. King Leopold had behaved disgracefully to his daughters. The eldest, Louise, had left her depraved and dissipated husband and gone off with an army officer and Leopold had countenanced their harassment. He had approved of the cashiering, dishonouring and illegal imprisonment of Louise's lover and of her own committal to a mental asylum; and when both had escaped, he would have nothing to do with either and forced them to live as beggars. His second daughter, Stephanie, was barely any luckier. Married to Crown Prince Rudolph of Austria, who either committed suicide in a hunting lodge, or died in an orgy – no one seemed to be sure which – she was left a lonely and wretched widow in a strange land because her father did not like returned goods. His youngest daughter he kept close by him to wait on his every need and would not let her marry the man she loved. All this was atrocious enough; but, since Sir Roger Casement's report on the atrocities committed in the Congo, published as a White Paper by the British Government, Leopold, as personal owner of the Congo, had been universally execrated. Therefore, when he asked if he might visit England, he received a forceful refusal from his royal relative through Lord Knollys:

> *The King cannot feel attracted towards a Sovereign whether he is a relation or not, who, he considers, has neglected his duty towards Humanity.*

Queen Victoria could not have made a point plainer than that.

16

Miss Charlotte Knollys sat up in bed and screamed.

It was a muted scream, more the squeak of a frightened governess, for Miss Knollys was a strictly self-controlled woman who did not shriek even when she woke to find her bedroom at Sandringham full of smoke.

She knew what to do, tugged on a bed-gown, dipped her face flannel in the water jug, held it to her mouth, and made for the door.

In the corridor it was worse. Dense smoke swirled round the dim lights, but no one had given the alarm. For a moment she removed the damp face flannel from her mouth and she shouted, her voice ringing out for the night-watchman. Then she picked up her skirts with her free hand and ran as fast as she could to the floor below. Immediately beneath her room was the Queen's, and the Queen, like everyone else, seemed totally unaware that the house was on fire. 'Ma'am, Ma'am,' begged Miss Knollys, tugging at her mistress' arm. She choked on the smoke.

The Queen woke up. Against the low light of the votive lamp she always kept burning she saw Charlotte and a great deal of smoke. She found a wet flannel being pressed against her mouth. Automatically she resisted. Was Charlotte trying to suffocate her?

Then she understood and climbed stiffly out of bed. Charlotte seized the Queen's bed-gown and a shawl and wrapped them round her.

'Quickly,' she shouted hoarsely. 'Quickly'.

The Queen allowed herself to be run out of her own bedroom, down the length of a corridor and along another until they were clear of the smoke. Both were gasping. They sat simultaneously on an Egyptian chaise-longue which stood against the wall. Simultaneously what Charlotte Knollys had feared all the time actually happened. The smouldering, wherever it was, was blown up into flames. A fire burst out. Wood began to crackle. The two women clutched each other. One, but not the other, heard a bell.

Charlotte Knollys placed her lips close to the Queen's ear. 'The estate fire engine is outside.' She said it twice.

They waited on the Egyptian chaise-longue. The Queen's chief dresser appeared, her face lined. She whitened in relief. Lord Knollys had sent someone to fetch his sister and then followed himself. Eventually he found her with the Queen. Two rooms had been gutted and several more drenched by the excited fire brigade before the King appeared.

'All well?' he enquired cheerfully.

'Yes, thank you, Sir,' replied Miss Knollys. She said nothing else, though she would have dearly liked to do so.

Her unspoken thoughts were reflected in a letter written by the straight-forward Grand Duchess of Strelitz, who sometimes was more tolerant of her Rumpenheim relative Alix than her Brunswick relative Edward.

> *'I was horrified hearing of dear Alix's danger, too awful to think of! We must give credit to old Charlotte for* really *saving her life. What order will the King decorate Charlotte with to reward such readiness of thought and action? Though* he *was in no hurry to hasten to see Alix after her merciful escape.'*

No one discovered the cause of the fire. Sir Dighton Probyn, who had a totally unselfish devotion to the Queen and called her 'the Blessed Lady', was appalled by the danger she had stood in. He made the most searching enquiries, but to no avail. Miss Charlotte, as she was known by the family, received no decoration but she was warmly thanked by the King. She said, quite truthfully, it was her duty and her pleasure, and she had done it. In her privileged position she was prepared for any sacrifice and, with a twinkle in her eye, she reminded him of his would-be assassin who had missed the royal target at Brussels station and fired a bullet through her bun. She also made fruitless enquiries and discussed her failure with Sir Dighton. United in their affection for the Queen, it was generally understood they must be on the edge of a mutual understanding, but, though the old soldier went as far as to give Miss Charlotte an expensive if unusual Christmas present in having her bathroom at Sandringham entirely re-walled in looking-glass – a curious mark of esteem in view of her cheerful acknowledgement that she was exceptionally plain – they never fell over the edge. They finally put the fire down to what Probyn called 'the electricals'. He had no faith in this already well-tried experiment in lighting, confessing that he would rather repeat his charge across the plains of India which had won him the V.C. than ever touch anything connected with 'the electricals'.

Miss Charlotte, sharp-eared as a mouse, missed little of what was going on in the great world beyond the Queen's small Court, and this was not because she went out seeking news. Indeed she was never known to take a single day off in all her long service with the Queen: but she absorbed information from those about her by some sort of osmotic process, and enamelled it with an exciting touch or two if she thought it would please the Queen or, if it was necessary for the tranquillity of her adored friend, she would dilute it.

The Queen's old rival Daisy Warwick was much in the news early in 1904. In January her daughter married Viscount Helmsley and the fact that the bride's mother was carrying a child was not missed by many of the thousand wedding guests. It added a piquancy to the situation that five months before Joe Laycock's first child had been born to the former Kitty Downshire, and she was already carrying her second. In March Daisy warned her Socialist friends that they should cancel all her platform work and Joe Laycock was warned she was going to die. Probably she wished to, and being confined at forty-one was a considerable risk. But she came through it. 'Mercy!' she cried, when she was presented with her second daughter, and Mercy the child was baptized. With Mercy she tried to hold on to Joe, but after a motoring accident which was entirely Joe's fault and in which his wife lost a leg, he decided to finish with Daisy. She had lost him for ever.

The saga lost nothing in its retelling by Miss Charlotte. As if adding a great *Amen* to this Balzacian romance, the Queen remarked: 'Well, they all still have their hunting.'

She was less placid when Miss Charlotte related a titbit from Balmoral, where Edward had gone in February. He had grown too stout for stalking and preferred a deer drive, which taxed the resources of all his gillies and those of his neighbours as well. He had also been entertaining Mrs George Cornwallis-West, formerly Lady Randolph Churchill, showing her over the Castle, and returning her visit to Invercauld where she was staying. Miss Charlotte believed there could be nothing racy, as she put it, about these meetings and actually the King had been pumping her about her sister Leonie Leslie's strange affair with the Duke of Connaught. Being a bottled-up character, unlike his brothers, Arthur Connaught had found the searing of his passion too much for his nerves, until his Duchess – a less odious Prussian than most, the Queen conceded – had made Mrs Leslie her friend and blessed the arrangement with a rare and civilized understanding. The Queen wondered if she had been as civilized and understanding with Edward. She was certainly put out to hear that the King had been heard criticizing his younger brother to an American lady whose impulsiveness and lack of discretion were well known. Edward ought not to let down the family, however much he disliked Arthur.

Miss Charlotte overheard the Queen as good as saying this to the King when they all met in London for the funeral of the Duke of Cambridge. It was a family occasion which underlined the principle of family loyalty. The King took his lesson well and was gentler to his soldier brother than he had been for a long time. Alix, too, put herself out to be agreeable to Arthur although he had married a Prussian. The Duke of Connaught supposed it was because they were all so sad about Uncle George, which he himself thought a mistake. The old man had had a full and marvellous life and had enjoyed himself. Theoretically married to an actress, Mrs FitzGeorge, he had fathered three sons – all of whom had given him a son's due of anxiety and pleasure, and he had had other affairs with rich, interesting and complaisant ladies. Miss Charlotte, who was a realist like Arthur of Connaught, would have agreed with him. Both agreed with the old Duke's decision to be buried in Kensal Green Cemetery in the same vault as Mrs FitzGeorge.

No one else was. The King thought it disgraceful that a Prince of the Blood should be laid to rest in Kensal Green, until he was reminded that his mother's uncle, the Duke of Sussex, had been buried there between his two morganatic wives. His son George, the Prince of Wales, still thought it dreadful. The Princess of Wales, who had already begun to make the collection of family treasures and keepsakes for which she was to become famous, was extremely concerned about Uncle George's property. He had inherited from his father and his mother a mass of plate, jewellery, and portraits, and, as these could be regarded as possessions of the Royal Family, he had given Queen Victoria to understand that he would leave them back to the family. But either he overlooked his undertaking, or he had not forgotten his virtual dismissal from the post of Commander-in-Chief, and he carefully willed everything to his sons. A man of punctiliousness to the last, he also left strict instructions to the valet who had been with him for thirty-five years that, if it was raining on the day of his funeral, only his *second* best pair of boots was to be hung from his charger.

It is difficult when a person dies full of years, honours and riches to estimate the depth of sorrow of those who mourn. The Queen's grief was sincere. Miss Charlotte and Sir Dighton realized this and did their best to comfort her. The King too, had cared for jovial Uncle George and wept at the military funeral accorded him. The crowds who lined the route of the cortège afforded the old soldier their deepest sign of respect, total silence. Lady Geraldine Somerset, a Lady-in-Waiting of his mother's, had longed to be his duchess for almost a golden jubilee of years, and she had grown used to waiting. His sister, the Grand Duchess Augusta, who was invariably late for family deathbeds, was intensely provoked by a scarcely veiled insinuation that she was an unfeeling woman.

'*I had a* vile *letter from Geraldine* (she wrote to the Princess of Wales) *really a nasty one, upbraiding me for not being there.*'

She would, most sincerely, have liked to be there, and raced over as quickly as she could to put Lady Geraldine in her place and sort out her brother's things in his second house at Kew because part of them belonged to her.

It seemed that almost everyone had fond memories of Uncle George. He would be missed as a family institution, always, at every grand ceremonial, correctly dressed to the last thread, erect, solemn, and puffing through his white moustache. His successor at the Horse Guards, with an ungentlemanly lack of respect, had termed him disparagingly 'that old bumblebee', but the nation as a whole had honoured him.

The Grand Duchess in ebbs and floods of tear tides wept over her gloomy task. The Queen and her daughter and the Prince of Wales and Miss Charlotte helped her and found she would burst into fresh sobs at every remembrance of her brother. 'Now, I am alone,' she said, sorting with bent, rheumaticky fingers through a cabinet tray of bibelots. 'Alone. Alone. The last. Alone.' Then, at the thought of an invention she had heard of only a few days before she looked up from the bibelots and remarked: 'And with dearest George's love of gadgets, *how* he would have loved a thermos flask. Oh! *how* I would love to have given him a thermos flask!'

They all felt dreadfully for the poor old lady until half-way through her probing and selecting she abruptly said: 'And now, Alix, as Kew Cottage reverts to the Crown, why should Toria not have her own establishment here?'

Miss Charlotte felt the Queen stiffening with displeasure.

'I should imagine,' cried the Grand Duchess, noting the change in Alix's expression, 'I should have thought that a woman of thirty-six required a place of her own.'

Princess Victoria went first pink with embarrassment, then white as if she was about to faint. Her sister-in-law took her arm and led her to a seat, but over her shoulder she managed to say. 'Very probably you are right, Aunt Augusta, and it would be a most convenient house for Toria. . . .' Her voice faded, giving place to a deadly silence broken only by Toria's sighing and the Queen cracking and clicking her knuckles in annoyance.

In the face of such cold hostility even the Grand Duchess felt at a loss. 'I expect of course, Alix dear,' she said weakly, 'that you would prefer to keep Toria with you.'

'Certainly,' said Miss Charlotte firmly, speaking for her mistress. The Grand Duchess returned to her melancholy task.

Miss Charlotte thought it noble of the King to accompany them to Copenhagen in April. She knew from Captain Ponsonby that the King had really wanted to go to Paris, but while the actual negotiations were going on for the Entente Cordiale he felt unable to do so. She also knew, from her own observation in the past, how the King hated the stiff protocol and boredom of the Danish Court.

Dining with the venerable Franz Josef of Austria at five o'clock had been bad enough but at least the old Emperor had gone to his iron cot at 7.30 leaving everyone else to enjoy the deliciousness of Vienna, but at the Court of Queen Alexandra's father, the eighty-five-year-old Danish King, they sat down to a ceremonious dinner of many dull and stodgy courses, at an equally ungodly hour of 6.30 without any chance of escaping afterwards. Dinner was preceded and followed by a formal *cercling* of the guests by the old King and his family, and Edward could only get away to smoke from eight o'clock until nine, when he was required again in the Drawing-room, there to play whist which he loathed, or Loo which he loathed more. At ten the King of Denmark retired, and Miss Charlotte had not the slightest doubt that had the company been larger and the facilities available, the King of England would then have gone on the rantan. But who, at that time, could go on the rantan in Copenhagen? Apparently he returned to play bridge and smoke in his own rooms, and groan in spirit because so many Danish days lay ahead.

Sir Dighton had been left in England and so Miss Charlotte had sole charge of 'the Blessed Lady' who, clearly, found her father's routine quite bearable and enjoyed every minute of her stay. Having known them for so many years, the Lady-in-Waiting considered it strange that husband and wife had grown so far apart. In the first years of their marriage Alexandra had easily kept up with the tremendous pace set by her husband and his set, but, while age hardly seemed to have altered her appearance, it had certainly subdued her – almost to the point of lethargy – while the King, despite his bulk, still had huge reserves of energy and required continual action, amusement and novelty. Having nothing to do made him fractious and the ominous drumming of his fingers on a table, or a tap-tap-tap of his right foot, was always a sign that Lord Esher should be sent for – the one man who had enough patience and charm to keep the King amused. Unhappily, on this three-week penance at the Amalienborg Palace, Lord Esher was not in the suite.

Miss Charlotte and Captain Ponsonby went to considerable trouble to prevent the royal fingers drumming too often and the King's right foot from going tap-tap-tap. He was shown every museum, gallery and historic house in the area. He was even reduced to visiting a farm which sent quantities of butter to England. They proposed a private competition to find the ugliest woman in the Palace – which Miss Charlotte was confident of winning herself, and she was rather put out to find herself put second to the Crown Princess of Denmark. Then Captain Ponsonby breathlessly reported that, on opening a wrong door by mistake, he had found Prince Waldemar's Bourbon wife dancing the can-can, which had given him the idea of surreptitiously importing a cabaret for the entertainment of his master. But Miss Charlotte, while disclaiming any real knowledge of cabarets, suggested that surely they were a little noisy.

In the event, the King was kept from the frustration of total boredom by deliberately interesting himself in politics. The red despatch boxes which followed him everywhere were for the first time a welcome sight. He even tried his hand at some personal diplomacy, talking with Isvolsky, the Russian Minister to the Danish Court, about the Russo-Japanese War which had just broken out. Because England and Japan had a treaty alliance this was not a wise thing to do, as Lord Lansdowne swiftly cabled in code from the Foreign Office. The King might have resented this move had not his Foreign Minister just signed a comprehensive agreement with France. The Entente Cordiale was close to being a reality. But then he heard from Knollys in London that Balfour had informed the Commons of certain minor cessions of colonial territory which were part of the Anglo-French treaty. Immediately Edward's hackles rose, as they always did when any part of his prerogative was threatened. He was already angry with Balfour who had steadfastly continued Lord Salisbury's policy of denying him the right to see Cabinet papers while decisions were actually being made, a privilege enjoyed by his father, and which Esher argued was part of the royal prerogative.

Angrily he telegraphed to the Prime Minister direct:

CONSTITUTIONALLY POWER TO CEDE TERRITORY RESTS WITH THE CROWN

Bluntly Balfour replied that his speech had been made on the authority of the Foreign Office and the Law Officers, but he would look into the matter.

Immediately the King telegraphed Knollys:

HE IS ALWAYS SO VAGUE THAT PROBABLY HE IS WRONG, BUT I MUST INSIST, IF HE IS, THAT HE ADMITS IT

It turned out that by precedent the Prime Minister was right and a very disgruntled monarch sent a further telegram to his Private Secretary:

MR BALFOUR HAS TREATED ME WITH SCANT RESPECT IN EVERY RESPECT

With such splutters of indignation going back and forth across the North Sea, the King just managed to survive his three weeks' ordeal in Denmark without noticeably losing his temper or his good manners.

Soon afterwards the same suite accompanied the King and Queen and the Princess Victoria on a private visit to Ireland. First they were entertained by the Viceroy at Viceregal Lodge and afterwards went to stay with the Devonshires on their Irish estate at Lismore Castle. This was more to everyone's pleasure. The King and the Duchess had their bridge. Miss Charlotte enjoyed keeping her mistress company on the interesting excursions which were planned for each day of their visit by the Duke's enterprising agent. So enterprising was he that the King wished to give him an M.V.O. and told Ponsonby to approach the Duke about it. The Duke was as vague as ever.

'M.V.O., Ponsonby, what's that?' he exclaimed.

Because, with the Order of Merit the Victorian Order was the only one entirely in his gift, Edward regarded it highly, and Ponsonby was glad his master had not heard the Duke's astounding question.

Politely and carefully he explained.

The Duke scratched his head when he had finished. 'Well, Ponsonby,' he said. 'If that's what the M.V.O. is, I don't think my man will want it.'

In fact the Duke was wrong and the King right. The agent was delighted with his Order. But Captain Ponsonby dreaded that by some eccentric piece of tactlessness the Duke's views on the Victoria Order should somehow reach the King.

'Sovereigns, Miss Charlotte,' he said on the day they left Lismore, 'are not easy to serve.'

Charlotte Knollys had temporarily been suffering the scratchiness of 'the Beloved Lady' who, on occasions, could be very, very scratchy indeed. 'You are right, Captain Ponsonby,' she replied.

And so, both thought, back to London for the end of the Season. But the Season was partially subdued by mourning. Aunt Augusta – still going through her brother's effects with his sons and their wives – once more showed her truly remarkable capacity for missing family deathbeds. Her blind old husband the Grand Duke of Mecklenburg-Strelitz died on 29 May while she was far away in London.

She was in a great taking.

The family gathered to see her off at Victoria Station on the 31st.

'The unluckiest day of the unluckiest month,' she sobbed. 'So I expect to be drowned on the crossing.'

'Poor Aunt Augusta,' said the Queen to her Lady-in-Waiting afterwards. 'The Grand Duke was not easy to live with, but at least she had her place at Neu Strelitz. Now she is simply a dowager. It cannot be pleasant.'

Miss Charlotte pressed her hand. She knew precisely what the Queen was thinking.

17

The Royal Navy was the passion of the Prince of Wales' life; indeed his eldest son David was to say that he had a blue-water approach to life, and he was typical of a very large percentage of naval officers in 1904. It was, therefore, to him – because as sovereign and heir they got on uncommonly well – that the King took his anxieties about a situation which was beginning to erode the Board of Admiralty.

Years before he had been a close friend of Rear-Admiral Lord Charles Beresford and, until a scandal which had involved darling Daisy Warwick, they had been on the best of terms. After that they avoided and disliked each other intensely, and gradually the business of hating mellowed into a less fiery antipathy. Now they respected each other's positions, but Lord Charles was anxious to bring his long experience to bear upon the King, who, he believed, was about to be led by the nose in naval affairs.

'By Admiral Fisher?' said the Prince.

His father nodded. 'Exactly.'

Sir John Fisher, the Second Sea Lord and Commander-in-Chief at Portsmouth had invited the King down to Admiralty House, and there had proceeded to pound him with vigorous opinions about reform in the Royal Navy. What Esher with Fisher's help was doing for the Army, Fisher with Esher's help wanted to do for the Navy. The Admiral's enemies, reactionary officers, said he was a mischief-maker, an office-grabber, better at dancing than at naval warfare (he certainly had a passion for the former as well as the latter), and that he had Malay blood in him. They were led by Rear-Admiral Lord Charles Beresford.

'Well, George?' demanded the King. 'What am I to do? Fisher's as explosive as a box of Chinese crackers. He has ideas, dozens of them. Some must be sound, especially his views on the value of submarines. But a good many officers can't stand him and that's a fact.'

The Prince of Wales agreed. His own blue-water approach to

life rather made him shrivel at Fisher's wild talk of redundant ships, obsolete personnel and supplies, worn-out strategies and Nelson's-time customs, and his own taciturnity made him dislike Fisher's vulgar noisiness. Like a Neapolitan, the Second Sea Lord never whispered if he could speak and never spoke if he could possibly shout. With fellow officers at full volume of persuasion Fisher made the din of a beaten copper gong. Nevertheless, because naval reform was so desperately important to him, he was prepared to give especially influential people special treatment and he had not failed to work on the Prince of Wales because of his power in naval circles. As a result, while the Prince deprecated Fisher's manner, he felt forced to admit that at least fifty per cent of his ideas were absolutely sound.

He said so and the King sighed.

'Your Mama,' he said, 'has the same view.'

The Queen had easily been scooped into the Fisher net – an easy prey because they had much in common, both being impetuous, single-minded, deeply religious and possessed of the same sense of humour. She invariably addressed him as Admiral Jack. What was good enough for 'the Beloved Lady' was enough for Sir Dighton and Miss Charlotte. Knollys, too, had been gathered up. Not even Captain Ponsonby had been neglected. He was always being written to by the Commander-in-Chief Portsmouth.

The Prince of Wales was never a garrulous man, but suddenly he found his voice and surprised his father by saying that the Entente Cordiale was excellent in its way but cousin Willy would now fear being encircled, and it was ten to one he would build up his naval strength. Therefore it was vital for the Royal Navy to be enlarged and show a united front. Bickering between the Beresford and Fisher parties could only do harm.

The King agreed hastily, then added reflectively: 'I wonder if I made a mistake by inviting Fisher's cook to the Palace.'

His son had the Hanoverian frog-eyes. They stood out in amazement. The King turned pink. 'Where he found her I can't imagine,' he went on hastily. 'But her foie gras cutlets quite carried me away. With her teal and sandpipers I was undone.' He looked apologetically at his son. 'How does an Admiral's cook turn out such food?' he asked as if in extenuation. 'Her Leopold Rothschild soufflé alone was worth a decoration....'

'You gave her a decoration?'

'A small one,' admitted his father.

'As well as an invitation to the Palace?'

'Yes, yes. As I said. Menanger could learn things from her and no doubt she could learn from him.'

'She is pretty?'

'As a matter of a fact, yes. A remarkably lovely young woman. . . .' He paused. 'Ah, I see. . . .' He paused again. Then sternly he said: 'Fisher knows I have the common touch. It's a gift he shares himself. To congratulate someone's cook is to give him a compliment. . . .' Then, noticing his son's frog-eyes were still standing out he rapidly went on. 'I absolutely refuse to credit that the Head of the Navy List has been fooled by a soufflé!'

The Prince of Wales suddenly smiled. 'There were the teal and sandpipers, too,' he reminded him. 'And foie gras cutlets, if I'm not mistaken.'

'And damned delicious, all of it,' his father chuckled. He put an arm round George's shoulder. 'Don't worry, I'll keep my eyes open in future, and as sovereign I do have a bit and bridle on Jackie Fisher. Now, promise me, if I try to quieten his uproar will you do your best to subdue Beresford's diehards?'

The Prince of Wales at once said, yes, he would; though, knowing the tempered feelings of his reactionary friends, he doubted if he would succeed.

'As for Willy's fear of encirclement,' continued the King. 'I shall sound him out at the Kiel Regatta. Almost certainly he will be indiscreet.'

Father and son suddenly smiled at each other.

The latest furore caused by the German Emperor had all Europe in laughter. It had been found necessary to remove a small polypus from the Imperial throat and he had expected his family and his subjects to be closely attentive to the operation. Congratulations had been showered on him on making a swift recovery and he had glowed until somehow he learnt that the Crown Prince, the heir to his throne, far from behaving himself in a filial fashion had actually been steeplechasing at the time of the operation. Without a moment's hesitation the Emperor had him put under house arrest and cancelled his leave for a year. Since, of course, he had regretted it, but Europe was still laughing.

'Very probably you are right,' agreed the Prince of Wales. 'He is bound to bungle things at Kiel, by showing off his naval strength.'

'Poor Willy,' said the King. His smile died. For a moment he was in deadly earnest. 'I believe his stupidity will be his downfall, but it is not all his fault. He is surrounded by flatterers who make up to him. Our Ambassador tells me General von Mackensen has set the fashion of kissing his hands before and after an audience.'

'Eh?' The Prince could scarcely believe his ears.

'It is true,' insisted his father. 'No wonder the fellow is stupid. Pray God his downfall will not be the ruin of us all.'

But the Prince missed the nervous anxiety in his father's voice. He was still thinking of the hand kissing. 'Just who do they think Cousin Willy is?' he asked. 'The Emperor of China? The Pope?'

Until fourteen years before, the island of Heligoland, which commanded the approaches to the Kiel Canal, had been a British possession. Then Lord Salisbury had done a straight swap with it for the more productive German island of Zanzibar. It had not been entirely to Queen Victoria's pleasure. She thought it a pity to give up 'what one has'. As the Germans had promptly constructed the canal and made Kiel at the Baltic end into a great naval shipyard and arsenal, the Queen had probably been right. Certainly King Edward thought so as his royal yacht steamed along the canal on the way to the regatta of 1904. The Royal Navy could have kept better control of the North Sea with Heligoland as a base.

This was planned as a friendly visit to his nephew – the first of his reign, because his proposal to visit Berlin the year before had been rudely turned down.

Edward was determined to do his best for England, to control his temper and impatience when Willy was irritating, in particular to control the almost irresistible temptation to tease him for arresting his own heir, and to soothe away his suspiciousness by persuading him the Entente Cordiale was not part of a grand scheme to surround Germany, and, at the same time, keep a sharp eye open in the German dockyards. His suite had been carefully chosen. To show Willy that the Entente Cordiale was a serious treaty and that Frenchmen did not have forked tails as Willy possibly supposed, he included two as his own guests. One, the Prince of Monaco, was very acceptable to the German Emperor, being a deep-sea fishing enthusiast with a scientific bent, but the other, Baron d'Estournelles de Constant, though he had a profound respect for royalty which ought to have appealed to Willy, was also an ardent pacifist and had written pamphlets on the necessity for peace, and this on reflection was not likely to endear him to the warlike Prussians. Besides these Frenchmen the King had with him his relative Admiral Prince Louis of Battenberg, Lord Selborne, the First Lord of the Admiralty, and no fewer than five post captains in the Royal Navy. Ponsonby, by now promoted major, was to act as Private Secretary.

The Kiel Regatta was not merely a social occasion in the German Empire. It had its official importance. So often was the Emperor away from the capital that it was the one chance in the year for many of his ministers to speak to him. As a rule they submitted their ideas and projects through a Civil Secretariat, and saw their Sovereign only at Kiel.

This year, as the King of England was to be a guest, the Kaiser took immense trouble to impress, summoning every available vessel to line up for a review of his navy, overcoming his own careless attitude to food – for only mincemeat could make him greedy – by a thorough inspection of menus to be enjoyed by his gourmet uncle, and, on board his own yacht the *Hohenzollern*, interfering in everyone's work, having a special canopy fitted over the promenade deck, and everywhere banking flowers and ferns. There were even fountains and waterfalls for the delectation of his guests.

Unhappily his hopes of stunning his visitors with luxury and plenty were thwarted because the *Victoria and Albert* did not dock until after dark, and when the two monarchs met it was sheeting down with rain. Out beyond the reach of the dockyard lights were thousands of the Emperor's soldiers – unseen but heard. The King inspected a Guard of Honour as well as anyone could in such teeming rain while a band with drenched instruments made what it could of 'God Save the King'. At any rate, he would not hurry, and showed the men the courtesy of moving slowly along their ranks, water trickling down his neck to soak through his hated Prussian uniform.

Following this, both uncle and nephew dripping, they went to the *Hohenzollern* for the presentation of suites, and, after a change, there was dinner, an excellent meal of Scandinavian, Russian and Pomeranian dishes which made the chief guest murmur softly to himself in fond appreciation.

Comfortable and very much at his ease, King Edward replied to the Emperor's toast with aplomb, and, being a master of German idiom, he had the company in laughter before he said, apparently in all sincerity: 'May our two flags float side by side to the most remote ages even as today, for the maintenance of peace and the welfare not only of our own countries, but also of other nations.'

He sat down to an enthusiastic ovation and lighted an oversize cigar.

His nephew bowed and tried to smile. In fact, under the table, he was nervously clasping and unclasping his right hand, wondering if his fat bully of an uncle would taunt him for arresting William. It had been done in the heat of the moment. No one seemed to appreciate that. He was anxious, too, that something might go wrong with his plans for the regatta. He reflected gloomily that if his uncle was there to sneer, something almost certainly would. . . .

It nearly did. Count Eulenburg, head of the Emperor's Household, took Ponsonby by the arm after dinner and handed him a list of some two hundred persons whom he knew King Edward would wish to honour. Ponsonby gasped. He tried to explain what Eulenburg already knew quite well, that English Orders were not handed out with the liberality of European decorations. The King, he said, would never consent. Nor did the King. He grew a deep crimson when he saw the list. Some of the names on it were of people who were not even at Kiel. Under protest he eventually agreed to give minor Orders to the Emperor's ministers who were actually at Kiel and to no one else.

Major Ponsonby passed this on to Eulenburg who simply handed the matter on to someone else. The King, through Ponsonby, having so far proved inflexible, the decoration-hunters ended by going to their own Ambassador to the Court of St James, at that time Count Metternich. Metternich called to see Ponsonby aboard the *Victoria and Albert* and asked particularly if they could sit on the upper deck. There they enjoyed talk about trivialities until the Ambassador rose to go. Then he admitted that the telescopes of many decoration-hunters were fixed on them from portholes in the *Hohenzollern* and other ships, and he had asked to sit on the deck so that he could actually be seen persuading the obdurate Major. Then, at least, he could say he had done his best. It amused Ponsonby a good deal, but then he found he had to face Order difficulties of another kind.

Sitting quietly working in his cabin after breakfast, he was interrupted by the First Lord of the Admirality, Lord Selborne, who came in clutching the Prussian Order of the Red Eagle.

'I won't have it,' he burst out. 'I won't have it under any circumstances. I can't accept it as a Minister of the Crown. And I don't want it as a British peer.' And he repeated twice: 'I won't have it; I won't have it,' and threw it on to the desk. It half lodged itself beneath a small pile of papers and on raising the pile, Ponsonby found two Orders of the Red Eagle. One was evidently meant for him, and he had simply missed it. He pressed a bell and a steward came into the cabin. In answer to a question he said a German officer had come aboard while everyone was at breakfast and gone from cabin to cabin.

Ponsonby was decisive. 'My compliments to the Officer of the Watch and no one is to be allowed ashore for the moment. Meanwhile you will go from cabin to cabin and collect all Orders you find which look like this.' He held up the Red Eagle.

Then personally he tracked down the Emperor's A.D.C. who was being entertained in the wardroom.

He was profuse in his thanks for the honour done to the King's suite by the Emperor but, as he returned all the Red Eagles, he explained that no one in the King's service was permitted to receive a foreign Order without his express permission, and especially not Lord Selborne who, as Minister in Attendance, could under no circumstances accept such a kindness. If a list of names could be prepared for the King to look over the formalities would soon be concluded. Puzzled by this British way of going about things, the A.D.C. put all the Red Eagles in a box where there were a good many more and went ashore to report. An hour later he returned with the required list, and an hour after that with a further clutch of Red Eagles plus a huge print portrait of the Emperor for poor Lord Selborne, who was barred from receiving an Order.

The King enjoyed the social side of the yachting week, but his nephew's nervous strutting grew more fantastic each day. The Emperor threw his weight about like an overgrown schoolboy boasting of the might of the High Seas Fleet, and, to his Admirals' despair, he seemed bent on disclosing closely guarded secrets merely to prove the strength of his navy. He did not quite go so far as that, but even the inexpert eye of his uncle could not fail to be impressed by a cursory inspection of the German fleet from iron-clads to tugboats. The experts in his suite were struck by the variety in type of vessel, and making a shrewd appraisal of the docks, wharves and facilities at Kiel, they estimated that while at maximum production the Germans could not begin to compete with the British fleets for several years, it might one day become a possibility.

This reflection hardly cheered King Edward. In an after-breakfast talk with the Geman Chancellor, Bülow, he tried his best to be pacifying by saying there was absolutely no point in an alliance between England and Germany because evidently they were such good friends. Such straightforward talk puzzled Bülow. He read into it a subtle interpretation: that because King Edward did *not* want an alliance it followed he *did* want to encircle Germany.

Such casuistry was a little beyond the Emperor who temporarily had forgotten his dread of encirclement and was eager to wean his uncle from the British Alliance with Japan. It was an offence to Christian Europe, he declared. Let the King look to the East. The Yellow Peril was a very real thing.

But then he caught the faintest glimpse of a smile on his uncle's face. Willy and his Yellow Peril was a long-standing family joke. A dozen years before he had commissioned and distributed to all the Courts of Europe and all the members of his family an allegorical picture showing the nations of Europe with their Guardian Angel confronted by a horde of slit-eyed orientals and entitled 'People of Europe, defend your most sacred possessions!' The Sandringham copy had passed from room to room and ended up in a guests' lavatory.

That faint smile stung the Emperor. He promptly sulked, and his uncle, although he knew it was wrong, could not stop himself from making matters worse. He pricked the bubble of the Emperor's self-esteem by remarking softly after a great Naval Review: 'Splendid! Splendid! But then you've always been fond of yachting!'

It was imprudent and neither forgotten nor forgiven. Later it provoked a like remark from the Emperor William when he heard that his uncle was sailing with Sir Thomas Lipton: 'Ah, yes, I heard he was boating with his grocer.' Thenceforth regular reports came from Germany that the Emperor was scandalized by the royal goings-on in England, and he was saying some very unpleasant things indeed about Mrs George Keppel. This never failed to make King Edward smite his desk with rage and say the most dreadful things about the Emperor.

Not much, in fact, came of the Kiel meeting save that uncle and nephew's mutual dislike and mistrust were underlined; that and a declaration by King Edward to his ministers that perhaps it might serve England well for them to pay closer attention to Admiral Fisher's ranting and roaring.

In Marienbad that August Edward also had an opportunity to speak to the Leader of the Opposition on the same theme.

Whether or not it was constitutionally correct for them to do so neither the King nor Sir Henry Campbell-Bannerman cared. Both were on holiday, or, rather, they were applying themselves to dieting and purging, and, for the first time, they were enjoying each other's company. They had been acquainted for years, and Sir Henry was a regular habitué of Marienbad, but the King had never really approved of his pro-Boer sentiments during the war. Now they were brought together by Major Ponsonby and his brother, the radical Arthur Ponsonby, who was Sir Henry's Private Secretary. The Liberal Leader was invited to luncheon and, to the Ponsonby brothers' delight, host and guest took to each other at once.

The son of a Lord Provost of Glasgow, Sir Henry was a baronet in the drapery business, but the King was the least snobbish of European sovereigns and he tended to like or dislike men for what they were, not on account of their background. Clearly he liked Sir Henry.

Each was surprised to find they had so much in common. Both loved France, were fluent in the French language and had many mutual French friends. Both practised old-fashioned courtesies. Both were excellent raconteurs. Both enjoyed the risqué story. Both were outspoken: Edward because he was royally accustomed to speak his mind; Sir Henry because he was Scotch. Neither could easily be fooled, and they discovered they shared reservations about Prince Ferdinand of Bulgaria who also happened to be taking the cure in 1904.

To Sir Henry the Prince was a political mess. To the King he was a social one – so unpopular in European society for his biting tongue and love of causing trouble that he was called Foxy Ferdinand. Moreover he had deeply affronted Edward by ostentatiously banqueting in Sofia on the day of Queen Victoria's funeral. But for diplomatic reasons Foxy had to be received and, though he caused raised eyebrows by boldly declaring he had been to see the Austrian Emperor in the hope of getting the Golden Fleece, but *ce sale vieillard*, as he called him, had denied him the honour, his mordant wit was some compensation for his unattractiveness. He could amuse.

Sir Henry and Lady Campbell-Bannerman gave a luncheon for the two monarchs and some of the regular habitués of the spa; including the King's old friend Harry Chaplin and a brand new one, Mrs Hall Walker, the young and lovely wife of a very rich elderly man who bred racehorses by astrological prognostications. The restrained magnificence of the meal entirely won the King's heart. It was perfect. Evidently Sir Henry and his lady cared for and knew about food, which was another bond between them.

Frequently their talk was serious and confidential. As they walked together beneath the plane trees for their daily glass of the spa waters they confessed mutual anxieties. Both feared that out of all the vaunting and vanity and cockscombery and competitiveness amongst the major powers, especially as expressed by the French, German and English press, which were getting wilder and more frenetic and inaccurate each day, there would eventually be a war, or rather, a holocaust. It was essential, warned the King, that if the Liberals came to office they must have a realistic naval policy. Cheese-paring over estimates could endanger England. Sir Henry agreed. He also provisionally accepted the King's view that only Admiral Fisher had the ideas and the strength to avert a war or – if that was not possible – at least to win one.

But their talk was not all serious. The King enjoyed the unconventionality of Marienbad. There was some excellent shooting offered by a neighbouring prince, balanced dieting, dinners of plain food, bridge naturally, and tea visits to Mrs Hall Walker's hotel, where elaborate preparations were made daily for his reception – the suite decorated with heavily-scented flowers and sprayed with patchouli, the curtains pulled to, and the crimson velvet cushions plumped up. . . .

Nevertheless as their King and the Leader of the Opposition were frequently seen and photographed together there was a good deal of guesswork by the press. It was surmised that they must always be talking politics, and a sketch appeared in a London periodical of the King and Sir Henry strolling on the Marienbad promenade, their heads close together, with the King characteristically smiting one hand with the other. Beneath was written: '*Is it peace or war?*'

This much amused them because, in fact, the King had been asking his new friend's opinion whether halibut was better baked or boiled.

18

Quietly and with great adroitness Lord Esher had been urging independent members of the Cabinet to consider Sir John Fisher as the best possible candidate for the post of First Sea Lord. With one or two exceptions they allowed themselves to be persuaded. By a majority it was decided that Fisher should be promoted. On 21 October 1904 his appointment was announced. At the same time the King appointed him his principal naval A.D.C., though not without the rueful reflection that probably he was sacrificing a certain amount of peace of mind because the appointment gave Fisher direct access to him at all times.

How right the King was.

On that very day Fisher availed himself of the privilege, reporting as First Sea Lord and bounding into the audience roaring: 'October 21st, Sir. Trafalgar Day! Trafalgar Day!' He appeared to equate Nelson's victory over Napoleon with his own over Rear Admiral Lord Charles Beresford. And though, in fact, the interval was about sixty hours, it seemed to the bemused monarch that barely had the ebullient First Sea Lord gone away than he was back again.

He reported, this time his face damson-coloured with choler, that the Russian Baltic Fleet steaming through the North Sea on its way to the Far East had just fired on some English trawlers fishing off the Dogger Bank. A steam trawler had been sunk, her captain and a hand killed, and other ships had been damaged and the crews injured. 'And the black, base part of it, Sir,' roared the First Sea Lord 'is that those Ruskies steamed on, gave no assistance at all.'

'You may be seated, Fisher,' said the King, fearing that the Admiral would have an apoplectic stroke in front of him.

Telegrams went backwards and forwards between St Petersburg and London. The Russians claimed their Admiral had thought the British ships were Japanese. No one believed this.

An apologetic telegram from the Tsar to the King ended:

> TRUST NO COMPLICATIONS WILL ARISE BETWEEN OUR COUNTRIES OWING TO THIS OCCURRENCE BEST LOVE...
>
> NICKY

The Tsar was over-sanguine. King Edward was busy preventing his First Sea Lord from uttering his wild opinion in public. As it was, Fisher had already sent out an order that warships were to be detached to shadow the Russians. But the King found time to send a sharp reproof on his own account, telegraphing his nephew:

> WHAT HAS CAUSED ME AND MY COUNTRY SO PAINFUL AN IMPRESSION IS THAT YOUR SQUADRON DID NOT STOP TO OFFER ASSISTANCE TO THE WOUNDED AS SEARCHLIGHTS MUST HAVE REVEALED TO YOUR ADMIRAL THAT THE SHIPS WERE BRITISH FISHING VESSELS

Edward and his government were for pressing for the strongest measures, but not to the point of going to war. Fisher had to be told firmly by his master to call off the shadowing British ironclads. The Queen, the Prince of Wales, Lord Esher, Lord Knollys and Miss Charlotte joined the King in begging the Admiral to modify his rage or Russia would be put in a position which made war inevitable.

Fortunately the Russians appeared to make no attempt to escape the consequences of their Admiral's mistake and were anxious to make any *amende honorable* consonant with their dignity. Ultimately it was agreed that an international enquiry of admirals from five countries should look into the matter. It found for the British trawlermen and the Russians had to pay adequate compensation, but Fisher was not appeased. Nor by now was the Tsar. The English press had been outspoken and united in demanding abject apologies, severe punishment of the admiral responsible, compensation, and had added a further goad that the Royal Navy should forcibly prevent the Germans from re-fuelling the Russian fleets throughout the world. It had angered the Tsar who, as an autocrat, was not accustomed to being told what to do, and it had driven the German Emperor frantic.

King Edward heard through Alix, whose sister was the Tsar's mother, that the two cousins were fulminating against him. Then, through agencies in Germany, he heard Tsar Nicholas had proposed an alliance of Germany, Russia and France 'to abolish Anglo-Japanese arrogance and insolence'.

Considering how restrained England, in fact, had been, this made King Edward exceedingly indignant. Thank God, at any rate, for the Entente Cordiale. France would not, could not, turn on her brand-new ally. Nevertheless he was troubled. He begged Esher to make enquiries as to the authenticity of the reports.

Lord Esher did so. He checked and he found that *'to abolish Anglo-Japanese arrogance and insolence'* had been the Tsar's actual expression.

'How damned cool!' exploded the monarch.

Esher agreed. He then threw the King into a temporary panic by saying that Entente Cordiale or no, French financial investments in Russia were vast and, in modern European diplomacy, fiscal policies were playing a larger and larger part. Moreover he had learned that the Emperor William was sowing distrust of England everywhere.

'Good God, Reggie!' exclaimed the King. 'You don't mean to say this alliance thing is a possibility.'

'No, Sir,' Esher reassured him. 'Our rapprochement with France is built very solidly. Like the most enduring marriages it is based on sound legal settlements. I simply wanted to make the point. After all, you did ask me to make an enquiry.'

The King breathed heavily. 'Always the bad news first. Hurry, please, to something more welcome.'

Lord Esher smiled. He said he had it from several independent and reliable sources that despite the size and resources of the

Russian Army and Navy she could not win her war with Japan, and though the German Emperor aspired to be as autocratic as the Tsar, his ministers would not wish him to ally himself irrecoverably to a defeated state. 'Russia, Sir, is in a sad muddle,' he said. 'And if I may speak plainly, the Queen's sister, the Dowager Empress, is not favourable to the Germans.'

The King nodded. It was no secret that the Empress Marie was jealous of her German daughter-in-law's influence over the Tsar, and that she had never lost her intense dislike of Prussia. She would do all she could, and she still had great power, taking precedence as Dowager even over the Tsaritsa herself, to make sure there was no Russian–German alliance.

'Thank you, Reggie.' The King lighted an Egyptian cigarette with hands which actually trembled. 'What a relief.'

Lord Esher refused a cigarette. 'I think, perhaps, Sir, you ought not to underestimate the German Emperor's powers as a mischief-maker.'

'Eh?'

'He has been cultivating the Americans.'

'Our rough-riding President?'

'The President himself. If you were to re-open a correspondence with Mr Roosevelt it might be to our advantage.'

'Under Lord Lansdowne's supervision?'

'I think not, Sir. If you will be guided by me, you will simply write a series of friendly letters which prove you are not the master of intrigue His Imperial Majesty has made you out to be.'

'Reggie,' said the King. 'I am constantly being guided by you. Very well.'

Edward was not pleased with his wife.

Her nephew George, the King of Greece's son, had been appointed High Commissioner of Crete by four interested powers, England, France, Italy and Russia – an appointment which by now had proved disastrous for the Cretans. Not only was Prince George inefficient but he made bad appointments and grew increasingly despotic. The *Daily Chronicle* said that he had Out-Sultaned the Sultan, and clearly he would have to be removed. Nevertheless Alix, who ought to have held her tongue, was clamant in her defence of the High Commissioner. She protested to her son. She begged him to see Lord Knollys and the Foreign Secretary to explain how her poor nephew had been maligned.

The King felt obliged to intervene. 'My dear Alix,' he said when she returned from Denmark. 'You are absolutely wrong. Your nephew has not been calumniated, nor is he the victim of a plot.'

More guttural than usual, the Queen said defiantly: 'George is as innocent as a baby.'

Edward threw his hands in the air. 'He is inept, has favourites, and on occasion he has been exceptionally cruel.'

His wife glared at him. 'And you are such a model monarch!' she said viciously. The protective shell she had built about herself usually prevented her from being spiteful to her wayward husband; but now she was too angry to hold her tongue.

Edward left her sitting-room feeling very much like a smacked spaniel. He wondered how she could already have heard about Sophie Hall Walker.

Possibly he was being naif. When Beatrice's young daughter Ena first came to Court in November, he lodged a mild protest that she had been brought out at an Infirmary Ball at Ryde on her seventeenth birthday. 'An Infirmary Ball! Beatrice,' he protested. 'And on the Isle of Wight!'

'There was no other suitable occasion, Sir,' his sister snapped. By carefully phrased insinuations she managed to express her point of view that as Ena lacked a father it had been the King's duty to make appropriate arrangements for his niece and not waste such a good deal of his energies tea-timing in darkened Marienbad drawing-rooms drenched with the scent of tuberoses and patchouli.

Edward gave a start, and panicked at this cleverly veiled hint that Beatrice also knew all about Sophie Hall Walker.

'I should think, Beatrice,' he said, regretting that he blushed so easily nowadays, 'I should think we might count that initial coming out at Ryde as a practice run. Let Ena come out officially from here, the home of her family. And between us I believe we could give a ball at Kensington Palace. How would that arrangement strike you?'

It struck Princess Beatrice very well indeed, but she was not over-effusive in her thanks. From long experience she knew this was the best way with her brother.

'The King and Queen of Portugal will be with us soon,' he

added. 'So you and Ena and your elder boy must stay on with us. Carlos is a jolly man, and Amélie is a rosy, cosy Queen. You will enjoy their visit.'

He had been generous, decided Beatrice. Given a push Bertie was always like that, impulsively generous. She curtsyed. 'Thank you, Sir,' she said. 'I feel sure we shall enjoy ourselves.'

When she had left the room he lighted a cigar. For one moment Beatrice had very much reminded him of their mother. It had been rather frightening.

His nerves were in no state to receive the bouncy First Sea Lord, who arrived for an informal audience soon afterwards. Nevertheless Fisher was principal naval A.D.C. He had been given that special privilege of direct access to the monarch which could not now be denied.

It was unlike Edward to drink between meals but he rang for a brandy and soda and drank it down before he sent word for the First Sea Lord to be admitted. The brandy gave him just that necessary force to face the Admiral, but after Fisher had bounded in and walked up and down and roared out his latest idea, the King felt he needed a second and stiffer drink.

'Fisher,' he declared feeling for the bell pull and tugging it. 'Don't agitate yourself and take a seat.'

When he had drunk his second brandy Edward wondered if the First Sea Lord had actually taken leave of his senses.

'It'd be the easiest thing in the end, Sir. Cost a few lives, but save thousands.' Totally unable to sit still, the Admiral leapt to his feet. 'Gambier did it to the Danish fleet in 1807. I'd like to do it now.'

'Fisher, you must be mad!' muttered his sovereign. 'To take our Home Fleet to the Baltic and bombard the German High Seas Fleet and Kiel dockyards without any declaration of war would be monstrous.'

'That's what I'd do, Sir. I'd do what Gambier did at Copenhagen. War's coming. Depend on it. I'd anticipate it, by God!'

'This is 1904 not 1807,' the King reminded him.

'No matter, men are the same. Give me the word and I'll Copenhagen them right away. Right away.'

'You will do no such thing,' said the King sharply. 'And you really must put the idea out of your head.' He stood up. 'I shall try to do the same.'

'What a pity!' bellowed the First Sea Lord. 'What a pity! I'd Copenhagen them!'

19

The year 1905 would be recalled by many because it was then that Freud published his *Theory of Sex*; Einstein propounded his theory of relativity; a one-reel moving film was made, entitled 'Rescued by Rover'; and both Melba *and* Caruso sang at Covent Garden.

It was memorable to the Jewish community as the year of the death of Baron Alphonse de Rothschild, head of the French part of his illustrious family and a lynchpin of world Jewry. Others remained of that great house; Alphonse's son Edmond in Paris, Albert von Rothschild in Vienna, and Lord Rothschild with his brothers Alfred and Leopold and their brother-in-law Baron Ferdinand in English mansions; but Baron Alphonse had been spectacular amongst the *haute juiferie.* In the 1870 war he had fed a starving Paris and under-written the five-billion-franc indemnity claimed by Prussia. Once he had found himself side-tracked and kept waiting while travelling to dine with the King of the Belgians by a special train which contained only the evening clothes he happened to have left behind. And, fabulous to the last, he left by will '25,000 gold francs to my dear son-in-law Albert . . . so that he may buy himself some chocolates'.

The year was recalled by the supporters of Women's Rights and by their opponents as the turning point when militancy without quarter became the policy of the suffragettes. Neither the ex-Registrar of Births and Deaths in Manchester, Mrs Pankhurst, nor her eldest daughter, Christabel, would give an inch. They were carried bodily and roughly from meetings, screaming women's rights and, if a policeman attempted to gag their shrieks with his fingers, they bit. Many political meetings were interrupted. Everywhere there were demonstrations, processions of women, tightly corseted, with huge plumed hats and parasols, carrying the purple, green and white banners of the W.S.P.U.

In Russia it was a year of bloodshed and revolution.

A bewildered Tsar prayed about his own personal tragedy. At last a son had been born to inherit the Russian throne, the Tsarevitch Alexis, but the boy had incurable haemophilia.

He prayed, too, about his country's tragedies. His armies were being driven back by the Japanese. There were protests against mismanagement of the war, strikes, processions. Then came Sunday, 22 January. From all parts of St Petersburg workers carrying icons and portraits of the Tsar and singing the Imperial anthem converged on the Winter Palace to petition their Little Father, the Tsar. They were led by a socialist priest, Father John Gapon, an honest but muddled man. The Little Father was equally honest and muddled. Between them were troops who, without warning or on any specific order, fired on the workers' procession. Ninety-two men, women and children were shot dead. Many more were wounded on that Bloody Sunday. Three weeks later the Tsar's uncle, the Grand Duke Serge, was blown to fragments. His wife, a sister of the Tsaritsa, found nothing of her husband when she ran down the grand staircase, nothing but pieces. Bravely she tried to comfort the dying coachman.

The Tsar prayed on.

In forty-five minutes his Grand Fleet was destroyed by Admiral Togo. Eight Russian battleships, seven cruisers and six destroyers went to the bottom of the Strait of Tsushima. Through President Roosevelt the Tsar negotiated peace terms. They were neither too demanding nor humiliating, but Russia was turbulent with discontent. The Autocrat of all the Russias rather wished he had the democratically elected President's strength and decisiveness, for that energetic ex-colonel of the Rough Riders, in commenting on America's class struggles had declared his conviction: 'The sentiment now animating a large proportion of our peoples can only be suppressed . . . by taking ten or a dozen of their leaders out, standing them against a wall and shooting them dead.' Yet in his heart Tsar Nicholas knew this would not answer.

Ultimately he was forced to do what he had vowed he would never do and grant some sort of constitution to his people. But it made little difference. His Prime Minister was a sleepy elderly man with Piccadilly whiskers who spent most of his time on a sofa reading French novels. It was a fateful year for Russia. . . .

In the other Courts of Europe it was a memorable year because, while making an exhibition of himself on the one hand, the German Emperor managed to win a considerable diplomatic victory on the other. Cruising in the Mediterranean, he visited a castle of Frederick II and there struck an attitude and made a remarkable and widely reported observation: 'It is wonderful to think what this great Emperor achieved. If I were able to have people beheaded as easily as he could, I could do more.' This caused a ripple of laughter through Europe. But then the German Emperor had slapped at France and her Foreign Minister, Delcassé, who was particularly disliked in Berlin – by landing personally at Tangier to declare German support of Moroccan independence from France. It was impossible not to pity the Emperor because what should have been a grand and dramatic occasion turned into a piece of opera bouffe. The sea was choppy and the short trip ashore from the *Hohenzollern* in a bobbing motor boat proved too much for the Emperor's stomach. Then, ordinarily a fine horseman despite the limitations imposed by his withered arm, he was given a huge, white and highly strung charger which reared when the Arab troops excitedly fired off their rifles in salute and charged pell-mell up the road. He was met by what he called a 'senior Arab' and, presuming he was the Sultan – though, in fact, he was his uncle – he made his speech on protecting the Fatherland's great interest in Morocco and the independence of the Sultanate, and galloped back to the bobbing motor boat. Opera bouffe or not, his visit had the desired effect of angering both England and France. King Edward declared his nephew was a political *enfant terrible*, but then what could anyone expect when British foreign policy was in the hands of Lansdowne, a minister apparently so indifferent to what was going on that that year he took a six-week holiday in Ireland to look over his property there. The French, always excitable, were hysterical in their attitude to M. Delcassé, and he was forced to resign. The Emperor William had achieved a notable diplomatic triumph, but, spurred on by his success, he quickly lost his new reputation by meeting the Tsar secretly in the Baltic and persuading his cousin to sign a draft treaty of mutual aid. Possibly it was the Emperor William's fate to appear the strutting clown, but the Tsar was quickly advised not to ratify the treaty and the humiliating secret was revealed. So one diplomatic triumph was balanced by a failure which caused more laughter in the Chancelleries of Europe. 1905 was not, after all, one of the Emperor's vintage years.

To the members of the English Royal Household it was much like any other year, twelve months of dullish routine spotted, like currants in a duff, with occasional diversions.

An internal boil threatened to erupt when Lord Knollys discovered that the Palace *éminence grise* had persuaded the King to let him edit Queen Victoria's earlier papers and letters for publication. His sense of outrage at the impropriety of such a thing was tinged, of course, with bright green jealousy; and Esher made tension tenser by preserving a bland indifference to the views of the Private Secretary. There were many difficult moments at the Household dining-table: Lord Knollys sulphurous, Lord Esher calm.

A light diversion was provided by one of the King's Physicians Extraordinary, Sir Felix Semon, who wrote to Lord Knollys that 1905 marked the centenary of Manuel Garcia, the inventor of the laryngoscope and celebrated singing master. This was duly passed on to the King who asked, irritably, what he was supposed to do about it. Sir Felix was referred to. It seemed that as the maestro's sovereign the King of Spain intended to honour him, and so – purely out of interference – did the German Emperor. As the old gentleman had lived half his span in London perhaps it would be appropriate for the King to honour him as well. Hearing of his nephew's intention the King at once agreed to confer on the maestro the Victorian Order, and said he hoped the centenarian would be able to manage the journey to the palace. Not only did he manage it, but turned out to be a spry, forceful little man, as shrivelled as a lizard. The King was affable and, congratulating him, presented the old man with an M.V.O. Knollys signed to him that he must now bow and retire, but the maestro paid no attention and continued staring at the King. To keep a conversation going the King said clearly: 'No doubt you are a great Wagnerian?' which, as Knollys remarked afterwards, should have been a safe enough thing to say in all conscience. But it turned out to be the worst thing the King could have said. Garcia narrowed his eyes, then opened them wide. 'No,' he said shrilly. 'I am not. I detest him!' With which the inventor of the laryngoscope bowed smartly and left.

Other currants in the duff of routine were provided by the press. The King was always courteous to reporters unless they behaved badly and followed him when he wished to be alone. He was always ready to wait while they photographed him. And he was even tolerant of newspaper proprietors, all of whom were parvenus and some of whom had been ennobled. But in his heart he detested the press, and this was suddenly revealed by the German Naval Attaché in London, who had an audience with the King and talked of the war scare ballooned out of all proportion by the international press. 'The press,' said King Edward forcibly, 'is mad in all countries'; an opinion which, via Berlin, was leaked to the press itself. No one was pleased, from Lord Northcliffe to the most insignificant teaboy. As if in penance, the Queen astounded the press by, for the very first time, granting an interview to a French journalist of the *Gaulois*. She was reported as saying:

> *'I always have had a dread of these warlike preparations . . . of all the inflammable material which they are accumulating, and which may break forth into a conflagration such as may plunge humanity into mourning.'*

It hardly sounded like Queen Alexandra. Wagers were laid in the Household as to the authorship, Miss Charlotte or Sir Dighton? A lone soul thought it *might* have been Princess Victoria. All were wrong. The Queen was as surprised as anyone to see the sentiments attributed to her. Certainly she had never uttered them.

There were other fond remembrances of the year, chief of them an increase in the monarch's motoring mania and the arrival of a newcomer to the Department of the Master of the Horse. The

King's fleet of claret-coloured motor cars had grown, but there being always a chance of a breakdown, and chauffeurs being, as they put it, coachmen, not vets and farriers, he decided to add a motor engineer to his establishment. This expert, named Stamper, now accompanied the King on all his drives, riding in the front beside the chauffeur, alert to leap from his seat and make minor adjustments and running repairs. Thereafter he took the praise for an uninterrupted ride at high speed. 'A very good run, Stamper,' the King would announce. 'Very good indeed.' But he also bore the blame for any hold-ups which, reasonable or not, thwarted his master into tremendous rages; and, too, for accidents, of which, happily, there were few. An equerry riding with the King to Newmarket witnessed a minor accident not long after Stamper's arrival. The royal Mercedes was bowling along at fifty miles an hour, the monarch leaning forwards on his cane, willing the machine to go faster, when there was an appalling jolt. They had hit a culvert. 'Stop! *stop*, STOP! *STOP!*' roared the King. 'I will *not* be killed. Look, Stamper, at my hat!' And he held out his brown bowler hat, its crown crushed and dented.

Equally worth recalling was Major Ponsonby's rescue at Cowes. He was using a steam pinnace from the *Victoria and Albert* to visit friends when he saw a woman waving her parasol with a handkerchief attached, on the deck of a large and elegant yacht. A courtier's seventh sense made him turn the pinnace about and climb aboard the yacht which, like a ghost ship, appeared to be deserted. There was no one on watch, no one at the bridge, no one below. At length Ponsonby saw a huddled form swathed in black in a folding chair on the promenade deck. His courtier's seventh sense had not failed him. It was the Empress Eugénie, widow of Napoleon III. It appeared that the first mate had died and all the crew had gone ashore for the funeral at the Empress' express wish. It was only then, after she had been left isolated and stranded, that she remembered she was due to drink tea with the Queen. Would Major Ponsonby kindly take her to the *Victoria and Albert*? Ponsonby did, though getting a black-draped, none too agile, eighty-year-old ex-Empress down the yacht's side into the pinnace was not easy. In their hurry they failed to leave a note, and when captain and crew returned after the funeral to find no trace of the Empress, signals were sent flying everywhere.

All these took the edge off dull routine, but the chief event of the year to the Royal Household was what Sir Dighton termed 'the Arnold-Foster Business'. Since his appointment as Secretary for War Arnold-Foster had made no attempt to soothe his sovereign. On the contrary, he appeared to enjoy tormenting him. Pinprick followed pinprick. When the King's brother was made Inspector-General no special salute was afforded him as had been the case with former Inspector Generals. The King had been obliged to ask for this honour due to the Duke of Connaught, but Arnold-Foster had not replied and simply handed the question over to the Army Council, and they, unbelievably, had turned it down. Esher's committee of three for the reform of the Army had powers of recommendation but nothing more, and some of their most cherished ideas had coolly been disregarded or drastically distorted. Automatically, it appeared, Arnold-Foster opposed anything his sovereign proposed, and things came to a head in 1905 when he announced in the Commons an Army Order of great importance which the King had not yet signed. He then had his Private Secretary send the Order to Lord Knollys for the King's signature which he said he would like to have 'before luncheon'. Having received no reply by that hour, Arnold-Foster's Secretary telephoned Lord Knollys to say he hoped his Minister would be saved the embarrassment of having to explain to Parliament that an important Army Order was being held up by the King for no good reason. Icily Lord Knollys repeated this insolent and casual ultimatum, not from the Minister, but from his Secretary, into his royal master's ear. The effect was shattering. Major Ponsonby was of the opinion that King Edward could frighten even his most intimate friends by his gusts of anger. Ponsonby's own daughter recorded that the King's 'angry bellow, once heard, could never be forgotten'. On this occasion his anger filled the huge room. It was palpable. Swiftly he went to his desk and signed the Army Order. He had been taught well that as a constitutional sovereign he ought not to reject ministerial advice. This he flung into a despatch box, locked it, rang for an estafette and sent it off. Then he let himself go. Housemaids dusting in different rooms heard the din. Grooms far off in the stables claimed they had heard it too. Never in anyone's experience had King Edward been so terribly, thoroughly angry. Lord Knollys begged him for his own sake, for everyone's not to excite himself – and was lucky not to have something thrown at his head. After that he said nothing, holding his own head bowed as though it was a thunderstorm not simply a storm of royal rage which beat over him. Lord Esher, not in the least calm for a change, stood white-faced in another corner of the room. Eventually the lion roars died down. Grimly the King sat at his desk. 'Reggie,' he said, 'you will please go at once to see Balfour's Secretary and tell him of this offensive, ill-mannered behaviour.' Then he turned to Knollys, 'And if you, Francis, would send simultaneously the strongest possible protest to the Prime Minister I should appreciate it.'

Arnold-Foster apologized. He had been under stress, he said, and had had a headache. Arthur Balfour apologized for his Minister. He meant it. He appreciated how sensitive the King was to bad manners. He was himself. But his Ministry was in a sorry state, crumbling to pieces in a schism between those who wanted free trade and those who did not. He felt obliged to play the sort of card a Cecil would play for the sake of his party. He offered to dismiss Arnold-Foster if Lord Esher would take his place. This, he was well aware, Lord Esher would never do. It was an *amende honorable.* The King's contempt for Arnold-Foster was such that he barely ever mentioned him again. No one in the Household or amongst the royal servants ever forgot that awful, terrifying roaring.

Amongst the King's closest relatives 1905 was remembered for a variety of experiences; some pleasant, others unutterably sad.

The children of the Prince of Wales were aware that soon they were to have a new brother or sister. It had been explained to them in various ways; that is, to David who was eleven, Bertie who was ten, and Mary who was eight. Harry and George at five and three were not told anything. When the news came that the new baby had arrived and that it was a little boy named John, they were permitted to see him in his cradle, and said the right things, in other words what they had worked out to say beforehand. They presumed, of course, he would have his own nurse and be absorbed in the nurseries at York Cottage, Marlborough House, Frogmore and Abergeldie. But to their surprise, he simply disappeared. They accepted the explanation they were given without much comment, and in time forgot their brother John. Their stricken parents at first clung to each other. John was not as other children. He had distressing epileptic fits. On the advice of their medical household they decided he should be segregated and brought up with his own Household at Wood Farm in Wolferton not far from York Cottage. The Prince tried to forget his sorrow in sailing and shooting – and forever remembered the year because he got a right and left at woodcock in County Galway – Princess May in preparing for their visit to India which was planned for that autumn. With her accustomed thoroughness she read a good deal about the subcontinent, its religions, languages, geography and general affairs. She also devoted herself to a careful selection of clothing, which were duly listed in the newspapers, and carefully studied by Aunt Augusta in Neu Strelitz.

> '*Your dresses amuse me to read about* (she wrote) *so many too! and* who *is to pay? the one for the Tiger hunt gave me the shivers!*'

Princess Victoria spent 1905 as she had spent 1904 and was to spend 1906, worrying about her health, growing more dispirited, longing to break away and be no longer Beck-and-Call, longing, as well, to be Lady Lonsdale.

Her sisters were more fortunate. Louise, who had given up her royal dignities on marrying the rich and elderly Duke of Fife, was secretly pleased when the King ordered that in future her children should be styled 'Highness'. Maud, always lucky, landed a throne. Norway divided itself from Sweden and proceeded to elect a King. Their choice fell on Maud's husband, Charles of Denmark, who as a second son, counted himself fortunate to be elected and thenceforth called himself King Haakon VII. The Grand Duchess of Mecklenburg-Strelitz was not in the least enthusiastic, consistently spelt his name 'Hakoon', and declared an elected monarch seemed a *non sequitur*.

> '*Too horrible* [she wrote] *for an English Princess to sit upon a Revolutionary Throne. . . . he making speeches, poor fellow, thanking the revolutionary Norwegians for having* elected *him! no really, it is all too odd!*'

Nevertheless, everyone else in the family was contented.

Princess Beatrice's humbler branch of the family caught that same year a non-elective, far more illustrious throne; but, because the Battenbergs were of morganatic stock, this did not really please the redoubtable Grand Duchess either:

'Ena is to become Spanish Queen! a Battenberg, good gracious!'

The young King of Spain was a small, smiling man, and evidently had great courage. On the last day of a State Visit to Paris that spring an assassin hurled a bomb under his carriage. It failed to go off, but King Alfonso did not move a muscle. Later the same day, when his train was being shunted at Cherbourg there was a jarring crash which caused the King to enquire laconically of a member of his suite: 'Another attempt?' From France he went to England to meet and woo Princess Ena. Within four months he was asking for her hand. Princess Beatrice put on her grandest jewels and motored to Windsor. Then she told the astounded King that Alfonso wished to make her daughter Queen of Spain.

1905 was a turning point in the life of Queen Alexandra.

Firstly, she made an official State Visit all by herself to Portugal. It was a successor to King Edward's visit and complemented it, and she found her warm welcome and the Portuguese Royal Family's eagerness to make her comfortable very touching. Nevertheless, it was a sign to her that more and more her path and Edward's were diverging.

Secondly it was brought home to her how close she stood to being a widow. Edward's annual cure only partially controlled his increasing weight and girth. With it he was still huge. Without it he would have become as vast as Georges Pigache, son-in-law to the owner of the Café Royal, whose interest in the kitchens of that celebrated establishment resulted in a frame so colossal he required the assistance of three porters and the stationmaster of Surbiton to lever him into a carriage every morning and out of one every night. The chief trouble, as the King's physicians repeated frequently to the Queen, was his temperamental inability to take warnings seriously. Rather like a schoolboy he did what he was told when he was ill and he was frightened, as he was in the February of 1905, but after a week of chronic bronchial catarrh and a high fever which was a week of great anxiety for everyone and which depressed him and made him apathetic, he made a sudden recovery and decided he would dine the following night at the house of a friend. Thenceforth he paid small attention to his doctors calling them Jobs and Jeremiahs and offering them huge cigars.

The physicians' united appeals made the Queen do something she had not done before or even contemplated. She decided to forgo her annual spring visit to beloved Copenhagen with poor Toria for her father's birthday and instead join the King at Marseilles for a Mediterranean cruise. The physicians were adamant that the King must be got away from the chills and fog of London. His own grey features – for he looked very unwell and rundown – were a dreadful warning.

From Marseilles the royal party sailed to Minorca and Majorca, then on to Algiers and back by way of Sardinia and Corsica. The three-week cruise had brought some colour back to the King's cheeks. Everyone had done their best to take him out of himself and he was no longer depressed, though his irritability had not been lessened by catching Major Ponsonby slipping ashore to pay an official call on the Governor-General dressed in a faded greenish-blue frock-coat which, he declared, was a disgrace to the Household. Nor was he very pleased when he and the Queen and all the party were ashore walking to see a garden of tropical plants and a huge car forced them into a ditch, covering them all with dust, and the occupants proved to be a rich old man and, of all people, Ponsonby's French servant. It was only bridge which saved poor Ponsonby from becoming the butt of the royal displeasure, for only three bridge players could be found on board and this trio included the new Marquis of Salisbury who was inclined to bouts of melancholy, suffered frequently from seasickness and played an appalling hand at bridge. No one else could play or would admit to it. And so nightly the King lost his temper with poor Salisbury and asked Ponsonby if he didn't think such and such a bid or piece of play might have done that much better. Anyway the King had recovered sufficiently to reassure the Queen that she was not about to become a widow, and she happily fell in with his plan that she should continue cruising, perhaps as far as Greece, while he returned to England by way of Paris.

When they docked at Marseilles and the King's luggage was being put ashore, the British Consul came aboard with a large folio and the King and Queen, who were eagerly awaiting telegrams and letters, were both put out when the portfolio proved to be quite empty. '*Where*,' roared the King, 'are my letters?'

The Consul was so alarmed that he said nothing but simply bolted. For an hour the King strode up and down the deck cursing him as a half-wit. He was expecting a good many letters relating to his approaching visit to Paris and hated to be kept waiting. At the end of the hour the Consul arrived and begged Major Ponsonby to take in the mail and retrieve his portfolio. He also begged to be excused from paying his respects to their Majesties on this particular occasion....

As for the King himself, 1905 was the year he returned to Paris, to joyful, delectable Paris.

No sooner had he arrived there, and moved into a splendid suite at the Hôtel Bristol as the Duke of Lancaster, than he discovered his delightful Jeanne de Sagan was ill, not seriously, it was hoped, but, all the same ill, and not in Paris. Cast down, he wrote to her. Affectionately he ordered a posy of violets to be sent to her each day until she recovered.

And then a second discovery made his face fall further. Alice Keppel and her husband were also in Paris. Really, he thought, it was too bad of them. Since that stiff, diplomatic visit to Paris of the year before he had been looking forwaard to being *le Grand Boulevardier* once more, and, dearly as he cared for her, he did not want Alice about just at that moment. He was surprised by her lack of *savoir faire*. Happily sense came to his aid. No doubt the visit had been a spontaneous idea of George's which Alice had been happy to fall in with. She had never made demands on him yet and was unlikely to do so now. Naturally he would see the Keppels. It was a politeness which he intended to extend to a large number of people, but his private plans need not be altered. Flowers were sent to where the Keppels were staying, together with an invitation to luncheon.

The Duke of Lancaster's entourage was large. At the head of the Secretariat Major Ponsonby toiled with despatch boxes, and a constant stream of visitors who came to sign the visitors' book. The fact the King was using an incognito did not seem to diminish the work. So far as the Parisians were concerned 'Notre Edouard' was back again and they wished to pay their respects. Eventually Ponsonby had to send most of the official letters to the Embassy and deal solely with the private correspondence. He was also the

Duke of Lancaster's mouthpiece to general enquirers, reporters and the police. The last were as concerned for their reputation as they were for King Edward's safety. Should he be assassinated, even as Duke of Lancaster, wrath would descend upon the *Sûreté.* The better-known anarchists were being watched. A number had quietly been shut up for the King's visit. The King himself would be constantly followed by detectives in disguise.

The King was no fool. On his first stroll out he became increasingly familiar with two ever-present faces, and knew precisely what was happening. Though aware it was for his own welfare he intensely disliked this surveillance. Ponsonby was given a piece of his mind, so the Major sent for the head of the French police and passed some of it on. The Prefect of Police took umbrage. If he were given clear and written instructions not to have the Duke of Lancaster guarded, he would call off his men and the Duke of Lancaster would almost certainly be robbed and quite probably shot, stabbed or bombed within twenty-four hours. Ponsonby calmed him. They reached a compromise that the guard must be maintained but less obviously so that the King was unaware of it.

That very day the scheme was put to its hardest test. The King was giving luncheon to the Keppels and Madame Standish and the Breteuils and chose a restaurant at St-Cloud where he and his guests could sit at a large table in a garden arbour. Major Ponsonby was there as Equerry and, in view of what had just passed between him and the Prefect of Police, he was alarmed when Mrs George Keppel whispered confidentially that she did not care for the look of one of the men at the next table. He looked so villainous, she said, and capable of anything. Was the King absolutely safe? Ponsonby assured her the French police were close by in plain clothes. She need not worry. But he himself worried. The man certainly did look capable of assassination. He excused himself from the table on a pretext and went in to telephone the *Sûreté,* and there, in the inside restaurant, he found the Prefect of Police himself eating a substantial luncheon. In great relief he explained his dilemma. The Prefect laid down his knife and fork. Had the good Major not noticed a gardener working on the hedge round the arbour? He was a policeman. 'But the people at the near-by table?' asked Ponsonby. 'There is a dreadful-looking man amongst them.' The Prefect laughed. 'All are police and their wives, and the dreadful-looking one is one of my best detectives.'

Ponsonby was delighted by the success of the scheme and became friendly with the Prefect of Police, whose name was Lépine. When the day's work was done he would chat idly with Lépine and discover what surprising roguey-poguery the King was enjoying in his moments off duty. It really was startling that a sixty-three-year-old could carry on in such a way, especially after almost dying of bronchitis a short time before. He hoped the detectives would show the utmost discretion.

'But of course,' exclaimed Lépine. Then he closed one eye. 'In any case who would believe them if they told all?'

Ponsonby smiled. 'No one,' he agreed. 'No one could.'

Larded with official functions such as dining with the President at the Elysée, visiting Versailles, going racing at St-Cloud and to the Théâtre Français for a performance of *Le Duel,* and seeing that year's Salon, Edward was enjoying himself immensely.

A privileged few from the Faubourg Saint-Germain and the Faubourg Saint-Honoré were permitted to feast and pleasure him, but it was in the Latin Quarter and in places of assignation that he tucked into lobster and oysters and pink champagne, and enjoyed the caresses of cocottes. For comfort he preferred an ample, generous-hearted woman; but he still had a discerning eye. One evening at the Théâtre des Capucines he ogled a slender beauty with long-lashed, winning eyes and could not prevent himself from writing a note begging for an assignation. Considering how much trouble he and his friends had suffered from letters, he knew it was madness. But with surprising speed and chivalry his billet was returned with a note scribbled on the reverse. He turned scarlet. The note thanked His Majesty King Edward of England for the excessive compliment, but an assignation in this case was sadly out of the question. It was signed by one of the richest of all Russians who was indeed beautiful to look at and had wrought havoc in many homes, but who had a fondness for jewellery and dressing *à la mode* in Paris, wearing sensational wigs. His name was Felix Youssoupov. Edward crunched the note in his hand. He had tried to make an assignation with one of his nephew's noblemen and a kinsman, a boy of eighteen. . . .

Major Ponsonby found himself again in trouble on account of the police. The King had made an assignation with a noted beauty at the Jardin des Plantes and, in a moment of passion in a fernery, had noted faces he had seen before peering through the greenery.

They could only be plain-clothes men. 'Which, Fritz,' thundered the King, 'was damned embarrassing. We all have our private moments. Call off those French bloodhounds.'

M. Lépine agreed with Major Ponsonby that it had been an unfortunate lapse. On the behalf of his department he apologized; his men would be more discreet than ever. Nevertheless, it was amusing, was it not, to think of the Duke of Lancaster being passionate in a fernery. Ponsonby frowned. He was not going to have his sovereign laughed at. Privately he was amazed at the King's vitality. Shakespeare had been wrong to pity Falstaff 'the desire so long outliving the performance' – for there was the King of England, a Falstaff if ever there was one, proving himself with astounding regularity. 'We all have our private moments,' he had said. Ponsonby was inclined to believe that the King had more private moments than anyone he had ever met.

His embarrassment at the Jardin des Plantes made the King decide not to tell anyone when he had a special assignation, so that the police could not be warned where he was. Again and again he gave Ponsonby the slip. Ordering the motor car for four, he would change his mind and go out in it at three. Or he would quietly let himself out of a rear entrance to the Bristol. Busy as he was, Ponsonby could not watch his master all the time, and warned the Chief of Police that the King was dodging them. Lépine tried to prevent this by having all doors under surveillance, but the King slipped through even this net.

A secret grief was soothed that spring in Paris. Edward's unfortunate Hanoverian physical inheritance had prevented him from being the great lover he wished to be, and this impediment was made worse by his bulk. Nevertheless with the deft use of a barber's chair draped in velvet, one enterprising *demi-mondaine* managed to raise him to exhilarating heights never reached before. Edward was so triumphant and so grateful that he gave her the equivalent of a life's pension in jewellery. If only he had known before . . .

Major Ponsonby suddenly found his master sweet-tempered, even willing to carry out a score of royal chores before they left for England. One included dining the British Ambassador and his wife at Voisin's and afterwards taking them to the theatre to see Granier in *Bonne Intention.* It so happened that the detested King of the Belgians was also in Paris and unhappily had chosen the same evening to go to see Granier. King Edward saw him in the stalls and glared. It was a glare that few could withstand, certainly not Leopold II of Belgium. He sank down in his seat and remained out of sight until the entr'acte, when he fled the theatre. Another duty was to pay a courtesy call on the Empress Eugénie, who was staying incognito at the Grand Hôtel as the Comtesse de Pierrefonds, and, on being invited to go up, the Duke of Lancaster strode to the lift at exactly the same time as a large American tycoon with a cigar in his mouth. Edward being a King was accustomed, naturally, to everyone making way for him. The tycoon, being a tycoon, was also accustomed to pushing his way first through everything. The two collided as they strode into the lift, but the King's weight won. The American stumbled and the cigar shot out of his mouth. Afterwards, as the lift took them to the first floor, he muttered and rumbled. The King simply looked through him, indignant at having been jostled.

M. Lépine saw the Duke of Lancaster's party leave with a sigh of satisfaction. The royal visit had tired him. From what he heard from his men it ought to have worn 'notre Edouard' to the size of a wafer. But he was as large, as smiling, as ebullient as ever.

The Prefect of Police and Major Ponsonby shook hands at the Gare du Nord and said *au revoir*.

When the royal train had gone M. Lépine began to wish he had told the Major about that velvet-draped barber's chair. Half Paris knew of it. It seemed strange that the King's closest advisers and servants appeared to know nothing at all.

Weeks passed. Under the pressure of work and fast-moving events, the King forgot his order of violets to be sent daily to Madame la Princesse de Sagan.

And then, at the beginning of October, came a letter from the Duchesse de Mouchy to tell him Jeanne was dying.

Edward was at Balmoral when he read the letter. His hands began to tremble and the thin, folded sheet fluttered. He wished with all his heart he had gone to see Jeanne in the spring, that he could rush to her now. But Anna de Mouchy made it clear she was not receiving visitors, and true or false, he could not escape the inexorable royal pattern which planned his days for weeks and months to come. In any case, this time was for her two boys, the elder who had once thrown all his clothes in the Mello fountain and the younger who had quite startling blue eyes. At her death Edward no longer had a place, though he believed he still had a place in her love.

He moved to the desk which had been his father's and drew a pen from the standish. Even with his perfect command of French he used clichés and mixed metaphors, but no one could have doubted the sincerity of the sentiments he tried to express.

He sent off the letter at once, but never discovered if Jeanne de Sagan received it.

She died on 12 October in that memorable year of 1905.

20

On a dank November day when walking slowly to a shooting stand, the King put his foot in a rabbit hole and by the curses and roars which followed everyone judged he had sprained his ankle.

He had, and wrenched a leg tendon, and done something complicated to his heel.

Two beaters and two peers carried him on a wattle gate to the game cart. Thence, cushioned by many dead hares, partridges and pheasants, he reached home. He affected not to mind the pain while his physicians did what was necessary, but he was instantly gripped in anger when told that he would have to keep the leg up for some weeks.

'Weeks!' he exploded.

Being restricted or bored or in any way frustrated was the worst sort of torture to him.

Fortunately Alice Keppel had just arrived and was there to pacify him, and, in no time at all, she had him in tucks of laughter because, fearful of missing her train, she had leapt into the nearest cab at the Portman Square rank calling 'King's Cross' – and the sympathetic cabby had put his head on one side and said: 'Oh, dear! But never mind. He'll be all right again soon!'

Alice, who understood him so well, could always make him laugh at the absurdities of life. She was prepared to play endless bridge, as well, and tell him endless home truths and share confidences. Nevertheless the thought of his energy being penned up for weeks, made Edward so savage that one comforter was not enough. And so the Prince of Wales, on his own initiative, sent for Lord Esher – the soother, the conjurer-up of novelties, a man with sufficient imagination to make the commonplace extraordinary for the King. Cleverly he chose to make the pending change of Government a game as exciting as, and far more sustaining than, any rubber of bridge.

The situation in late November, 1905 was this. The Conservatives were impaling themselves on the issue of trade. The philosopher Prime Minister, Arthur Balfour, had let the King know he felt he ought to resign.

In a sense Edward regretted this. He disliked any sort of change, and the policies of the Conservatives were more to his liking than those of the radical element in the Liberal Party. Nevertheless, he had never lost his sense of uneasiness when in the presence of his highly gifted, inscrutable Prime Minister. And Campbell-Bannerman, the alternative, he really liked. Again that summer at Marienbad he had seen a good deal of the Liberal leader. His old boyhood friend Charles Carrington had given a dinner for them and as a leading Liberal had reassured him: 'If we come in, Sir, Campbell-Bannerman will make a first-rate Prime Minister.' Edward was sure of it, calling Sir Henry a 'gay old dog with a twinkle in his eye'.

Esher, needless to say, had the correct procedure to be followed at his fingertips. This he formally passed on to Lord Knollys as the King's Private Secretary, but simultaneously he gave the same information to the King. If Mr Balfour should resign, Sir Henry should be asked to form a new Ministry.

But, while this was undoubtedly the right thing to do – and both Esher and Knollys, being mild Liberals themselves, were in agreement with the King that Sir Henry would make a good Prime Minister – a *coup* was attempted within the Liberal Party. Asquith, whom the King regarded as secret and reserved, with the Scotch advocate-philosopher Haldane who commanded at least £25,000 a year at the Bar, together with Sir Edward Grey, plotted to have Campbell-Bannerman moved to the Upper House while Asquith wielded effective power as Prime Minister in the Lower.

The reason was a clash between the new Imperialism and the Liberalism of Campbell-Bannerman, which had a distinctly Gladstonian flavour.

The excuse was that Sir Henry was not really fit enough to lead the country at such a difficult time.

Esher scotched the former by insisting it was correct for the King to send for the Leader of the Liberals. Edward himself scotched the latter by getting a medical report from their joint physician in Marienbad, Dr Ott, that at present there was little in Sir Henry's bill of health to exclude him from the highest office.

When Arthur Balfour resigned, the King gave him appropriate thanks for all he had done as Prime Minister, and gleefully sent for his new friend. The question now was, could Sir Henry form an effective government which included those who had tried to turn him out of the leadership? Sir Henry could. He produced a new Cabinet comprehensive enough to include the King's old friends Lord Carrington and 'Priscilla' Morley, Winston Churchill, who, to Edward's disgust, had crossed the floor of the House exactly like his father, and the feather-plucking radicals John Burns and Lloyd George.

There followed, inevitably, a general election.

By this time the King was on sticks and lame, but getting about. He followed the course of events with the keenest interest and thought Darling Daisy very game to speak up for the Socialists, electioneering from farm wagons, and shaking hands all round. Not that he cared for Socialism himself, but he appreciated her humanitarian ideals and her pluck. Other people failed to be so charitable and said she was letting down her class. The Queen was far more shocked by her rival's politics than by her numerous affairs. In public she declared the Countess of Warwick was an enigma. In private she wrote to her son about Daisy addressing *'her "comrades", the scum of the labourers, and then taking off her glove to shake and feel their horny hands.'*

While the country polled its votes, the King and Queen with many friends were invited as usual to the Chatsworth January party.

Their host was as amiable and as vague as ever and Louisa Devonshire in splendid form. Her latest sharp rally had been to an impertinent enquiry if Devonshire House was to be sold. 'Perfectly true,' she replied at once. 'We propose instead to live at Clapham Junction. The train service is so convenient.' She was still as excellent in entertaining guests as she was at putting people down. From the Chatsworth kitchens streamed an endless supply of magnificently prepared dishes. No one was permitted to be bored or idle. Patsy Cornwallis-West's daughter, Daisy of Pless, was especially invited to declaim monologues. Hawtrey was brought down from London to act in a sketch with two of the guests. The King hobbled about and managed to shoot from a chair, and enjoyed playing bridge with his hostess. He also enjoyed talking politics with Devonshire.

The old Liberal statesman was caustic about the new fellows, as he called them. Shrewdly he guessed that John Burns, for all his socialism, would probably snub his docker friends and turn respectable. Lloyd George would cause more trouble, a thruster if ever there was one. 'But on the whole, Sir, C-B's lot will do. There's a deal of rubbish there, of course. There always is in every Cabinet. Balancing between extremes. But C-B, Sir, should manage them. He's capable enough. If he has the country's backing, he'll manage.' He caught his wife's eye. 'Dinner, Sir,' he said. 'If you'll permit me to hoist you out of that chair.'

Grumbling about his sticks, and eager to get to Louisa Devonshire's table, the King temporarily put politics out of his mind.

The election proved memorable.

As a token of what was to come the King heard that Arthur Balfour himself had lost his seat. It was the beginning of a flood of changes which altered a Conservative-Liberal Unionist majority of 130 to a Liberal majority of 200. There were also 54 Labour members to vote with the Liberals and 83 Irish Nationalist Members who were inclined to support them.

His friend Sir Henry certainly had the country behind him, but the King found himself very anxious about the type of Members who now sat in the Commons.

He wrote a courteous letter of sympathy to Balfour and received a worrying reply through Knollys.

'If you had asked me when we last met whether I should much mind permanently leaving politics, I should have answered in

the negative. But I am so profoundly interested in what is now *going on, that I should return a very different answer today . . . We are face to face (no doubt in a milder form) with the Socialistic difficulties which loom so large on the Continent. Unless I am greatly mistaken the election of 1906 inaugurates a new era!'*

A new era! The thought depressed the King. Change, unless absolutely necessary as it clearly was, for example, in the Russian Empire, had no appeal to a man of his years. And he had absolute faith in Balfour's judgement. He had never much liked the man, but there was no denying his political acumen. He knew what he was talking about.

Esher and Knollys agreed. Glumly they laid further facts before their sovereign.

The House of Lords itself stood in some danger if the threats of some returned Members were ever implemented.

Then there was the matter of religion. It disturbed Edward as titular governor of the Established Church, to note that more dissenters had been returned than at any time since the days of Cromwell. The Commons contained 180 non-conformists, all pledged to prevent religion being taught in schools in case children were 'contaminated' by Church of England or Roman Catholic doctrine.

Finally, as the head of Society, Edward was concerned. The delicate balance of class which the English generally managed so much better than other people was clearly going to be upset by public announcements of class warfare up and down the land. And though commercial and industrial interests had been ousting the landowers and small gentry since the first Reform Act, the latter were now conspicuously rare in the ranks of the Commons. Knollys gave it as his considered opinion that the old idea that the House of Commons was an assemblage of gentlemen had quite passed away.

The King thanked them both and indicated that he would like to be left alone. They bowed themselves from his sitting-room. For quite five minutes he looked thoughtfully into the fire. Everything seemed to be getting out of hand. The suffragettes were behaving disgracefully. Strikers wanted to legalize peaceful picketing – as if industrial action could ever be really peaceful. Even the farmers were using more and more barbed wire despite the protests of M.F.H.s and the squirearchy was slowly being dethroned.

With a sigh Edward heaved himself to his feet and, with the aid of two canes, made his way to the bow window which overlooked the Park. For support he leant against the sill and, opening a bird-cage which stood there, he let out a canary which by habit perched on his finger and trilled. Caesar his dog sat at his feet. All appeared to be the same. Outside everything was dripping in a thin lemon fog. It was disconcerting to realize that out there, in the world's commercial capital, things were no longer as they had been. A new era had begun.

PART TWO

1

At the end of January, 1906, King Christian IX of Denmark died.

Queen Alexandra at once left for her father's funeral but King Edward's physicians would not allow him to accompany her. Instead he was chief mourner at a memorial service held in London two weeks afterwards.

He realized that Alix would be feeling the loss of her home in Denmark almost as much as the loss of her father because, though she got on well enough with her brother the new King, his Queen was quaint and did nothing all day but illuminate vellum. Bernstorff and Fredensborg and the Amalienborg would not be Alix's home any longer. Therefore he was not surprised when she announced that she and her sister, the Dowager Empress of Russia, had jointly bought a little villa for their own private use. It was by the sea not far from Bernstorff and was called Hvidøre. Evidently Alix had no intention of curtailing her Danish holidays, which, in a sense, was a relief to Edward because it gave him the excuse he needed to holiday *en garçon*.

When the Queen returned to England she brought with her sketches and photographs of Hvidøre. The King made appropriate comments, though breathlessness made it difficult for him to exclaim enthusiastically over the designs for decorations and furnishings.

Pleading that grief made it impossible for her to remain in London, the Queen swept Miss Charlotte off to Sandringham, possibly unaware that she was leaving the King still far from well, though cheered up by receiving a long and devious letter from his detestable nephew in which Willy really let himself go.

Declaring that his uncle's sympathetic friendship was a cherished gift, the Emperor went on:

'There is no denying the fact that the political relations between the two countries had little by little become charged with electric fluid to such an extent that its discharge might have created endless woe to both . . .'

Nevertheless, all he was certain would be well and Queen Victoria would have approved.

'I feel sure that from the Home of Eternal Light she is now looking down upon us, will rejoice when she sees our hands clasped in cordial and loyal friendship.'

Then, in deploring the death of Alix's father, he added a peevish note on its unexpectedness.

'One was so accustomed to count on his fine constitution.'

Edward balled the letter in his hand. Slush! Rot! But he had to uncrease it so that it could be sent to the Foreign Office and Knollys could write a suitable reply on his account. He did not feel quite up to writing himself. Then momentarily he smiled. Under diplomatic pressure, because Japan was an ally, he had consented to give the Mikado the Garter, and quite soon his nephew, young Arthur of Connaught, accompanied by the dependable Redesdale, was to go out and invest him in Tokyo. But not even the thought of Willy's apoplectic reaction to the Yellow Peril being so honoured could keep him amused for long. He felt far too jaded.

Still lame, still breathless, he sat about most of the time, and his energies at last flagged. Not even a glorious run down to Brighton on a summer day during which his Mercedes exceeded sixty miles an hour could shake off his lethargy. Not even Fisher, who pounded in to tell him of the launching of a new kind of battleship with eleven inches of armour plating called a dreadnought, could spark his old vitality. Indeed he begged Esher to steer the exuberant Admiral aside should he come visiting too often. He was so noisy and boisterous.

The King's coughing and gasping and his general lack of condition worried his physicians. After several examinations and tests, they conferred and agreed on the necessity of getting him into the sun as soon as was practical. Quite clearly except for his annual cure at Marienbad he was not prepared to abate his eating or his smoking in the least. He would need to be cosseted through the early part of each winter and sent abroad as soon after opening Parliament as was possible.

The Queen was informed and she volunteered once again to join her husband on a Mediterranean cruise in April. Without alarming her unduly and, in view of her great anxiety over the King's bronchitis the year before, it was deemed both unkind and unnecessary to overstress his present condition to the Queen, Reid, Laking and Semon still decided he ought to be removed from the fogs of London and the mists of Windsor as soon as possible. On their own initiative they decided privately it would be prudent, even if a little unprofessional, to confide in and seek an alliance with the King's great friends Miss Agnes Keyser and Mrs George Keppel.

This informal consultation between the King's physicians and his greatest friends resulted in the evolution of an annual regimen.

Sister Keyser sent to the Cavendish and asked if Mrs Excelsior Lewis would kindly step round to Grosvenor Crescent, and afterwards they went to the Cavendish together to work out a scheme for re-arranging the King's suite so that he never need exert himself unduly. Rosa Lewis was even prepared to make slight modifications in her culinary arrangements for the King, if it really *was* for the dear royal soul's health. Agnes Keyser assured her solemnly that it was.

Thereafter Sister Keyser was to have general overall charge of the King until February when Mrs Keppel took over, travelling with her daughters Violet and Sonia, a maid, a nanny and a courier, to stay in what had once been the Empress Eugénie's private villa and was now leased by the Government to Sir Ernest Cassel as the Hôtel du Palais.

At Biarritz there was the fresh sea air and the sun King Edward needed and he had a special fondness for the place. His mother had also cared for it and had decided Biarritz was France's answer to Osborne – so much quieter and cleaner than the Riviera – and she might have gone there frequently if it had not been for an unhappy contretemps on her very first and only visit. The Pavilion had been lent to her by the Comte de La Rochefoucauld but, on arrival and not before, Queen Victoria had discovered her hostess was the guilty party in a divorce, and therefore presentation was out of the question. This made everyone uncomfortable to say the least. Then the Comtesse had made everything worse by begging to be allowed to peep at her royal guest from behind a door but, overcome with loyalty, she had burst from her hiding place, thrust a bouquet at the Queen, and declared she was respectable once more because her ex-husband had just died of drink. As Victoria afterwards remarked to her eldest son, the dilemma had been most unnerving and had spoilt her taste for Biarritz.

Edward's fondness for the little town had naturally attracted his friends there. The Dudleys liked it. So did the Roxburghes and the Manchesters. Best of all vague old Devonshire and his Ponte Vecchio were frequently there – he gazing at the Atlantic rollers like a Celtic bard, she delighting the King, but not Sir Ernest Cassel, by being constantly at the Hôtel du Palais to indulge her passion for bridge. Edward was very eager to go there and join Alice early in the spring of 1906, though, what with one thing and another, he did not get away as soon as his physicians could have wished. Cheerfully remarking as he left that he hoped the Prime Minister would not abolish the House of Lords in his absence, he went to do diplomatic chores in Paris and enjoy a little private roguey-poguery supervised at a distance by the ubiquitous M. Lépine. Then his train took him down to Bordeaux and on to Biarritz. There Alice told him excitedly she had been given semi-royal treatment on her way through France. Chefs de gare, sleeping car attendants and porters en route had all wished to honour her. It was strange that in a republic *Madame la maîtresse du roi* should count for so much.

This, their first visit to Biarritz together was to be followed each spring by others. Sir Ernest looked after everything. Apart from being the King's financial adviser and a powerful representative of *haute juiferie* at the very centre of affairs in England, he liked to play host to the King for his annual spring holiday. His sister was hostess, and she and Mrs Keppel looked after the King. The children would be brought to him twice a day. Sonia, the younger and far more shy, seldom distinguishing between the King and Sir Ernest – because both were bearded, bald, stout and wore many rings – would give each a royal curtsy just in case. Violet, aged fourteen and already aware that there must be a significance in the uncanny coincidence which threw her mother and the King together – before Christmas at Crichel, at Biarritz for Easter, and in Scotland during the shooting and stalking season – maintained silence in company and privately confided to her young friend Vita Sackville-West that she thought men took advantage and were 'diskie' – a current piece of slang which meant disgusting.

After 1906 the lives of the Keppel children fell into a distinct pattern. From Biarritz the King would leave for a cruise, and they would go to Paris to be Sir Ernest's guests at his apartment in the Rue du Cirque. Thence they would return to Portman Square for the Season. Sometimes their parents were at home. More frequently they were not. On occasion the King would call at teatime. Then, in the high summer, there was an exodus northwards to Scotland where they quite often saw the King. He would shoot with Papa and tease Mama about her Scotch relations – her brother Archie who, despite the fact that he lived at the top of one tower of Duntreath House and his wife at the bottom of another had managed to produce three strapping sons, and her eccentric cousin Gladys who, convinced she was the Young Pretender, dressed in man's jacket and the kilt, and always went to the gentlemen's lavatory in hotels. Violet was mortified by having such lunatic relations; Sonia never, she thought them so interesting. What their father really thought about these annual peregrinations no one ever knew. Colonel Keppel kept his own counsel. A magnificent figure six foot four inches tall, in his Gordon Highlander bonnet he stood almost eight feet, and, with one brother an Equerry to the Prince of Wales and another sitting in the Upper House as Lord Albemarle, his life could not have been easy – dining often at his clubs, keeping out of the way, sometimes having to be where he did not wish to be in order to keep up appearances. But, then, he might have reflected ironically that his family held its earldom and lands from a favourite of the homosexual Dutch sovereign William III, and his deep love for Alice showed through a long marriage.

Princess Beatrice and her daughter Ena were also in Biarritz in the spring of 1906, and the King of Spain drove over all by himself from San Sebastian, tearing along at forty miles an hour in a Panhard. He took Ena and her mother for motor drives; a method of wooing which the Grand Duchess Augusta castigated as *'Love-making in the Motor-car!'* She strongly disapproved of the match, writing to her niece, the Princess of Wales:

> *'Did you see the ridiculous Photo of them all,* laughing, *Beatrice leaning down over the young lovers spreading her arms out like an Eagle . . . no, too funny & not Royal!'*

The Grand Duchess was not the only one to disapprove when the engagement was announced and King Edward had formally given his permission. There was uproar in Protestant circles.

The King remained quite unmoved. He made it clear that his niece was renouncing all right to succession to the English throne, that her conversion to the Roman Catholic religion was a private affair, and that the marriage had his blessing and the full approval of the British government. Then he made Ena a Royal Highness and left to join Alix and Toria aboard the royal yacht at Marseilles.

2

King Edward and his queen, with Toria in tow, met the Waleses at Corfu. They were the guests of Alix's brother, the King of Greece, who had gone there to avoid the fasting, abstinence and mortification of an Orthodox Holy Week in Athens.

The Prince and Princess of Wales were on their way home from the successful tour of India and May was full of it. Her father-in-law, who had always liked clever women, listened enchanted to her description of the places he himself had visited and so much enjoyed many years before. She told him the voyage home had not been so pleasant. She did not care all that much for Egypt. The Pyramids had been too tall to climb. Riding a camel was not easy. The Sphinx she thought disappointing.

King Edward respected though he did not always agree with her views. They were in accord, though not for the same reasons, when Lord Charles Beresford, commanding the Mediterranean Fleet, brought his battleship squadron to Corfu and offended the mild Greek monarch by receiving him aboard his flagship without troubling to change into full-dress uniform. King Edward thought Beresford's slovenly conduct an insult and telegraphed the Board of Admiralty. The Princess of Wales deplored it because she saw it was simply part of the Fisher–Beresford quarrel and it had made an English Admiral rude to a foreign sovereign, which would never do. Again they were in accord, but again for different reasons when they heard at Corfu that the Liberals had framed an Education Bill which proposed that no doctrine of any kind should be taught to children, and religion must be taught entirely on undenominational lines. The King wrote an angry letter to Esher denouncing the bill as 'deplorable' and asking 'What *can* the government be thinking of?' His daughter-in-law was equally shocked but because she saw who was behind it, the Welsh Merlin, Lloyd George, who had led a revolt to bend the existing law four years before and, as an inflexible believer in royalty, she did not hold with elected demagogues.

A little after Easter the whole party went on to the Piraeus and Athens for a State Visit and there encountered a huge collection of royals who had gathered for the Olympic Games. May, King Edward noted, was never still – always rushing from monument to monument, work of art to work of art. She took in Classical Greece, Byzantine art, the Olympic Games, and family gossip with the eagerness and apparent insatiability of a fledgling swallowing insects. How shrewd she was, too. A score of doctors had begged him to give up smoking or, at least to cut it down from his daily ration of one small cigar, twelve huge cigars and twenty-two Dambergi cigarettes. May quietly told him one day in the garden she had heard from the Grand Duchess of Strelitz that a kinswoman, a Duchess of Mecklenburg, had died less than a fortnight before of over-smoking. 'Such a pity,' she remarked quietly, 'that people can't do things in moderation!' The King dropped a half-smoked cigar on the brushed gravel path whence, no doubt, it was swiftly retrieved and either smoked by a Greek or sold off as a royal relic.

In a way he was sorry when George and May set off for England, to see their children, read up Spanish history, and represent him at Ena's wedding in Madrid. But in a way he was not. He and Alix had planned to separate at Naples, where she would continue cruising and he would go north to Paris. He hated humbug, as his mother had done, and he was never a hypocrite; nevertheless he did his best to separate the faster side of his life from that which belonged to the family, and he respected May's obvious wish to keep herself and her husband and the children apart, ready against the day when a new code of manners would be *de rigueur*. Live and let live was an excellent motto for them all.

He had May much in mind during the next few weeks. He was a trifle preoccupied, for at Naples Vesuvius was erupting and causing considerable damage, and Rosebery committed the heinous sartorial crime of wearing a white tie not a black one with his Yacht Squadron mess-jacket at a dinner. Then in France there were strikes, a general election and new ministers to call on in between enjoying himself under the scrutiny of M. Lépine. But he kept in touch with George and May.

May wrote to say King Alfonso was on the Isle of Wight, carving his name on a tree with his beloved Ena, and planting another with her to commemorate their betrothal, though in such a state of euphoria that it was oblique rather than perpendicular at the end of it. She wrote to say also that she personally was taking care of the King and Queen's wedding present of a parure of diamonds and oblong turquoises. Reliable, efficient May. For George the King had an uncomplicated devotion – the sort of manly affection Evangelical clergymen praised so frequently – and, while their roles as sovereign and heir, father and son, were never forgotten, they were, as far as possible, true friends. At Cowes they were almost on an equal footing, and if George took second place at race meetings, then his father did at shoots, because the Prince of Wales was one of the three best shots in the kingdom. But the King sometimes asked himself, and very frequently at this juncture, where would George be without May? Mama had known well she would give George muscle as a monarch, and he had appointed Mama's Private Secretary, Sir Arthur Bigge, as George's Private Secretary confident that it would have been her wish. George had also promised to take Ponsonby into his Secretariat when the time came, and Bigge and Ponsonby had served Mama for years. With May they might make his reign memorable, but May would be the lynchpin. She really was a first-rate wife and Princess of Wales. One day she would make a first-rate Queen.

. . . . .

The royal physicians, Sir Francis Laking, Sir James Reid, and Sir Felix Semon were much gratified with the King's physical condition when he returned to his capital after a seven-week holiday. Either the sunshine of Biarritz, or the Mediterranean cruise, or the plush pleasures of Paris in the springtime, had toned him up. He was a different man; full of portly bounce; prepared to get back to work with his ministers, even ready to tolerate the Welsh Merlin's invective – Lloyd George's latest thrust had been to declare all peers were bulls in the china-shop and bulls were safer as beef – and endure the gale-force boisterousness of Admiral Fisher; looking forward to the Season though, as a token of mourning for her father, Alix had asked that his party for Ascot week be entirely male, which would be dull to be sure; and eager to do his best for his niece Princess Ena.

He did his best so thoroughly that Princess Beatrice was in floods of tears of gratitude for hours. He gave her daughter a farewell banquet at the Palace, drove with her to Victoria Station through streets lined by cheering crowds, and walked her along the platform to her carriage. Her mother and her brothers Leopold and Maurice were to travel with her. King Edward was at his most charming and encouraging.

A few days later he saw off his son and daughter-in-law who were to represent him at the wedding; bidding May tell him every detail on her return.

He was hardly prepared for the story she ultimately told him.

By protocol royal weddings were not attended by reigning sovereigns, but everyone else went to enjoy the chance of seeing one another amidst the luxuries of a Court clearly on its mettle for a grand occasion.

Trains de luxe thundered to Spain carrying Heirs Apparent, Grand Dukes, Archdukes, Princes and Princesses and the envoys of republics with all their suites, everyone getting hotter and hotter and grumbling at the lack of *luxe*. At the Spanish frontier, in a gaslit soldier-guarded station waiting-room, what Queen Victoria had called 'the royal mob' gradually collected, and when the mob and their suites had been counted and recounted, they were transferred to a Spanish *train de luxe* where they drank cooling drinks in a dining-car at midnight, and still grumbled about the lack of *luxe* as the train thundered towards Madrid.

Their arrival at three on a blazing afternoon was a trying business. Greeted in turn by King Alfonso's sister and the widower of the Princess of Asturias, to the martial sound of their own national anthem, given attachés and put into mule-pulled carriages, they were taken to the Palacio Real, brilliant and splendid and incredibly uncomfortable, where there were more national anthems, and where, to the *rat-tat-tat* of fifty drums and fanfares of silver trumpets, they were received in a long file by the King and his mother in a heat so powerful that Prince Albrecht of Prussia in his tight-fitting uniform fell senseless at his hostess' feet.

The Prince and Princess of Wales suffered all this with truly British phlegm. Because of their high rank they were given apartments in the Palacio Real itself, cool, cathedral high rooms – as May put it – to and from which for all meals and ceremonies and entertainments they were escorted by a bowing Spanish duke. The Prince of Wales, accustomed to a more leisured and less supervised coming and going, was put out. The Prussian Court he found uncomfortable, the Austrian Court far too rigid, but Spanish protocol had not altered a jot since Philip of Spain married Mary Tudor of England. His wife, with her love of history, was thrilled by the formal etiquette. He was not. Every time he left his apartments, to smoke in the gardens, or stroll a little in the city, an officious servant would clap his hands in signal, and halberdiers stationed at intervals along all the corridors would present arms as he passed and cry to one another. 'Arriba Principe! Arriba Principe!' It was a far cry from York Cottage, Sandringham.

Everything was arranged in the same magnificent style on the day of the wedding itself. Forty state coaches drawn by horses wearing pink or orange ostrich plumes carried the royal mob and the republican envoys to the Church of St Hieronimo where the ceremony was not overlong and slipped by, as the Prince of Wales put it nautically, without a hitch.

But afterwards – as the bridal coach was passing the Italian Embassy and was a bare two hundred yards from the Palacio Real – an anarchist's bomb was thrown, wrapped round with flowers. It exploded beneath the horses drawing the royal coach killing the two wheelers and another and mutilating the rest. Twenty people were killed, some blown to pieces, and at least sixty were injured. But by a miracle, though they were covered with broken glass, neither King Alfonso nor his bride was harmed.

Enquiring for his mother and mother-in-law, and hearing they were safe, and ordering that all possible should be done for the wounded, the King refused to take shelter as he was advised. Instead he took his Queen by the hand, and they transferred to another carriage for the short distance which lay ahead.

His bravery was astonishing because he had been warned before that an attempt would be made, and his care for his guests reassured them of their own safety – though already they had heard that the anarchist had first tried to get into the church for the wedding and, had he succeeded, the succession and composition of a number of royal houses would have been considerably altered. No praise was too high for the King, reported the Princess of Wales. He had behaved perfectly in a grisly situation when his bride's gown had been soaked in the blood of his subjects, and his mother-in-law, Princess Beatrice, had watched human heads roll down the street like so many footballs. The royal luncheon which followed was not a lively meal.

The widow of King Edward's brother, the Duchess of Edinburgh and Coburg, did not improve things by saying gloomily and continuously that she personally was accustomed to such things, both her father and her brother having been blown to bits. The Princess of Wales had to take her in hand and suggest that she might be more cheerful. Such a suggestion, in particular when expressed in Princess May's most severe tone, was tantamount to a command. Aunt Edinburgh and Coburg relapsed into a gloomy silence.

At the appropriate time the Prince of Wales had to propose the health of the bride and groom. Happier at giving orders on a gunboat, or formally opening a bridge, he was never a great speechmaker and had laboriously committed to memory something which his Equerry had thought appropriate to the occasion. He tried to alter it, but nothing could have been more muddled or dispiriting.

The anarchist was not found for seventy-two hours, which caused the Duchess of Edinburgh and Coburg to break out into fresh complacent jeremiads, and the Prince of Wales to say in public 'Damn the Spanish police!'

'And I fully agree with him,' said King Edward warmly, when May told him the story in full. 'What a shocking, shocking affair!'

Princess May nodded. 'Most unpleasant!' she agreed. 'And so

very hot. But I enjoyed the fine pictures and our visit to the Escorial.'

'You went sight-seeing?' said the King in amazement.

Again his daughter-in-law nodded. 'It seemed sensible. Once I had sent off reassuring telegrams to you and Motherdear and Aunt Augusta, and had done what I could for poor Aunt Beatrice and Ena, it seemed a pity to miss such an opportunity.'

The King smiled, took her hand and gallantly kissed it. 'May,' he said, and very sincerely. 'Sweet May, you are a remarkable woman.'

3

While, on the surface – and certainly during their usual cure at Marienbad – they were good friends, Lord Knollys doubted if Campbell-Bannerman could ever get on with the King politically. C-B, he averred, no more understood King Edward than Gladstone had understood Queen Victoria. In breadth they were in agreement, yet the King was vexed by Sir Henry's casual habit of withholding full information.

The King also deplored the Liberals' over-liberal distribution of peerages. He knew the party 'needed to be blooded', as he put it; but Sir Henry's Birthday Honours List that year included the name of a Belfast shipowner who was heartily loathed by everyone and about whom nobody had a good word to say except that he contributed handsomely to the Liberal Party funds. As the Fount of Honour the King had the right to object and did so strenuously; but, as was his right as Prime Minister, Sir Henry disregarded the royal wishes, and the Belfast shipowner began to grace the Upper House.

Sir Henry's equivocal attitude to the House of Lords was also a worry to the King. The radicals and Labour members wanted it disposed of altogether. Even Liberals to the Right thought it ought to submit to extensive surgery. When, as everyone expected, the peers defied the Commons by wrecking the Education Bill, Campbell-Bannerman began hinting that one day he might have to advise the King to create sufficient Liberal peers to get a measure through the Lords. The King was aghast. Precedents were hurriedly looked out. Queen Anne had actually done it. William IV had obliged his First Minister by agreeing to create sufficient peers. Esher, Knollys and, naturally, Admiral Fisher, were all for the King refusing to go along with C-B; but Edward preferred to take Alice Keppel's moderate advice to wait. After all Sir Henry had only hinted at what might happen. The King respected Alice's womanly intuition that such a crisis might never arise.

In foreign affairs Sir Henry was more communicative, believing as few in his party did, that the King was in a strong position to implement his Government's policies. He was *l'oncle d'Europe*, and, except in Prussian circles, he was already being called Edward the Peacemaker. Sir Edward Grey, the Foreign Minister, was in agreement and begged the King to greet the Inter-Parliamentary Union which was to meet that July in London, especially as representatives of Russia's first elected Parliament, the Duma, would be there. The King fully agreed to do all he could, and instructed his Prime Minister to welcome the delegates in his name. There was almost an hiatus, for on the morning of the opening the Tsar telegraphed to say that he had summarily dissolved the Duma. But Sir Henry Campbell-Bannerman adroitly saved the situation by interpreting the dissolution as an act of suspension not total abolishment, and he reminded the assembly that most Parliamentary systems had gone through a stormy youth. Adapting the ancient phrase, he concluded: 'The Duma will revive in one form or another. We can say with all sincerity, "La Duma est morte: Vive la Duma!" '

His words irritated the Tsar intensely. Protests were made through the Russian Embassy to the Foreign Office, and a plausible explanation offered. But it was King Edward who, through the medium of a personal friend and member of his Household managed to soothe his ruffled nephew. Tsar Nicholas was in desperate straits. Revolution was flaming all over his empire. To combat it he dismissed the languid Goremykin who lay on a sofa reading French novels and put in his place a rosy-faced countryman, Peter Stolypin, a whirlwind statesman who hanged so many terrorists during the summer that the hangman's noose was renamed 'Stolypin's necktie'. Nicholas wanted the understanding if not the sympathy of England and France, and because of their close family relationship he looked to King Edward to tell the world that, while Stolypin was executing terrorists, he was also initiating land reforms which gave nine million Russian peasants the right to own their own farms.

The King and his Ministers agreed that there could be no thought of a formal *entente* with Russia until things were more stable – but it was an ideal they were to aim at.

Meanwhile there was, as ever, the Emperor William to appease. He had dreamt up a list of fresh grievances against his uncle which Edward made no attempt to comment on. Instead he thought it would be tactful if, on his way out to Marienbad, he asked Willy to meet him. This was arranged and, not at all looking forward to it, King Edward stepped down on the platform at Homburg to charm his odious nephew for the sake of his country.

The Emperor, wearing a spiked steel helmet and leaf-green uniform with a crimson collar, looked splendid against a background of courtiers and officers, all in uniform and Orders. King Edward in his tight-fitting Prussian uniform, and with only a small suite, felt immediately at a disadvantage. Nevertheless he allowed his nephew to dazzle and chatter and joke and even tease him. Why, asked the Emperor, were the English aristocracy going into trade? He understood the Marquis of Londonderry – the man who never spoke to his poor wife, added the Emperor with a wink – had become a retailer of coal; that the Countess of Essex was thinking of setting up a laundry; that his uncle's old friend, the Countess of Warwick, had opened a shop for women's underclothing in Bond Street.

Refusing to be baited, the King presented the Emperor with a copy of Elinor Glyn's *Vicissitudes of Evangeline*, a work he was sure to enjoy. Then he allowed himself to be driven in the Emperor's motor car, which had a trumpeter on the box to blow bugle-blasts at every corner, out to his sister's dower home at Kronberg.

There everything was much as it had been at the time of her death, and they ate a great luncheon in her dining-room. It was a place full of hurtful memories to the King. He kept largely silent through the meal, while the Emperor gave a lengthy lecture on archaeology. It was a prelude to an expedition to Salzburg to see a Roman camp which, under Imperial superivision, had been excavated and reconstructed. Bloated, because he never missed a chance to eat until he actually reached Marienbad, and longing for a nap, the King found himself being walked round the site and into a museum where he had to stare at dozens of exhibits while his nephew ran on and on. Coffee was served in the museum before the return run to Homburg, the trumpeter showing off as much as his master all the way.

Still it was not over, and by now the King had a headache.

Hardinge, his Minister in Attendance, and his Ambassador in Berlin, talked over controversial problems with the Emperor and his Foreign Minister, and the King left them to it. His part, he realized, was to be pleasant – even if it killed him. At a huge dinner he ate a great deal and grew positively affable to his nephew.

What either said about the other in the privacy of their rooms that night was not known, but Hardinge assured the King as they travelled on to Marienbad on the following morning, the Emperor had been decidedly pleased with the visit, his uncle's benevolence especially.

Badly in need of a rest, the King discovered their arrival in Marienbad coincided with the Emperor of Austria's birthday – a fact which, he said bitingly to Ponsonby, ought to have been noted by someone or other so that he would not have had to dress up and rush about at the very moment of arrival. The town was *en fête* and even as Duke of Lancaster he had to dress in the trappings of an Austrian field marshal and attend the local church and hear a *Te Deum*. Afterwards he went back to his hotel to relax, and there was Sir Henry Campbell-Bannerman to pay his respects and congratulate the King on the happy outcome of the Homburg meeting. Tired as he was the King would have cut the audience short, but Sir Henry was clearly a worried man and eventually admitted that, since arriving in Marienbad, his wife had been taken seriously ill. Instantly King Edward was full of sympathy and asked if there was anything he could do. No, said Sir Henry unhappily, there was nothing anyone could do.

Sad for his Prime Minister the King saw him leave and, just as his carriage drove away, another took its place. A top-hatted monk descended, followed by another. Edward groaned. It was the Abbot of Tepl come to pay his respects.

The first few days at Marienbad were never easy; adjusting to the routine, taking the waters, dieting, re-meeting old acquaintances, and avoiding those who, until the Austrian and English police had a system of surveillance running smoothly – and this invariably took time – were inclined to mob him for one reason or another. Some simply wanted to be able to say they had had a word with or touched the King of England. Some had grievances to air, notably on this occasion an exasperating American lady who claimed she had been badly treated by a British Consul somewhere in Austria. Others had the strangest requests; a military gentleman who had invented a sword with a telescopic scabbard and wished the King to patent it, an Austrian countess who wanted the King's authority to avoid the quarantine laws when she took her dogs to England, and an Austrian *demi-mondaine* who had taken a ticket from Vienna so that she could oblige him. The last he did not see himself, which he regarded as unfortunate, especially as Fritz Ponsonby, who dealt with this particular problem, told him the lady had been undeniably beautiful and, frustrated in her chief design, had offered herself to him as second best in order not to waste her fare. The King hoped Ponsonby had been kind to this enterprising girl, but rather feared that he had not.

Once the settling-in process was past, and the crowds kept at bay, the King began to enjoy himself – until a Protestant bubble of protest burst in the English press about his having been to a Roman Catholic Mass on the day of the Emperor's birthday. Very angry, he be-rated Ponsonby for not making sure the press was aware he had only attended to hear the singing of the *Te Deum* and afterwards had left the church. The Secretary pleaded that the press was uncontrollable.

'Then, my dear Fritz,' said the King warmly, 'you must find some way to control it.'

Ponsonby thought for a while and sent out a general invitation for all reporters and correspondents in Marienbad to meet him in the hotel lobby. He expected six to a dozen and was astonished when thirty-seven people arrived in the lobby. They were of all nationalities. Some were women.

Quickly he told them how small mistakes could cause trouble to the King and, as he was visiting Marienbad privately, it was imperative that exact reports, and not approximations, should be printed. For this purpose he was prepared to write out each day a detailed list of the King's public activities and this he would hand to an appointed representative for him to pass on to the rest of the press. He then left the reporters to elect a representative, but, when he returned in ten minutes' time, he found a furious discussion raging in English, German, French, Russian and Italian, as to who should be elected. Ponsonby promptly solved this by saying he personally would appoint Reuter's correspondent, and give him notes for passing on each day. He hoped that would satisfy everyone. It did, with one notable exception, a female reporter from the *New York Herald*, who refused point blank to agree, accused Major Ponsonby of trying to muzzle the press, wagged a finger at him and said: 'I shall have to report you to Mr Gordon Bennett, and *he* will be very, very angry with you.'

Appalled by this unfeminine, impolite and totally unjustified attack, Ponsonby informed her icily that he was not personally acquainted with any person by the name of Gordon Bennett, and at the same time he instructed Reuter's correspondent not to pass on the day's release to the reporter from the *New York Herald*.

Afterwards he came to the conclusion that amongst journalists, if nowhere else, dog docs eat dog, because, well satisfied with the new arrangement, not one of the thirty-six who had answered his summons to the hotel would pass on a word to the woman who had insolently threatened him with the displeasure of a totally unknown man. Within ten days she was asking for an interview, apologizing for standing out against his plan, and begging to share the advantages her colleagues enjoyed.

Ponsonby eventually consented, though he kept her waiting a day or two for trying to schoolma'am an Equerry and Private Secretary of the King of England in the name of, presumably, the proprietor of a newspaper.

As a sauce to the compliment he had already been paid by the King's visit, the Kaiser was to receive a private visit from the British War Secretary, Richard Haldane, who had asked if he might attend the German Army Manoeuvres. Any chance to show off the military might of Germany delighted the Emperor, who at once agreed.

On his way out Edward wished him to stay a day or two at

Marienbad. Haldane's intellectual accomplishments almost matched Balfour's, but he did not alarm the King because his feet were fixed so very firmly on the ground. And, while Edward always thought that Balfour rather looked down on him, it was obvious that Haldane did not. In fact, more than most in the Cabinet, he knew why the King was being referred to as Edward the Peacemaker in certain circles, and believed that his power for good or bad in foreign affairs was considerable. He also admired his sovereign's mastery of languages. His idiomatic French was perfect, as was his German, and he could even manage the silky drawl of the Austrian aristocracy, Schönbrunner Deutsch. And Haldane admired the King's preparedness to take trouble over people, and the gusto with which he lived. Furthermore, being from a middle-class Scotch background, he was snobbish enough to enjoy being his sovereign's guest. The two got on splendidly.

Haldane received a fair summing-up appraisal of the German Emperor's character; that he had been indulged by his grandfather and Bismarck, and that his atrophied arm had made him acutely sensitive. In general affairs William was only as clever as his flatterers and his secretariat permitted, although he was kept fully informed on the state of his Army and Navy. The King advised Haldane to notice the excellent military organization. Parts of it, or modifications of certain features might well be worth adopting in the British Army.

All this was their official business, conducted in the presence of Major Ponsonby who corroborated all the King had said and added to Haldane afterwards that, considering how the two disliked each other and there always seemed thunder in the air when uncle and nephew met, the King had been generous.

In private sovereign and minister drove out into the fragrant pine forests, both wearing green Styrian hats bought from the famous Marienbad hatter Fraülein Pistl, stopped to buy coffee, the King remarking that one could always tell when one crossed the frontier into Germany because the Germans, without exception, made it so badly; played a little golf and a lot of croquet and bridge; and took the daily promenade.

One morning a special plain-clothes policeman arrived at the hotel to say that several well-known anarchists had arrived the night before and would the King please remain in his apartments until they had been located and removed. No, said Edward, he would not. Anarchists or no anarchists he was going along the promenade to get his tumbler of spa-water.

Haldane admired his courage while, at the same time, he thought him foolhardy. To his dismay the King invited him to join him on his walk, an invitation he could hardly refuse. He could not stop himself from glancing here and there in the crowd looking for anarchists.

'Haldane,' teased the King. 'Evidently you are unaware that the police here are a very nervous lot. We shall be quite all right.'

To his War Secretary's great relief they were.

On the very day Haldane left for Berlin, Lady Campbell-Bannerman died. Understanding what the loss must mean to Sir Henry, for the two had been exceptionally close, the King's formal letter of condolence had a warmth of feeling and sincerity which raised it above the commonplace. He was not normally adept at letter-writing, lacking the careful style of his father and the rambling yet lively and coherent dash of his mother, but Sir Henry's distress moved him greatly. Ironically it was to Lady Londonderry, that sufferer from a totally loveless, silent marriage, that the King confided:

It is a terrible blow to him, as they were so devoted to each other

Sir Henry being desolated, the King took over all the necessary arrangements. He organized the funeral service, half to be in German, half in English, personally attended it, walking with Sir Henry as chief mourner, laying a wreath on the coffin, and holding his Prime Minister's trembling arm as Job's lovely song of triumph was sung on a September day in Marienbad:

I know that my Redeemer liveth, and that he
shall stand at the latter day upon the earth. . . .

And then, through Ponsonby, he arranged for the body to be taken for burial on the Campbell-Bannerman estate in Perthshire.

. . . . .

Brought closely to personal suffering few people could be kinder or more generous than King Edward. But he was also a realist. Life must go on, and, as always with him, it went on with a verve which, considering he was supposed to be on a cure and was sixty-four years of age, was a miracle of endurance.

He shot regularly with princely landowners close by, and the Abbot of Tepl, evidently thinking it was up to him to provide the best sport in the neighbourhood, set about it in a truly unworldly way which was a credit to his calling. First he instructed the ranger of the monastery estates to buy a large number of cartridges and a large number of partridges. The latter he had placed strategically, and kites were flown over them to resemble birds of prey and prevent them from scurrying or flying away. Secondly, the King of England's reputation as a gourmet being what it was, he thought he ought to provide a very special meal before the shoot. Expecting Lenten fare, but pretending not to mind as, after all, they were taking the cure, the King and his party arrived at the Abbey for a preliminary luncheon to find a Lucullan feast prepared. One course followed another. The accompanying wines were superb. The cure-takers hurled themselves on the delectable viands and the Abbot and his monks beamed to see their guests' happiness. Unfortunately it had the effect of making accurate shooting quite out of the question. Unfortunately, too, the ranger forgot to remove his kites so that even when the beaters moved towards the torpid guns few of the bought partridges could be persuaded to rise. Thirty-six were accounted for, though the ranger out of self-respect felt obliged to add the corpses of those partridges which had died in the train to Marienbad the day before, and brought the score up to 150 brace.

The King had enjoyed his luncheon so much that he did not mind in the least about the abortive shoot. He also appreciated Ponsonby's calculation that, considering the cost of importing partridges, hiring beaters, providing cartridges, and giving such a splendid banquet, each dead bird at the end of the shoot had cost the poor Abbot at least £8. The royal guest tried to cheer up his crestfallen host, and did so by inviting him to come to Windsor in the following year to enjoy his royal hospitality.

'For shooting?' asked the Abbot anxiously.

'There need be no shooting,' the King reassured him with a smile.

4

Society troubles spread like influenza during that autumn.

Esher, in a candid moment, told the King he believed it was because the old disciplines were no longer respected; not those of chastity, of course, a virtue which very rarely in history had been strictly imposed by the members of Society, but the valuable disciple of circumspection. In the fastest set it had been considered *de rigueur* to take a lover, either platonically like Lady Elcho, who lavished love on Arthur Balfour, or even passionately, as could be exemplified in scores of cases – just so long as there were already plenty of thriving heirs in the nursery and schoolroom, and so long as husbands were not humiliated as Lord Londonderry had been. Corridor boards had squeaked at night-time in country houses for years and years, and there was a score of stories of people like Lord Palmerston and Lord Charles Beresford leaping into the wrong bed by mistake, with other marvels like the pair who made a trysting signal that the lady should place outside her door the plate of sandwiches always provided for guests; but which the gentleman found empty, took for a warning signal and fled. Only by accident did they discover that a fellow guest, the German First Secretary and Counsellor and a very greedy man, despite a big breakfast, bigger luncheon, huge tea and vast dinner had found the strange offering in the corridor too tempting and had gobbled the sandwiches up. Such adventures had been part of the late Victorian, early Edwardian scene in many country houses up and down the land; but now, Esher declared, people lacked the sense of propriety or the fortitude which kept couples like the Londonderrys together and sustained the whole fabric of society.

In fact, he believed that not only had the House of Commons initiated a new political era but the cult of individualism was initiating a new social one.

There had always been divorces in Society but generally for very good reasons and they were given rarely, but suddenly people were beginning to accept the noxious American doctrine that divorce was not only permissible but even desirable.

The Marlboroughs had been setting a particularly bad example. The eighth duke had been divorced by his wife and now the ninth duchess, Consuelo, who on instructions from her mother had brought £6 million to the Marlboroughs and the Vanderbilts into Society, was separating from her husband.

Furthermore, people were not simply rich, they were gaudily, offensively so.

Knowing how the King respected his daughter-in-law's opinions, Lord Esher passed on a remark she had made recently that Society was suffering from a surfeit of gold and orchids, and he believed she was right. It signified a great deal and corresponded with another shrewd judgement he had heard, that they were living in an Age of Jade and Lobster. Taste reflected much and taste was undoubtedly altering. Solidly comfortable furniture was being replaced by papiermâché chairs, 'Lady Teazle' screens, day beds draped with silk shawls in wishy-washy colours. There was talk now in restaurants of 'frenchified' food as though it was an opprobrious term. Begonias and petunias were out, malmaisons and orchids were in. Especially the latter. The Princess of Wales was quite correct, Society was surfeited with orchids. It was all very well for the Rothschilds to finance orchid hunters and collect fabulously rare and beautiful varieties, but it was surely going too far when Lord Digby sent his scug of a son at private school a weekly orchid to wear at church on Sunday. Think of it, said Esher warmly. And think of the lavish entertainment of the Gibson Girls, named after the American artist who designed their clinging dresses of black velvet, a dozen dancers with appetites like horses – one reputedly ordered for her supper 'A porterhouse steak, please, liberally sprinkled with kidneys and cutlets' – who were being snapped up by the aristocracy one by one.

'If I did not know you better, Reggie,' said the King reflectively, 'I should say you were lecturing me for leading people astray, for setting a bad example.'

'No, Sir,' said Lord Esher sharply. 'Your standards and the new ones are very different. You have the strongest possible views on what is permissible and what is not. You value honour, devotion, good manners, courage, initiative. In some circles, which are widening, these are not valued as highly as before.'

Edward put the fingers of both hands together. 'Then what would you propose I do?'

Lord Esher smiled. 'Nothing save be yourself, Sir. No one expects you to change. And your consistency will indubitably keep the decay from covering too much ground too rapidly.'

'Decay!' the King considered. 'You think matters are as serious as that?'

'I do, Sir,' replied Esher emphatically.

'So!' Edward considered. He stroked Caesar's scruff. The dog turned and licked his hand. 'Possibly a *petite guerre* with the Churchills might make people imagine I am becoming increasingly autocratic – that *le roi* by no means *veult* all these changes of standards.' He chuckled. 'Ours may be lowish standards, Reggie, but at least they deserve the name.'

Esher seized on his suggestion. He would pass the word that as long as the Marlboroughs seriously considered divorce, the King would prefer not to meet them. He would also let Winston Churchill know that the King expected him to put country before party, which he showed no sign of doing, and that he did not care for the way he was chiselling away at his own class by constant talk of abolishing the House of Lords. Then there were the Cornwallis-Wests....

'Yes, Reggie?'

'He almost went bankrupt during your stay in Marienbad. I gather some trouble with a solicitor. But Winston and his brother, and his brother-in-law Westminster, came to the rescue. Nevertheless he is edgy, very quarrelsome with Lady Randolph.'

'Then let West know,' said the King immediately, 'that having made a decision to marry a woman old enough to be his mother in the face of everyone's advice, including mine, he is expected to keep to his decision.'

Lord Esher rubbed the palms of his hands together. 'Most wise, Sir. I really think your idea of a *petite guerre* might delay or stop the decay.'

While the *petite guerre* was waged, not without success, and certainly to the consternation of many in Society, the King put his life at hazard by grouse-shooting at Abington. It was politically important for him to get on with the First Secretary of the Russian

Embassy and no one knew if this gentleman was reliable at this most dangerous form of shooting. Fortunately he turned out to be safe, if not particularly expert.

After that the King went to Londesborough, where the shooting was sure to be safe, though he teased his host because twenty-four years earlier he had contracted typhoid there and had almost died. He said to Londesborough that he hoped the drains had been adjusted since.

Lord Londesborough failed to see anything amusing in the remark and said something snappishly about fate. Indeed he was renowned for his peculiar views on fate and if things went wrong was inclined to blame the Almighty with some force. Having once had an outdoor evening *fête champêtre*, plus a thousand candles and lanterns, entirely ruined by a suden deluge, he had remarked, 'Oh, God, how *like* you!' On this occasion, peeved by the King's teasing, he shot badly, so badly that he stamped with anger, praying angrily, 'Oh, God, you *know* how much I enjoy shooting. *WHY* won't you let me hit these partridges?'

5

The King returned to Windsor (in November 1906) to face an entirely new experience. It was not without misgivings that he gave an audience to the extremely left-wing radical John Burns, the ardent socialist who had brought Dockland out on strike some years before, and was a militant of militants. Edward hoped he would not be rude, either through nervousness or deliberately. He also hoped that Devonshire's prophecy might have been correct and that, on taking office, the old docker had begun to glow less radically, had snubbed his old associates and turned respectable. When he arrived for his audience Burns was the more nervous of the two.

Once the preliminaries were over the King considered he might properly ask if Burns was acquainted with any nihilists. Did he, he asked shyly, know any terrorists?

The confidence seemed to give Burns confidence. Why, yes, he said, and he told the King how at Queen Victoria's Diamond Jubilee he had met seven very well-known anarchists in the crowd and had expected them to blow up the procession. But instead, as the royal carriage bowled by, they all took off their hats and bowed.

'They bowed, Mr Burns?'

'They did, your Majesty. With my own eyes I saw it.' And John Burns went on to say that except from the attacks of lunatics or men with deep grievances the English royal family was safe from anarchists – simply because they were so unprotected by the police.

'It sounds illogical, your Majesty,' he admitted. 'But that's the truth. Nobody fusses the Communists in England, so their sting is drawn. In Russia, where Stolypin strings up scores and scores by his necktie, they are all terrorists.'

'Mr Burns,' said the King. 'You reassure me for my personal safety. Thank you. But I feel you should have more sympathy for Stolypin. Though he is pitiless with revolutionaries, he is trying to improve matters for the people. I understand his land reforms have given many benefits to the labouring peasants. Besides, his daughter has just been blown up by anarchists.'

Having cheered himself by the unexpected success of the audience with Burns, the King was buoyed into a false confidence that he might even be able to resolve the stalemate which now existed between the Liberal majority in the Commons and the Conservative majority in the Upper House.

On his own initiative he invited Campbell-Bannerman and the Archbishop of Canterbury for a Saturday to Monday at Windsor, and in long private discussions he begged them to explore every possibility of compromise. He was concise and frank. He did not wish to create the many peers necessary to pave a measure for the reform of the Lords. Nevertheless he could see the injustice of the wishes of an elected assembly being blocked by a house containing chiefly hereditary members.

Esher was there, of course, to guide, warn and advise behind the scenes. Knollys, whose judgement was beginning to fail him, was there to persuade from a very prejudiced point of view. Fisher roared in and out again. Mysteriously the Archbishop, a dearly loved friend of Queen Victoria, had the happy effect of muffling the old sailor's zest. Edward decided to bear that useful information in mind for future occasions.

Yet it all came to nothing. There was almost agreement that at least there should be no public wrangling between the two Houses, that Balfour and Campbell-Bannerman should have further meetings with the Archbishop and certain selected peers, but it never came to anything.

Failing as a reconciler actually made the King ill. His days and nights were racked with asthmatic bouts of coughing. In order to sleep he had to sit almost bolt upright. Eventually he found the courage to tell his resident physician, Sir James Reid, that he often had a pain between the root of his nose and his right eye and when he pressed the place he could feel a lump.

Sir James gave him a careful examination and said that radium treatment ought to clear his trouble. It was an incipient ulcer. The King need not worry....

But, naturally, Edward did. Having had a brother and a sister die of cancer, the disease terrified him.

Sir James sent for Sister Agnes. Possibly only she had the necessary force to make the King understand his case was not necessarily as bad as he thought it.

Sister Agnes half managed it. She helped him subdue his fears although they were merely lightly buried until Reid assured him the ulcer was responding to radium. Then he brightened. But Agnes Keyser was not letting him out of her care until he was himself again: neither coughing nor cursing, and properly nourished for a change. She supervised the continuing radium treatment, hurled open and banged-to windows in the royal apartments at different intervals, gave the King's valets syrups and strict instructions, and caused commotions in the royal kitchens. From M. Menanger, the Chief Cook, down to Mr Etherton, the Steam Apparatus Man, there were daily grumbles at the interference from the Matron of King Edward's Hospital for Officers in Grosvenor Crescent. They were there to magic up the dishes their sovereign loved: the *Velouté de Poulet au lait d'amande*, *Suprême de Sole à la Samaritaine*, *Ortolans pochés au Clicquot*, *Jambon de Prague au paprika rose*, and *Désirs de Mascotte*, not sago, broths and jellies, plain steamed tripe and whiting, with coddled eggs and pap.

Louisa Devonshire's New Year's Party might in 1907 have undone Agnes Keyser's work, had the King had more of an appetite. But he was still not feeling fit, and his infectious despondency could easily have proved the ruin of the New Year had not Sir James arrived, uninvited and unannounced but very welcome, on the second day to assure the King, and quite positively, that his face ulcer was completely under control. It had been entirely cured by radium.

'Reid,' King Edward said, clasping the doctor's hands. 'I am determined to found a Radium Institute in London.'

Sir James warmly approved and at once the King wrote to two of his richest friends, Iveagh, the Guinness baron, and Sir Ernest Cassel. He left it to them, he said, to follow him and to lead others on to a subscription list.

Everyone noticed the difference in the King after Sir James' visit. He was able to eat more of the Chatsworth delicacies, was very content to play bridge by the hour, and was as affable as Louisa could wish to all her guests.

Arthur Balfour was there and rather surprised him by attempting to join in the fun. Somehow it seemed wrong for so notable a philosopher–statesman to wear a paper hat at dinner.

And Alix surprised him by playing baccarat for high stakes, an illegal game which had been at the back of the Tranby Croft scandal, causing him endless trouble seventeen years before. Wryly he judged that she had not the least idea what she was playing because Lord Rosebery, who played a great deal with her, called the game Lotto.

The fiercely moustachioed Portuguese Minister was there to delight everyone with his wit, the Queen with the perfection of his waltzing, and the King with his bustling good humour: he who had once confessed to Edward he quite saw the Importance of being Ernest Cassel, and who alone at the English Court had not a single enemy, earning the affectionate nickname of 'Soveral überall'. He was also called, even more affectionately, the 'Blue Monkey', because his beard grew so fast he had to shave twice a day and invariably had bluish features.

And naturally Alice Keppel was there to soothe the King when he grew fractious, which he instantly did when Louisa clapped her hands and announced there would be 'revels'. The word was an omnibus one which covered several of the King's aversions, notably charades, recitations, one-act amateur theatricals, and musical turns.

On this occasion the King was very good. He professed to enjoy the drama especially staged for the Queen. He even professed to enjoy a display of virtuosity by Daisy of Pless, who sang three songs in rapid succession: first a piece from the *Mikado* while wearing a brown wig; then an American folk song; and, finally, a song about snow in French while striking attitudes in an artificial storm dressed as an Eskimo in short skirts and vermilion high boots. But he refused to pretend to enjoy Lady Maud Warrender's contribution to the fun, a piece sung in such a shrill and piercing voice that the King gazed uncomfortably at a chandelier and even the Duke of Devonshire was kept awake.

The Duke was certainly becoming sleepier and vaguer. Ponsonby told his master that Devonshire had just 'discovered' *Paradise Lost* in his library and, declaring it 'capital stuff', had settled to read it through, missing a meal, and having to be prodded back from Paradise to Chatsworth by the point of his indignant Duchess' umbrella. But Edward enjoyed talking with him all the same, touring the glasshouses in his company, telling him Lloyd George's latest impertinence in dragging the King's name into a political speech – 'Nothing offensive, naturally; but he must learn the monarch is above the arena', and confiding that, despite the reckless extravagance of the Queen, his triumvirate of financial advisers, plus the excellent Dighton Probyn, had reassured him all was well fiscally and he never need worry about money again.

'Just imagine it, Devonshire, just imagine it.'

The Duke could not imagine it at all. He was far too rich.

Nor could the Duke quite understand when the King told him Admiral Fisher's name was now being used as a bogy in Germany. Not only that but for two days there had been real panic at Kiel when a false message came through 'Fisher is coming! Fisher is coming!' He laughed politely because his sovereign evidently thought it amusing but personally he considered Fisher a loud and vulgar sort of fellow.

'Your nephew's subjects, Sir, evidently scare easily,' was all he said.

This sparked a flash from Edward who declared warmly that his nephew was as ever rattling his sabre and playing the fool simultaneously. He was enlarging his High Seas Fleet in the most provocative manner, and, at the same time, had sent a huge cast statue of William of Orange as a present to his uncle. This had turned out to be equally provoking because of the high passions it aroused in inflammable Ireland. The Orangemen of Ulster had insisted the statue ought to be raised in Belfast, better still in Londonderry; a suggestion which had driven the Green Irishmen frantic, and neither side had been placated when Campbell-Bannerman, a Scotchman, had announced in the Commons that it would be placed in a far more appropriate position – before Kensington Palace, close by the orangery.

This did get through to the Duke. He pulled at his long beard and chuckled.

Just before the house party broke up the King informed his Assistant Secretary, now Major Sir Frederick Ponsonby, that because he valued Devonshire's friendship and services to the Crown so highly, he intended to give him the G.C.V.O.

Ponsonby said something appropriate. Actually he was much alarmed. Recalling the Duke's extraordinary views on the King's personal Order, and how much the King valued it himself, he sought to avoid an embarrassing scene by warning the Duke in private of the intended honour.

True to form, the Duke merely grumbled and said it would simply complicate dressing for dinner. Couldn't the Order be given to somebody else?

'The King would be awfully hurt to hear you say so,' remarked Ponsonby.

'Would he, now?' The Duke pondered. 'How odd.'

Eventually he was persuaded. Ponsonby exerted a little pressure by reminding the Duke of his gaffe a few weeks before. Forgetting that the King and Queen were to have luncheon at Devonshire House, the Duke had eaten a chop or two in his club and napped there until one of the score of footmen sent out to find him tracked him down. Even the Duke had been a little disturbed at having forgotten Louisa's royal guests and keeping them from their luncheon. It was moral blackmail to remind him that he owed the

King special consideration, but under the circumstances Ponsonby felt it was justified. He begged the Duke to look pleased even if he did not feel it, and when the King sent for him and presented him with the Order as a token of his long friendship, Devonshire said all the right things.

Nevertheless, before dinner, he appeared in Ponsonby's room followed by his valet bearing a tray heaped with collars, sashes, crosses, and insignia of the Garter. Peevishly he demanded to know if he had to wear the Victorian Order as well as the Garter that evening. For some reason he appeared to blame Ponsonby for his sartorial difficulties.

Warning the Duke that he was no expert in such things, Ponsonby said he understood that Knights of the Garter should always wear their Order, but on this special occasion the King would probably expect him to wear his Grand Cross of the Victoria Order Riband and Star, with the Garter Star and the diamond Garter on his leg.

'Then dress me up, dress me up,' said the Duke irritably and between them, Ponsonby and the valet rigged him out for dinner.

Apparently Ponsonby had judged correctly. The King instantly looked to see what the Duke was wearing and nodded approvingly.

'*Notre Edouard*' amazed Paris, and possibly surprised himself a little, by taking his Queen with him on a week's visit to the French capital at the beginning of February. They stayed at the British Embassy, putting no one to any inconvenience, as the ambassadress informed them with a chill in her voice which matched the weather, and, while the visit was supposedly entirely private, the formalities of calling at the Elysée and receiving the President and Mme. Fallières were, of course, obligatory. Ponsonby, delighted that the French Sous-chef du Protocole was in despair at the difference between the elegance and natural charm of the King and Queen and the hesitant bumbling of his own Head of State, found himself unable to resist saying: 'Ah, it is to be expected. Ours, after all, are professionals. Yours are amateurs.'

The King was very good, and made it plain at once he had not come in the mask of *Le Grand Boulevardier*. He permitted himself few private diversions while the Queen and Miss Charlotte, both inexpressibly happy, went shopping, and walked in the snow, and drank coffee in public places – always, of course, under the supervision of the ubiquitous M. Lépine.

When the King and Queen went out together his task was easier. Once they went to a circus – which was trying for Lépine because the noise and lack of crowd control was a feature of the circus; and once they went to see La Bernhardt act in a modern poetical play which had no trace of a plot – but that, surmised M. Lépine, would not worry '*Notre Edouard*', who had once been Bernhardt's lover. On another occasion when they went to a play – and this did have a plot – M. Lépine had no leisure to enjoy it because a crowd of five thousand strikers had gathered outside the theatre in the hope of getting a speech from the King of England as he left. He was not worried about the inside of the theatre. He had an appropriately dressed plain-clothes man in the gallery; another in the upper circle, and a third in the balcony stalls dressed impeccably in evening clothes, white waistcoat, opera hat, kid gloves and a gold-topped cane, but he was anxious about the strikers. In the entr'acte he asked if the Duke and Duchess of Lancaster would consent to leave by a back entrance. King Edward considered it a great deal of nonsense, and said so, but Alix and Miss Charlotte thought it so romantic an idea that smilingly he consented.

On the whole it was a successful and happy holiday. The two had not been closer for years. It was only marred by an attempt by the German Press to see a political motive behind the visit. Spitefully the *Reichsbote* declared that the King had gone 'to look after his branch establishment in Paris'.

On their return, Alix was overjoyed to be able to receive a visit from her sister Dagmar, Dowager Empress of Russia. For almost thirty years it had been deemed politically inexpedient for the Dowager Empress to come to England. Now, though she was not warmly welcomed by the radicals, she was able to make a visit and the two sisters had the prospect of a long spring together in England. They would go sight-seeing. They would go to the theatre. They would see the splendours of Windsor.

Their plans were somewhat modified by the King falling ill on St Valentine's Day. He had another bout of bronchitis, and much more severe than the two previous attacks. Down in the mouth, lethargic, irritable, suspicious of politicians and members of his Household alike, he talked much of abdicating and giving way to George.

Alix and her daughter-in-law were in the classical mould and not overfond of one another, but they combined in their attempts to make the King change his mind; Alix because she wished to remain Queen; May because she was a realist and knew that George was still not quite ready for the kingship. Given a year or two and he would be, but, at present, no.

Such was the King's lowness that it was only with the greatest difficulty and persistence that he was dissuaded from giving up the throne. His vitality was quite sapped away and he had little interest in life – he who normally took an absorbing interest in everything which went on round him. His hacking cough through the nights prevented him from resting. His fever weakened him. His physicians admitted to no one but Lord Knollys and the Prince of Wales that in a man of his build there was always a danger of a coughing attack rupturing a blood vessel. Chandler, the Superintendent of the Wardrobe, and his second valet, Hawkins, sadly missed the sharp edge of his tongue. As much as the physicians they knew he must be very ill indeed to be so quiet and calm.

Then, as abruptly as on previous occasions, and for no explicable medical reason, his temperature dropped and his spirits rose. He ordered Kinema shows. Esher was sent for to distrust him, Agnes Keyser to bully him, Alice Keppel to soothe him. Chandler and Hawkins were almost glad to be once more the victims of a very, very impatient and irascible master....

The Queen felt she could carry on with her programme for entertaining her adored sister, but fate again stepped in to prevent it. Dagmar contracted lumbago and she was kept to her bed in Buckingham Palace. To divert her Alix sought the aid of their nephew, Prince Christopher of Greece, who was also staying at the Palace. She had assembled in her room a collection of dresses, mantles and bonnets which had belonged to Queen Victoria, and bade him dress in the tartan taffeta topped with a feathered bonnet which Victoria had worn in Paris on a visit to Napoleon III in 1855. The Prince was not large, but several times larger than the Queen had ever been. However, after a struggle and a burst seam here and there, he managed it – then to be taken by the Queen down endless corridors past servants with popping eyes to be presented to the Dowager Empress of all the Russias as 'Her Majesty Queen Victoria'.

Privately Prince Christopher thought it a poor joke, though the Empress laughed so much that she had a relapse.

Nor did the King think it a joke. Very angry indeed, he did not trust himself to speak directly to Alix.

Miss Charlotte was sent for. Even she, accustomed to displays of majestic wrath, found herself unnerved by the King's rage at this 'tomfoolery playing about with the memory of a great Queen and my mother'.

Afterwards, considerably shaken, she sat on a chair in the corridor outside the King's apartments. Watered down, the rebuke she was charged to convey would cause her poor Alix great distress. On her own initiative Miss Charlotte decided to say no more than that the King had failed to see the joke. Her protective deception remained undiscovered because the Empress recovering from her lumbago and her sister immediately began on the itinerary she had planned; and once the King was fit enough to travel, he and Alice Keppel, plus children, servants and dogs, left for Biarritz.

6

The Atlantic rollers and the spring sunshine did their work again. Biarritz had become almost the only place where Edward could literally do nothing without becoming too fretful. Work with despatch boxes was reduced to bare essentials. Occasionally the King would walk out, play a game of croquet, which he preferred to win, or go for what he thought were delightfully spontaneous picnics – which, of course, had to be well thought out in advance by a nervous staff.

He was touched to hear from friends that, although his son and daughter-in-law were staying in Paris, and doing their best as quasi-ambassadors for England, there could only be one *Prince de Galles* to the French. He was also amused to hear of May's tireless sight-seeing – she even refused the offers of the greatest couturiers so that she could concentrate on packing in as many sights as possible – and to hear of George's short bursts of daring. Accompanied by Derek Keppel and, of all people, by his sons' French tutor – presumably for purposes of translation – George had penetrated some of the brightest spots in Montmartre and had seen a play, *Occupe-toi d'Amélie,* which he acknowledged was 'the hottest thing' he had ever witnessed. Dear George and May. Somehow the King could not imagine them in Paris; certainly not in the plush milieu where he himself fitted so snugly.

It was at the back of Edward's mind to honour his niece Ena by paying a State Visit to Spain from Biarritz, but everyone advised against it, even King Alfonso. His nephew-in-law regretfully admitted that his capital was riddled with anarchists and his police force was a negligible quantity. Instead he suggested a friendly meeting at Cartagena in the south of Spain where King Edward could call on his Mediterranean cruise. He would have with him his Foreign Minister to talk officially with Sir Charles Hardinge, while he and his uncle-in-law could dine and talk of family affairs.

The suggestion suited King Edward admirably.

On 8 April, escorted by the entire Mediterranean Fleet, he was greeted by King Alfonso, who delighted him by appointing him Captain-General in the Spanish Army. He wore his new uniform that night at dinner while his host wore the full dress uniform of his English regiment, the 16th Lancers.

Afterwards while the politicians talked Alfonso spoke excitedly of Ena's approaching confinement. Spain blazed from end to end with burning candles lighted for the birth of an heir to the Crown, and, according to her medical advisers, Ena was in excellent condition. Edward congratulated him and wished them both all happiness as parents. Then he asked if Alfonso had heard of Willy's latest act of folly? Alfonso had. Suffering from indigestion at a banquet given by the Knights of St John, the German Emperor had vented his spleen on his uncle, telling three hundred astounded guests that the King of England was intriguing against him and ending: 'He's a Satan. You can hardly believe what a Satan he it!'

'It's scarcely credible!' consoled Alfonso.

'I know that Willy is excitable. I know he dislikes me. But this is surely going too far?' complained his uncle. 'And to rub salt in the wound I am instructed by my government that it would be politic to invite Willy to Windsor this autumn.' He spread his hands. 'And so I have to invite him – though,' he added through his teeth, 'I had far rather horsewhip him. He has disgraced the family all his life.'

Alfonso did all he could to soothe his guest. He was kind, affable, absolutely charming to his uncle.

King Edward was bitter and sad to hear a little more than a month later that while Queen Ena had been delivered safely of a boy, and Spain had her heir to the throne, the baby prince was an haemophiliac. Both Russia and Spain were now in the same case.

After a long cruise, accompanied by Alix and Dagmar, and a brief, invigorating visit to Paris, the King returned to his duties and the Season.

He lent a sympathetic ear to the Inspector General of Cavalry, Robert Baden-Powell, who had an idea for mixing classes together and getting boys into the fresh air by interesting them in tracking and natural history. He gave his blessing to a first Scout camp to be held on an island in Poole Harbour. To have young people healthier was vital to the Empire's interests, and possibly the good manners inculcated in some of the boys would spread to the others.

Good manners. His own were put to a curious test at a palace banquet given that May for an Indian prince who began to hurl asparagus stalks over his shoulder. The King at once decided he could only do the same. Everyone followed suit. Footmen bravely withstood a barrage of buttered asparagus. Their livery was not quite the same afterwards, but courtesy mattered more.

To the King's delight George Edwardes had listened to his personal plea to stage *The Merry Widow,* a musical play which he had seen in Vienna. It opened on 8 June, and within a month Franz Lehar's music was being sung at garden parties, played in restaurants, and whisted by tradesboys and scullery girls all over the kingdom.

Excellent.

Not so excellent was Cromer's curious refusal of the Garter. As British Consul Lord Cromer had virtually ruled Egypt for many years and his country owed him much. But to have the offer of the Garter refused – and a personal offer by the sovereign at that – and a request for a money grant put in instead, was a trifle cool.

Parliament voted national heroes pensions and houses, but the heroes did not generally ask for them.

Edward had a little brush about this spare Garter. The Liberal Foreign Minister thought it would do for the King of Siam. The King reminded him that it had been agreed no more non-Christians were to receive this Christian Chivalric Order, and to offer it to the king of a comparatively new country would reduce it from its position as the pre-eminent Order in the world. He was quite determined, and quite unpersuaded even when informed that the Siamese Ministers, having led their monarch to believe he would be offered the Order, were in real fear of being decapitated. With an imperiousness as regal as his mother's he indicated that the pre-eminence of the Garter mattered more. As it happened no heads rolled. The King of Siam was not in the least put out, but he did want to lure King Edward's Palace Steward back to Bangkok – and when that functionary courteously refused, he was promised the White Elephant instead. Unaware that this was an Order, the Palace Steward spent an unpleasant hour telephoning the zoo for elephant accommodation until the insignia of the Order arrived and set his mind at rest.

It was the King's view that people were not sufficiently careful about the importance of Orders, and Chandler and Hawkins had a particularly bad time when they accompanied the King to Dublin for the International Exhibition in July and he discovered that the Crown Jewels of the Order of Saint Patrick had been stolen without anyone missing them. Though an investigation revealed that Ulster King-of-Arms was culpable in not looking after the safe key properly and was dismissed, the jewels, which included the Diamond Star of the Grand Master, never were recovered.

The King was not placated by the attitude of the new Liberal Lord Lieutenant who evidently thought he was making a great deal of unnecessary fuss.

'Unnecessary!' rumbled the King, thinking aloud. *'FUSS!'*

But he said nothing directly to the Lord Lieutenant, Lord Aberdeen. Obviously he was one of those hare-brained egalitarians. When Governor-General of Canada Aberdeen had taken his wife and children to dine once a week in the servants' hall – an undignified act of condescension which must have been very uncomfortable for the servants. Even in Ireland the Aberdeens were eccentrically taking their servants to a club where the Lord

Lieutenant would lecture on railways, his estate jack-of-all trades would recite, and his lordship's valet would sing 'Will o' the Wisp'.

Edward did not exactly cold-shoulder Aberdeen, but he made his disapproval felt.

Unveiling a statue of Uncle George in Whitehall – a statue so lifelike that one almost expected his whiskers to puff out – Edward wondered what that stickler for correctness would have thought of the fast-changing world. Haldane, the War Secretary, was no longer in the royal favour. He had been tinkering with the ancient auxiliary forces of the realm and produced a Territorial and Reserve Forces Bill which, had he known about it, would have made the old Commander-in-Chief squirm like a corkscrew in his grave at Kensal Green. But then, reflected the King, how the gadget-loving old soldier would have revelled in the invention of the cathode ray tube in Russia and that spidery-looking flying machine called a helicopter which could go up in the air, hover, and come down again. They would have enchanted him.

Caesar lay ill in the King's bedroom at Marienbad. A local vet. was summoned who, chirping with nervousness at having so grand a client, recommended purging. This was done, but it simply weakened the dog who lay curled up on his master's bed. He would eat nothing, but he lapped more water than was normal. Hawkins was in a great taking. Normally Caesar was in the care of the English second footman who also brushed the King's clothes and had his own beeswax and champagne receipt for cleaning the King's shoes. But this functionary did not always travel abroad with his royal master, and now Hawkins found himself with the unenviable duty of using a proprietary polish for the royal boots and being responsible for Caesar. He hardly took his eyes off the dog for twelve hours. Then, the King, anxious and vexed by the local vet's incompetence, summoned Sir Frederick Ponsonby and asked that Sewell, the London vet., be telegraphed at once.

The Secretary was aghast. 'But, Sir, his fee would be enormous.'

'No matter.'

Ponsonby had done some costing after the previous year's cure at Marienbad and Sir Dighton Proby had been appalled at his figures. The royal suite of rooms was always entirely refurnished, the previous lot being sold off at an inflated price to souvenir hunters, and the cost of hiring a car came to far more than buying a new one outright. This year the Secretary had promised to prevent needless expenses, and here was the King insisting on Sewell coming all the way from London to examine Caesar.

'Sir,' he said, and not without courage because the King could be as angry as a hornet. 'Will you permit me first to try and locate a specialist in Vienna?'

'No,' snapped the King. He stroked Caesar's nose. The dog put out his tongue. 'Oh, very well,' he said, suddenly changing his mind. 'It might be quicker. Yes, it might. But I warn you, Fritz, if anything happens to Caesar simply because you prevented me from sending for Sewell, I shall not be pleased.'

Ponsonby hurried to telephone Vienna. His relief, in fact everyone's, was profound when a portly Austrian vet., recommended by the British Embassy, arrived post haste and pronounced that the King's fox terrier had a minor ailment which he would attend to directly. With the help of Hawkins he did so. His fee was reasonable.

The King personally thanked him and ordered that he should be given a Royal Warrant of Appointment.

At dinner that evening he told the company that Caesar was well again. 'Which,' he added grimly to his Secretary, 'is just as well for you.'

Ponsonby did not care to imagine what would have happened had the dog died. Several times he had been the object of the King's unreasonable fury, but on one awful occasion, which stood out in his mind, he had been, figuratively speaking, scalded by the royal rage of his master. It had been in Paris where he had politely suggested that a silver cigarette case with an enamelled Royal Cypher was not quite good enough a present for someone of importance and the King's reaction had been immediate and drastic. In bellows which could be heard all over the hotel he had been in danger of choking. But he had not choked and both he and Ponsonby survived to become good friends again. This was chiefly because his Secretary was not a yes-man and, at the same time, was aware what ill-health was doing to his master. He understood perfectly how increasingly difficult the King found it to control his temper, and even before his anxiety about Caesar, he had been severely tried.

Chief vexation of all had naturally been caused by his nephew.

On the way out they had paid the obligatory courtesy call on the German Emperor who, true to form, had made a family meeting into a political occasion and an informal meal into a chance to get on his legs and give an oration which was printed the following day in all the newspapers.

After that Emerald Cunard had thoroughly displeased the King by accepting his invitation to dine and then discussing Elinor Glyn's most risqué novel *Three Weeks.* It was not so much that, properly, at a formal dinner the sovereign or his consort ought to initiate any subject for conversation. King Edward was not over-particular and he would never have expected an American like Sir Bache Cunard's wife to be bound by the courtesies of English Court protocol. But he was incensed because a young unmarried girl happened to be present and he held strictly to the old proprieties that such topics were not for the ears of *une jeune fille*. Oblivious to the menace growing in the air, Lady Cunard twittered on in her birdlike way about the seduction of an Englishman on a tiger skin by a Balkan Queen – a royal lover of great prowess who, according to Mrs Glyn 'Purred as a tiger might have done while undulating like a snake'. The King had choked with rage at this, literally choked, but no sooner had his throat cleared that the unsquashable Emerald was off again reciting the current rhyme:

'Would you like to sin
With Elinor Glyn
On a tiger skin?
Or would you prefer
To err with her
On some other fur?'

– finishing with a shrill peal of laughter before popping a titbit into her mouth.

There followed a dreadful silence.

It came home at last to Emerald Cunard that she was not popular. Her host, his face thunderous, turned his shoulder on her, and began to talk in German on another topic. Afterwards Ponsonby had the unpleasant task of carrying a reprimand to her hotel, a missive so fierce that she kept to her suite for several days.

As if these unpleasantnesses were not enough the King had

walked out of a play called *Die Hölle* because he had thought it would be a melodrama and found, instead, that it was a type of music-hall performance which bored him. At once he was being clapped on the back by sad puritans for standing up for virtue. Bishop Boyd Carpenter of Ripon went so far as to write him a letter expressing the satisfaction of the whole Church at his stand against impropriety in the theatre. The King was impatient and angry at being so misunderstood. He instructed Ponsonby to write to the Bishop the exact truth; that he had no wish to pose as a protector of morals, especially abroad, and that boredom alone had driven him from the theatre.

Then the Austrian Emperor unwittingly upset the King by asking that his Hoffourier be given the G.C.V.O. – to which King Edward felt obliged to consent, but he was horrified to see the Hoffourier standing behind the Emperor's chair at dinner. Afterwards he sought out Ponsonby saying he had given the Grand Cross to 'a blasted footman', and was only with difficulty persuaded that the Imperial Hoffourier was a Comptroller of Supplies with the rank of a colonel, and that he had already been honoured with the Iron Cross.

Really, thought Ponsonby, it was small wonder that his master's flash point was low. Even the French Prime Minister vexed him by coming over from Carlsbad with a gift of plums and staying to luncheon. Mr Clemenceau was anxious to impress the world that it was right for the King of England to see the Premier of his closest ally because he had just taken the salt of the Emperors of Germany and Austria. It was, actually, a neat piece of diplomacy, but King Edward felt out of sorts. This year he thought perhaps he was overdoing the cure and losing weight too rapidly. He did not want to listen to the French Premier pontificating on certain English games and giving his opinion that croquet and tennis were merely excuses for bringing young people together to make love. Golf he was inclined to exclude because he had seen a young man and a woman drive from the tee at a links near Paris and while he had marched off firmly to the left, she had marched with equal firmness to the right. After this conversation, Clemenceau had suddenly started talking real politics, asking what would happen if the Germans marched on Paris through Belgium. . . . The King, appalled by his indiscretion, rapidly drew the meal to a close and took the French Premier off to his own private rooms.

With Clemenceau safely back in Carlsbad, and Caesar on four legs again and as good as new, the King found it easier to enjoy himself. The ageing Mr Hall-Walker told him in great excitement that he believed he had bred a perfect horse through astrological prognostications and, while he doubted the validity of such an unusual breeding method, the King was impressed by the old man's enthusiasm and telegraphed to his trainer to have a look at the beast and, if it looked at all promising, to buy it. In this way Minoru came into the royal stables.

Mr Hall-Walker's young wife was equally willing to pleasure her sovereign. She received him frequently at tea time in her scented rooms with the blinds down, and arranged for him to dine at her hotel one evening and afterwards see a performance by the famous dancer Miss Maud Allen. The King immediately said yes, which put Ponsonby into a great state of perturbation. Miss Allen was an advanced sort of dancer, the pianist who was to accompany her was the leader of the Marienbad orchestra and the correspondent of the *Daily Mail.* Ponsonby contacted the latter and begged his co-operation in making sure that the private display was not reported. He also saw Mrs Hall-Walker and confessed his dismay for someone had told him Miss Allen danced in nothing but two oyster-shells and a five-franc piece. Mrs Hall-Walker reassured him. While diaphanous, Miss Allen's clothing was a little more substantial than he had heard. And would Sir Frederick please accompany the King to dinner and to watch the display so that he could see there was nothing indecent in the dancing.

Ponsonby did this. Indency is difficult to measure. Certainly the dancer and her dancing were remarkable. And King Edward was highly entertained. He sat in his tall backed chair, a little to the front, leaning on his cane, his eyes twinkling. Lewd or not, the dancing pleased him. That was obvious.

7

Three visits in the autumn of 1907 consumed a great deal of Edward's nervous energy.

The first was the easiest, possibly the most pleasant. His friend the Abbot of Tepl came over from Austria and stayed at Windsor.

The entertainment of Roman Catholic prelates was bound to cause rumbles of Protestant thunder. The Defender of the Faith shut his ears to them, showed the Abbot the royal treasures, gave him an honoured place at table and caused even that gourmet to close his eyes in appreciation of some of Mr Menanger's dishes. Then he gave him the K.C.V.O., which the Abbot wore proudly round his neck, and each promised the other the pleasure of renewing their friendship in the following August.

The second visit of the King and Queen of Spain was both informal – at Sandringham, and formal – at Windsor. As much as anything King Edward wanted Alfonso there to serve him against the third and most dreaded visit; that of their Imperial Majesties, the Emperor and Empress of Germany.

Having overcome his revulsion at the very idea of having to invite his nephew for reasons of diplomacy, Edward was determined that the visit should superficially be a success, and he went to great personal trouble to make all the necessary arrangements. Therefore, when he was at Newmarket on the last day of the autumn races, with less than a dozen days to go before Willy and Dona arrived, he was enraged to receive a telegram calmly announcing that the Emperor had had influenza, felt far below par, and under the circumstances would not be coming to England.

It was a golden day outside, the wind blowing leaves across the heath, and the King's private quarters at the Jockey Club were luxuriously appointed. He had had a good day at the races and Alice Keppel was coming to dinner. But now everything was spoilt.

He took off his spectacles, flung down the telegram and rang the Equerry's bell. Fritz Ponsonby answered it. He was at Newmarket in his double capacity as Equerry and Assistant Secretary.

The King speared the air with his beard. 'What,' he asked angrily, 'am I to do about that?'

Ponsonby had seen the telegram earlier, and, conceiving it his duty, had already telephoned Sir Edward Grey in London. He was in a position to pass on the Foreign Minister's view that the discreet hint given to the German Emperor that, on account of the shortage of space at Portsmouth, he should not be escorted by the whole of his High Seas Fleet, had given offence. Hence the diplomatic illness.

Again the King put his head back and speared the air with his beard. 'And you, Fritz, what do you think?'

To his surprise, Ponsonby did not at once reply.

He looked at him sharply. 'Come now, you've something up your sleeve.'

'Rather, in my pocket, Sir.' He drew out a number of German newspaper cuttings and handed them to his master.

The King replaced his spectacles. All the cuttings were from a Berlin newspaper, *Die Zukunft.* He began to read them, at first standing, then sitting at his desk.

Vituperative articles disclosed that Prince Philip zu Eulenburg, former German Ambassador in Vienna and a close friend of the Emperor, who had just been presented with the Black Eagle, together with Count Kuno von Moltke, the City Commandant of Berlin, were notorious *Soldatentanten;* that is, they were emulating the most notable of all Prussians, Frederick the Great, and had a taste for young soldiers. Further, it claimed there was a large company of such offenders against Article 175 of the German Penal Code who were described as the Kaiser's 'camarilla'.

'Muck-raking,' muttered the King. 'And we heard it before when Krupp blew his brains out and Bülow made that offensive remark in the Reichstag.'

Ponsonby sadly shook his head. 'It has been going on all year, Sir,' he said. 'I did not wish to worry you unduly and said nothing because, like you, I thought it was simply a press campaign led by *Die Zukunft* –'

'It isn't?'

'I'm afraid not.' Ponsonby looked away from his master. 'Recently I made it my business to find out how true these charges are. And through our Ambassador and others I hear that a secret military enquiry has resulted in the enforced resignation of certain high-ranking officers.' Involuntarily he paused because the King had made some sort of exclamation, but then, inexorably, he continued: 'There is now much talk of the Emperor of Austria banishing his youngest brother the Archduke Ludwig-Viktor and banishment, for a similar reason, of a blood relative of the Kaiser's, of his A.D.C. and leader of the Regiment Garde du Corps, Count William Hohenau.'

Ponsonby then took from his breast pocket a cutting from a

Munich newspaper and gave it to the King. It was a cartoon showing a crowd of well-dressed gentlemen queueing at a railway station. The caption read 'Moltke's and Eulenburg's friends leaving for Italy'.

'My God!' said the King softly.

Still looking out of the window, Ponsonby went on. 'The scandal has been ballooning for months, and kept from the Emperor because no one dared tell him. Finally the Crown Prince – despite the fact that his cousin was on the list of suspects – has thought it right to inform his father of the facts.'

'My God!' said the King again.

In the same matter-of-fact voice his Secretary continued: 'Eulenburg and Moltke are to be dismissed and the Emperor is almost out of his mind with shame and anger and anxiety. He blames the Jews....'

'He does *what?*' broke in the King.

'The Jews, Sir – he blames the Jews. The owner of *Die Zukunft* is of Jewish origin and the Emperor says a trusted group of friends have been broken up through Jewish insolence, slander and lying.'

The King crushed one hand into the other. 'So that is at the back of his diplomatic illness? That is why he will not come?'

'He is afraid of being laughed at,' said Ponsonby simply.

'Emperors and Kings,' said the King, 'are not afraid of such things.'

He immediately sent a telegram to Berlin to say a cancellation at this stage, unless his nephew were mortally ill, was out of the question. He also directed Grey and his Ambassador in Berlin to bring the strongest possible pressure on the embarrassed Emperor. The embarrassed Emperor gave way. He agreed to come.

The King and Queen of Spain arrived for a private visit to Sandringham on 4 November.

'Alfonso,' said King Edward, drawing him aside after dinner on the first day of their arrival, 'I cannot begin to say how thankful I am to have you both here for Willy's visit.' He suggested they smoke a cigar together in the library. There, after two false starts, he confided what had occurred. To his surprise Alfonso confessed he knew all about the German scandal. He smiled. 'All nations have their troubles, but the German scandal had naturally to be *kolossal.*'

King Edward's smile was only polite. 'You know?'

Alfonso nodded. 'I believe everyone did except Willy.'

'And I.' His uncle mused. 'I had heard bits and pieces, yes; but I took no account of them. So only Willy and I were kept in ignorance. He for obvious reasons. . . .' His voice trailed off. Hurriedly he looked away from his guest. Ponsonby had only revealed the facts when he judged it was unavoidable. Knollys still did not refer to them. Grey had been unusually vague for so crisp a diplomat. Now, at last, he realized why. Eighteen years before one of his own equerries had fled the country just ahead of the police for having an affair with a telegraph boy. But worse, worse by far, his own elder son had been intersexual and so indiscreet that he had had to be rushed out to India for a time. Dearly as he had loved Eddy, both he and Queen Victoria had seen his early death as perhaps providential for the throne. Eddy had been too unstable, too unreliable, too easily led, altogether too naïf to manage the Crown of England....

Knowing all this, and aware of his deep feelings on the subject, his Household had kept quiet about the German scandal, not wishing to wound him afresh. The King felt he was well served.

'Alfonso,' he said. 'Did you know my son Eddy?'

The King of Spain said yes, but not at all intimately, simply as part of 'the royal mob'.

King Edward told him the story, keeping nothing back, and felt the better for it. He confessed it made him more understanding of the German Emperor's present predicament. 'Not,' he added, drawing on his cigar, 'that it will make him any easier as a guest. He is always difficult to please, so particular and prickly. This time he will be more prickly than ever.'

'If he is,' advised King Alfonso with a laugh, 'I should silence him with two words "Tutu" and "Phili".'

'Moltke and Eulenburg?'

The other nodded. 'His own names for them. You can understand how distressed he is.'

'I can,' said the King. 'But, if he is difficult, I shall remember those names.' He repeated them. 'Phili and Tutu. God bless my soul! Tutu and Phili!'

. . . . .

From the moment he stepped ashore from the Imperial yacht *Hohenzollern* to be greeted by the Prince of Wales, the German Emperor was on the defensive. This made him strut and appear more like the caricature of himself than he really was.

His host had been provided with a long list of subjects the Emperor might wish to discuss, for his nephew was temperamentally incapable of keeping politics out of a conversation for long; but when any subject was broached the King took the easy way, confessed he was out of his depth in such diplomatic waters and advised the Emperor to discuss the matter with his ministers. Their antipathy to each other was barely varnished over by King Edward's good manners.

A number of the royal mob were in England for the marriage of Prince Charles of Bourbon to Princess Louise of Orleans, and they were invited to Windsor to meet the Emperor and Empress of Germany and the King and Queen of Spain. Twenty-four senior royalties sat down to a sumptuous luncheon; an assembly which in no one's experience had ever been rivalled. What an opportunity for the anarchists, exclaimed the King, and his nephew Willy, who seldom saw a joke unless it was a practical one and caused someone else distress, immediately demanded to know full details of the arrangements made for everyone's security. King Alfonso quickly and charmingly soothed the difficult moment by relating an anecdote of Bernadotte, the General whom Napoleon had made King of Sweden. None of the royal family, not even his closest attendants, were aware until his death that King Bernadotte had tatooed across his chest: '*Mort aux Roi.*'

Three days later the Emperor was invited to shoot at Virginia Water, and made the greatest possible fuss of his Uncle Arthur, the Duke of Connaught, to demonstrate that he was by far his favourite uncle. The Duke was not all that fond of his brother, but he thoroughly disliked his nephew and, aware of what he was up to, was positively chilling towards the Emperor. By the time a *déjeuner de chasse* was arranged in George IV's Fishing Temple – an extravaganza of Swiss chalet mixed with Chinese pagoda – and the ladies had joined the party, not even Alfonso of Spain could keep the peace. There were mince pies because Alix, recalling that mincemeat was a favourite of the Emperor, had deliberately included them on the menu, but he declared that to eat a mince pie in England before Christmas was unlucky and forbade his suite to touch them. King Edward, his brother, and their sister Beatrice promptly ate barely anything else.

What the politicians were up to the King neither knew nor cared. All he longed for was the 18th when the official visit came to an end. But when the 18th did arrive only the Empress returned to Germany. The Emperor said he was staying on a further month as the private guest of a friend in Bournemouth.

The King fumed, but he could do nothing about it.

His bad temper spread in various directions. He ordered that Florence Nightingale was to be given the O.M. as much as anything because Willy had no one in his Empire quite like that apparently indestructible old lady. When, on Guy Fawkes' Day, the Cabinet voted that he should accept the Transvaal's gift of the Cullinan Diamond, he agreed with enthusiasm because a diamond weighing about a pound and a quarter in the rough would make his nephew's mouth water. He complained because Campbell-Bannerman's ministerial reports were so brief that he was being denied information and the suspicion grew in him that the Liberals regarded him as a cypher. When old Lord Roberts, the champion of the Boer War, complained about the new Territorial Army, the King thoughtlessly took his side, declaring that Roberts ought to know what he was talking about, whereas Haldane was 'a damned radical lawyer and a German professor'. When a trade-unionist told a congress of his fellows that the King was 'almost the only statesman left and certainly the greatest of our kings since William the Conqueror', Edward swallowed it whole and swelled like a toad with pride.

In fact the Emperor's childish behaviour had so got on his nerves that he responded by being childish himself. He badly needed to be shaken back into his real self again.

An event which, because of its commonness, he might have ordinarily accepted as sad but inevitable, did this for him.

A man of whom he was not particularly fond, indeed, whom he did not fully trust, but who was his President of the Board of Trade, had recently concluded a brilliant piece of negotiation between railway directors and railwaymen and averted an almost certain strike. Sir Henry had congratulated David Lloyd George at a Lord Mayor's Banquet, and the King had noted with approval that even such a jack-in-office was getting something done. Now, without warning. David Lloyd George lost his eldest and best-beloved daughter, who died of appendicitis at the age of seventeen, and he was a stricken man, refusing to leave his office, sleeping there on the floor where his friends remained with him in case he lost his reason or tried to take his own life.

The King heard of it by chance. He was at Sandringham. Sir Dighton Probyn mentioned Lloyd George's loss and how badly he had taken it. Edward asked Probyn what the girl was named. Neither he nor anyone else appeared to know. He requested that enquiries be made by telephone. The name was brought to him, written on a square of paper: Mair Eilund Lloyd George.

He excused himself from the company and walked upstairs to Eddy's room. After the fashion of the day it had not been touched, save by cleaning servants, since the day his eldest son died after seven hours of fevered heavings. Even then, at the moment Eddy died, his father had known it was better for England, but simultaneously he had suffered more than at any other time in his life. He knelt at the foot of the bed where George had knelt at the moment Eddy died. He knew quite well what agony David Lloyd George was suffering in his London office.

Suffering put things into proportion.

Suddenly he realized his detestation of Willy and their long vendetta put the important things of life out of all proportion.

Wordlessly he prayed for Mair Eilund and for his son Eddy that they would rest in peace. He prayed, too, for the suffering man he would never be able to like.

8

The King had a few close patrician friends who loved him simply for what he was, but others in the aristocracy who, almost without exception, were less close to him, were critical because he was so free with American kings of commerce, *arrivistes* and Jews.

He was at pains to defend those to whom he had given the entrée to his Court, asking how England could manage now without them? The American kings of commerce had buttressed a number of crumbling noble houses with well-dowered daughters, and the stability of the Empire now depended on the capitalists who had risen to the top in the industrial revolution. As for the Jews he reminded their critics that hospitals and other charitable organizations had benefited enormously from his Jewish friends, and asked roguishly how he and many other spendthrifts could possibly have managed without the expert advice of the Rothschilds and Sir Ernest Cassel.

His argument did not impress those who disliked his Court. They deeply resented the parvenus, especially the Jews. No doubt this was because the Jews had been so successful in the tolerant Society of England. Cassel, for example, had started life as an apprentice banker in Cologne and his acumen brought him such riches that he imported eight hundred tons of Carrara marble for his Park Lane house and had it entirely decorated by Duveen. But the Rothschilds especially made their detractors cross. In four short generations one family had managed to dominate much of international finance. And the Rothschilds particularly offended the natural English distaste for the flaunting of riches. Their opulence allowed their excesses to be towering: they kept packs and packs of hounds, huge yachts, strings of racehorses and built mansions in London and palaces in the countryside, creating pleasure grounds out of wildernesses, moving fully grown trees to stud their parklands and make pheasant coverts, and provided the most lavish and eccentric entertainments in Society. Added to this, Lord Natty was a despot and, now that Lord Randolph Churchill was dead, the rudest man in England. King Edward, however, missed the most cutting edge of his old friend's tongue, and he enjoyed the Rothschild opulence. Indeed, having the same luxurious tastes and much resembling a Jew, the old story was dragged up that the King's father had been the bastard of a half-Hebrew army officer.

Good naturedly Edward took little notice of these barbs. Nevertheless, feeling as he did, and because he thought it disgraceful that the German Emperor should automatically blame the Jews for the Moltke–Eulenburg scandal, Edward made a demonstration of his partiality by accepting the advice of his Jewish physician, Sir Felix Semon, and running down to Brighton to stay with the Jewish family of Sassoons just after a strenuous though enjoyable house-party at Chatsworth.

The Sassoons, via Baghdad, Bushire, Persia and Bombay, had travelled from Spain to England in the course of four centuries and now enjoyed a special position in Society as sportsmen and cultured philanthropists. The King went stalking with Arthur Sassoon in Scotland, racing with his brother Reuben, and was frequently the guest of their brother Edward Albert who had a charming villa in the bracing air of Brighton. Worried by the critical bronchial attacks the King had suffered in the last three winters, Semon wanted him to escape the fogs and infections of London, the mists of the Thames Valley, and that piercing wind which swept uninterrupted from the Arctic Circle to the Great House at Sandringham. There were few people about in Brighton and the King liked to walk as the Prince Regent had done along the promenade, not being pestered by gaping subjects, and able to do what he called his 'Brighton Exercise'. This included marching at a steady pace, breathing in and breathing out while counting under his breath and then crying 'Ozone! Ozone! There's nothing like it.'

Fortified by a week of this Brighton Exercise, he was obliged to return to London, and there, within days, he suffered another bronchial attack. Sir Felix Semon was hurriedly sent for. He found the King impatient with the inhalations, camphor rubbings, and sponging. It was actually a good sign. If he had the spirits to be vexed by the constant ministrations of his nurses, the attack was unlikely to last long. Nevertheless the King gave Semon a piece of his mind. 'Here I am,' he said petulantly, glaring at his physician. 'Here I am. In bed again. And I've taken the greatest care of myself. The *greatest* care.'

'As soon as we can,' said Sir Felix, 'we must get you to Biarritz.'

'Semon, you sent me to Brighton to keep me clear of all this.' Edward waved at the battery of phials, kidney dishes, evaporators, towels and other medical supplies which stood on a table against the wall.

'For one moment, Sir, I must ask you to stop talking and roll over. I wish to listen to your wheezes.'

Ordinarily he would have asked a patient to lean forward. In the King's case it was becoming increasingly difficult. Hawkins removed the mountain of pillows behind his master and helped him to ease himself down the bed. The King grumbled as he rolled over, grumbled as the physician applied his stethoscope, grumbled still more when he firmly tapped his back with the ends of two fingers.

'Hawkins!' he croaked. Lying on his front was particularly uncomfortable to him. Hawkins helped to roll him back. 'And now,' said the King sourly, 'I suppose you wish to push and prod all over my chest?'

'That, Sir, is my intention. From my preliminary examination it seems you are on the mend. In fact you are much better. But I must make sure or you will be smoking those terrible cigars again. And be comforted, Sir. You will not have me to push and prod you much longer.'

'Eh!' The King sat up.

'I must beg you to lie down, Sir,' said Semon, gently pressing his sovereign's abdomen. He and Hawkins eased the patient back on to his pillows. 'You have forgotten, possibly, that I am retiring very soon.'

'But not from me, Semon? I beg you, not from me.'

Sir Felix smiled and began to tap and listen. Afterwards he pocketed his stethoscope.

'I am at liberty to retire from my practice,' he said. 'But as a subject I can never be free from Your Majesty's commands.'

Edward eyed him. 'Do you understand Sir Felix, Hawkins?' he demanded.

'Yes, your Majesty.'

'Well I don't,' snapped the King.

Lord Knollys explained a little later when he came into the King's room with a despatch box. He suggested that Sir Felix could be made a Physician Extraordinary and so still remain in the Royal Household.

'An excellent plan.' The King rubbed his hands together. 'If, of course, he gets me through this.'

Lord Knollys seized on the opportunity. He had not quite known how to present his bad news. 'Of course he will, Sir, and have you away to Biarritz as soon as possible. You are, in fact, more fortunate than some other sovereigns.'

The King looked quickly at the despatch box.

His Private Secretary did not at once open it. 'There is bad news from Portugal, Sir.'

The King sat forward. Hawkins hurried to put yet another pillow to support him. Portugal had been seething with political trouble for months and finally, with the King's approval, a dictator had seized power, ruling subject only to the throne.

Knollys opened the box and handed the King a despatch. Simultaneously Hawkins placed a pair of gold-framed spectacles on his nose. The King's hand was already trembling. It trembled further as he read that on driving to Lisbon with his Queen and two sons, the King had been fired on by a pair of Republican riflemen. He and his elder son the Crown Prince had died instantly. The second son, Don Manoel, had his arm smashed by a bullet. Only Queen Amélie had miraculously escaped. The assassins had immediately been cut to pieces by the escort and the dictator had fled the country. . . .

King Edward dropped the paper. Genial, bluff, portly Carlos who so loved sport and English beef and pork, and who had been his guest so short a time before, was dead.

Knollys returned it to the despatch box. 'I regret that you have lost a friend and a fellow sovereign, Sir. My profound sympathies.'

The King nodded. When he found his voice he thanked his Private Secretary. 'Will you see to all that needs to be done?'

'I shall, Sir.'

A quarter of an hour later Sir Felix Semon came into the room. He had been quietly summoned by the valet Hawkins. He took the King's wrist to measure his pulse and listened as the King told him what had happened, his voice choked with sobs. 'The tragedy is that it was unnecessary,' he cried. 'Carlos was a good, good man. But he was not wise as a king. A constitutional king cannot allow dictators to take over the duties of Parliament.'

Sir Felix mixed a draught at the medicine table and gave it to the King, who pulled a face. 'You said I was much better,' he pleaded.

'You are, Sir, but this will do you good.'

When he had drunk it, the King smiled. It was champagne and brandy. 'Now I feel better still,' he said. 'Semon, will you help me to do something? You will not wish to. But under the circumstances I hope you will.'

'No physician should commit himself,' came the cautious reply.

'All I wish for is your permission to attend a memorial service. No,' he added, holding up his hand because Semon's mouth had already opened to object – 'hear me out, please. It must be soon to show my feelings and the feelings of my people. And you shall have permission to wrap me in layers of wool, if it is necessary. But I must mourn King Carlos publicly. He was not only a friend. He was a King. A member of my trade union.'

Sir Felix did not reply for a moment. Then he shrugged. 'Perhaps,' he admitted, 'royal physicians are apt to be overcareful with their patients. It is natural. Very well, Sir, you may go, but only on condition that you do wrap up well and that you do not try to strain yourself in any way.'

'That,' said the King solemnly, 'I promise.'

'And soon we shall get you off to Biarritz – where you will stay twice your normal length of time?'

'Very well,' agreed the King.

By way of expressing their disgust at the assassination of King Carlos and his heir the King and Queen of England, with many members of their family, not only attended a memorial service in St Paul's, but also attended a Requiem at St James' Church, Spanish Place, with a full Sovereign's Escort. It was a touching gesture but it raised howls of execration from the Protestant Alliance. It was the first time an English sovereign had attended a Roman Catholic service since the reign of James II, and the bigoted invective which burst over the King simply served to depress further a man who was already depressed enough. He longed to get away, but his doctors would not permit it until he had sufficient strength for the journey. When he had, and he was officially cleared, he went at once to Downing Street.

Sir Henry Campbell-Bannerman had not been at all well for some months. Advised by the King to try Biarritz, he had gone there, but the sun and sea air had failed to do him any good. He had managed to move an Address to the Crown on 4 February in which Parliament expressed its 'indignation and deep concern' at the assassinations in Portugal, but afterwards he had returned to be in his official residence. Far too unwell to go and see the King, he was deeply moved by the sovereign's concern in personally coming to see him in Downing Street.

'They say, Sir, I should resign,' he murmured in dejection. 'And perhaps I should.'

The King sat on a high-backed chair beside Sir Henry's bed and pressed his hand. 'You would be the first to tell me the

Sovereign must keep himself apart from party affairs and so I cannot advise you. But I can and do say my doctors are at your disposal, that if you wish to try the air in Norfolk or Balmoral you must feel yourself free to go there when and for as long as you like, and that champagne, taken in moderation, is the best medicine in the world.'

'Dear Sir,' said the Prime Minister.

'Dear Sir Henry,' returned his King.

Before he left on the following day King Edward consulted privately with Mr Asquith, who was deputizing for the Prime Minister. He was not over-fond of Asquith, a scholar and sharp lawyer who varnished over his skills with a dreamy, even careless attitude. He believed that beneath all this varnish he was as much an upside-downer as the full-blooded radicals Lloyd George and Burns, and found the eccentricities of his second wife, Margot, quite intolerable. Nevertheless he was prepared to tolerate, if not trust him, and was glad to hear that, should it be necessary, Mr Asquith would gladly travel out to Biarritz to talk with the King about future developments within the Government. This was a dressed-up way of saying he would go there to accept the office of Prime Minister if Campbell-Bannerman died.

Biarritz was particularly lovely in March 1907. Day after day the long unbroken Atlantic waves rolled on to the shore, but the Duke of Devonshire was not there to watch them like a Celtic bard. He had been taken to Cannes by Louisa, and there he died quite unexpectedly of pneumonia and with a characteristic last utterance: 'Well, the game's over and I'm not sorry.'

Pulled down by his own illness and Sir Henry's, and the assassinations in Portugal, the King found it hard to bear the death of his old, old friend. It meant, too, that there would be no more Chatsworth winter parties because Devonshire's heir was a nephew. Louisa was now a Dowager Double-Duchess.

In order to lessen the strain of stair-climbing the King had been given apartments on the ground floor of the Hôtel du Palais and not his usual first-floor suite. This did him as much harm as it did good, for he could no longer enjoy the full panorama of the coast.

The modification of his diet was almost as useless. Feeling despondent he only wished for certain dishes. Denied them, he either deliberately pushed away the recommended, nourishing food and ate nothing, or glowered with anger until he got what he wanted.

The beginning of the King's six-week holiday could hardly be counted a success.

For the first time Sir Ernest Cassel got on his nerves. No man with pains in the small of his back and in his thighs and who wheezed and blew like a sea cow was in the frame of mind to be soothed by stories of fiscal triumphs, no matter how well recounted. And Sir Ernest's risqué jokes, culled from many sources for the King's delectation, barely achieved more than a wan grin. Ordinarily most would have triggered off a burst of that happy, gurgling, infectious laughter.

Ponsonby, who was there as Secretary, had to bother the King with work. He recognized it was essential, because it looked as though Campbell-Bannerman was dying and Asquith would have to come out to Biarritz, and he knew Fritz Ponsonby would not bother him with trivialities. Nevertheless he felt old and bad-tempered and utterly jaded and he did not want to work at all.

Hawkins failed him too – or appeared to – by not being sensitive to his needs. If he wished to sit in a particular chair at the window Hawkins was as slow as a carthorse in finding him a footstool. If he wished to rest on the sofa at the end of his bed, Hawkins piled too many rugs on him. If he wished for an extra pillow Hawkins brought a hard one. If he wished for a little hock and seltzer, almost certainly the drink would be too warm or too cool.

The King even managed to find fault with Alice Keppel.

Mrs George had minor worries of her own. Sonia was old enough to be reasoned with and yet she paid small heed to her mother's strict warning to keep out of the King's way, and tended to bother him by being bright and active when he felt at his most bearlike and simply wanted to be left alone. And Mrs George's elder daughter was also continuing to cause her anxiety. She and her friend Vita Sackville-West and another girl had gone off with chaperones to see Florence for the first time. Her letters were infrequent and what she said a mere gush of girlish excitement at travelling apart from her mother, but Mrs George read in between the lines a condemnation of her own double life and what Violet openly called the dreary round of Crichel, Melbury, Biarritz, Duntreath, and Portman Square. Violet also made no secret of the fact that apart from her handsome saint of a papa, she found all men objectionable, in fact foul.

Made distrait by these worries and the invalidish atmosphere in the Hôtel du Palais, Alice found herself unable to attend one hundred per cent to all the King's needs and moods. And this he required. She managed to show sufficient interest when at last the Prime Minister resigned and Mr Asquith travelled out to kiss hands on taking office, but she was not up to comforting him when this simple act provoked widespread criticism, especially from *The Times*, where, in a vitriolic leader, it was implied that the King had failed in his duty. He was so angry at this that he made enquiries and discovered it had been written by an ex-army officer, Colonel Repington, who had nursed a grudge against King Edward for not intervening on his behalf when he had been obliged to send in his papers on account of some discreditable divorce proceedings. It was nothing more than a personal vendetta, raged the King, and a disgrace to serious journalism; and he berated poor Alice for not being more sympathetic.

His anger jolted her into a better appreciation of his condition. Still dejected by the physical effects of his illness, he needed special understanding. From that time she gave it, unremittingly, telling the nurse to keep Sonia away from the King on pain of instant dismissal, and devoting as much time as Edward wished to hearing a recitation of his woes.

Some were imagined grievances which no one could soothe.

Of the real woes, they varied from his distress that, barely a fortnight after his resignation, the genial Sir Henry had died, and his grief that Queen Ena had given birth to a second son who was a deaf mute, to his indignation that the suffragettes were behaving in so frightful a fashion: a Miss Ogston wielding a whip in the Albert Hall and thrashing several men. He had other troubles too. It was not his wont to criticize his wife, but not being himself he did so on this occasion. In April they were to make a State Visit to the three Scandinavian Kingdoms and getting Alix to agree to prearranged plans had been an infuriating business, only made possible because he had written to the King of Denmark begging his co-operation in compelling his sister to be reasonable. Arguing and pestering Alix had worn his nerves to shreds. It might be, he added with an uncharacteristic touch of malice, that this anxiety alone had been sufficient to start off his illness again.

Without committing herself – and probably it would have shocked the King if Alice had been outspoken about his wife – his mistress managed to soothe this particular grudge. She soothed too his anxieties that his grandson Prince David might have inherited the Danish family deafness pointing out that, if this was so, he would have heard about it by now.

Because she knew Edward so well, and because by now the bland air of Biarritz was soothing his inflamed lungs, Alice chanced raising his spirits by a method which sometimes succeeded but, if it failed, would have brought down his wrath upon her. This was to exasperate him about matters which were really insignificant but which he happened to think important.

Cleverly she began by telling him that a Daylight Saving Society had just been formed by a Chelsea builder who wanted to put the clocks back one hour. Instantly the King was on his feet – a week before he could not have managed that – and, pacing the room, sternly asked what everyone proposed to do with the daylight that was saved. He got himself quite worked up about it and had to ring for Hawkins to bring him a pill.

Mrs George's second move was more adventurous. Casually she mentioned that, as if to keep one jump ahead of his fellow monarchs, the German Emperor had bought from the King of Greece the villa in Corfu which had belonged to the Austrian Empress. There, it was announced, he intended to give his patronage to eminent archaeologists, the German Imperial Court being the last repository of royal culture in Europe.

The King refused to believe it. It was a leg-pull. No Emperor could make so arrogant a claim. But when persuaded that his nephew had done just that, Edward stamped up and down his sitting-room, his voice vibrating with his annoyance. It was perfect medicine to enliven his spirits.

Biarritz did the rest.

At the end of his six-week stay the King returned to make his State Visit of the Scandinavian Kingdoms, a journey which earned each member of his suite the stars of three Orders, and so was renamed by one of them the Hennessy trip.

As ever platitudinous, the King's talk and letters were suddenly full of reference to silver linings, more than one fish in the sea, things easily being far worse, and *nil desperandum,* the wish being father to the thought, and never saying die.

Things *were* looking up.

One of the greatest triumphs of his time as Prince of Wales had been leading his Derby winner *Persimmon* into the box at Epsom in 1896. Certainly the brightest jewel in the crown of the Sandringham stable, Persimmon had died earlier in the year. Now the Natural History Museum wanted the skeleton of such an exceptional horse, and the museum, founded by Papa, should have it. The King rubbed his hands.

Then there was the story which made Edward laugh so much that he fell into a dangerous fit of coughing. Patsy's daughter, Daisy of Pless, had had her bottom pinched at a religious function in Seville Cathedral during Holy Week – instantly she had turned and slapped the nearest male face.

Finally, he had a photograph which Probyn had given him, and which gave him endless pleasure. It showed the gallant Sir Dighton himself, dressed elegantly in a grey top hat, his foot-length white whiskers blowing madly in the wind, sitting beside 'the Blessed Lady' Queen Alexandra – she in a toque and veil and with her hand on a parasol. But it was no ordinary picture of his Consort and his Privy Purse sitting side by side on a garden bench or a drawing-room sofa. On a visit to the White City, Alix had amazed everyone by insisting on taking a trip on the Canadian Mountain Railway, and there she was with Sir Dighton amongst a crowd of fellow daredevils photographed on their up and down switchback affair. It must surely be counted as one of the most extraordinary portraits in the history of English royalty.

9

King Edward's platitudes were of a different kind when describing the abrupt and painful eruption of a boil which had festered in the Senior Service for years past. But then the Fisher–Beresford quarrel had been kept within the Service. Now it was threatening to be divisive in Society.

Fisher was sure he had the Royal Family on his side, noting breezily in his diary:

'I had a private séance with Princess Victoria by her wish at Buckingham Palace, and she told me about all Society being worked up against me but the King and Queen and herself solid as a rock, but George rather wobbly.'

Fisher, however, was a simple man as well as a visionary – a not uncommon combination amongst reformers.

His diary entry was something of an exaggeration.

While the Queen found him an attractive character and supported him to the full, Princess Victoria was the cleverest member of the family and she was not entirely taken in by his gaiety and charm. The King liked him, yes; but he was a constitutional monarch and would be led by his First Lord of the Admiralty not the First Sea Lord. As for George, Prince of Wales, whilst genuinely approving of Fisher's keenness for dreadnoughts and essential reforms in the Navy, he deeply regretted the man's cut and thrust methods of trying to get his own way.

Fisher's chief opponent, Admiral Lord Charles Beresford, had the die-hard's unintelligent suspicion of any innovation in the Service. He also had an unlikeable lofty attitude to Fisher because of his humble origins, and had been known to enquire offensively in the hearing of the First Sea Lord's most ardent supporters: 'Who, I wonder, is Fisher?' But he got as good as he gave – Fisher describing him publicly with boisterous alliteration as 'that bloody, rebellious bastard Beresford'.

At a Levée held at Buckingham Palace on 11 May 1908, the ripe boil burst.

Fisher was there in his capacity as Senior Naval A.D.C. to the King, and Beresford was there as Commander of the Channel Fleet.

Fisher, as was his duty, approached Beresford and put out his hand. The Irishman looked at the proffered hand with unfeigned disgust. He then deliberately turned his back on Fisher.

There was a gasp from a large crowd of officers, ministers and members of the Household who saw this happen. It was followed by a silence in that part of the Throne Room. Then everyone desperately started talking at once, glancing covertly to see if the King had seen this overt piece of insubordination to a senior officer and his own A.D.C. at a royal Levée. From the King's high colour they judged he had.

King Edward sent for Mr Asquith and the First Lord of the Admiralty Mr Reginald McKenna.

He told them what had occurred, though it was quite unnecessary; almost everyone in England, certainly all the matelots and ship's boys in the Navy, already knew.

He said he knew that he, as sovereign, must be impartial, that they as his ministers could only advise what was best in the country's interests. Nevertheless, his own Court had been insulted. His Senior Naval A.D.C. had been ridiculed by a junior officer at a Levée. He trusted that the Cabinet would see its way to order Admiral Lord Charles Beresford to haul down his flag and retire.

There was a fluttering of hands in almost oriental deprecation. Lord Charles had seriously offended, of course....

'Well?' said the King loudly. He realized he was about to see the opening of a political box of tricks, and in this, at least, he was not disappointed.

Mr McKenna pleaded that he had not been long enough at the Admiralty to be fully informed on the unfortunate schism which existed in the Navy. His predecessor, Lord Tweedmouth, while passing on certain facts had not been quite explicit in this matter.

There was more oriental fluttering of hands in deprecation while the King reflected that if only people had appreciated much earlier that Tweedmouth was going off his head, the split would not have become so wide. And it was rather obvious the poor man was doing so. Besides causing great mischief by mishandling a private but unhappily phrased letter about naval affairs from the Kaiser, he also formally submitted, through the King's Private Secretary, that he had fifteen young and unmarried nieces who would be delighted to stage a little variety entertainment for their monarch, followed by a stand-up supper. Clearly Tweedmouth was off his head. Yet Asquith on discovering this had merely moved him from the Admiralty where he had done colossal harm to be

Lord President of the Council – which Tweedmouth gratefully described as 'a charming post'!

'Well, Prime Minister?' said the King, to force something from the silent man.

Asquith was as vacillating as the First Lord had been, repeating that his Ministry was a new one. Lord Charles' rudeness to Sir John Fisher was known to all his colleagues, but, individually and collectively, they did see a difference between regrettable conduct in the Palace and regrettable conduct on any of the naval establishment. . . .

'What,' cut in the King relentlessly, because he was already tired of Mr Asquith. 'What is your advice?'

The Prime Minister at least gave the impression that he was considering, and had not worked it all out before the audience. At length he said: 'As your Senior Naval A.D.C. has been insulted, Sir, we believe you should request an apology from Admiral Lord Charles Beresford.'

'To whom?' snapped the King.

'To you, Sir, of course.'

'Not to Fisher?'

Evidently not to Fisher.

Asquith and McKenna went on and on. Very skilful they were, too.

Eventually the King said. 'I shall ask for nothing from Lord Charles. I leave this matter, gentlemen, entirely in your hands.'

It was the most abrupt ending of any audience he had given during his reign.

In all Edward's experience only two people of consequence had ever dared to threaten him with publication of his peccadilloes, proclaiming arrogantly to their friends that they held the Crown of England in their hands. One had been Jenny's husband, Randolph Churchill, a man long dead; the other was that mischief-making busybody Charlie Beresford. So far as the King was concerned it had put them beyond the pale and Edward could never bring himself to forgive either. Yet he was determined to be correct and show strict impartiality in the war which blazed between the naval diehards and what was known as 'the Fishpond'.

Therefore, when invited by Beresford to review the Channel

Fleet he did so, but he and Alix went to Portsmouth without enthusiasm and their letters of thanks afterwards were not entirely sincere. And both were models of circumspection, restraining their elation when, that December, Beresford was at last relieved of his command. Far more surprising and creditable, both managed to restrain their indignation when somehow Beresford still held on to his post for a further six months and then was carried shoulder high through Portsmouth dockyard and given a hero's send-off. Neither was surprised to hear that within two days Beresford was threatening Asquith with the press nor as a result that Asquith promptly undertook to appoint a Commission to look into charges brought by Beresford against Fisher.

But Charles Beresford's high-handedness marked an end of the royal patience. The Queen became an out-and-out member of the Fishpond. The King was acid in his comments on the supineness of Asquith's cabinet, and from that time would hear nothing in Beresford's favour, not even from his own son, George. He was sick to death of the intrigues in the Senior Service and thoroughly shocked because Beresford intrigued for as long as the Commission sat. He did not go unrewarded. The government had given way. When the Commission's findings were made public they vindicated everything Fisher had done, but in such milk-and-water terms that Beresford had really won the battle.

Edward was disgusted. When McKenna hinted that Fisher would be asked to retire in a few months' time, the King instantly told him that Sir John would remain his Senior Naval A.D.C. and demanded a peerage for him. A viscountcy at least was his desert. Asquith, with a meanness the King thought intolerable, would not give him more than a barony.

When the time came for his retirement the King wrote in his own hand to Fisher thanking him for all he had done for England.

> *'Time will show what admirable reforms you have created in the Royal Navy, and you can afford to treat with the contempt that it deserves "those backbiters" who have endeavoured to calumniate you!'*

The King was sad to see Jackie Fisher go, and dumbfounded by the baseness which was at the back of his dismissal. Almost totally disillusioned by the manners of the new politicians and the ways of the new diplomacy, he reflected that there must be something wrong with the world.

Edward had reached the age when he liked to plan well ahead and not have his plans upset. He wished life to flow like a calm sea, but, even before they had finally stabbed Fisher – and given two or three twists to the wound – Asquith's Cabinet contrived to make the life of their sovereign toss and heave like the Channel in a gale.

First, quite reasonably, they advised a State Visit to Russia, but Chandler barely had time to look out the King's shaggy uniform as Honorary Colonel of the 27th Dragoon Regiment of Kiev before Asquith had changed his mind. For reasons of security it was decided the visit should only be a quasi-State affair; the two monarchs meeting on their respective private yachts off the Baltic port of Reval.

Readjusting his mind to this unwelcome but possibly sensible change, Edward was aghast to hear it might not take place at all. Asquith was under heavy bombardment from his left. The radicals in his party and all the Socialists were strongly against any sort of discussions with an autocrat. To the King's indignation Keir Hardie, the Leader of the Labour Party, accused him of condoning atrocities, and another Socialist, Ramsay MacDonald, called his nephew the Tsar 'a common murderer'. In a division many members of the House of Commons voted against the visit.

Edward declared he had had enough. The names of three particular offenders were at once struck from the list of invitations to a Royal Garden Party for parliamentarians. One was Fritz Ponsonby's brother Arthur, who, declared the King, ought to have known better.

Instantly there was a flare-up. In the radical press the monarch was accused of unconstitutional behaviour in bringing pressure to bear on the Commons. Hardie stated he would never again attend a royal function. Ramsay MacDonald, quite unable to separate in his mind the personality of the Tsar himself and the régime he headed, became more acidulous and offensive about Nicholas II, and his public strictures on the King – who by custom could make no public reply – were such as had not been heard since the days of Ruby Nose Cromwell himself. The King's postbag was packed with condemnatory letters. His only solace was a letter of explanation and apology from Arthur Ponsonby who was persuaded he had done wrong to attack the King for accepting what was, after all, official Cabinet advice.

It was in a mood of deep despondency that the King prepared to leave with the Queen for Russia. Seeing a picture on show of the uncompleted Victoria Memorial he murmured audibly: 'Well, we'll all be in our graves long before *that's* finished!' A remark which was widely reported in the press. It was typical of his state of mind and perhaps accounted for his permitting Sir Ernest Cassel to interest him in floating a Russian loan, an idea which the King's wiser friends considered deplorable. He was warned by Knollys and Esher that he ought not to be mixed up in any sort of financial transaction. Earl Carrington and Lord Redesdale murmured that it would never do. But the King had been stung by the Socialists and on this occasion he refused to accept good advice.

Simultaneously he received from his good friends the Rothschild brothers an entirely disinterested but sincere appeal for him to speak to the Tsar about the fate of the Jews in Russia. Pogroms against Jews were a regular feature of Russian life and no one, not even the revolutionaries, had any thoughts of altering it. By both the Foreign and Diplomatic Services the King was advised under no circumstances to mix himself in a question of such considerable political importance.

The royal yacht *Victoria and Albert* weighed anchor on a fine day in June. For political discussions Hardinge and the British Ambassador at St Petersburg were on board. Admiral Fisher and General French were also there as special guests. Escorted by cruisers and torpedo-destroyers, the yacht got under way for Kiel.

It was not an uneventful voyage.

A gale blew up in the North Sea and threw the royal yacht about. The Queen and Miss Charlotte who were pouring out tea were hurled across the dining saloon and ended in a corner heaped with bread and butter, cakes, biscuits and sugar.

After that they were made to feel small by the German Emperor. In order to point out that any sort of agreement with Russia would constitute the encirclement he feared, he made the *Victoria and Albert* run the gauntlet of his imperial strength. Greeted at the approaches to Kiel canal by nine-tenths of the entire High Sea

Fleet – which made the King thank God for Jackie Fisher – the royal yacht then had to steam along mile after mile of canal lined with masses of the finest and largest cavalry regiments in Europe.

It was a relief to drop almost immediately into a pea-souper in the Baltic.

Whether the Reval meeting could be counted a diplomatic success or not the King was never informed. He and his party were exceedingly well looked after by the Russian Imperial Family aboard the yachts *Standart* and *Polar Star*. There were many exchange visits between the royal and imperial yachts, deck games, banquets and balls – at which Admiral Fisher whirled about in the *Merry Widow* waltz with the Grand Duchess Olga and declared he adored her – and even a concert given from an adjacent steamer on which was a massed women's choir – all the ladies having been stripped and searched for bombs and daggers beforehand. There were talks with Stolypin and his Foreign Secretary, and, as a politeness, the King created his nephew an Admiral of the Fleet.

But on his return no one seemed satisfied.

Sir Ernest was told that the Tsar would receive him if he cared to go to Russia, which was as far as anyone could expect him to commit himself, but this did not altogether please Cassel, who had hoped for more.

The Rothschilds were informed that the King had spoken to M. Stolypin about ameliorating the lot of Jewry in Russia, but a frigid reply came from Lord Rothschild who said he had little confidence in Stolypin and was disinclined to express a satisfaction he did not feel. He was also curt about Cassel, saying his self-interest in the Russian visit was a disgrace.

As for the government, Asquith lectured the King for making the Tsar an Admiral of the Fleet. His back benchers were being difficult again. . . .

Edward was not having this. He insisted that no matter what the coal heavers and dockers in Asquith's party thought, the Tsar was a good-natured gentleman, easily led, maybe, but not the man of blood they said he was. What was done was done. Nicholas II of Russia was an Admiral of the British Fleet. He also told Asquith that he deplored the soft attitude he was taking about Women's Suffrage, and he point-blank refused to give Grey, the Liberal Foreign Minister, the Order of the Garter. He offered the G.C.V.O. instead, but this, with atrocious manners, Grey promptly declined.

More and more mistrustful of the new men in power, the King pined for the decent, reliable statesmen who had worked with him in the past. Their ranks were thinning rapidly. It seemed that even the best men in the Liberal Cabinet were being weeded out. Charles Carrington was still there as a small steadying influence, but 'Priscilla' Morley had gone, and, simply through inefficiency, Asquith lost the services of Lord Ripon.

Ripon was a Roman Catholic and Privy Seal in the Government, and quite naturally made strong protests when, at the conclusion of a Roman Catholic Eucharist Congress, a formal procession of witness had to be shorn of its meaning and its colour solely because of the vacillation of the Cabinet under merciless pressure from the Protestant Alliance. He considered the government's delay in coming to any definite decision as lacking in courtesy to some of the very highest dignitaries of the Roman Catholic Church, and did more than protest. He resigned.

> *'It would be impossible for me to support or defend the course which has been taken by the government'*

he wrote to Asquith.

The King's personal religion lacked fervour. Like his mother he had a sanguine belief that all would turn out well in the end – even for royalty. To others he was largely tolerant, though he enjoyed teasing Alix and Miss Charlotte and the High Churchmen amongst his cronies that one day he would attend a Keswick Conference and enjoy a little open-air self-cleansing in the best Evangelical manner. Frankly he did not want no-popery riots in his capital, yet he had not forgotten those supposedly charitable souls who had impertinently threatened to pray him out of his youthful and middle-aged wickednesses, and who never did anything but complain. They had been vociferous when he had been to see that good old gentleman and fellow sovereign, the Pope; vociferous when Ena had changed her religion; vociferous when he had tried to honour the memory of his dear friend, Carlos of Portugal. Now they had been positively clamorous and he did not care for pope-hunting.

Deeply as he regretted Ripon's departure from the Government, he warmly approved of his high standards and courage, and so he was contemptuous of his ministers when, rather than give the true reason for the Privy Seal's resignation, they persuaded him to say it was on account of ill-health and age.

'It has saved us from embarrassment, Sir,' explained Asquith, to his sovereign's disgust.

Even more dramatic evidence for his belief that things were worsening in the political scene, was Austria's sudden annexation of Bosnia on 5 October 1908.

Only a short time before Edward had been enjoying the Austrian Emperor's hospitality, but the *Pechvogel* had not said a word of warning, and the first intimation he received of this grave international incident was a letter, in Franz Josef's own hand, delivered to Balmoral where he was entertaining a large house party.

Because the letter was personal and delivered by the Emperor's accredited Ambassador to St James' – a man whom the King despised as a purely social race-goer 'who knows not a horse from a cow' – and he presupposed it might be important, he asked one of his guests and intimates, Lord Redesdale, to be there while he read it.

The Ambassador and Redesdale watched in silence. Neither was prepared for the sudden eruption of anger. Flinging the letter to the floor the King roared out that it was a vile plot hatched by scoundrels.

Redesdale, who thought he knew him as well as anyone, was astounded by his old friend's outburst. It was not only that he was furious with the Austrian Ambassador, and the variation in his expression of displeasure – from the most chilling hauteur to roars of rage which made Balmoral ring – made that unhappy man fly from Deeside as fast as he could, but Edward was very deeply upset, moved almost to the point of tears by Austria's outrageous contempt for the common courtesies of international diplomacy.

'So much that we value, Redesdale,' he said with great emotion, 'is slipping away. Slipping like sand through our fingers.'

10

The *Daily Telegraph* of 28 October 1908 contained an exclusive report of table-talk between the Emperor of Germany and his host at Bournemouth a year before, Colonel Montagu-Stuart-Wortley.

It had been concocted by the Emperor himself, with a little aid from the Colonel, to prove that he was not an Anglophobe, and he considered it a triumphant piece of personal diplomacy. Proudly he had sent a copy to his Chancellor, but Bülow was on holiday and passed it on to the Foreign Office without bothering to read it. At the Wilhelmstrasse its potential for harm had boggled the minds of the bureaucrats, who hurriedly threw it from one to another, none of them having the courage either to cool such a very hot potato or to criticize the Emperor's prose; and, supposing that it had the approval of his Secretariat, the Emperor sent it off to the *Daily Telegraph,* confident that possibly he had at least made the English see that he was their friend.

On that morning of the 28th, his ambassador, Count Wolff-Metternich, read the Bournemouth Table-Talk, laid down the newspaper with trembling hands and said in his excellent idiomatic English: 'Now we might as well shut up shop.'

His uncle, King Edward, read the article in his Jockey Club apartments in Newmarket. Then, not believing his eyes, he roared for Hawkins to come and read it out loud. But Hawkins had scarcely reached the third line – and so proved to the King that this astonishing conversation really had been printed – than he found the paper torn from his hands, his royal master leaping from bed in a way he had not done for years, and bellowing demands for his clothes, his Secretary, and for telephone calls to be put through to the Prime Minister and Sir Edward Grey.

'Your bath, your Majesty!' said Hawkins daringly.

'*Bath*? This is no time for bathing. My nephew has gone off his head!'

In the article intended to show the Emperor was England's

friend he had announced with unparalleled insouciance that the English were 'mad as March hares' and 'like mad bulls, seeing red everywhere'. And to demonstrate his friendship he casually mentioned that he himself had drawn up a plan for crushing the Boers, had submitted it to his own general staff, and then had sent it to Windsor for his Grandmama's use. 'I ask you,' he declared rhetorically, 'was this not the behaviour of a man who wishes England well? Let England give a fair answer!'

England's fair answer would have been unprintable in any newspaper in the world.

Wolff-Metternich in an interview with the Foreign Secretary could only shake his head. He had had no clear instructions about anything. He had not been aware of his Emperor's intentions. He did not care for Sir Edward Grey's retort: 'If, by this article, his Imperial Majesty hoped to convey Anglophile views, he must be clearly informed of the magnitude of his failure, and of the offence he has caused.'

With his intimates the King quite seriously discussed the possibility that Willy had gone mad. 'You know how he has fretted and galled us this summer. Could they have been signs?'

This was certainly true. On Edward's annual penance, that is at his meeting with the Emperor on the way to Marienbad, there had been an open discussion on naval affairs and afterwards the Emperor had taken Ponsonby on one side – to say quite angrily that as he was an Admiral of the British Fleet *he* knew far more about the Royal Navy than a mere Equerry and Assistant Private Secretary. Ponsonby had not attempted to quarrel with this eccentric point of view, but the Emperor showed he was offended. Then somehow or other the Emperor had been informed of Cassel's projected loan and, because of his uncle's part in forwarding it, he had referred to him at a full Court as 'a jobber in stocks and shares'. Afterwards there had been trouble about a replacement for Lascelles who was giving up the British Embassy in Berlin. Only a nonpareil would have really suited Willy, but Grey and the King between them had gone to the trouble of finding and proposing a Mr Cartwright because he was said to be friendly with the Emperor who constantly called him by his Christian name. But this proposal had not been viewed with favour. It appeared that twenty-five years before Cartwright had written a satirical exposée of Berlin Society. Only four copies had been printed but they had circulated fast enough. Then the King suggested Sir Edward Goschen who was in every way suitable, but the Emperor had merely made an unpleasant remark about the ghetto. With a sudden flash of impatience, and to support his friends the Jews – for he still felt he had let down the Rothschilds – the King had insisted on Sir Edward's appointment and there he was now, in Berlin, to handle this extraordinary situation.

He sent coded messages to Grey that the endeavour to show friendship for the English had not endeared the Emperor to his own people. There was an outcry against him in the Reichstag, and he had promptly gone for a diplomatic hunting trip leaving everything in Bülow's hands. Bülow thereupon threw his hands in the air in a gesture of despair.

Both Grey and Goschen were inundated with letters from their angry monarch. How was it possible, he asked Grey, for the Emperor to fly in the face of his own Foreign Office and publish his Bournemouth Table-Talk? Grey was an expert on the German constitution and declared that because parliamentary democracy and the absolutism of the Emperor could not work side by side, it ended up by no one being truly responsible for anything. Goschen, asked how German society was reacting to the scandal, sent a brief unsatisfactory report. Because of his Jewish blood he was finding it difficult to gather confidence, and he was not quite fixed in the saddle of his post.

King Edward considered and came to the conclusion that here was an occasion to make good use of that irritating female, Patsy's little Daisy.

Princess Daisy of Pless was no longer a firm-fleshed, radiant beauty, and to think of her as little was preposterous; but she did know the Emperor and rather liked him, and she did know the Empress, whom she compared with a 'good, quiet, soft cow – that has calves and eats grass slowly and then lies down and ruminates'. When asked, via Queen Alexandra and her mother, Patsy Cornwallis-West, what exactly was happening in Germany, she reported back that there *was* talk amongst the princely houses of asking for the Emperor's abdication, but this ought not to be taken too seriously; and evidently the Emperor was going through a *crise de nerfs*. Prince Phili Eulenburg at the command of his one-time friend had been forced to sue his detractors in the press for criminal libel and evidence had been dragged up proving a brief liaison with a Bavarian carp-netter of twenty-five years before. This, reported Daisy, had brought the excitable Emperor close to a nervous breakdown and his condition had worsened on his diplomatic hunting trip when the Chief of his Military Secretariat had donned a ballerina's *tutu* to dance a marvellous *pas seul* on the table at a riotous all-male supper and had dropped dead before his much-embarrassed imperial master.

These, pleaded Patsy's little Daisy, surely made it plain the poor Emperor was to be pitied rather than blamed for his wild journalism.

King Edward was not impressed.

True to his character the Emperor panicked and made an abrupt and startling move. Hoping to regain his lost popularity with his subjects he gave an interview at his hunting lodge to the American newspaper *New York World* in which he said an Anglo–German war was inevitable, England heading for disaster, the Royal Court rotten, and his uncle, King Edward, personally corrupt.

There was pandemonium the world over; laughter in many countries, deep suspicion in certain chancelleries, dismay and crimson embarrassment in the German Empire, a deep sense of outrage in England, and King Edward was mortally offended.

The despairing German Foreign Office brought diplomatic pressure to bear and, despite the fact that it had had every right to print the Emperor's views, the *New York World* was asked to make a public apology. From London Count Metternich demanded that the All Highest send an apology to the King of England.

Threatened on all sides, Willy did as he was told. He went one better than apologize, he boldly repudiated the remarks attributed to him. Then he went to Potsdam, announced he was sick with nervous prostration, and told his Household and his family that he was going to abdicate.

There could have been a *coup* which would have guaranteed this, but the Empress firmly prevented it. Daisy's estimate that she was a brainless ruminator proved sadly awry. It was the Empress who directed her son the Crown Prince that under no circumstances could he accept a throne abdicated by his father. It was she, with the Crown Prince, who spent hours with the Emperor, listening patiently to his remorseful pleadings and his claims to be the most misunderstood man in Europe; and between them they gave him the mental muscle he needed to reconsider. Nevertheless, although he agreed not to abdicate, his self-confidence was considerably shattered.

In England the King showed how profoundly he had been affected by the two newspaper articles. He snappishly agreed when his Cabinet suggested that a State Visit to Berlin in the New Year when the German Season started was now absolutely essential or cordial relationships between the two countries could never be re-established, but he warned Asquith and Grey that if the Queen or he were in any way insulted he would leave Germany at once. He sent the same warning to Sir Edward Goschen who, still not sitting prettily in his ambassadorial saddle and dumbfounded by the events which had taken place, was made nervously irritable for weeks.

Edward wrote to his oldest adviser, Lord Knollys:

> *My dear Francis,*
>
> *After your leaving me with Count Metternich's letter, with the German Emperor's emphatic denial, I have, I presume, nothing more to do than to accept it. I am, however, convinced in my mind that the words attributed to the German Emperor are perfectly correct. I know the Emperor* hates *me, and never loses an opportunity of saying so (behind my back) whilst I have always been civil and nice to him.*
>
> *As regards my visit to Berlin. . . . The Foreign Office, to gain their own object, will not care a pin what humiliation I have to put up with. . . .*

All his immediate Household saw with concern how deeply he had been affected by his nephew's infamous newspaper articles.

11

Though they had met at Kiel and many times privately in Germany and the Emperor had paid State Visits to England, King Edward had not yet been able to return the compliment. Berlin was, in fact, the ninth and last of all his State Visits to the Courts of

Europe. It was, therefore, considered vital by both sides that all should go smoothly.

Everything in Berlin was organized with Prussian efficiency, and his more realistic courtiers prayed that the Emperor would not make an idiot of himself. Clearly he was still in a nervous, overwrought state, and blaming Bülow, who did not appear to care that the days of his chancellorship were obviously numbered.

In England there was the usual concern about the King's health. The royal physicians and Hawkins did everything in their power to keep him free from bronchitis and, fearful of being ill away from home, he did attempt to ration his heavy smoking and was careful to take the linctuses prepared for him and avoid going out in fog.

But, as it happened, the Queen caused far more anxiety. She contracted a virulent form of influenza and was so ill that even the Prince of Wales was not permitted to visit her. In her convalescence she suffered from neuralgia and, far worse to her, an acute form of depression. She poured out her woes to Miss Charlotte: that as a Dane all her instincts rebelled against going within a hundred miles of the German capital; that as a wife she objected to visiting people who had been so overtly hostile to her husband; that as a practical person she seriously doubted if the King's temper could stand the strain of being with his odious nephew for three long days; and that as a Queen, she considered Mr Asquith's government was demanding far, far too much of an elderly couple to make them travel so far at the coldest and dreariest time of the year.

Irritable and utterly dejected in turn, merely contemplating the hateful visit which lay ahead made her weep and, for a long time, the Queen could take no pleasure in anything. Agnes Keyser's dieting she detested, but knowing in her heart that the Berlin visit was very important and quite unavoidable, she forced the unpalatable foods down and slowly regained her strength. As she did so she was lifted out of her depression by the united efforts of Miss Charlotte and Sir Dighton and the Marquis de Soveral, who said he would call on her every day until she was ready to waltz with him again. He kept his promise and once she felt herself again she made a real effort not to slip back.

Sir James Reid in giving her a clean bill of health said he relied on her to help him look after the King. Excitement and apprehension had brought on Edward's asthma. If he, Sir James, could have his way, the State Visit would be cancelled but his irascible patient had wheezed angrily: 'Don't be absurd, Reid. After my nephew's attempt last year at a diplomatic illness no one would believe me. They would say I was frightened of appearing in his capital.'

'So I threatened him, Ma'am,' Sir James told her, 'as more than once I had to threaten his mother. I told him bluntly I'd no wish to reach Berlin with a royal corpse.'

Reid's forthrightness at first alarmed the Queen and then amused her. At any rate she saw the seriousness of the situation and undertook to do all Sir James wanted and more. Momentarily she forgot herself and her own health and became the enchanting, totally irresistible Queen Alexandra of twenty years before.

The Royal Household was amazed by the transformation. So was her husband, and then he, appreciating why she was making such an effort, was deeply touched and more affectionate towards her and more patient with her than he had been for a very long time.

It was evident that whatever might befall in Berlin the Queen of England was going to delight everyone. On the train from Calais a footman, unused to the rocking motion, sent a dish of quails flying as the royal suite ate luncheon. To his horror one lodged in the Queen's neatly dressed and netted hair, in fact upon the *toupet* she was known to wear; but she made light of the accident, adroitly disentangled the greasy little bird and afterwards declared that perhaps it would have set a new mode in Berlin to arrive there *coiffée de cailles*.

When the mirth had died down, she kindly reassured the red-faced footman by telling him of a far graver mistake made by one of his number at a dinner given by Lord Rothschild at Tring. Catching a wig on his sleeve button, a footman had plucked it from a gentleman's head and, as speedily as he could, returned it – but to the wrong bald head. Happily neither of the gentlemen, both of whom happened to be Ministers of the Crown, minded any more than she had done. Accidents did happen. . . .

That evening, as the train racketed to Germany, the King's Assistant Private Secretary sat over a whisky and soda with his Household Physician. Ponsonby made a half serious, half joking toast that on this occasion at least there might not be the usual battery of absurdities and misunderstandings always associated in his mind with the Emperor.

'Ponsonby,' said Sir James his eyes alight with amusement. 'I'll drink to that, but only because I'm fond of whisky. Man, you might save your breath.'

Only a few hours afterwards he was proved correct.

A Guard of Honour, and the Germans attached *en suite* to the visiting English party, met the royal train on the Brandenburg frontier. King Edward had expected to be met in Berlin itself and was not ready. In any case Hawkins, not accounting for the change of time at the frontier, had not wakened his master. The result was a Gilbert and Sullivan mêlée. The suite to be attached, in full ceremonial uniform, was lined up on the platform. A Guard of Honour stood rigidly to attention at the present. And a military band, instructed to play the British Nattional Anthem the very moment the train stopped, had to play it again and again and again in the icy air while the King struggled into the uniform of a German Field Marshal and his suite leapt into appropriate uniforms. Driven mad by ten solid minutes of 'God Save the King', Edward inspected the Guard of Honour at double quick time, wondering if this unannounced or misunderstood piece of protocol had been thought up by his nephew simply to provoke. . . .

Duties done, and the attached suite on board, the train continued on to Berlin. There the King did not descend from his own carriage where there was a red carpet and the German Imperial Family, but from Queen Alexandra's carriage five coaches down the train. As the imperial entourage scurried in an undignified way down the platform to meet the King and Queen, the Emperor wondered darkly if this had been thought up by his uncle simply to provoke.

A long procession of carriages was formed outside the Lehrter Bahnhof and off went the King and his host gravely saluting the crowds who lined the route to the Palace. But behind them was confusion. The horses in the Empress's carriage had refused to move and she and the Queen had to transfer to another. Reshuffling followed, and odd horses pranced in and out to make a mockery of what should have been a dignified entry to the Imperial capital. Queen Alexandra, with her own secret mastery of horses, was not altogether tactful when she laughed outright at the Germans' inability to manage them.

It was not the end of a series of mishaps, deliberate or otherwise. The King was honoured by a permanent guard of specially chosen officers who, dressed in uniforms of the time of Frederick the Great, flanked the wide staircase up to the royal apartments. But he would have far preferred a lift. Wheezing his way up and down the flight of stairs several times a day aggravated his asthma and overheated him. What everyone had secretly dreaded took place. Sir James Reid informed the Household and the attached suite that despite everyone's care, King Edward had contracted a bronchial chill.

Not feeling at all well, the King was anxious to get through everything as quickly as possible, and was short and quick tempered. But the programme was a heavy one. There were family luncheons and dinners, a civic reception, luncheons with the Army, a motor drive to Potsdam and a visit to the Rathaus at which he suddenly found the energy and inspiration to make a perfect diplomatic speech which won enthusiastic applause from the Burgomaster and the people of Berlin, and envy from his nephew. It could be seen in the Emperor's face.

He had his petty revenge at a gala performance of *Sardanapalus* at the Opera. During the last scene in which, with German thoroughness, the funeral pyre which immolated Sardanapalus was made enormously realistic, King Edward woke from a doze and seeing the flames and smoke asked anxiously if the Fire Brigade had been summoned. The Emperor chuckled merrily and spread the joke against his uncle, not only in the Imperial Box, but afterwards to his whole Court.

Daisy of Pless was there. She wore a lily which, apparently, was her custom at the German Court, and she cornered the King and bored and wearied him by prattling on and on and on about her brother George betraying Winston's mother and flirting openly with Mrs Pat Campbell. Then, abruptly, she changed the subject and archly suggested that the English royal party stay on in Berlin for a charity concert she was organizing. Only an uncontrollable burst of coughing prevented the King from failing his own high standards and being rude to a lady. Charity concerts, when all he longed for was to fly from this beastly Court and city and get to Biarritz. . . . The Queen hurried over to his rescue, taking Daisy's arm and leading her away.

But Daisy was insistent. Perhaps, as the daughter of one of the

King's ex-mistresses, she thought she had some claim on him. Barely an hour after luncheon at the British Embassy where she had been a guest, she caught the King, attached herself to him, sat by him on a sofa, and chattered and chattered, though she elicited very little response. Then, suddenly, to her terror, he coughed and fell back against the sofa-head. The cigar he was smoking dropped to the carpet, and his face grew whiter and whiter. Feebly he tried to claw at his collar. Daisy half screamed and attempted to loosen the fasteners and the Queen rushed across the room to help. Neither could unhook the eyes. 'Oh! oh! oh! oh!' panted Daisy until the Queen bade her please to be quiet.

The King's eyes fluttered. He brought his head forward and managed to undo the collar himself.

Sir James Reid was hastily summoned and the room cleared. Before she left Daisy begged the King to permit her to summon a man who had a special inhaling machine which she herself had found very beneficial.

'I don't believe, your Serene Highness,' said Sir James quite firmly, as he ushered her from the room, 'that it would answer in this case.'

'Well,' enquired the King huskily when Reid had made a brief examination.

'You fainted, Sir. A bronchial symptom. Nothing serious.'

'My God!'

Reid retrieved the cigar from the carpet. It had burnt a substantial hole. 'You are better without these, Sir.'

'Yes, yes,' said his sovereign testily. 'I know all about that.' He paused. 'You are sure it is not serious?'

'Yes, I am sure. Though it takes the stuffing out of you.'

'A good description.'

'And,' added the physician, tapping the King's heart, 'it is not good for this.'

'I really don't feel the thing.'

'You must rest, Sir, until the next function.'

Reid was confident, but neither Hardinge nor Ponsonby, to whom he reported the incident, could share his sanguine view. In fact Hardinge wrote to Knollys in London to suggest that on their return the King should be given a most thorough examination by all the Medical Household. Ponsonby, practical as ever, tried to make his master rest.

Fortunately there were four and a half hours before the next item on the programme. He persuaded the King to go to bed for that time and helped Hawkins make him comfortable. He reflected it was a pity that at the German Court a State Ball began at 8.30. In England they scarcely ever began before 11.00. Those extra hours in bed would have made a great deal of difference.

The King leant on his Queen when they made their entrance at the ball.

Alexandra was magnificent. Smiling and gracious, her deportment perfect despite her limp, evidently anxious for her enfeebled husband, she yet managed to bewitch the Court she secretly detested. Her own innate good taste, with the help of Monsieur Worth, made her look absurdly young. Beside her the Empress and all her Ladies looked overdressed or dowdy. She was attentive to everyone, as winning as she could be, because she heard very little and was not expert in German, and was evidently trying to take her husband's place.

Edward was grateful. He touched her hand and smiled wearily as she left him to *cercle* and greet a large number of people on his behalf.

He was left sitting with a footman behind his raised chair, a chamberlain to explain in a hushed voice to princes wishing to pay their respects, that His Britannic Majesty was for the moment resting. Feeling exhausted by climbing the stairs he asked for a glass of whisky, only to be told there was none. Nor did any functionary attempt to provide some. It was an aggravation – promptly soothed, to the chamberlain's astonishment, by Major Ponsonby who produced a hip flask – but only the first in a series of annoyances. Tired of watching young German officers dancing minuets and gavottes, the King asked why the dancing was so old-fashioned. After all, while he himself was old enough to prefer traditional quadrilles and waltzes, they were living in the age of the two-step and *le Boston*. He was told that the Emperor considered people did not attend Court Balls for amusement but to learn deportment. Bored by sitting on the edge of a gilded chair, King Edward asked for a game of cards, to be told it was not the custom at the German Court. By now thoroughly vexed, he gave a defiant look in the direction of Sir James Reid and demanded a cigar, to be told smoking was forbidden.

Furiously he got up to leave, but good manners and diplomacy prevailed when the Emperor came over to enquire after his health. He said he was sorry to hear of the attack that afternoon.

The King made light of it, but said he felt exceedingly tired and would have to be excused the remainder of the ball. Before going he asked about the doctor with a patent inhaler recommended by the Princess of Pless. Was the doctor well known? Indeed, replied the Emperor, very well known indeed, though whether or not he was qualified was problematical, his chief employment being the clearing of the throats of opera singers before performances. Should he turn up at the Castle with his machine the Emperor thought he would probably have him forcibly ejected. A straight answer to a straight question. The King appreciated it. One last point, because the visit finished on the following day: would it be possible for him to see the Dr Renvers who had looked after his sister during her last illness? To his astonishment the Emperor replied there would be no point as Dr Renvers had never been acquainted with her.

Sir James accompanied the King to his apartments.

His patient was in some excitement. 'Now why did he say that? Why did he emphatically deny that Renvers was my sister's doctor? Damn it, I met the man many times. If I'm not mistaken he lives here in Berlin. Why should the Emperor deny it?'

Sir James could offer no explanation, but to calm the King he promised to try and get in touch with Renvers before they left.

'Do that. Do that. Do that,' said the King. 'I should be very grateful.'

Reid saw him into bed and measured out some syrup.

'What about that patent inhaler?' asked the King, the spoon sticking out of his mouth.

'Sir,' said Reid bluntly, 'I have a general practitioner's dislike of quackery.'

'Oh, very well.'

When the physician had gone, the King rang for Hawkins. 'Sir James would not approve,' he said. 'But I have a blinding desire for a cigar, Hawkins.'

His valet looked at him sadly. 'You are sure, your Majesty?'

'Absolutely, Hawkins. Absolutely.'

Sir James Reid found Dr Renvers in Berlin. That gentleman's opinion of the Emperor's disregard of the facts he said was *Pseudologia phantastica,* a tendency to live in fantasy.

'My God,' breathed the King. 'How absolutely right! I think it important enough to pass on to Goschen and our people in London, don't you, Reid?'

'It was an opinion not a diagnosis,' Reid carefully pointed out. 'But I think you are right, Sir.'

'There is a cure?'

Reid nodded. 'A remedy rather. Bodily and mental quiet are essential, so are composure and self-discipline.'

They looked at each other and smiled.

'I found Renvers a most interesting man,' continued Reid. 'It appears Chancellor Bülow is in disgrace because of last autumn's newspaper articles. And the high probability is he will eventually be replaced by a patient of Renvers, Bethman Hollweg. In fact the Hollwegs have been friends of the Emperor's for many, many years and a long time ago Bethman senior told him he would always find life intolerable unless Prussia applauded him daily, Germany weekly, and Europe once a fortnight.'

'Someone told my nephew that?' said the King incredulously.

'So it appears, Sir, but a long time ago.'

'No matter,' said the King. 'I think you had better pass on that information as well.' In his excitement he began to cough and splutter and could not find his handkerchief and had to be held in a bolt upright position by Sir James and Hawkins until he could get his breath again. When his wheezing had died down he managed to smile and mutter: 'Prussia daily, Germany weekly, and Europe once a fortnight! Dear Lord! How absolutely true!'

Patsy's little Daisy was not easily put down. She sent a message to Major Ponsonby and, to make sure, a copy to Charles Hardinge, that she and her special doctor, plus his patent inhaler which would do the King so much good, would be waiting on the day the Royal Train left Berlin at a little station in the suburbs. It was only necessary for the driver to be forewarned and the train could stop for a short time for them to leap on board.

True to her word she was standing on the station platform, furred from head to foot and with the inevitable lily, and beside her was a tall, bald cadaverous man, holding a small box of dark brown wood edged and studded with brass. She curtsyed and he, bare-headed, bowed; but the slow-moving train did not stop. Ponsonby and Hardinge stood together at a saloon window and courteously returned the salute.

Crestfallen Princess Daisy explained how hard it was to get at the English King. He was so hedged about with deleterious protocol. But if the good professor would care to accompany her to the Pless house in Berlin he might kindly treat her throat with his special inhaler, and then she could practise her contribution to the Charity Concert – '*When the Birds go North Again*'.

Impulsively, to the amazement of the station authorities and the professor, she there and then trilled a couplet in the raw February air:

For every heart has its sorrow, and every heart has its pain,
But a day is always coming when the birds go north again. . . .

12

The Queen was astonished to see the difference in her husband when in Paris he climbed into the special train which was to take them to Genoa.

She had last seen him in London a pathetic, grey-faced gasping man, cursing Asquith for allowing the Germans to catch up with England in the naval race; cursing Lloyd George for standing out against laying down the eight dreadnoughts England needed now; and cursing all politicians in general. Now, after a few weeks at Biarritz he was a much better colour, and if he did not precisely leap into the saloon carriage he could at least grasp the rail and climb aboard without aid, chattering excitedly about seeing Wilbur Wright fly his aeroplane from a field near Biarritz.

And Edward was equally pleased to see his wife looking well, for she had had a mild attack of pleurisy after the State Visit to Berlin, but now looked radiant. Poor Toria was there as well, sniffing into a handkerchief and advising her father not to kiss her as she had another cold.

Evidently the Princess thought levity between her parents was somehow shocking for she refused to do as much as smile when the King chattily confessed that the recently introduced rule about Privy Councillors appearing in formal uniform had already gone by the board because the Archbishop of York, a very big man, and huge in his episcopal robes, while backing away from the throne had scooped up and entirely enveloped Lord Northcote who was a very little man, in the folds of his scarlet rochet.

'So much for formality, my dear! Not one of us could keep a straight face!'

And to Toria's distaste both laughed.

She was even more disapproving when Mama told Papa a most undignified story about George who was, after all, Prince of Wales.

An old lady, said the Queen, had recently sent George a stamp collection because a dealer had offered her £50 for the lot and by some sort of intuition she guessed it might be worth more. It appeared her intuition was right. In a jumble of stamps was one George had been wanting for years. He returned the collection, told the old lady to sell it through Puttick and Simpsons, and gave excited instructions to his collection curator to buy the 2½d. Bahama at any price.

'He would,' declared the King. 'How much did they squeeze out of him.'

The Queen help up her hand. 'Patience, my dear.'

She told him that a week later one of the equerries had occasion to telephone the Prince and afterwards remarked that he had seen in the paper that some damned fool had just given £1,400 for a 2½d. stamp. A quiet voice told him. 'I was that damned fool!'

Major Ponsonby, who knocked and entered to say that the Chef de Gare reported all was ready for an immediate departure, found the King choking with laughter and Princess Victoria, looking very sour, thumping her parent on the back. The Queen was all smiles. 'Fritz, a glass of water if you please for the King. I have been telling him about the tuppence ha'penny Bahama.'

The train sped south to Genoa where the royal party met the Dowager Empress of Russia. As she had left Buckingham Palace at the same time as her sister, and had travelled from Paris in the splendour of a Russian Imperial train, King Edward wished to know why they had had to pig it on their special. 'With all that room,' he cried to his sister-in-law, waving at the luxurious royal blue saloon carriages, 'you might well have brought your poor relations with you.'

'Now, Edward,' said the Empress firmly. 'You know that with protocol and one thing and another . . .'

'Never mind,' he said. 'We shall be revenged. You now have to suffer the squalor of the *Victoria and Albert*.'

'Now, Bertie ——' began the Empress a second time until she caught her sister's eye and realized she was being teased. Her massive husband Alexander and her solemn son Nicholas had got her out of the habit of being teased. Nor had she ever fully understood her stout brother-in-law's sense of fun. 'I am sure,' she continued firmly, 'that I shall be very comfortable, thank you.'

She was. There was only the family and a small suite aboard: Miss Charlotte and another Lady-in-Waiting with the Queen; Seymour Fortesque and Fritz Ponsonby with the King, and the yacht commanded as usual by George Keppel's cousin, Admiral Sir Colin Keppel, and there was a great deal of space for everyone's comfort.

Only one jaring note threatened to spoil the King's pleasure and that was the deplorable unpunctuality of the two sisters. As he grew older precision and perfection mattered more and more, and as they grew older the predilection of Alix and her sister never to be on time became worse and worse. Thoughtfully Sir James Reid had provided just the thing for this sort of contingency; a large bottle of syrup containing an opiate which Hawkins would produce whenever his master became jumpy or nervous. A teaspoonful became an indispensable prelude to every meal. Sir James was telegraphed to forward a prescription to Malta so that another large bottle could be made up on arrival there.

The King of course believed that part of the joy of cruising was that no definite plans had to be made about destination, a theory which was about as tenable as his views on the joys of 'impromptu' picnics at Biarritz; but so far as he was concerned there was only one positive 'must' on this cruise before he returned to England

and the ladies continued cruising in the Athens area. That was to visit Malta and see his brother the Duke of Connaught.

A scheme for making a military federation of the Empire had been conceived by the Esher committee and taken up and developed by the Army. It had the King's enthusiastic support, and he had insisted on his brother being given command of the Mediterranean section. This, in effect, had put the Duke of Connaught in sole charge of all British garrisons bordering on the Mediterranean and for a year now he had been settled in the Palace at Valetta as Field Marshal Commander-in-Chief and High Commissioner in the Mediterranean. The Jack Leslies were there to make the Connaunghts feel less cut off, and because, as the Duchess and Mr Leslie had learned to understand and appreciate, the Duke found life quite intolerable without his beloved Leo. Malta was not a popular station, and was considered one of the most unattractive clumps of rock in all the Mediterranean, with an insufficiency of polo grounds, tennis courts, and croquet lawns; and, because of its total lack of decent trees, resembling Nebuchadnezzar's furnace in the 'parasol months' from June to September. But these defects apart, the Duke had never made any secret of the fact that he did not like Esher's military federation idea at all, had not wanted the Mediterranean command, and had only accepted it under protest. Now the new War Secretary had told Asquith, who had rapidly passed it on to the King, that the Duke was not giving a very good account of himself either. Perhaps it might be advisable to transfer him elsewhere. Determined to find out the facts for himself the King headed straight for Malta.

He was on the deck enjoying the sunshine and a mammoth cigar, and reading the programme arranged for his reception at Valetta, when Seymour Fortesque took him a signal from the C-in-C of the Mediterranean Fleet to say that he had been ordered away from Malta to Lemnos.

The King promptly flew into a passion and sent for Major Ponsonby, hurled the signal at him and asked what he proposed to do about it.

'I will not, not, *not* dock at Valetta if my Fleet is not there to receive me.'

The Queen and the Dowager Empress hurried to calm him. If anything, this enraged him further. It flashed through his mind that

Alix's sister had often looked and behaved like a sad sort of Yorkshire terrier, and it was on the tip of his tongue to say so. Fortunately, by concealed means, Major Ponsonby managed to convey to the Queen that this was an affair in which she could lend no assistance and with great presence of mind she dragged her sister away.

As they swiftly walked along the deck the King repeated: 'I will not, not, *not* dock at Valetta if my fleet is not there.'

Ponsonby suggested that possibly a situation had arisen which made a demonstration urgently necessary.

'Keppel,' said the King. 'Do we or do we not have a telegraphic sending and receiving instrument aboard this vessel?'

'We do, Sir.'

'Then, Fritz,' said the King triumphantly, 'I should have been informed of this situation.'

'I agree, Sir, that is the chief point,' soothed Ponsonby. 'The Prime Minister or the First Lord had a duty to keep you informed.'

'Quite.' The King began to wheeze so much that, although he had consumed barely a fraction of it, he threw his mammoth cigar overboard. 'Kindly write two cables for me, Fritz. The first is to Asquith. The second to McKenna.'

Neither could have been sent in the forceful form in which they were dictated, but Ponsonby was by now an artist at conveying the sovereign's displeasure without forcing resignation on the recipients and without his master really being aware of it.

Asquith was grumpily accepted back into favour because he made a handsome apology. But McKenna was unrepentant. He expressed reasonable regret explaining that the situation in South East Asia had made it necessary for the Fleet to move there, but he claimed that as the King was cruising, he could not expect to be kept in touch with day to day naval affairs.

This bellicose reply caused another barely smoked mammoth cigar to be hurled into the Tyrrhenian Sea.

McKenna, the King recalled, had hardly done anything to discipline Beresford and he had merely pretended to support Fisher. Now the despicable fellow was daring to insult the King's intelligence.

'You may reply to the First Lord of the Admiralty,' he instructed his Secretary, 'that in settling into his new post he will soon discover it has always been the custom for the Royal Yacht

Commander to signal her position when she arrives at a port. This was done from Girgenti and so communications could easily have been established. You may add that it has also been a scrupulously kept custom in the past for the Head of the Navy List to be informed of Fleet movements. That, I think, should be sufficient to bring him to heel.'

In this he judged wrongly. McKenna was a cocksure young minister and an incorrigible flatterer of those he thought might be useful. But as this category did not include his ageing monarch he was not in the least disposed to show more than a minimum of respect or consideration. The Fleet remained off Lemnos. King Edward arrived at Malta to be welcomed by what he called 'the bilges of my Fleet'.

It was not a happy beginning to the visit. Nor did his brother Arthur mollify him by saying the Royal Navy was a law unto itself, which ran its own course in its own way and took not the slightest account of the C-in-C Mediterranean.

'But then,' said the Duke mournfully over cigars and billiards that evening, 'can you expect them to tie themselves to such a curious arrangement as this Imperial military federation?'

The King frowned. They were playing a foursome of one hundred up: the King and Jack Leslie against the Duke and Major Ponsonby. He missed an easy pot and irritably seized the chalk. The chain which attached the chalk to the table snapped.

'You don't seem to be in form, Sir,' said his brother in the same sad voice. 'Would you care to change your cue?'

'This, thank you,' said the King stiffly, 'is quite adequate.'

His girth made it more comfortable to play with a rest. None of the rests at the Palace at Valetta were very long. 'Do you generally play with dwarfs?' he snapped at his brother.

All four were relieved when the game ended in an overwhelming victory for the Duke and Major Ponsonby. The latter and Jack Leslie, guessing that the King was going to speak openly with his brother, rapidly excused themselves.

'More brandy, Sir?' asked the Duke when they had gone.

The King shook his head. 'What,' he asked belligerently, 'is wrong with this carefully thought-out scheme for an imperial military federation?'

'Ask any soldier, Sir,' came the brief and irritating reply;

doubly irritating to Edward, who had always envied his youngest brother's professionalism as a soldier.

'The Committee for Imperial Defence and the War Office do not, on the whole, agree with you.'

'Kitchener does,' replied his brother laconically. 'He knows this command is the fifth wheel to a coach.'

The King's frown screwed up to a scowl. 'I think, perhaps, it might be less of a fifth wheel and much more effective, Arthur, if you were here more often. You take a considerable amount of home leave. Do you think you have given the experiment a fair chance?'

For a brief moment the Duke of Connaught wished he possessed that electrical spark which could throw all his brothers and sisters into formidable rage. But he was by nature placid.

'I think,' he said mildly, 'that if you care to check on the amount of leave due to me in the past few years, you will find I have not been away too much.'

'It has been checked,' said Edward briefly.

This stirred the Duke. He flushed. 'And you approved, Sir?' Turning to the window he said carefully: 'What an extraordinary thing for a sovereign and a brother to do.'

'It has been checked,' went on the other ruthlessly; 'and, while in aggregate you have not taken too much leave, that is simply because you failed to take what was due to you some years ago. That leave is no longer allowable. Your present amount of home leave is unquestionably not in order.'

The Duke sighed. 'Very well,' he said. 'I was unaware that the aggregate system had been altered. I accept the fault.'

'And this is perhaps why the experiment in this new command has failed?'

'Very probably.'

'Arthur,' said the King sharply. 'How can you be so casual about an important part of imperial defence?'

Pouring himself more brandy the Duke replied: 'When against my wishes you persuaded me two years ago to take on this new post, I quickly reported that in my opinion the command is quite unnecessary and, in the overall scheme of things, a mistake. It is superfluous, a cause of inefficiency in peacetime, and it would be a positive danger in time of war.'

'Arthur!'

'And I have not changed my opinion in the slightest, Sir.'

The King stood up. 'More concentrated application to the job on your part, a careful training programme and regular inspection and having your staff think out new strategies instead of all this polo and tennis and billiards . . .' He waved a hand in the air.

'And lemonade parties?' added his brother with uncharacteristic asperity. 'In Malta we are famous for our lemonade parties. Bridge, croquet and clock golf are offered as diversions.'

'Good Lord, Arthur,' exclaimed the King in genuine astonishment. 'I never expected to hear you say such things.'

'I respect your crown, Sir, and I respect you as the head of our family, but I do not agree with your Ministers and I intend to resign when my tour of duty ends in October.'

The quarrel was continued, and with less dignity, the next day. The Queen and the Duchess found themselves involved in a family squabble. The Dowager Empress would have been dragged in too, had she not been firmly taken by Miss Charlotte to watch a tennis tournament. Things were said by both sides which were afterwards regretted.

The Duke insisted that as the only professional soldier present he ought to know what he was talking about, at which Edward coloured and said offensively that Arthur had shown little professionalism as Colonel-in-Chief of a newly founded Cyclist Corps when he fell flat off his machine the very first time he had to take a salute.

This roused the Duchess, who never failed to defend Arthur. She declared that they had both been temporarily exiled from England so that the King and Queen should have no rivals in popularity. The Queen's subsequent remark about the odious Prussian habit of exaggerating was bad enough. Worse was the King's declaration that Arthur's judgement could not be relied on. He had never been the same since, as a young man, he had fallen out of a window at Buckingham Palace, crushing a policeman below, and getting bad concussion. . . .

It was all most unfortunate and led nowhere. The Duke refused to consider being reappointed to what he called 'a superfluous post' when his tour of duty ended in October, and he asked for other employment.

'If you leave Malta, Arthur, you will cease to have any employment in my Army whatever.'

'That is for you to decide, Sir.'

There was the thunder of a royal salute from the battery.

On the highest terrace of the Palace the Duke and Duchess of Connaught watched the *Victoria and Albert* steam out of Valetta harbour.

'I am so very glad you were firm, Arthur.'

'Thank you, my dear.' He slipped her hand into his. 'I grieve for Bertie's health. It is that which makes him so bearlike.'

'He was shockingly rude.'

'Yes, I fear he was. But at least Ponsonby warned us why he was so very touchy.'

'And Alix has become rather difficult.'

'We are all growing older, my love.' Then suddenly the Duke chuckled. 'You know, I do not envy him cruising with Alix and her sister, and that poor girl Toria. She is positively fettered to her selfish mama, and have you ever known her admit to feeling well?'

'Never. On this occasion it was head, back, a cold, and something to do with her feet.'

The Duke sadly shook his head. 'No one could envy the poor fellow,' he repeated.

'No. Poor Bertie.'

The Duke did his final duty and formally saluted the royal yacht. Then he turned and, his wife on his arm, went to look for Leo and Jack.

The guns thundered on.

13

'He was exceedingly upset at Malta,' Major Ponsonby told Lord Knollys. 'A quarrel with his brother put him out and then he seemed to lose all taste for the cruise. He certainly lost all patience. I tell you, Knollys, I need a good rest.'

They were better friends now. Possibly it would be more accurate to say they understood each other better. Knollys had greeted Ponsonby from the cruise with the news that his promotion to Lieutenant-Colonel had come through.

'You can relax now you are out of waiting,' he suggested.

But Ponsonby shook his head. 'Not until after the Derby. I have a white-hot tip.'

'Minoru?'

'How did you know?' asked Ponsonby.

'He has done remarkably at Newbury and captured the Two Thousand Guineas. And who gave you your white-hot tip?'

'The King,' replied Ponsonby.

Lord Knollys smiled. 'No wonder he looked a little grey and anxious after his cruise. He will worry until Derby day.'

The stallion bred by the ageing Mr Hall Walker by astrological prognostication was promising to be the most extraordinary horse in all the King's string of twenty-three. In fact the colt's performance had already caused Lord Marcus Beresford, the King's manager, and Richard Marsh, his trainer, to look with fresh respect on the hocus-pocus of astrology.

Soon after the King's arrival in England on 8 May Lord Marcus asked for an audience and confirmed his master's highest hopes by saying that if Marsh could judge the extremely difficult balancing of rest and exercise, Minoru might well win the Derby. Twice Edward had won the great race as Prince of Wales. It was his great ambition to do so as King and his excitement grew as Marsh sent in daily stable reports which were never unfavourable. The King's red despatch boxes did not get half the concentration he devoted to studying form.

The favourite Bayardo kept ahead for days. Then, to the King's frantic delight, Minoru was favourite. But not for long. Unexpectedly he was replaced by an American-bred colt, a two-year-old with a fine history in the United States, but tried only once at Newmarket. Named Sir Martin, he still stood at the head of the list on 26 May when crowds flocked to Epsom.

There was something about Derby Day which always went to the King's head, an excitement shared by thousands of his subjects from his own family and friends gathered closely round him down to the Londoners in their 'Derby best' who had come down by donkey-cars or in decorated carts to picnic on the Downs.

With his light grey silk hat and whitening hair and beard the King looked patriarchial as he stood in the royal box regarding the field, but he lacked a patriarch's tranquillity and repose. His blue eyes were brighter than normal and darting here and there. He was as punctiliously polite as ever, raising his hat to all his acquaintances and to those of his servants who were off duty, but he was easily distracted by what was going on in the paddocks and on the course. He would talk briefly to his friends and then with a quick word of apology, break off to examine a colt through his race-glasses. Strung up to a pitch he found almost unendurable, he felt far more tense than usual on Derby Day.

There were several causes. To begin with it was May's birthday which might possibly bring him luck. Then Beresford and Marsh had come to report with something close to a glow in their faces. After that he had interviewed his jockey Herbert Jones, a shrimp of a man, dieted to precisely the right weight and looking somewhat oriental in the royal colours of scarlet, violet and gold, and Jones had said nothing beyond what was expected and polite, yet the King sensed he really wanted to say a great deal. Then the abundant champagne had exactly that dryness and exactly that temperature which to the King's palate made it perfect, and which was a combination very rarely achieved. And the cold collations in the royal box might have been chosen by himself. Menanger had surpassed himself and the royal digestion was in excellent condition.

All these little things were happy auguries. More important was the ground. The going would be exactly right for Minoru, and the May sunshine was neither too hot nor too cold, nor did it cast shadows where they might conceivably affect a colt running at full crack.

With an exhilarated, quivering, hardly bearable feeling of agitation, the King sensed that the investment he had made on a far, far-off chance through an eccentric acquaintance at Marienbad was going to pay off.

He watched the field of fifteen colts as they paraded past the stands. Sir Martin, the American-bred favourite, looked to be in marvellous form. Bayardo was too. And so was William the Fourth. The King lowered his glasses. Perhaps for sentiment's sake he ought to have had a side bet on a horse named after his great-uncle. But he did nothing about it. Raising his glasses he studied Louviers, a superb colt to be ridden by a French jockey brought over for the purpose. . . .

'Papa.' A voice broke into his concentration. It was the Prince and Princess of Wales both wanting to offer their good wishes.

'Thank you, thank you,' he said, when they had done so. 'May, I am sure you will bring me luck, and Marsh thinks he will win.' Then he surprised and delighted his son by adding 'George, I should like one day to see that famous tuppence ha'penny Bahama. Could you arrange it?' The Prince said yes indeed, it could be easily managed. 'Excellent,' said his father. 'Now if you will both excuse me. . . .' He raised his hat to them and settled to study the field.

Minoru was drawn on the inside, not exactly the best place. But from the moment they were under starter's orders, and he saw how his jockey was handling Minoru, the King had a deep-seated certainty he was going to win. He lighted a cigarette and nervously crushed it out after one deep inhalation. A roar told him they were off.

It was an extraordinary race.

At the mile post Minoru was pacing beautifully and independently, letting others force the general pace. There came another roar. The King's glasses had partially steamed and he could not see. He grasped the nearest lady by the shoulder. 'What's happened, Ma'am?'

'Sir Martin's down, Sir, and Bayardo's drawn back.'

Breathless with excitement the King re-focused his glasses to see Jones had not been affected. He was out in front with Louviers and William the Fourth. At Tattenham Corner he was next to the rails. Then his colt's long-legged action took him temporarily out of the King's view again. He let his glasses fall to bang against his chest. Grasping the balcony, he leant forward to will his horse along the last furlong of the straight. Minoru was neck and neck with the Frenchman . . . neck and neck . . . neck and neck. . . .

The noise from the crowd increased. In the royal box people were quite unable to restrain their excitement and the hubbub was colossal as Minoru and Louviers sped past the post.

Suddenly the noise was checked.

The King, white-faced, stood panting, gripping the rails.

There was a second's silence, then another second, and half another. There were only whispers on the Downs until the numbers were hoisted at the judge's direction, and then came one clear shout: 'He's done it.' After that the shouts grew to a thunderous ovation.

The Queen took the King's hand and bade him sit for a moment. He did, wiping a tear from his eye, taking a thimbleful of brandy from a footman as the roaring grew louder and louder. Then he took off his race-glasses, straightened his hat, picked up his cane, and, with Lord Marcus before him, he went to meet his horse, as tradition laid down, and lead him into first place.

Through tumultuous cheers, and crowds patting him on the back, he at last reached the gate of the little enclosure, and Marsh, forcing Minoru through the press, managed to bring him to his owner.

At that, when the King took the leading rein, pandemonium broke out.

Edward was deeply moved. He had been hurt by his sister-in-law's hasty and afterwards much-regretted remark that he and Alix were jealous of the Connaughts' popularity, and this upsurge of loyalty was abundant proof he was loved by his people. It was extraordinary for a nation generally so restrained to make such a demonstration of sheer joy, waving their canes and hats and handkerchiefs and chiffon scarves, throwing flowers in the air, and shouting themselves hoarse – peers, jockeys, bookies, policemen, soldiers, the picnickers from London's East End – all his dear people.

Much affected, the King raised his hat to the crowd, which, by no observable sign and by no known control, abruptly ceased cheering and followed the lead of a hearty voice in singing the National Anthem. Gradually it was taken up in all the stands and enclosures, growing right round the course and spreading into the fields and up into the Downs, swelling into a vast chorus. There were tens of thousands at Epsom that day and all spontaneously sang 'God Save the King' with a volume and feeling never known before.

Beside his magnificent colt Minoru their sovereign stood bare-headed, trembling with emotion, his eyes misted with tears.

14

To know that he was loved by his people and to love them in return was a privilege few monarchs ever enjoyed. It was a tonic to Edward when he faced what otherwise would have been a tiring Season, and, in addition to the many engagements assembled round the general framework of levées, Courts, State dinners and balls, regattas, horse shows at Richmond and Olympia, and racing at Ascot, Goodwood and then Cowes, Knollys was keeping his nose to the extra-social grindstone far more than was customary.

Edward well understood from his own mother's mistakes that showing himself to the people was an important part of a sovereign's work, and opening things was an inescapable duty. Therefore he had made it his practice to visit an important industrial centre at some time in July each year. But his engagement book for the summer of 1909 was formidable.

Rosa Lewis, by providing a secret escape, made the hot and busy summer far more bearable. When he could slip away to his apartments in the Cavendish she pampered the King and, though by no means as successful as Sister Keyser would have been, she did try to make him rest, or, as she put it, not hop about in such excitement. She paid him the most elegant compliment by altering some of her receipts for his sake. The small birds he loved were sauced with milder relishes. Her shellfish and oysters were prepared more plainly. And she kept him exclusively on porter and dry champagne. Under the dominating influence of the Matron of King Edward's Hospital for Officers, Rosa's motto appeared to have changed from 'No letters, no lawyers, and kiss my baby's bottom!' to the far more practical 'Bland delicacies, no piquancies, if you please!'

An occasional disappearance into the Cavendish made Edward feel more able to face the problems which assailed him. He certainly had enough.

There was for instance the business of Arthur to settle. His brother was being obdurate and had asked why he should wait until October to be relieved of his duties. Not wishing to fall out with him further, Edward agreed that Arthur might come home in July and Kitchener was nominated to succeed him: a post which that old soldier accepted with the greatest repugnance, saying it was 'a damned rotten billet'. Possibly Arthur had been right after all. . . .

As for Parliament, Lloyd George's People's Budget of that April with its proposal to tax land had madly provoked the peers. Edward detested any form of class warfare or threats to overturn the *status quo* with violence, but he remained convinced that Balfour had been right to say the election of 1906 had inaugurated a new political era, and it upset him to discover amongst some of his friends an ostrich-like attitude which could do nothing but harm.

Natty Rothschild for instance pained him by leading a quite absurd reactionary movement in the Upper House. His views were nonsense in a fast-changing world, and in Edward's opinion they might so easily harm the tolerance he and his brothers had won for English Jewry.

Lloyd George, of course, charged bull-headed at his adversary.

> '*Are we,* [he asked] *to have all the ways of reform, financial and social, blocked simply by a notice board: "No thoroughfare. By order of Nathaniel Rothschild"?*'

Not in the least afraid of Jewry, Lloyd George also showed scant respect for dukes, saying in Limehouse that 'a fully equipped duke' cost as much to maintain as two dreadnoughts – and was far more difficult to scrap.

Young Churchill was as offensive. Though himself the grandson of a duke, he publicly compared their graces to goldfish peering at the world from within glass bowls, a sentiment which caused the Duke of Beaufort to call him an insupportable pup and say he wished he could see him torn to shreds by his pack of hounds.

Vexed when he heard of Winston's impertinence, the King remarked glumly to Esher over the breakfast table: 'Do you know, if it had not been for me, Churchill would not exist.'

Esher was not ignorant of the King's friendship with Lady

Randolph, but so surprised by the candour of the remark that he choked over his toast. Eventually he managed to say: 'How is that, Sir?'

The King eyed him, then, realizing what was in Esher's mind, he smiled: 'You misunderstand me, Reggie. My point is that both the Marlboroughs objected to Randolph's marriage. It was I who persuaded them to give way.' Then his smile died. Evidently at that moment Winston's rebelliousness was making him regret his act of kindness.

The political scene worsened during the summer. The King was heartily sick of it intruding everywhere.

As he had feared, even the Rothschilds could not entirely withstand the damage caused by Lord Natty's obduracy. Here was too convenient a political weapon, too juicy an opportunity for the anti-Semites to resist. The ripples widened to embrace Sir Ernest Cassel and the Sassoons, until the King himself stopped it all by making far more of his friends in public than was usual. It added to all that he had to do that year, but did manage to contain the poison to the place where it had begun, in the party political arena.

There the two Houses of Parliament were moving towards a second head-on clash, which would undoubtedly be more serious than the first. The King's advisers differed, and passionately, as to what he should do when, as was inevitable, Asquith asked for guarantees that he would create sufficient Liberal peers to get a budget through the Lords.

Knollys and Esher said one thing.

Alice, Ponsonby, Carrington and Redesdale said another.

It did not make for a comfortable life. And not only were Asquith's uncontrollable Ministers leading the country into a most dangerous state, but the Women's Suffrage movement also stepped up the militancy of its campaign.

On one memorable occasion the two clashed. Asquith had already been the target of militant suffragettes who had seized him after a public meeting, tugged at his coat and dented his hat. They now pursued him in his mild pleasures, finding him playing golf with that notable heart-breaker Harry Cust. Seizing clubs the ladies commenced to batter the Prime Minister until he was saved from their fury by the inimitable Cust.

'Ladies!' he cried in a voice so ringing that they hesitated in the attack. 'Ladies, your quarrel with Mr Asquith is no doubt a personal matter, but, as Secretary of this Golf Club, I must *beg* you to obey the rules and not walk on the grass. *'Not'* he repeated firmly, 'walk on the grass.'

The suffragettes involuntarily looked down at the grass, laid down the golf clubs and left the links.

At first Asquith could only gaze at Harry Cust. Then he managed a smile. 'Secretary!' he exclaimed. 'I did not know you were even a member.'

'I am not,' replied Mr Cust.

Cowes rounded off the Season. In 1909 it was made spectacular by a State Visit of the Tsar and Tsaritsa and their children.

A return courtesy visit after the meeting at Reval of the year before was obviously in the interest of both countries, as Sir Edward Grey firmly pointed out in the House of Commons, but the Labour Party raised all of its old objections to having anything to do with the Tsar, and raised a few more besides. It published an offensive manifesto against the Tsar's visit.

When he had read it the King merely threw it on one side. 'Destroy it,' he begged Ponsonby, 'for it is not worth putting in any archive.' And he confessed he was tired of the upheavals which came up like perennial weeds. The socialists were so blinkered by prejudice that they did not appear to realize the havoc they might be doing to humanity. He said nothing in public, but privately he let the Labour leaders know that if the bloodbath in Russia which they so confidently predicted ever came about, they themselves would bear some degree of blame. For himself he intended to do his duty as a constitutional monarch, accept the advice of his government and receive the Tsar with all the warmth an uncle would naturally give a nephew.

Though his opinion had been expressed privately to private persons, it was soon widely known and caused widespread displeasure.

'Humbug!' retorted the King when someone drew his attention to the outcry. 'Hypocrisy and humbug! I'll have none of it.'

For the same security reasons which had prevented King Edward actually landing in Russia during such a troubled period, the Tsar was not to land in England for fear of anarchists who could not be contained by the police. The Isle of Wight and the surrounding waters could be virtually sealed off by carefully placed squadrons from the British Fleet.

The King went to a great deal of trouble to make certain that the hospitality he had received from the Romanovs was amply repaid, and, in order to impress the naval attachés to all the ambassadors who would be present, he ordered the Channel Fleet to be augmented and made as splendid as possible.

Three days before the Tsar's visit he personally reviewed the fleet, which contained twenty-four battleships, sixteen armoured cruisers, forty-eight destroyers, and over fifty additional naval vessels. Then he ordered the three largest battleships to Cherbourg to escort the imperial yacht *Standart* across the Channel. Aboard the *Victoria and Albert* accompanied by his family he waited on the Solent for England's visitors.

On 2 August, the very day of the Tsar's arrival, a letter of protest, addressed to the Foreign Secretary, appeared in a daily newspaper. It was signed by two bishops and another peer, seventy Liberal and Labour M.P.s, and a sprinkling of dissenting ministers. Ponsonby considered that his master ought to see a copy although it would probably make him wrathful. To the contrary, the King was simply disgusted. He refolded the paper and handed it to Ponsonby: 'How damned ill-mannered,' was all he said.

Evidently he was determined to let nothing spoil the day.

He greeted the Tsar with the courtesy which had now won him his great-uncle's envied title of Europe's First Gentleman, and to it was added a warmth of sympathetic feeling for a man known to be under great stress. He did not approve of Nicholas' stubbornness, nor did he think autocracy proper or even possible in 1909, but he felt for him in his dilemma. And besides this, Nicholas looked so absurdly like George that he might have been his twin, and part of the King's love for his son spilled over on to his nephew.

Nicholas was evidently moved by the warmth of his reception. So, too, was the Tsaritsa, a woeful figure on account of her beloved son's haemophilia, dressed as ever in lilac, and exerting, so King Edward understood, a continuously unhealthy influence over her husband through some sort of peasant priest, a very unholy holy man – as rumour said – who called himself Rasputin.

But to Edward the Tsaritsa was Alicky, daughter of his favourite sister Alice, who had spent much of her orphaned childhood in England. He kissed her with obvious affection, and though shy and reserved and, by her crushing experiences, only spontaneous with a very few people, she found her burly uncle's charm and love overwhelming. With tears starting to her eyes she returned his kiss, whispering in his ear that she was so very glad to be in England, the country she loved above all others.

The Tsarevitch evidently did not share his parents' feelings of security with their bearlike relative the King of England. Pushed forward to make his bow, he side-stepped and when the King chuckled and held out his arms to him, Alexis darted behind his mother. His sisters, the four Grand Duchesses, were not so retiring. Possibly more than any of the others they had enjoyed the jollifications at Reval the year before and hoped there would be more now.

There were indeed.

There had to be formalities of course. Stolypin was in the Tsar's suite, as was his Foreign Minister – though not, the King noted to his relief, that highly embarrassing young Prince, the soigné Felix Youssoupov – and the English ministers wished to hold certain discussions. But the King was determined that his royal guest should not be bored.

The *Victoria and Albert* with all the royal visitors aboard steamed through the lines of the British Channel Fleet, the Tsar, dressed in the white uniform of an Admiral of the Fleet, saluting each vessel, while Royal Marine bands played the two National Anthems in turn, and cannon thundered salutes, and English matelots, hanging like little white clothes-pegs from the rigging and the sides of every ship, broke into hearty cheers.

That evening *Standart* and *Victoria and Albert* lay alongside in Cowes Roads and there was a great dinner aboard the royal yacht. The statesmen were there, naturally; they had to be; and both sovereigns had to say the right things, which, in the world of diplomacy, were quite unimportant; but King Edward somehow managed to make the state occasion into a family party. Political commentators, seeing him in deep conversation with the Russian Foreign Minister, noted their affability towards one another, the conservatives amongst them hoping it presaged a fresh cordiality between the two nations; the radicals showing appropriately glum faces. The fact was that the Russian Minister was fascinated by the legend of Robin Hood, and the King, for his country's sake, was racking his brain trying to recall the adventures of Friar Tuck, Will Scarlett, Maid Marion, the Sheriff of Nottingham and Guy of Gisborne.

The Tsaritsa smiled more contentedly than for many a year. The Queen, though she believed Alicky was responsible for much of Russia's trouble, buried her suspicions, ate an unusually hearty dinner and was charming to her niece and nephew.

The feeling that, despite all the protocol, this was a family reunion continued the next day when the likeness of the Tsar and the Prince of Wales was recorded for all posterity by Messrs Debenham and Son in Cowes; the Tsarevitch and his sisters went on 'shore leave' to buy picture postcards and collect shells; and the Tsar and Tsaritsa were rowed to Queen Victoria's Maritime Residence where David, or Cadet Prince Edward as he was now called, showed them the sparse comforts enjoyed by him and his fellow cadets in the Royal Naval College.

Then there were the races. Cowes Regatta sealed off the English Season, or, as the Prince of Wales tried to explain ponderously to the young Tsarevitch Alexis, it gave every English gentleman just sufficient time to scramble to a grouse moor before the holy twelfth. In addition to the men-of-war there were hundreds of yachts lying in the Solent and there were luncheons, dinners, balls and garden parties, as well as races.

All of the Russian Imperial family were enchanted. Unaware, or, by the magic of Cowes, able to be unaware that behind most of the brass funnels of private steam yachts and almost every tree on the Isle of Wight there lurked a British policeman to keep them safe, they momentarily forgot their closed-in life at home, the terrorists and the revolutionary bullies, the grief of trying to live an ordinary life in extraordinary circumstances, and the utter lack of hope for their future. The riding lights glowed and the lights of the fleet dressed over-all twinkled in the evening sky; orchestras played the most chic dance music; wine glasses tinkled; and their English relations laughed over happy family memories; and, finally, there were arcs and wheels of fire, exploding circles growing larger with each burst, arrows of silver light cutting the dark sky, golden rain and Roman candles, Bengal lights and set pieces of fireworks glowing over Portsmouth.

'Nicky, my dear boy,' exclaimed his host expansively, his tulip brandy glass reflecting the myriad lights, 'Alicky, my love. I drink to your safe voyage home and to your swift return to England.'

Tsar and Tsaritsa clasped hands and watched him as he toasted them. Behind his white hair and beard the Bengal lights burnt a steady blue.

15

The King and Queen had other royal visitors that autumn.

Victor Emmanuel and Queen Elena adored Windsor and on this occasion the King of Italy was to be invested as a Knight of the Garter.

And a second crowned head to receive the same Order was the boy-King Manoel II of Portugal. The boy-King was a soubriquet which had clung to him ever since he had witnessed the butchery of his father and elder brother eighteen months before, but evidently he had a Latin's maturity and fire. He already kept a mistress in London, the spectacular dancer and soubrette in musical comedy Miss Gaby Deslys, and, while he was to stay a fortnight at Windsor, it was understood he would both precede and follow the visit with icognito trips to see Miss Gaby. Kept informed by Rosa Lewis that the girl was fleecing him, the King wondered if he ought to give his young guest a warning, but, putting himself in the boy's place, he decided against it. Rosa's reports were like something out of the Arabian Nights. Already Don Manoel had given the girl a rope of flawless pearls as long as herself and he was spending a king's ransom on her. It was to be hoped the royal Portuguese treasury could stand it.

This fortnight at Windsor was a very happy occasion. At the investiture of the Knights of the Garter the Prince of Wales and the Duke of Connaught escorted the two monarchs one after the other to have the Garter buckled over their white silk stockings below the knee. Afterwards there was a banquet. Queen Alexandra was there in her full robes as the only Lady of the Garter, and all but four Knights of the Garter were present. The Duke of Marlborough had been at the investiture by right, but he was not asked to dine because he had defied the King's known wishes and the divorce proceedings from Consuelo Vanderbilt were going through. But amongst the banquet guests were Winston Churchill and his bride, and Mrs Lloyd George, though without her husband. Why he had refrained from attending no one seemed sure. It was remarked that he was scarcely ever with his poor wife anyway. His universal nickname of the Goat was not meaningless. Or possibly there were too many dukes present for his comfort. Neither the King nor the Queen really cared one way or the other.

There was a good deal of shooting on the royal demesne, most of the game being shot by the Prince of Wales and the King. Victor Emmanuel blazed away but simply gave himself a headache. Young King Manoel, his thoughts undoubtedly elsewhere, invariably pressed the trigger when the birds were well away over his head.

After a shooting luncheon there was an unfortunate contretemps, in fact the only failure of perfect hospitality in the whole fortnight. Sadly it was a flare-up between the King and his brother, because, on being presented with an easy shot, the Duke fired and feathers instantly fluttered in the Queen of Italy's great picture hat.

'Arthur,' snapped the King angrily. 'You're a damned bad shot and should apologize to the Queen.'

And as the Duke of Connaught's face flushed scarlet, the King was audibly heard to mutter that, if field marshals shot so dangerously, God save the British Empire.

Another gun, hoping to joke over the matter but only making it worse, stupidly remarked that the bird on the hat was out of season. . . .

'I feel certain, your Majesty,' said the little King of Italy rapidly, 'that a breeze moved the feathers.'

'Shot, Sir,' said the boy-King, also trying to mediate, 'would have done more than flutter the feathers.'

Queen Elena declared no harm had been done either way, and if no one minded she did not wish to remove her hat without the assistance of a maid to see if it was damaged.

'If the hat is damaged, Arthur—' began the King angrily, turning to his brother, and stopped abrubtly.

The Duke of Connaught had already handed his gun to his loader and with uncovered head was bowing.

'With your permission, Sir, I will retire,' he said.

The King was so taken aback, and then so angry that he was close to telling his brother to go to the devil.

The Prince of Wales coughed. 'I really think, Papa,' he said tactfully, 'that King Victor Emmanuel is right. There was a sudden breeze.'

The King did not reply. Nor did he give his brother leave to retire, nor did he press the question. But a patina of anger, of which he was at once ashamed, made him refer obliquely to an accident of long ago when a stray shot from the Duke of Connaught's gun had blinded his brother-in-law, Prince Christian.

'To your stands gentlemen,' he said and nodded to his chief keeper to keep the shoot running. Cold with fury, the Duke did as he was told and took back his gun. It was much to his credit that he did not remind the King that he himself had recently peppered a beater at Sandringham.

That evening the King sent for the Duke of Connaught. He asked his pardon and admitted his temper was atrocious. 'Something inside goads me on,' he said, and then added pleadingly. 'I beg you to forgive me.'

'I forgive you, Sir, and willingly,' said the Duke calmly. 'I am aware that often you are not quite yourself and bronchitis is a very wearing disease to the nerves.'

'But really it was unforgivable,' said the King, bitterly reproaching himself. His genuine sense of guilt utterly depressed him.

'That is for you to judge,' returned his brother. 'For my part I am willing to accept your apology and assure you I understand the strains to which you are subjected.' He added frankly. 'I should not like to be under them myself.'

They shook hands and the Duke went off to write all about the day to his beloved Leo. Later he was forced to reconsider his brother's sincerity when he overheard him discussing Prince Christian's blind eye with the young King Manoel.

'A very easy-going man, my brother-in-law,' exclaimed the King. 'Not in the least peppery like me. Has the excellent notion of counting up to thirty whenever faced with something inexplicable. A good rule for kings, eh?' he smiled at Don Manoel. 'But he lives a great deal in the past, and dries up like a loofah when he's entertaining.' He chuckled. 'And so in desperation he sometimes sends a footman upstairs to get his tray of false glass eyes and then he discusses their merits with all his guests.'

Both laughed. Then King Edward took his guest's arm and they walked on down the great gallery; one at the beginning of his reign, the other so close to the end of his.

After long and careful thought the Duke of Connaught decided the King had not intended to insult him further, but he came to the conclusion that after this, except for Courts and special State occasions, their ways must part. His brother had one programme; he and his Duchess, Leonie and Jack another. In future he would stick to his homes in Clarence House and at Bagshot, with occasional visits to Castle Leslie and the Leslies' shooting box at Glaslough.

The King did not endear himself to his chauffeurs or to Stamper by thinking out new routes so that he could see more of the countryside. They were particularly put out when on a raw November day he decided to go to Sandringham by a little used, hardly known way from Ely to Littleport and then to Downham Market and King's Lynn. Despite their fears all went well until they reached the river Ouse between Littleport and Downham where there was a hump-backed bridge.

It was an attractive enough bridge as they could see approaching from the south, with willows near by and a small beer house with lighters moored to the tow-path, all of which broke the interminable flats of the peat fens. It was also silhouetted against a beautiful reflection in the water of the western sunset.

But the bridge was far too hump-backed.

The front wheels of the long Mercedes went over the hump, high into the air and then came down, all tyres whirring, the heavy chassis settling comfortably on the hump.

'Well, Stamper?'

The motor engineer got down without a word, but the expression on his face was sufficient for the King to say 'Stamper, that will do.'

'If your Majesty would care to descend with Colonel Ponsonby, the machine will be less heavy.'

'Descend! Certainly not. It is arctic in here already despite your stone bottles and these rugs. Do you wish me to catch my death, Stamper?'

'No, your Majesty.' Stamper turned to the chauffeur. 'Down with you and see if there's anyone at the beer house.'

There was a tall gangly boy with a beaky nose and a cap pulled well over his head leaning against the door. He gave the unwelcome information that the beer house was closed and would not open for an hour or more.

'Closed?'

'There's no one here, they've gone to Littleport,' said the youth.

The chauffeur called Stamper over and gave him the gloomy news.

'We'll need horses,' decided Stamper. 'Where's the nearest farm, boy?'

'Southery.'

'Well, where's Southery?'

The boy waved vaguely to the other side of the river. When a coin changed hands he was more explicit. 'It's a Fen mile or more. That means a good step. And the teams'll be stabled by now.'

'Then they'll have to be unstabled,' said Stamper crossly, and asked directly if the boy would go and get out a team.

'Can't,' said the boy. 'I have to guard the beer house.'

'Guard it?'

'Against passing strangers,' said the lad screwing up his eyes. 'Who might want to break in.'

There was a creaking noise from the motor car. What to the boy looked like a well-furred bear in a bowler hat climbed down on to the bridge. He stumped down the road followed by a tall, anxious-looking man in a drab coloured coat.

'Well, lad,' said the well-furred bear, 'and who are you?'

'Jack,' said the boy. When sixpence was pressed into his hand he volunteered more information. To Stamper's fury he even opened the door and took them into a snuggery where there was a strong smell of tobacco and damp corduroy, leather, beer and smoke from a badly burning fire.

The well-furred bear looked around. He sent Stamper and the chauffeur off to Southery and eventually they returned with a team of horses to drag the motor car forward on its chassis. By this time the fire had been made up and smoked no longer. A dense liquid called sweetened tea had been produced by Jack, plus a drop of something warming, and the King and Colonel Ponsonby both felt exceedingly cosy.

When they climbed back into the car it was to find the stone bottles had been refilled by Jack. Yet another coin was passed over.

'And d'you know,' said Jack to a gaping audience of ditchers and fowlers and lightermen and fen tigers that evening. 'Not till he'd gone did I know who it were.' He waved at a brightly coloured sporting print showing Edward as Prince of Wales, leading Persimmon his Derby winner. 'Believe me or believe me not, it was the King.'

'And you gave him rotten old tea with a drop! Why not port wine?'

'He never asked,' said Jack thoughtfully. 'But next time he calls, I will.'

By this hour the King was dining with Colonel Ponsonby, the local parson and the Sandringham agent.

He had barely any appetite. So far as he could see he had made a fruitless journey. The shoot would take place as arranged but he believed he himself would have to return at once to London. A clutch of telegrams told him on his arrival that while he had been enjoying thick tea with a drop in it at Southery the Lords had thrown out Lloyd George's Finance Bill.

It was despite all his own plans for moderation and meant that Asquith would request a dissolution and go to the country asking for a mandate to quell the peers.

Without any doubt at all it was the gravest political crisis of his reign.

He merely jabbed with his fork at a helping of *Poularde toulousaine*, which was the supreme art of the chef who had prepared it: a poached pullet coated with *sauce allemande* and garnished with truffles, Paris mushrooms, slices of veal sweetbreads, cocks' combs and kidneys, and quenelles of chicken forcemeat. Very little could he manage, and he did not do justice either to the roasted lapwings which was a Sandringham speciality. As for the dish of *canapés à la Cadogan*, he simply ignored it.

After dinner he went to the bowling alley with Ponsonby. They talked more than played, and, seeing how cast down the King was, the Colonel asked permission to telephone Knollys and the Prime Minister to see exactly how things stood.

Twenty minutes later he returned to the bowling alley. A bored footman who usually set up the pins stood idly at the other end. Evidently the King had not sent down a single ball.

'Both Asquith and Knollys agree, Sir, that things being what they are, there is no real necessity for you to return to London.'

The King brightened. 'Really, Fritz?'

'Most definitely, Sir. The Prime Minister and Knollys will be in constant touch with you here, but both beg you to keep away from the London fogs.'

16

On 3 December Asquith scored by pointing out that through dragging peers, who rarely ever attended the House, all the way to London solely for the purpose of destroying the Finance Bill, the Lords had acted irresponsibly. The vote had, therefore, been an artificial one. Then he threw down the gage, asking the Commons to vote on a motion that the action of the Lords was a breach of the Constitution and a usurpation of the rights of the Commons. The motion was carried by 349 to 134.

On that date there was a large house party at Sandringham.

In the afternoon the King had a tooth drawn without any anaesthetic, a matter he made light of, saying he could quite easily bear physical pain. What he did find unbearable was the plot-hatching in both Lords and Commons.

Ponsonby now wished he had not telephoned Knollys or the Prime Minister. Though the King's health was of great importance, so was his presence at the centre of things. Cynically Ponsonby considered that Asquith could be trusted no more than any other politician. Certainly some indiscreet disclosures by his eccentric wife Margot seemed to prove he was capable of anything. Moreover, in this particular matter Ponsonby thought Knollys' judgement might not be sound. The Private Secretary had reached a euphoric state about 'going down with all colours flying', and unless checked, would persuade the King it was better to abdicate than give way to the Liberal proposals, either that the King permanently transfer to the Prime Minister the right to create peers, or that he create sufficient to overtopple the enormous Conservative vote in the Upper House.

Whatever the outcome might be the King was sadly aware that he now had before him many conflicting opinions, all honestly given and conscientiously held, and he could not refrain from telling his thirty guests at dinner that night that he had never spent a more miserable day. It was an action which puzzled and worried his Household. Not in the least secretive, and acknowledged as an emotional man, it was, nevertheless, unusual for the King to confess his distress so publicly, or to take house guests into his royal confidence.

Sir James Reid especially was alarmed as he listened to the King telling everyone that Parliament would now be prorogued and the Prime Minister ask for a Dissolution so that the matter might be put to the people in a General Election.

Late that night – actually it was two in the morning – with the King's permission Sir James visited him in his bedroom. Edward was sitting up in bed, propped against a white hill of down feathers, drinking a hot whisky.

'I know you must be feeling the strain, Sir. Is there anything I can get you?'

The King put down the glass. 'Merely peace of mind, Reid. It's all I ask, but I can't see how to get it.'

The Liberal onslaught on the House of Lords was relentless. It was characterized not by Winston Churchill, who won Asquith's approval because, sensing social disaster, he had moderated his tongue, but by the squalls blown up by that working-class demagogue, David Lloyd George.

In a speech at Wolverhampton he hissed in the sibilant and mildly sinister accent of Caernarvon, a diatribe against the peers.

'They have no qualifications – at least, they need *not have any. No testimonials are required. There are no credentials. They do not even need a medical certificate. They need not be sound*

either in body, or in the mind. They only require a certificate of birth – just to prove they are the first of the litter.'

And then, after a sustained dramatic pause, a raising of brows over eyes alight with humour, and a hand gesture of ridicule, came the peroration, whispered with the S's hissing like Chinese geese or rather like bolts from a hidden crossbow:

'You would not choose a spaniel on these principles. . . .'

The pressure on the King was equally steady and relentless. No one amongst his friends and advisers held any hope that the Conservatives would be returned in strength at the General Election. But several insisted he had a constitutional right to tell Asquith that if his government was returned, a second General Election would be necessary. The general Liberal attitude in this election of 'doing something about the House of Lords' was far too vague. To secure a proper mandate definite and exact proposals would have to be put to the public in a second election so that the people could choose the fate of the Upper House. It was a delaying tactic and the King seized on it, yet he felt in himself that, unless a most unlikely miracle happened, the matter would ultimately rest with him.

Either he would have to create literally hundreds of Liberal peers which would make the Upper House a mockery.

Or he would have to do everything in his power to persuade the Conservative peers to let a Liberal budget through.

Or he would be obliged to abdicate.

17

Directly after the New Year the King and Queen and several of their Sandringham House Party went to Lord Iveagh's in Suffolk for a week's shooting. Naturally many of the guests had nostalgic memories of the New Year parties at Chatsworth with the dear old Duke and his magnificent Louisa. But while Eleveden Hall bore no comparison with Chatsworth, the Earl of Iveagh had undoubtedly gone to great trouble to entertain the royal party. He had seventeen thousand acres of some remarkable shooting, and Elveden was so grand that even the ladies' maids were waited on by footmen. His guests were most carefully chosen and included four of the King's dearest friends, Mrs Keppel, Mrs Willy James, the Marquis de Soveral and Lord Carrington. It was proposed by the last that politics be banned for the week, a suggestion which delighted the King and much relieved Lord Iveagh and Sir James Reid. The last proposed privately to everyone that bed at midnight should be a second golden rule. It was important that the King should rest.

Lady Fingall was also a guest. She had always been a favourite with the King, a small bustling Irishwoman of great charm who had broken hearts by the score, and, with Daisy Warwick and Daisy of Pless, was known as one of the three Daisies of the era. Daisy Fingall's admirers had included such good friends of Edward's as Sir Horace Plunkett and the Irish Secretary, George Wyndham: indeed there was once a story told in Rome and Ireland that His Holiness only had any hold over Dublin 'through the Parish Priest at Dansany, who talks with Lady Fingall, who mentions it to dear Sir Horace, who naturally tells Mr Wyndham what to do'.

On their first night at Elveden, Daisy Fingall paid the choicest compliment to the King by telling him there was a new popular song in the repertoire of Pelissier's Follies about Edward the Peacemaker. Urged on by her fellow guests, and after a false start or two, she attempted to mimic it:

> There'll be no wo'ar
> As long as there's a King like good King Edward.
> There'll be no wo'ar
> For 'e 'ates that sort of fing!
> Peace with 'onner
> Is his Motter;
> So God sive the King!

Edward was delighted. Beaming, crimson with pleasure, he thanked Daisy Fingall twice, and got himself into such a state of excitement that during the night Sir James Reid had to give him oxygen and a sedative, for he was rambling on about the peace of Europe and peace between the Lords and Commons, and the peace he so earnestly sought himself.

On the following morning Sir James sought out his host and told him what had happened. 'It was scarcely Lady Fingall's fault,' he admitted, 'but the King is so very tense about this war between the Houses. In fact,' he added grimly, 'Pelissier's popular song could be altered to read: "There'll be no King, As long as there's a wo'ar".'

The Earl of Iveagh was greatly distressed. 'I had no idea he was so delicate....'

'Not delicate, I assure you, merely worn out.'

Quite unwittingly the charming Daisy Fingall was partially the cause of another bout of distressing sleeplessness. At dinner on the last night of the visit she sat next to the King, who gently mocked her for being a suffragette.

'I am all for female fireworks,' she remarked, but she laughed with all the table when he quoted W. S. Gilbert's remark that it was as sensible for women to chain themselves to Parliamentary railings demanding a vote as for men to chain themselves to hospital railings saying they would not move until they had had a baby.

After dinner, in a very different mood, when the men went into the Eleveden drawing-room, the King led her to a quiet corner and asked if it was true she was acquainted with a Miss Haig.

'Quite true,' agreed Lady Fingall.

'And she has a brother, Douglas, who died some time ago and sends messages through a planchette board?'

'Just so, Sir,' said Daisy Fingall, nodding; 'and a lot of trouble it causes everyone. In fact someone rightly remarked that Douglas was a dreary enough bore when he was alive, but he's much worse now he's dead.'

The King laid a hand on her arm. 'Be serious, Daisy, I beg you.'

'But I am being, Sir,' she replied, astonished.

Moodily he stared at a lamp on the small table beside them. 'My mother had a planchette board,' he said suddenly. 'She used it to try and communicate with Papa.'

Daisy was astonished to hear it. 'I'd no idea, Sir,' she said. 'I'd no idea.'

'Nor had anyone else. Nor do many people know she used that drunken proud Highlander of hers as a medium. He'd the power, they said.'

Lady Fingall was momentarily startled, but then she nodded understandingly. Very probably Brown had had the second sight. A fey Irishwoman like herself could believe that without any difficulty at all. What she could not understand was the King's present mood.

'How do you come to know about Douglas Haig and his sister, Sir?' she asked.

'Because,' replied Edward slowly, 'he has sent me a message through her, purporting to come from my sister Alice. . . .' He paused.

'Who died in Darmstadt of diphtheria,' added Lady Fingall.

The King nodded.

After a moment's consideration Lady Fingall asked: 'And did George give any sort of proof that this message really came from your sister?'

Again the King nodded. 'He mentioned a day when she and I were on Ben Nevis together and, finding a piece of white heather, we divided it.'

Daisy Fingall decided to check this here and now if she could, not because she disbelieved in Douglas Haig's messages, but because she saw how upset the King was. 'I have always understood Princess Alice was your favourite sister,' she said rapidly. 'Dividing white heather is quite a natural thing to do, and very common. Servants see these things and talk. Perhaps your sister wrote of it in a diary? She could have mentioned it to another member of the family. I can think of half a dozen ways how that dreadful bore Douglas Haig could have heard of it. . . .'

The King was not persuaded. 'You may tell Miss Haig,' he interrupted, 'that I am not in the least grateful for her trouble in writing to me. And would you please add that I am deeply hurt she considered it her business to transfer this message from another world.'

'You may be sure, Sir,' said Daisy Fingall grimly, 'that I shall tell her exactly that.'

'Thank you.' The King put two fingers into his waistcoat pocket and took out a folded slip of paper. 'This,' he said opening it, 'is what purports to be a message from my sister.'

He held it out, and though she did not want to accept or read it, Lady Fingall felt obliged to do so.

Though in a scrawl the letters and the message were plain. It read

THE TIME IS SHORT *YOU MUST PREPARE*

She returned it to the King who put it in his pocket, offered her his arm, and led her back to the main company.

Mrs Arthur Sassoon did not care to use what she termed the telephone instrument and generally would only do so through the medium of a third party, but she found herself obliged to when a call came through from King Edward's Hospital for Officers and Sister Agnes Keyser demanded to speak to her and to her alone.

No, Sister Keyser informed Mrs Sassoon's butler, a confidential maid would not do; nor, she regretted, could she confide what she had to say to anyone but Mrs Sassoon or, perhaps, if really necessary, her husband. Mr Sassoon, said the butler, was out of the house. He would ask Mrs Sassoon if she could overcome her dislike of telephoning on this one occasion.

Realizing there was no help for it and trembling a little but encouraged by the solid presence of the butler at her elbow, Mrs Sassoon took hold of the listening handle. 'Are you there?' she asked.

'Of course I am here, Mrs Sassoon,' came the brisk voice of Sister Agnes. 'I have a favour to ask you. A most particular favour.'

'Yes?' said Mrs Sassoon feebly.

There was a clicking noise from the other end. 'I believe we have been cut off. How tiresome....'

'Yes?' repeated Mrs Sassoon more loudly.

'Oh, so you are there again. This line is troublesome. I shall complain. Now, Mrs Sassoon, will you please do me a particular favour?'

'Yes?' said Mrs Sassoon a third time.

'The King is not well ——' The butler caught Mrs Sassoon's elbow and steadied her. In her concern she missed a good deal of what Sister Agnes was saying so crisply and concisely about pressures, and the weather in London, and could Mrs George Keppel accompany the King as a house guest until this deplorable election was over? But she caught just enough to say 'Why, yes, of course.'

'I cannot hear you,' hooted Sister Agnes. '*Dear* Mrs Sassoon, do please speak more loudly.'

'I shall be delighted,' said Mrs Sassoon clearly, 'to entertain the King and anyone who cares to accompany him.' She passed the telephone instrument to her butler whose deep voice, assuring Sister Keyser that Mrs Sassoon would expect His Majesty at any time convenient, took that lady by surprise.

18

The General Election, which was spread over a period of fourteen days, began on 14 January 1910.

On the same day the King and Mrs Keppel arrived at the Sassoon's in Brighton. Mrs Willy James was not far away at her home in West Dean. It was arranged that the King should be given plenty of fresh air by drives to Worthing and Shoreham where he could walk unrecognized on the promenade in the company of his friends. He also liked to go on the beach at Shoreham and throw pebbles in the sea, his chauffeur picking them up so that he did not have to bend, but even this mild exercise caused him to cough and wheeze and lean for rest against a breakwater green with seaweed.

The Sassoons' house was not large enough to accommodate his Equerry and Assistant Private Secretary, but they were given a workroom and dined with the family. Mrs Sassoon's chef was excellent, but, being a sensitive soul, she was deeply concerned because four of the King's favourite dishes, flounders, lobsters, trout and whitebait, happened to be out of season. Shyly she asked Colonel Ponsonby if it would be too much of an imposition to ask for M. Menanger at the Palace to send down some recommendations.

Ponsonby warned her that even with plenty of salty air, the King's appetite was not what it had been, but surprises were most likely to please his palate. 'So let your chef try to delight the King, Ma'am; and I make no doubt he will succeed.' This advice seemed sound. Anxiously Mrs Sassoon watched her chief guest enjoy himself at table, and he was truly appreciative of her attentiveness in providing jugs of his favourite champagne, Duminy *extra sec* of 1883. Afterwards there was generally bridge until Hawkins appeared to take his master to bed.

Despite the many diversions made to keep his mind off the election, it seemed that the King could not stop brooding. This made him exceedingly melancholy, so much so that he lost his sharp temper as well as his infectious laugh. Only one event in the whole fortnight made him laugh outright and that was when a boy, kicking his heels on the Hove esplanade, said crossly to the King that he'd been waiting two blooming hours for his blooming Majesty to appear, and he wasn't going to waste a second more of his precious time in doing so. 'Sensible lad,' remarked the King. 'Nor am I.'

From the result of the Election it appeared that the British people were totally indifferent to the fate of both the House of Lords and Mr Lloyd George's Finance Bill. Asquith had a lead of only two votes over Balfour and his supporters. The Liberals actually lost 104 seats, and the majority of 86 which they had secured in the landslide of 1906 had become a minority of 120. But they could still govern with the support of the Labour Party and the Irish, and the same sort of new people whom the King didn't really care for were on both sides of the Commons. He looked at the results with his host and Colonel Ponsonby.

'Equal as a champion at Wimbledon,' he remarked with a sigh. 'And where do we go now? The Irish don't like Lloyd George's whisky tax. And they could turn on him.' He threw his arms in the air. 'If it was not so deplorable I should laugh. The fate of the Lords now appears to rest with the seditious Irish and their appetite for whisky.'

The Archbishop of Canterbury offered to mediate between the two parties; a very considerate and archiepiscopal thing to do – but of doubtful use when the strife had scarcely begun. However, the King thought it worth trying and went up to Windsor to meet the Archbishop and the warring parties. But evidently Asquith did not. Commanded, no less, to appear, he made the King exceedingly angry by going off to rest in the south of France.

'That,' said Edward with some asperity, 'is exactly what we should all like to be doing!' and he was vexed still further by a request for an audience from Mrs Asquith who wanted to see him personally, explain the nature of the Prime Minister's tiredness and say exactly why he had gone off to Cannes in the middle of a political crisis. 'Interfering female!' shouted the King to Knollys when he made the submission. 'Certainly not!'

The mists of the Thames Valley affected his chest. Friends and members of his Household begged him to return to Brighton. There at least the air was good. The Sassoons were perfect hosts. And he could walk about freely as the Prince Regent had done years before.

It was very different abroad where photographs were taken of the King walking on the sea front with a lady but, to excite the public's speculation and therefore make the postcards more saleable, the lady was ghosted out. Edward had a copy of one of these strange pictures, and frequently wondered who the wraith beside him might have been. In the Sussex coastal towns people behaved and left him alone; that is, until one unfortunate afternoon on Worthing pier.

It was 9 February. Cast down by problems and still feeling groggy, the King left his car and sat on a public seat on the pier to read a newspaper. He was wearing a huge fur coat and, in the heat of the sun, he began to doze. Then, suddenly, he awoke to find dozens of excited pairs of eyes peering at him.

He signalled with his cane to his Equerry in the motor car, and begged his subjects to leave him in peace. But curiosity overcame their respect. They drew nearer and nearer and, as the word spread, literally hundreds of people arrived to peer at their old King sitting in his big fur coat.

By the time a force of police arrived to clear a passage through the mob, Edward was shrinking with dread at the hundreds of eyes. He was close to tears. Elbowing, pushing, and even using their truncheons in a restricted way, the police got through to him, but it was only with the greatest difficulty that they got the King through the crowd to his motor car.

Inside he panted, feeling sick.

All round the car were swarms of moving bodies, faces looking in and suddenly being replaced by others.

At least twenty minutes had passed before the crowd was under control, by which time the King's nerves were close to snapping point. As the motor car drove off, the crowds clapped and gave loyal cheers. Their sovereign was unappreciative. He knew that from now on the south coast was closed to him. He could no longer walk out and enjoy the freedom of a private person.

On the very next day the Prime Minister arrived at Brighton.

The King was still nervy after his experience on Worthing pier. Nor had he forgotten Asquith's bolt to the South of France when he was most needed, and Mrs Asquith's impertinent attempt to interfere in official matters. He received him in audience in Mrs Sassoon's drawing-room.

'Well, Prime Minister, and how is Cannes?'

Asquith replied that it was much as usual.

'You left us at a particularly difficult moment,' the King persisted.

The Prime Minister could do nothing but flutter his hands in deprecation – just as he had done when Beresford had been so offensive to poor Lord Fisher.

'And Mrs Asquith?' asked Edward in a steely voice. 'She is well?'

'Thank you, yes, Sir.'

'I regret I could not see my way to granting her an audience during your absence. My secretaries advise me that political and personal matters should be kept separate.'

'No doubt,' said Asquith quietly, his hands fluttering again, 'they are quite right.'

Had he not been told the King was ill and that he had had a cruel experience the day before, Asquith would have been less abject. As it was, he judged it best to be quiet and unprovocative. But his first words when they talked of affairs drew more spleen from the King. Asquith was altering his government. The result of the election had made it imperative. And to begin with he wished to recommend a Lord-in-Waiting to replace one who had resigned three weeks before. Amongst his recommendations was Lord Tweedmouth.

The King glowered at him. 'As Tweedmouth made a nonsense of the Admiralty, and was possibly the most ineffectual Lord President of the Council known in history; and as he once offered me fifteen unmarried nieces for a leg-show to be followed by a stand-up supper, I imagine he is exactly the person to be one of my Lords-in-Waiting.'

Asquith was totally nonplussed and, in his confusion, mistook the King's irony for a request. By this curious method, Lord Tweedmouth received his last official appointment.

Quietly, anxious to get it all done with, the King accepted all the Prime Minister's suggestions for changes in his Cabinet. Then he asked how Asquith proposed to escape from the net the electorate had caught him in?

'By waiting on events, Sir.'

'I, too, am in a very tight place, Prime Minister.'

'That I appreciate and I regret, Sir.' Asquith evidently was sincere. 'You may be sure that I shall do all in my power to extricate you from it; and I believe I may say now, though I have not yet had the benefit of my colleagues' advice, that you will not be asked to create peers unless the House of Lords itself makes it imperative.'

The King was unmoved. 'That, if I may say so, Mr Asquith, is not very consoling.'

'The business of government must go on, Sir,' urged Asquith. 'Financial affairs are vital.' He hesitated. 'If only you could perhaps throw out a feeler to the Opposition, simply,' he added hastily, 'so that we may know where we stand.'

Edward stared at him incredulously. Asquith, not wishing to impair the Prime Ministerial dignity by putting out feelers to the Opposition, was as good as appointing his sovereign as a messenger boy, with no regard to the royal dignity at all. 'Very well,' he agreed at length, to Asquith's evident relief. 'I shall do as you ask.'

Unaware of the burning indignation he had aroused in the King's breast, the Prime Minister took himself back to London.

The Conservative leaders were duly approached through Knollys, and while, in general terms, they remained defiantly anti-Liberal, they said they were not prepared to block necessary Government business connected with finance.

With this assurance Asquith felt he could proceed. But, depressed by the King's coolness, he feared that he might show his displeasure over the constitutional crisis by refusing to open Parliament in State. It showed how little he really understood King Edward that he actually asked.

A cold, emphatic and brief message reached 10 Downing Street:

> *It is at present my full intention of opening Parliament with the Queen, as I have done on all previous occasions since my accession to the Throne.*

When this had been officially announced and the date set for 22 February, all the King's Physicians Ordinary and Extraordinary waited upon him in a body to beg him to change his mind. He was not in the least angry at what he might ordinarily have regarded as a piece of high-handedness. He was simply cordial. This made them more concerned, especially as he said he knew his duty and would do it to the end. They tried another tack. Would he then leave for Biarritz directly after opening Parliament, and not break his journey in Paris? The King smiled at this. He would consider, he said, but he rather thought he had established a custom of calling informally on the French President in the spring, and he did not wish to disappoint him or other friends by travelling straight through the city. Besides this he had written personally to M. Clemenceau asking that something be done to the drains at Biarritz to quell the fearful smells, and he heard that something had been done. Courtesy obliged him to halt in Paris and say thank you.

Sir James Reid who, though by no means the most senior, had known Queen Victoria so well, managed to bring the audience to a cheerful conclusion. The Royal Physicians Ordinary and Extraordinary bowed themselves from the presence.

'You'll not change him one jot,' Reid remarked outside the doors. 'Not one of you can. He's as obstinate as his Mama.'

Reid proved to be correct.

In the greatest style and with every particular correct, the King and Queen opened the new Parliament: the King reading Asquith's hot-potato speech with less emotion than he would have read out the wording on a wine bottle label. Commentators were impressed by his attitude of complete impartiality, almost of an apartness, which was far more closely allied to his subject's indifference as to who should win at Westminster than that of their elected representatives.

Afterwards, as though re-charging his cells for a brief stay in Paris, the King spent a week crowded with engagements while Sir James hovered over him like an anxious nursemaid. Actually the King was waiting to be reassured by the Prime Minister that no urgent and pressing crisis was imminent and he could safely go abroad. This Asquith could not give until he had placated the parliamentary members of the Labour Party, the Irish nationalists, and his own radicals led by Mr Lloyd George – a feat of conjuring some called marvellous and which others sneered at as slippery. By 1 March he told Lord Knollys it should be safe for the King to leave, but he gave no reason, which caused the King to say irritably he did not care to leave things entirely in the hands of so secretive a Prime Minister. However he promised Reid he would leave on the 6th – he had pressing engagements until then – and added with a twinkle in his eyes that he was very much afraid he could not disappoint his friends in Paris.

Sir James accepted his patient's rebelliousness with good humour and understanding.

The King was old and he was ill but he was enjoying a final burst of energy.

On his last night in England he gave a dinner at the Palace for men eminent in public life, and he confounded Colonel Ponsonby's view that even the salty Brighton air could not tickle up the royal appetite by cheerfully munching his way through a heavy masculine banquet course by course. A number of his closest friends were present. Carrington and Redesdale were astonished by his boyish high spirits, above all by the excellent account he gave of himself with turtle soup, salmon steak, grilled chicken, saddle of mutton, a number of snipe stuffed with foie gras, asparagus, dessert, an iced pudding and some sort of substantial savoury.

19

Having observed from her earliest girlhood what a thorough mess Queen Alexandra had made in bringing up her children, the Princess of Wales had long been determined not to make the same mistakes. Talented or not, they should learn certain disciplines. Languages were of prime importance to princes, as her poor George, with his schoolroom French and next to no German, had discovered to his cost. She thought it necessary that they should have a working knowledge of history, geography, mathematics and natural history. There was no doubting her zeal. Sometimes she probably made mistakes, but she did her very best.

Each evening at 6.30, when she was resting before dinner, she would send for her children and read to them or tell them the history of the Family, or give accounts of her travels. The children, in turn, were expected to be useful as well as attentive, and had to crochet or peg-top while they listened.

One afternoon in March 1910 she took Prince Harry and Prince George to an Aeroplane Exhibition, and they saw one in flight. And that evening, with their sister Mary – for David and Bertie were both now at Osborne as Naval Cadets – they pegged-topped while Mama read them a book about Africa. Africa was all the thing at the moment because she and Papa were going there in August, and Mama always read up a place beforehand. Frankly Princess Mary was bored. Not so her young brothers, who expected that one evening, through this dreary list of lakes, countries, mineral resources, natural vegetation and climatic conditions, there would emerge stories about big-game hunting and Zulus and Pygmies and even, perhaps (best of all), missionary-devouring cannibals.

That evening was memorable both because there was actually mention of Stanley meeting Livingstone and – far more important – because at that very moment, for the first time ever known, there was a knock on the boudoir door and Papa came in. He was carrying a letter and he looked disturbed. Three peg-toppers stopped immediately.

'My dear, I regret interrupting your rest but I have just received a letter from Papa.'

Automatically the Princess of Wales pulled the bell cord, took the shawl from her feet, and swung them from the chaise-longue. She slipped on her shoes.

Princess Mary's governess and her brothers' footman came to escort them to the schoolroom.

Goodnights were brief. When they were alone the Prince of Wales passed over the letter. It was dated 16 March; but the King's regular, strong and large handwriting was barely recognizable. Here and there it faded as though he had not sufficiently dipped his pen in the ink pot. But the most noticeable differences were the irregularities in the alignment of his lines and the tremulous formation of certain letters.

The Princess adjusted her eyeglasses and did her best to decipher the faint scrawl while her husband strode up and down before the fireplace, his hands clasped behind his coat tails.

Briefly the King wrote that on the same night as his arrival in Paris he had gone to a performance of Rostand's play, *Chantecler*, and found it very disappointing.

> *I never saw anything so stupid and childish and more like a pantomime! The heat in the Theatre was awful and I contrived to get a chill with a threatening of bronchitis....*

There followed a few shrewd observations on what Asquith was up to and what the enigmatic Balfour might do, and then suddenly the news that on 9 March, two days after catching his chill, he had travelled by special train with Mrs George to Biarritz, and on arrival, had collapsed. Reid was fussing him and he felt a little better, but he had little inclination to work at his despatch boxes....

'Your poor father,' said May gently.

'That is not the worst of it,' broke in her husband. He held out another piece of paper. It was a memorandum from his Equerry Derek Keppel.

Mrs. George had written to Mrs Derek with the obvious intention that it should be passed on that the King was in a pitiful state of nerves, unable to bear noise or the sight of strangers. He would not remain in bed but saw only Mrs George and Soveral and very occasionally his host, Cassel, and coughed and wheezed dreadfully from morn until night, and then it was worse at night-time. His dreadful dry cough, like the sound of tearing canvas, could be heard right through the building. Hawkins had hardly slept for ten days. . . .

'May,' pleaded the Prince. 'What am I to do?'

Instinctively she took him in her arms to soothe him. She could do little else. Having been, as a girl, forced to see so much of her screwed up, immobile and bald old Grandmama Cambridge who had lived to the immense age of ninety-one, she had a dislike for illness and invalids which she had never managed to overcome. Unknown to her husband she instinctively shrank from the thought of his father's suffering at Biarritz. It was all part of her sensitive dread of death and old age. But she could and did help George to face the probability that very soon perhaps he would be King and Emperor.

'It is not disloyal to Papa,' she urged. 'It is sensible and right for you to make certain private arrangements. It is not necessary for you to go to Biarritz unless you are summoned, but you do need to be ready.' She looked at him straight in the eyes. 'I know that you will have a triple loss in losing father, sovereign and friend – for you have been very close. Therefore it is important for you and your Secretaries to be ready.'

He kissed her hand thankfully, and brushed a tear from his cheek. 'You are right, May. Quite right. These damned politicians are never at rest and are driving Papa to his grave. I must have a private word with Knollys.'

'And Colonel Ponsonby?' suggested his wife. 'Davidson is at Biarritz at present but Colonel Ponsonby will soon be going into waiting. Until he goes he will be able to advise you.' She squeezed his elbow. 'It will be all right, my dear. Believe me.'

'I do,' he said quietly.

Queen Alexandra wrote to the King, recommending that he leave 'that horrid Biarritz' and join her for a cruise from Genoa. They had a new royal yacht, *Alexandra.* What a treat it would be for both of them, and for Toria, of course.

Despairing of making Alix understand exactly how things were, the King wrote once more to his son, this time in his familiar handwriting:

Her proposal is quite out of the question, as it might be necessary at any moment for me to return (and I can do so under 24 hours at any time) should the Govt. resign, dissolve, or commit any act which entails my presence at home.

'Now I should say,' said the Princess of Wales when she saw this letter, 'that Papa has made another of his miraculous recoveries.'

'You really believe so, my dear?' asked her husband eagerly.

'Yes, I think very probably he has. Mama, anyway, must think so as she is off to Corfu.'

20

Sir James Reid and Hawkins looked far more like invalids than King Edward. They had never been put to such stress in their lives. And their reward was one of his upsurges of energy which always followed a bad attack. It was by now a familiar part of the pattern.

The King received a long letter from Asquith warning him that he must be prepared at any moment to receive the Government's resignation. Vacillating, Asquith then telegraphed to say the King need not worry himself after all but suggested that if possible he should be back before 19 April. There would be a critical division in the House of Commons on the 18th.

The King replied through Knollys – who by now was almost hysterical with fury at the outrages committed, as he thought, against the monarchy – that he saw no point in returning until he knew the result of the division. When the time came Asquith telegraphed that the Government had won the division. Thereupon the King authorized Esher, Knollys and the Archbishop to meet Balfour and discuss the crisis, and he himself tried to put it out of his mind and enjoy his last few days at Biarritz.

At the bottom of his link box was the folded paper sent to him by Miss Haig and purporting to be a message from his favourite sister, Alice. Quite often he took it out and looked at it, but on his final day at Biarritz he tore it up and threw it in the waste paper basket. Then he went out on to his private veranda overlooking the Basque coast, which was bathed in sun.

Hawkins overheard him say: 'I shall be sorry to leave Biarritz,' and add, after a pause, 'perhaps for the last time.'

But there was an unquenchable puckishness in him which made Edward determined to stay a few days in Paris on his return journey. Sir James' craggy, tired face broke into a smile when he heard of the decision.

M. Lépine called out his gendarmes. Scores of young ladies prinked themselves out in the creations of Cheruit, Doeuillet, Redfern, Worth, Doucet, Paquin and Poiret. The chefs at Maxim's and some 'little places favoured by "*Notre Edouard*" ', were thrown into the most appalling nervous states.

The King did all that was expected of him, and found time to call on old friends. Three he had known since he was first presented to them as a boy of nineteen at Louis Napoleon's court at Fontainebleau: his dear Anna, Duchesse de Mouchy; Comtesse Edmond de Pourtalés who walked with him, not for the first time, in the Jardin des Plantes, and Comtesse de Greffuhle to whom he confided his conviction that very soon he would be dead and then the German Emperor would contrive to make war on England.

The King returned to London on the 29th, the very day his private advisers and Balfour had struggled unsuccessfully to find a way out of the political impasse without destroying the prestige of the monarchy and the peers. But Edward said he preferred not to hear Knolly's report until he had had time to settle down. He then at once changed, dined and went to the opera, waved to his cronies, wheezed his way through an opera supper and returned to the Palace gasping.

In the next three days the King showed extraordinary resilience, seeing his family, almost all his ministers, several advisers, and picking up all the complicated threads of the political crisis. But on the Saturday, four days after his arrival in England, he felt just a little unwell and decided to go down to Sandringham for the weekend accompanied, amongst others, by Sir Dighton Probyn and Colonel Ponsonby.

Because the Queen was cruising in the Mediterranean, orders were telegraphed not to open any of the drawing-rooms, and the royal party travelled by train, breakfasting on the way, and arriving at Wolferton at noon.

Almost at once the King was off with his agent Beck and his head gardener to see what had been going on during his absence. Nowadays he always did this on arrival anywhere, having once had the shock of his life on inspecting a newly laid out golf course in Windsor Great Park to find the whole thing had been bungled and that the contractor actually had a plan to make the last and most difficult bunker in the exact shape of the Victoria Cross. The walkabout, he said, did him good, and the alterations were to his satisfaction. But on the next day, although he took the precaution of driving to church in a clarence while his Household walked, he spent some time afterwards with Ponsonby in the office where there was no fire, and then strolled in the gardens prodding at this and that with his cane while a treacherous, cold, thin wind blew in over Sandringham from the Wash.

By the next morning, when he returned to London, he knew that he was in for another attack of bronchitis.

Utterly despondent at the thought, he proposed himself to dine with Agnes Keyser. She was concerned by his condition, but on this occasion she did not lecture him. Instead she encouraged him to hold on. It would soon be over. If he took care of himself he would be as right as a trivet in the warm English spring. She was anxious not to depress him further, but took the opportunity to telephone Sir James Reid the moment the King left her hospital in his carriage.

'I know, I know,' said the King irritably when he found Reid and Hawkins waiting for him at the Gardens Entrance to the Palace. 'It's back again, damn it! And we've all three got to go through it again.'

But, in spite of warnings that he should rest, Edward dressed each day and went on doing what he could. The Prince of Wales telegraphed his mother, who hastened back across Europe, to be met at Victoria Station by her son and daughter-in-law and her grandchildren, Princes David and Bertie. Her smile of greeting was forced. In all their long marriage the King had never failed to greet her personally at the station whenever she returned from abroad. It told her everything.

'But I am not particularly ill,' objected Edward, when Alexandra showed her concern at finding him hunched in his chair and grey in the face. 'It is simply my old trouble, Alix. And had not Laking and Reid absolutely forbidden it, I should have welcomed you at Victoria.'

'I am very glad you did not,' she said. 'You are better resting. Surely the doctors have told you to stay in bed?'

He nodded. 'Which I shan't do,' he said defiantly. 'But I really don't feel quite up to the opera tonight. The box is being kept for you at Covent Garden, but I beg you'll excuse me this once.'

Barely able to control her tears, the Queen said quickly she would not consider going without him.

That same evening the King sent for Colonel Ponsonby, who was going out of waiting on the following day. Clearly it was to say goodbye.

In a gasping voice the King thanked him for all he had done at Biarritz, in Paris, and since. Then, for the first time he admitted: 'I feel wretchedly ill, Fritz. I can't sleep. I can't eat. They really must do something for me.'

Deeply affected the Colonel took his hand.

'In case,' wheezed the King, 'just in case I don't see you again, Fritz, goodbye.'

Ponsonby bowed himself out, sure that he would not see the King alive again. He was utterly wretched.

The next morning the King insisted on getting up and dressing in frock-coat and formal clothes. Though he now frequently choked in gasping for air, he received Knollys and afterwards Sir Ernest Cassel.

He even tried smoking a cigar although he knew it was foolish, and he was obliged to lay it hurriedly aside.

He had only one object, to stay alive and see through the crisis which was threatening not only the peers but, with them, the throne. He forced himself to eat a little at a table in his sitting room. And he took a glass of brandy. He felt he had a duty to seize on any aid to strengthen himself, and he was determined not to weaken by sitting about or lying in bed.

Impulsively he went to the bow window where he had his caged birds. It was there he had stood on the day it had been made clear an era was ended and the make-up of the new House of Commons had altered the face of things for ever.

He stood there now, blinking miserably in the May sunshine, with a canary trilling on his stretched-out forefinger, scratching Caesar's scruff.

Hawkins in the dressing-room heard a thump, the trilling changed to a frightened squawk, and Caesar began to bark. He rushed to the bow window where his master lay.

Five physicians examined the King and pronounced he was dying. The Archbishop of Canterbury was summoned. One cardiac attack followed another. Morphia was administered by Laking who recalled sadly going all the way to Germany with the King to do the same for the Empress and being frustrated.

The King sat hunched and half-dressed in an armchair because he refused to go to bed.

'I must keep going,' he said over and over again; though occasionally he lapsed into unconsciousness.

With remarkable depth of feeling Queen Alexandra sent for Mrs George Keppel to come and say goodbye. She came. In a lucid moment the Prince of Wales informed the King that one of his horses had been placed first at Kempton Park that afternoon. The old man's face broke into a smile. 'Good, good,' he said, 'I am very glad.' He never spoke again.

Eventually Hawkins and Sir James got him into bed. Then the family came in to be with him. The Archbishop prayed. At a quarter to midnight, as Big Ben struck, with a single sigh, King Edward died.

After Lying in State, first at the Palace, and then at Westminster, King Edward's body was taken through the streets of London to Paddington with an orderliness and a pageantry he himself would have loved.

Immediately behind the coffin came his saddled charger and a solemn, half-frightened Caesar. And after them came a cavalcade of royal mourners, nine kings and a vast number of princes and nobles, and twelve State coaches of queens and princesses, more than Europe had ever seen before on one occasion.

The vast silent crowds, hundreds of them weeping openly, showed Edward was indeed loved by his people. And at Windsor, where his remains were lowered into a vault in St George's Chapel by the side of his eldest son, the tears of soldiers, statesmen, courtiers and servants as well as those of his family, showed he had equally been loved by those most closely associated with him.

Fittingly Colonel Ponsonby had been entrusted with the final ceremonies, and fittingly it was he who made the perfect panegyric about a master he had served and understood so well: that England had lost 'a lovable, wayward and human monarch'.

The Young Victoria

'The modes and manners of Victoria's childhood are sufficiently remote to be intriguing without being actually exotic, and the language avoids tushery and retains that peculiar tartness of flavour which one associates especially with Wellington.' *Sunday Times*

Albert's Victoria

'The book is highly entertaining and . . . highly instructive. Mr Whittle has most effectually whetted the appetite for the forthcoming final part of the trilogy.' *Guardian Journal*

The Widow of Windsor

'Completes the trilogy of Queen Victoria's reign, covering later years' relationships with family, household, servants – including John Brown – and Prime Ministers Gladstone, Disraeli . . . Vicky well focused, humanized.' *Books & Bookmen*

Bertie

'Edward VII was 60, and worn-out by his long wait in the wings, before Queen Victoria died. This meticulous account of his interminable apprenticeship is laced with a thousand delicious, revealing sidelights on the not-so-distant Royal Family. Mr Whittle makes the lonely Prince with a passion for parties a sympathetic, even touching, character.' *Sunday Telegraph*

Other books by Tyler Whittle

Common or Garden
The Plant Hunters
Some Ancient Gentlemen